SHADOW
OVER
ODIOME

SETH W. JAMES

BOOK 1

SHADOW
OVER ODIOME

CHAPTER 1

IN MADNESS, A CALL

EMILY WAS ALREADY dead. It hadn't been quick and it hadn't been painless but it was over. She no longer saw the bonfire nor heard the gunshots, feared the insane gibbering or shrill shrieks of the cultists who'd murdered her. Whether souls exist or death is just an off switch, whether the cult really could exile an incorporeal mind to an eternity of madness, naked before the thousand dreaming eyes of Cthulhu, Emily would know peace. Kane had killed the High Priestess before the rite could be completed.

Though the stars were in proper alignment for the sacrifice, a thick bank of clouds shrouded the night sky; the thrashing bonfire, scourged by the rising wind, threw as much shadow as light across the bloody glade. Kane had emptied three magazines into the forest clearing. Bodies of the dead and dying lay in heaps or struggled vainly to reach the trees, naked, anonymous, and finished. Except for Billy Trent. Kane had made sure Billy took the second round fired that night. Mr. Rush had been right: Billy was a bad kid. That

Billy no longer had a head, or most of his left arm, wouldn't matter to Mr. Rush, not in the long run, not much. Kane knew that, only too well, but he had no time to ponder the emptiness of revenge, not when a dozen cultists still stood between him and the grotesque statuette of Cthulhu.

The sentries on the far side of the clearing had come up after the shooting began. Some now fired across the glade, through the bonfire, while others circled both right and left, outflanking Kane. He'd caught sight of the cultist who'd fled with the statuette, heading toward the river, and knew the sentries would expend their lives to buy time for the statuette's preservation. The statuette of Cthulhu was important: only under the graven eyes of the unearthly stone could true rites and sacrifices be dedicated to Dread Cthulhu.

Kane dodged behind the trunk of a tree, dropping to the ground as he fished out another magazine for his pistol. The venerable M1911A1 only held seven rounds per magazine, which made laying down suppressive fire impossible. The sentries were armed with shotguns and semi-automatic rifles. One sprang from behind a tree to the left and sent a blast of double-aught buck at Kane's head, just as Kane released the slide on his pistol. The tree trunk splintered and blackened, burning powder from the point-blank shot scorching its wood. Kane didn't feel the slivers of oak enter his cheek, nor the 00 pellet slice burning over his left eyebrow: reflexively, he brought his pistol across his body and fired, dropping the cultist. He swung instantly back to his right as another sentry stumbled through the murky tree-line; Kane's first round took the man through the hip, the next one went through his head. Kane then pushed away from the tree he sprawled beneath and tumbled deeper into the woods.

He circled the clearing, orange and red and alive with gurgling cries. The wind covered his footfalls but also those of the sentries hunting him. A silhouette passed between trees, a man before the fire; Kane shot and then plunged forward. Returning shots rang out around him. He couldn't tell if they knew where he was, if anyone had drawn a bead on him, and couldn't take the time to find out. If he'd taken ten steps around the bonfire, the escaping cultist with the statuette must have taken thirty.

"Ai, ai, Cthulhu!" suddenly erupted ten feet away as a sentry who'd crawled through the clearing jumped to his feet and charged the tree-line.

Whatever the crazed man attacked, shadow or corpse, it wasn't Kane and Kane left him to it: he'd circled the glade far enough to leave it and head after the escaping statuette. The woods were alive with the sounds of searching. Occasional shots came from every direction and Kane couldn't tell if any of them were aimed at him. All he cared about was getting to the statuette before it was spirited away. He wondered if the cult kept a boat on this side of the river, or if the cultist who had fled with the statuette could swim across while carrying it. The lowering sky murmured in disapproval and then the clouds opened up with torrents of rain.

Under the storm's cover, Kane rose from his crouch and ran flat-out toward the river. He hated to leave even a single cultist alive in the woods; they'd continue to murder, sacrificing even without a statuette of Cthulhu. But the statuette was the key, what drew in potential cultists with the addicting madness the rites evoked. Like a torturing poison that a victim cannot stop taking, for its lack means death, the cultists of Cthulhu suffered under the lashing of his worship but suffered in ecstasy.

Trying to take his breaths only in quick gasps, hoping to hear something of his quarry between intervals, despite the storm, Kane heard footsteps pounding through the forest parallel to him. He threw himself to the ground, rolling to a stop, just before a shot-gun coughed fire and lead through the night. "Ai, ai, Cthulhu!" the wretch shouted with each racking of the slide and discharge of shot. Wild from rage, the blasts fell just over Kane or into the ground before him. Kane scrambled around a tree trunk on his palms and toe tips, the ground now slick with rain and mud. He tossed his pistol into his left hand and stretched to one side, just as his would-be killer fired again, and sent a round through where the man's chest should have been. The shotgun clattered to the ground and the chanted war cry was replaced by a dry heave. Kane lunged to the dying cultist's side, pawing the ground for the shotgun. If nothing else it would mean a few more rounds. He lifted it from the clinging leaves of the forest floor only to find it empty. "Shit," he growled as he tossed it aside. More sentries were approaching. Kane staggered to his feet and again raced off toward the river.

The trees failed without warning. Kane was in the open. He could feel the wind blowing freely against his skin but in the utter darkness of the storm he could see nothing. Somewhere not far ahead, the river hummed like tires on a highway. Kane dropped to a crouch, his left hand stretched out to the ground in front of him, his right bearing his pistol. He needed speed more than silence, but he still needed silence. If there was a car nearby, and someone flipped on its headlights, he wouldn't last long out in the middle of a field or wherever he was. His hand suddenly met wood. Not the bark of a living tree, Kane had come to the clapboards of a house. Pressing himself against it, Kane crept to his left, his hand gently probing the darkness.

"Fuck, man, fuck," a voice wept on the verge of hysterics.

"Shut up," another voice hissed.

Kane had come to a window. There was no glass and no light. Just past the window was the rough field-stone of the chimney. Kane eased himself up to standing, wedging into the corner, ear close to the window. The interior of the house was a deeper well of darkness than the night without. He felt certain that if he showed himself in front of the window, the contrast would give his enemies a target. Instead, he stood listening, waiting for fate to take a hand, open an opportunity. Fate played its hand.

Footsteps slapped against the soggy ground around the far corner of the house as several men approached.

"It's us, don't shoot," someone whispered harshly.

"Get in here, get in here," the voice that wasn't crying earlier said from inside.

Great, Kane thought.

"It's a fucking Venator, man," the weeper moaned. "A fucking Venator."

"Shut up," the other voice said as the remaining sentries filled the room.

The front door slammed and someone said, "Bar that door."

Kane knew that as long as they were inside and he was outside, they had the advantage. And the storm wouldn't last. The rain was coming down too hard and the thunder pealed too loudly and often for this to be anything but a passing storm front. When it let up, and more so when the sun rose, Kane would again be one man against several, out in the open. And with only twenty rounds left.

Putting the 1911 under his arm, in the battered holster he only wore when attacking a sacrifice, Kane looked up the height of the chimney and took a hold of the rough stone. It was slick with rain but by gripping firmly, the coarse texture of the stone bit into his fingers. He could climb, however slowly. Up he went, more worried about his foot scrapping loudly than falling off. It took a torturous few minutes to reach the second story of the house, all the while listening to the vague noises of the cultists within. The house must have been an old frame building, maybe a century old and barely holding together; there was neither paint nor glass anywhere. At the second floor window, Kane slipped one leg through and sat on the ledge, withdrew his pistol, and then ducked in.

The sudden lack of rain falling right next to his ear made Kane uncomfortably aware of his own noises. He took a minute to still his breathing, to let the water run from his dark suit until it no longer audibly dripped. The murmurs had ceased below. Kane hadn't heard them leave and assumed the cultists still occupied the ground floor though he heard nothing of their movements or words. Now inside and subject to the same cloaking darkness, Kane took a step to cross the room, to find the stairs down and finish his stalk. The floor creaked under him loud enough to shake the house.

"You hear that?" the weeper all but shrieked.

"Shut up," his partner shouted, followed by a chorus of hisses.

Kane wondered how thick the floor boards were, if they'd stop a round fired from below. *The shotguns, surely,* he thought, *but who knows if the rifles are of high-enough caliber to shoot through the floor.* With that cheery thought, he took another, much more cautious, step forward.

Each step was an act of balance, of slow-motion acrobatics as Kane traversed the second floor. He wondered if there was a door or a stairwell, if any furniture remained in the house for him to knock over, or some animal to disturb. The thought of throwing himself down the stairs, to trade rounds point-blank with however many cultists defended the house, only quietly murmured in the corners of his mind. He didn't think of the ten years he'd been stalking, didn't think about the night that brought his old understanding of the world to a catastrophic end. Emily had found an end and peace, however horrible the method, however against her will, and part of Kane—a part that he only ever looked in the face over a glass of whiskey—hoped to find that peace one grim night. His fingers, tracing his way through the dust of the abandoned house's floor, came to a wall and then across to a void; the doorway. Some faint glimmer from the bonfire in the forest clearing, dying under the storm but still burning, made a ghostly gray shadow through one of the windows below. The stairs were three feet away and Kane could hear the breathing and shifting of the cultists beneath him.

"We just wait," someone whispered. "We got the advantage in here."

"A Venator, man," the weeper repeated.

"He's just a man, like any other," someone else said. "Just like the ones we open and burn for the might and majesty of Cthulhu."

"Ph'nglui mglw'nafh Cthulhu, R'lyeh wgah'nagl fhtagn," they all replied in chanting unison.

Kane felt the tension drop from his features, tension he hadn't realized was pulling at the skin around his eyes, stiffening the muscles in his neck, shoulders. He rifled his pockets, not loudly but no longer actively concerned with noise, and withdrew his last magazines. He replaced the half-empty magazine in his pistol with a fresh one and then held it and the other three full magazines between the fingers of his left hand, like a bookie sorting different dollar denominations. A different sort of bill was come due, however, and the odds were all on one side. Kane threw himself forward and slid down the stairs on his side, like a ballplayer stealing second.

His first shot was intended to light the room, give him an idea of where to send the next seven, but it found a mark. The next seven and then the seven after that and then the seven after that and then the seven after that plowed to the edges of the house as Kane pressed his back to the wall and slid from one side of the room to the other, sometimes on his feet, sometimes on his knees. The cultists fired in all directions, out the windows, at each other, at Kane. The noise was impossibly loud, the smell of burning cordite overpowering, greasy and sick. Ancient drapes like spider webs clinging to one window caught fire and flickered dimly when the thirty seconds of madness came ringing, ringing, ringing to a halt. Kane was on one knee in the far corner, opposite the stairs he'd come down, his last magazine—the half-full one—loaded but not immediately needed. Fifteen cultists lay dead or dying on the floor. Kane slowly passed the pistol into his left hand and then, with his right, withdrew a stiletto he kept in his boot.

When the grim work was finished, Kane salvaged one of the

sentries' rifles and a few magazines for it. He then searched among the dead for the statuette of Cthulhu. Little more than a foot tall, it had the weight of eternity bound within its unearthly stone. Like jet in color and granite in texture, the statuette was of a creature squatting on a rough throne. Some said it resembled a dragon, surmounted by the head of an octopus, bearing vestigial wings and pincer claws. In truth, it looked nothing like the imaginings of man nor the beings of earth. Only its posture, one claw upon a hind knee and the other supporting its many-tentacled head, spoke vaguely to the human experience: Cthulhu upon his throne contemplating that which was beyond the ken of mankind.

Kane dragged the heavy statuette from under the weeper's body. A bullet or the dead cultist's fall had taken off one of the wings. In the dark, Kane couldn't find it. He left without it, knowing it held no power now. Though he had handled many such statuettes over the years, the touch of the stone disgusted him and he was glad that the darkness concealed its features. There was a watchfulness in the stone figure's gaze, as if it searched for a madness within the viewer's mind, evoked by the blood sacrifices made at its feet. Kane swathed it in the torn and bloody shirt he'd taken from the weeper, tied with his belt, and slung it over one shoulder before heading back out into the storm.

CHAPTER 2

SHADOWS OF THE TRUTH

I T TOOK OVER an hour of creeping through the woods to find the last of the wounded or hiding sentries, to make sure of those around the bonfire, and to carry Emily's body to the road. Kane knew it was stupid, knew he was giving in to a sentiment he could not afford to indulge. *Shouldn't have talked to her father*, he told himself as he drove back to town. He left Emily on Mr. Rush's front lawn, the weeper's shirt covering her as a funeral shroud, and then sped away, out of town, out of North Carolina.

Kane had smashed the statuette of Cthulhu with a small sledge-hammer he kept in the trunk of his '93 Cutlass convertible. As he crossed the Yadkin River, just before dawn, he hurled the pieces into the rushing water below. He knew it would not take long for the local sheriff to find the massacre, certainly not after Mr. Rush found Emily, and Kane needed to be as far away as possible. He drove north fast enough to get out of the state but not fast enough to lure a cop out of a speed trap. He just hoped his out-of-state license plates didn't prove irresistible.

A couple minutes after crossing into Virginia, the adrenaline wore off; horror at his own actions—no matter how many times he'd gone through it before—and the onset of physical shock caused Kane's hands to shake on the steering wheel.

"That's not something you want see the guy in the next lane doing," Kane said aloud, looking at his vibrating fingers.

An all-in-one roadside shop sat back from the entrance to the interstate, ahead on the right, and Kane decided he'd better pull in and fill his tank; and not just at the gas pump. He let the Cutlass roll slowly up to the gas station side of the parking lot, cut the engine, and then sat breathing the odor of gasoline fighting with the fried breakfast smells rising from the all-in-one's kitchen. His hands still shook and when he looked in the rear view mirror, he saw haunted eyes staring back. He shook his head and kept taking slow deep breaths of gasoline.

When he finally felt he could, Kane threw open the door and stood up, in time to see a young fellow in jeans and a *Panther's* jersey lean his head out of the all-in-one's entrance and shout if Kane needed service. Kane waved him off, went around to the back of the Cutlass, and put the premium nozzle into the side of the car. He listened to it gurgle for a moment and then opened the trunk.

Should've changed earlier and somewhere out of sight, Kane thought. *There's blood all over this sweater.*

The black wool hid the smear left from when Kane had lifted Emily's body, at least at a distance. Up close it—along with the spatter running down both legs from the close-range work in the abandoned house—would not look very much like mud. Kane rifled the suitcase he kept in the trunk and found his other suit, all but rolled into a ball. He sighed, shook it out, and hung it over the trunk lid before stripping off his sweater, blazer, and undershirt all in one sweep. He had to, to cover taking off the shoulder rig carrying his .45 without being noticed. Slipping off his shoes, he quickly stepped out of his black trousers and grabbed the blue ones.

For forty-three, Kane looked pretty fit. No longer as cut as he had been well into his thirties, his chest and arms still remembered high school football, a tour in the army, and the caresses of someone who had loved the breadth of his shoulders. His hair, however, told the tale of the past ten years. No longer the subtle graying anyone earns in these stressful times, Kane's hair was shot through with gray, the salt and pepper of someone looking down the barrel at sixty. It needed a trim, too; as did his chin, where the gray had long outnumbered the black. On his square jaw, climbing up drawn skin to high cheek bones, the mix of youth and age gave the impression of wisdom. Or would if he didn't look perpetually tired.

The suit he climbed into was so wrinkled it looked like he'd slept in it and not well. It's color was hard to make out: it was either a powder blue that someone had worn inside a coal chute once too often or a dark blue that had seen too many long days in the Mojave Desert. Though he thought about replacing it every time he pulled it out, buying off the rack for a six-foot-three-inch frame was never easy. It had also been with him since before his days as a Venator.

Dressed but not clean, his .45 at the small of his back, and his bloody clothes stashed in the concealed compartment on top of a few specialty items, Kane came around to the gas nozzle just as it clicked off. He checked the fee and then pulled the Cutlass up to the all-in-one, dropped off some cash at the attendant's hutch, and walked over to the breakfast counter.

The all-in-one had it all: beside the gas attendant and his racks of automotive gear there was a fishing tackle section, a grocery area on the other side of the large room, the checkout had lottery (of course), cigarettes, and a small but powerful array of bottled bliss. Kane eyed the scotch as he crossed to the back but pulled his head around reluctantly; in his condition, he'd fall asleep after one sip.

Sitting down at the counter, careful not to slouch in case the .45 showed, he smiled wearily as the waitress came over. She smiled, too. A wiry woman of indeterminate age, she had the shuffling gate of someone who'd been on her feet since the Ford administration. Her hair was pulled back so tight it look about ready to pop off. Her smile was warm, however, and not just from Southern Hospitality: her position behind the breakfast counter commanded a view of the parking lot—and the gas pumps. She'd looked Kane up and down as he'd walked over and liked something. What it was would have been hard to say but women had been finding it appealing for most of Kane's life, though he never had quite gotten used to it.

"Coffee?" she asked.

"And how," Kane said, affecting a parched voice.

She laughed soundlessly and took pot and cup and saucer from a shelf, pouring and placing at the same time and without spilling a drop. "You're not old enough to say 'And How,'" she said. "My *granddaddy* said, 'And How.'"

"They say you're only as old as you feel," Kane said.

"Yes, they do," she said, something like pride coming into her voice.

"In which case I'm old enough to say, Dame Van Winkle, where's my pants?" Kane said.

She laughed aloud this time and it didn't tinkle like tiny bells so much as rattle in a sauce pan, but she was doing her best. She put the pot back and said, "You don't need cream and sugar," knowing her customers.

"No, thanks," Kane said, raising the cup.

"You need this?" she asked as she slid a menu onto the counter. "Or do you know what you want?"

"I think I better get this into me first," Kane said and blew on the steaming cup.

"Sure," she said and leaned against the shelf behind her, crossing her arms.

Kane saw a paper left by a previous customer and dragged it over, flipping to the want ads and taking out a pen. He circled an insurance auditor position near the top of the page.

"You looking for work?" she asked.

"Always," he said without looking up. "These days? A fellah ought to keep his options open."

"The gals, too," she said.

Kane circled an ad for a cruise ship piano player. He couldn't play the piano but it sounded nice. His phone vibrated and he was glad of the chance to step out from under the eyes of the waitress (Gail, by her name tag), knowing who it would be.

"Hey," he said.

"You couldn't have called me to let me know you're okay?" Helen said.

"It's still early," he said. "Didn't know if you were up yet."

"Very funny," she said. "Can you talk?"

"Hold on a sec," he said and then put his hand over the smart phone as he stood up and spoke to Gail: "Can I have a couple eggs over easy, bacon, wheat toast, and hash-browns? I'll be right back."

Gail said yes and wrote it down for the cook as Kane went out to the Cutlass and leaned against the passenger door.

"Or a text message?" Helen said when Kane came back on the line. "A quick, hey I'm not dead?"

"I couldn't text you while driving," he said. "That's against the law."

He could practically hear her pinching the bridge of her nose and shaking her head, the way she did in person, but he knew she was smiling when she said, "Of course."

"I'm okay," he said and took a sip of coffee, having carried the cup outside with him. "I wanted to get out of state before I called you, away from the local cell towers. How many times, I wonder, after a mass killing in the woods—of some unidentified cult the police won't report anything about—has a call been made to Arkham, Massachusetts?"

"That all depends on whether the Venator in question stops for breakfast," Helen interjected.

Kane chuckled into his cup before saying, "Guilty. Though I wasn't kidding about that cell tower thing. How could authorities not put two and two together?"

"Kane, the number you call doesn't go directly to Miskotonic University," Helen said. "I'll leave the intricacies of call routing and IP addresses for when you come up here next."

"Time for the 'Kane, why don't you come up for a rest' conversation?" he asked.

"Because it's been so successful in the past," Helen said, chuckling in her turn. "It went okay?"

"Yeah, well enough, I guess," Kane said and set the empty coffee cup on the hood of the Cutlass. He rubbed his hand over his face, his stubble making a sound like sandpaper. "I should have gone in earlier, not waited for the night of sacrifice."

"You couldn't locate the leader any other way," Helen said gently.

"Maybe I could have," he said. "I have before."

"And when you can, you do," she said. "But that doesn't mean you should beat yourself up when it isn't possible. The girl didn't make it."

"Emily," he said. "No."

"I know," she said softly. "There's a police reader out on your car. It was seen across from her father's house. Local PD hasn't published their blotter yet and local news doesn't have the story."

"They won't," he said.

"Probably not," she said. "The reader didn't mention a license plate number but we'll have to wait on the blotter to see if Mr. Rush mentions any names. What alias does he have on you?"

"Clemens," Kane said. "The estate lawyer. I dropped the paperwork in the bonfire on my way out. I'm Clyde Markson, now. And Mr. Rush won't say anything."

"I hope not," she said, making a note of Kane's new alias.

"I told him enough, he won't," Kane said.

"And the statuette?" she asked.

"It's in the Yadkin River," he said and gave her the coordinates.

"You sound tired," she said as she entered the information.

"Then it must be a day that ends in Y," he said.

"I have something I'd like you to check out, if you can," she said.

Kane laughed and said, "So it's 'Kane, you're tired and need a rest' followed immediately by 'Kane, there's something I need you to do,' is it?"

"You never listen to the first one," she said, "so I'm trying to do both at once. Thought this might appeal to your particular talents."

"Shoot," he said.

"No, the other one," she said deadpan.

"Funny," he said.

"There's a town on the New Hampshire coast called Odiome," Helen said. "A woman there, the Mayor's wife—called, if you can believe this, Mayor and Mrs. Odiome; an Odiome having been mayor since the town was founded some four hundred years ago—Mrs. Odiome was found raving in the streets one night last week. Dread language, the words 'Cthulhu' and 'R'lyeh' featuring prominently, her moments of madness interrupted by lucidity only when terror overcame her. It all found its way into a local newspaper article."

"The cult has taken up advertising at last," Kane said. "That should help attendance."

Helen said, "No, I don't think so. I don't think this is a cultist losing her mind in a spectacularly public display; not that that's never happened. I think she might be an artist or a sensitive picking up a dream sending."

"Whoa, whoa, whoa," Kane said, coming off the car and pacing back and forth, the edge of his hand against his brow. "As in, artists picking up the dead dreams of Cthulhu as his sleep grows restless? As in restless because his fucking island city of R'lyeh is about to rise?"

"Kane, Kane, you're standing outside a diner, right?" Helen interrupted.

Kane froze for a second, looked over his shoulder and through the glass door to see Gail watching him, and then went back to sitting on the Cutlass's door. "Yeah," he said, "probably shouldn't shout Cthulhu too loud."

"Best not," she said. "And yes, an artist picking up a dream sending from Cthulhu could point to a rising door to R'lyeh but it doesn't always. If we were seeing dozens of these all over the world, then it would be time for me to make some phone calls, bribe someone at NASA to point the Hubble at earth and find where the island is rising this time. Artists and sensitives do crop up from time to time all on their own. If Mrs. Odiome happens to have an interest in the occult, happened to have read something about Cthulhu or a few lines from the *Necronomicon* or the *Unaussprechlichen Kulten*, it could have tuned her in to a dream sending, broken her mind. That's why I'm asking you to go up there, rather than sending one of the boys."

"Archie in town?" he asked.

"No," she said. "Hector."

"And Hector would burn Odiome to the ground," Kane said, "just to make sure."

"He's been doing this for twenty years, Kane," she said. "And his reasons for getting involved are just as good, or as horrible, as yours. But you're not wrong, in a sense. Hector would shoot first. And this sort of opportunity requires questions to be asked. If we truly have a sensitive eavesdropping on dream sendings, we can't possibly pass that up. You'll ask the questions."

"Yeah," Kane sighed.

"And, just to be honest about it," she said, "since you won't take a break, since you insist on driving yourself to exhaustion—and I won't bore you with the psychological motivation behind that—"

"Thanks," he said.

"—this is a good way for you to relax a bit while still contributing to the war," she finished.

Kane looked across the road at the weed-covered lot separating the on-ramp from the highway, just starting to buzz as the morning warmed up. After a minute, he said, "Yeah, okay. I'll head up to Odiome—after breakfast."

"You should stop and get some sleep first," she said. "Once you're a few states away."

"I won't sleep for the next couple days, Helen," he said. "Might as well spend them driving."

"You won't do anyone any good if you fall asleep behind the wheel and crash," she said, her voice connoting how much she expected from arguing. "And you should ditch the Cutlass."

"I've had this car a long time," Kane said, patting the door beside him.

"I know," she said. "And it has a lot of murders attached to it in blotters and APBs and in investigation notes."

"Part of the job," he said.

They finished up their usual back and forth of good advice and sentimental refutation before wishes of good luck and safe travel closed out the call. As she was for many Venators, Helen was the closest thing Kane had to a friend or family, anymore. Everyone else, everything else, was sacrificed for the war, for the stalking and slaughter of Cthulhu Cults. He put his phone away and went inside to a cold breakfast.

After eating and working on his flirt with Gail—a useful skill for someone who had to talk information out of people from time to time—Kane lingered over a second cup of coffee, despite knowing it would necessitate another stop an hour up the road. His hesitancy did not arise from what he thought he would find in Odiome; he expected Helen was correct, as she almost always was. Kane knew that once he was alone in his car with nothing but the droning of tires on pavement, the hot sun, and his own thoughts, that his mind would return to everything that had happened over the last four days, relive every conversation, chew over all the facts, question every decision, and in the end he'd find what he should have done differently. Rationally he knew that even if other choices could have been made, they would not necessarily have made things turn out better. But in the Cutlass, with hours of nothing but the road, rationality wouldn't matter for long. He paid off the seven-dollar tab with a ten, climbed under the wheel, and drove north.

"It's like this, Mr. Rush," he said aloud to himself, a few minutes down the highway. "There are whole eons of unrecorded history, even on earth. And I'm not talking pre-history, either. I'm talking before Mesopotamia, before Ur. Oh, there are a few books that tell of those days, tomes of evil knowledge that break the minds of those who read to deeply into them, but by and large this time before mankind ruled itself is forgotten. And with good reason. It was the time of the domination of earth by The Great Old Ones and their Dread Priest Cthulhu."

He drummed one hand on the steering wheel, shaking his head; what he had actually told Mr. Rush in the days leading up to the sacrifice in the forest, to Emily's murder, had differed significantly from what he *could have* said.

"What is Cthulhu?" he said aloud. "That's a good question, Mr. Rush; I hope I can never answer it. There are things in this universe that are beyond the power of man's mind to comprehend.

Cthulhu is one of them. Even trying to would cause madness, which is, strangely enough, what the cultists are after. But I'm getting ahead of myself, Mr. Rush. You see, once upon a time in the not-so-idyllic past, a race of beings so different from ourselves that we actually lack the necessary mental organs to entirely perceive them ruled this part of the universe. On the unremarkable planet earth, a creature known to humans as Cthulhu acted as the Dread Priest of their faith. A towering monstrosity, Cthulhu is described in many nightmarish ways but generally it is thought to be many stories tall with the skin of a dragon, the head of a squid, claws or talons, and vestigial wings hanging raggedly from its back. And eyes, Mr. Rush. More eyes than any squid, like pools of eternity where minds are ripped from their wills and sent fleeing into terror. That's poetry, Mr. Rush, the last bastion of the rational mind struggling with futility."

Kane was silent for many miles, as he crossed Virginia into Maryland. It had always been like this. After stalking a cult, discovering its members or just one who could lead him to a sacrifice, after attacking the blasphemous rites and hopefully saving the intended victims—and sometimes succeeding—after killing every raving cultist and smashing their unhallowed statuette of Cthulhu, after it all came the first memories. Those parts of the night that would never see morning, which would live in eternal darkness in the pit of his mind, would then thrash as they clawed out space in Kane's thoughts where they would live ever after. He knew it was better to get it over with, to talk and talk until his thoughts settled and he could focus again, on to the next investigation, the next sacrifice to stop, the next murder to prevent and murders to commit. It was always harder if he knew the victim's name.

"The domination of earth by Cthulhu, Mr. Rush," he continued, "was a time of fear and blood. Cthulhu, for whatever reason, requires human sacrifice. The Temple to Cthulhu in his drown city of R'lyeh was said to be painted in blood, from all the sacrifices. Mankind existed solely for torment, in those years. What Cthulhu or The Great Old Ones got out of it all, I can't say, Mr. Rush. I don't think anyone can. You'd have to understand them and that just isn't possible.

"Then, for reasons we don't understand—surprise, surprise—The Great Old Ones and Cthulhu died. Or something like death. There are words, Mr. Rush, words that men like me have heard all to often, words that are chanted at sacrifices, which are conducted to this very day in the dark corners of the world:

Ph'nglui mglw'nafh Cthulhu, R'lyeh wgah'nagl fhtagn

"It means, 'In his mighty house in R'lyeh, dead Cthulhu lies dreaming.' R'lyeh is a city and not a city; an island that exists many places and in many times simultaneously. When Cthulhu died, or what we understand as death, R'lyeh sank deep into the ocean. And there, beneath the waves, in his mighty house in ol' R'lyeh, Cthulhu lies dead and dreaming. They say that a time will come—when the stars are in proper alignment, if you can believe it—when Cthulhu will be reawakened from death and through his power recall The Great Old Ones.

"And attempts have been made. As crazy as all this sounds, Mr. Rush—to say nothing of my talking to myself here in the car—there are people today who would like to see that happen, to see Cthulhu revived and The Great Old Ones return. Some claim to be the remnants of the Cthulhu Cult of old, those willing slaves who carried out the blood sacrifices in the Temple of Cthulhu. Most, though, are victims themselves, in a sense. There are these statuettes of Cthulhu, made from a stone not found on earth, that can connect the mind of an observer to the vague whispers of Cthulhu's dreams. Those whispers become louder if a human is murdered before it. Eventually, if you're around a statuette long enough, if you witness enough murders in front of it, you go crazy—and that's what the cultists want. They need to lose their minds like a drug addict needs a fix. Some claim they'll join Cthulhu, or Cthulhu's dreams, if they finally go bonkers at one of their clambakes. Whatever happens to be true doesn't matter to us, though, Mr. Rush, not to you and me."

Kane was quiet then for many miles, watching the road thicken with other travelers as the day grew old. Maryland passed by, and then Delaware, and Kane paid more attention to slowing down at potential speed traps then he really needed to after ten years of stalking cults; pursuit was always at the back of his mind. When he hit New Jersey, though, he had to stop for gas and to let the coffee out. He grabbed another from the rest stop convenience store before continuing north.

"And how did I get involved, you ask, Mr. Rush?" he said after taking a sip from the Styrofoam cup and then wedging it between the dashboard and the windshield. "There are people who hunt the cults. They're called Venators, but I won't bore you with the details. It's enough to say that some of us who've lost family," Kane said but had to take another quick sip of coffee, scorching his tongue, "some of us who've lost family try to find answers. 'Getting into the war,' is how Helen puts it. You ask questions, you look things up, you hit dead ends and more questions. If you keep at it, you might eventually start to see shadows of the truth. You pick up a few things, you learn. And maybe, if you're lucky enough or cursed, you'll come upon a cult. The one that killed your little girl, Mr. Rush, or another one. For you, it'll have to be another one. *That* cult is out of the war. And when you find a cult, you wipe it out. For most Venators, it starts in vengeance. Hell, I'm not going to sit here and claim vengeance isn't still a part of it. But for most, after the first couple cults, after hoping you'll catch a bullet at the next sacrifice you crash, after the horror of killing a few dozen people regardless of circumstance, after all that, what drives most of us is simply to get there before they kill Emily."

CHAPTER 3

SEASCAPES AND DREAMS

I T TOOK KANE nearly twelve hours to reach Odiome, hitting traffic delays outside of New York and Boston. Driving up the New Hampshire coast, he had stopped in Rye and managed to find a copy of the week-old paper that detailed the crazy behavior of Mrs. Mayor Odiome, Layla. It was dinner time when Kane finally made it to the tiny port town.

Odiome nestled between the low hills surrounding it and the bay from which it drew its name. Too shallow for use by the commercial fleet, Odiome relied on tourism for its local economy. Quaint bed-and-breakfasts and artisan store-fronts made good use of the town's Victorian architecture. Period streetlamps and cobble-stone lanes, horse-drawn taxis and store clerks in costume, as well as an army of unobtrusive street cleansers and meticulous landscapers all helped to give visitors the feeling of having stepped back a hundred years, to a quieter time of parlors cluttered with knickknacks, dressing up no matter the occasion, and the simple enjoyment of walking. The restaurant trade could also rely on day-trippers from

Portsmouth or Rye, due to the excellence of the local shellfish. Down near the fishers' pier, the working class of Odiome kept an even quieter existence than what was manufactured on Main Street, in their mostly 1950s-era quarter of the city. Kane avoided the tourist-clogged streets of Odiome proper for a flophouse on the pier side.

The little man behind the counter couldn't make up his mind if Kane was a lost tourist on the wrong side of town or day-laborer in a borrowed suit. He gave Kane a room nevertheless; shellfish— Odiome's other industry—being handled mostly by locals who lived in a small hamlet on the south side of town, he had plenty or rooms to give. Kane trudged upstairs with his squashed suitcase half-filled with t-shirts and socks but no other clothes, to a corner room overlooking a tiny, scum-covered canal. He could imagine the smell even with the window shut.

Dropping his suitcase on the bed, Kane went to the TV sitting on the dresser and spun it around. It was an old CRT TV, not a flat-screen. Kane rummaged through the contents of his pockets until he found a small multi-tool and unfolded a Philips-head screwdriver. He then unscrewed the back cover of the TV and finessed it away from the front just enough to slip his M1911A1 inside, along with the six extra magazines he had for it. *You never know with these small-town police forces,* Kane thought as he screwed the TV back together; *not staying at one of the B&Bs or driving up with the wife and kids may just be enough to warrant a frisk.* With his pistol now hidden, and conveniently overlooking the dagger he kept in his boot, Kane spun the TV back into place and then looked longingly into the closet-sized bathroom. The sink practically sang of a steaming-hot shave, the shower beckoned like a Siren upon the rocks; Kane didn't dare look too long at the lumpy, sex-crushed bed, knowing he needed sleep badly and there was still a lot to do and time left that night to do it. With a sigh, he dumped the contents of his suitcase into a single drawer, threw the suitcase into the closet, and headed out.

Kane walked up to the tourist side of town and spent the better part of an hour just wandering the streets, learning their names and attaching businesses to city sections, watching the meandering crowd while appearing to window shop or reading restaurants' posted menus. No one seemed to take any notice of him expect to size up his likely spending limit: given the condition of his suit, no one was getting their hopes up. About eight o'clock, he went into what purported to be a steakhouse and took a seat under the disapproving eye of an impeccably dressed waiter.

While lingering over his scotch—much to the annoyance of the matre' d, who imagined a higher-paying customer would appear at any moment—Kane considered moving to the bar and pumping the lady behind it for whatever she might know about Layla Odiome and her recent hysterics. He decided against it, though, thinking that if Odiome did have a small-town Napoleon in the Police Department, he didn't want his first conversation to point at his investigation. It would only take an ounce of suspicion for a local cop to pull any readers on a Cutlass, and that would complicate things quick.

After another two hours of casing Odiome, the heat and vigor of his meal having long since worn off, Kane returned to the flophouse, unscrewed the TV, recovered his pistol, and lay down, still wearing his shoes and clothes except the jacket. He'd learned long ago to sleep with the .45 in hand without blowing off his own foot, even when the nightmares woke him. With the deep breath of a diver about to go into the shark cage, Kane closed his eyes.

The next morning, after what added up to maybe two hours of sleep, Kane finally had a shave and a shower, hanging his suit next to the steaming curtain to try the old traveling salesman's trick of getting wrinkles out of it. It didn't help much. After picking up a coffee-to-go from a truck that serviced the wharf, two streets down from the flophouse, Kane drank it on his way to the Odiome Public Library. A converted stable that once belonged to the largest hotel in town, the library was surprisingly modern with a bank of computers along one wall. The balcony that comprised the second floor was stocked primarily with novels of the sort tourists might want to borrow during their stay but the central stacks they looked down upon carried books on local history and documents of the town's existence dating back to Puritan times. Kane nodded to the affronted librarian who gaped at his not-much-improved suit. The unconcealed sigh of disgust she uttered when he sat down at the farthest computer conveyed her lurid suspicions. Despite the librarian's assumptions, Kane dipped into the local paper's—*The Odiome Courier's*—online backfile and examined every story that even remotely touched on Mrs. Layla Odiome.

Helen had been right about the Odiome family's legacy in the city named after it: an Odiome had been mayor since the town was founded in the seventeenth century. The current Mrs. Mayor Odiome, however, had started life as Layla Dryden, born in Portsmouth, and met Mayor John Odiome while she attended a small liberal arts college, of which he was a member of the Board of Governors. Their difference in age proved no bar to love, it was written, twenty years being never-no-mind between the dashing mayor-to-be and the sophisticated young woman. Kane learned almost all of that from their wedding announcement and the accompanying biography of the blushing bride. From the rambling obituary appearing after Layla's father's death, which Kane suspected she must have written herself and not well, he learned that she had originally majored in Art, while in college, but changed her major to Art History after a disappointing showing at a local gallery.

"Yahtzee," Kane mumbled to himself. "How do you do it, Helen?"

The next item on the list was the recent brush with madness that had found its way into the papers. Dream sendings were the psychic emanations of Cthulhu's deathless slumber. Sensitive people, usually artists, could occasionally pick up on these dream sendings, often with horrifying consequences. Visions of blasphemous rites from eons past, images of the future torment of mankind, prying into the most deeply hidden fears of individuals, of whole societies, stripped of all concealment to lie quivering in terror for the unknowable satisfaction of Cthulhu: it was never long before an artist subjected to dream sendings slipped into madness. Kane had little to go on, however, when it came to evaluating Layla's recent spectacular meltdown.

He read again the local paper from Rye but found little in it except a remarkably accurate spelling of Cthulhu and R'lyeh. *It is eerie how people totally uninvolved with the cults or the study of The Great Old Ones' mythos and literature can so often spell those things according to the accepted practice,* Kane thought; *maybe we're all receiving a little of the dream sendings.* With that comforting thought, he scoured the *Odiome Currier's* backfile again. There was nothing about the incident, not surprisingly. The town relied on tourism and a story about the mayor's wife losing it on Main Street, raving about the coming end of humanity at the hands of a dead monster, doesn't exactly read as inviting. Thinking he could perhaps talk a description of events out of someone close to the family—but not too close—Kane searched the archive for records of local events Layla would have attended. He hit pay dirt in a picture from a charity art auction the year before: Selma McKenzie. Side by side, the two women were described in the caption as being old friends from college. It also stated that Layla still painted. *That could explain why she still has the sensitivity to pick up a dream sending,* Kane thought. *Maybe this friend of hers, Selma, heard what happened on Main Street last week.* It took only a few seconds with the yellow pages to find

Selma McKenzie. She owned an art gallery a few blocks away, called *Seascapes and Dreams*.

Kane returned the librarian's glare on his way out, adding a wink just as he reached the door that sent her into an apoplectic fit. He chuckled to himself as he maneuvered around the meandering tourists on their way to lunch, wondering what sort of delinquents the librarian was getting in there. *It's probably all bluff*, he thought, *and she has a leather fetish and a dominatrix business on the side.*

Seascapes and Dreams took up the ground floor of a grand Victorian house at the top of a small rise, nearly dead center of town. All of the interior walls had been removed or shortened, and many additional windows added, making an art gallery out of what once had been a small and rather stuffy parlor, living room, and kitchen. What the second floor—and the over-sized turret above—contained was anyone's guess; the proprietor's apartment, Kane assumed. The etched glass double doors read, "Local Artists, Unbound Imagination." There were three people inside, other than Ms. McKenzie.

She stood with a couple who were decked out like war correspondents in khaki vests covered in pockets and cameras hanging all over the place, nodding her head to their museum-level whisperings. Above medium height, pale blond hair intricately braided, she wore a skirt that swept to the floor and a denim jacket, which she hugged tight against the air conditioning. The other party in the shop was an old-timer in a tweed suit who wandered from painting to painting having his good time spoiled by raising his pipe to his mouth only to discover it still wasn't lit and couldn't be. Kane checked a seashell-encrusted clock above the checkout counter, saw that it had just passed noon, and then padded out amongst the standing sculpture and hand-thrown pottery planters to wait for the customers to head to lunch.

It took longer than expected and so Kane passed the time

looking at what was for sale. In one corner there was a six-foot
sculpture of a mermaid splashing up on a rock in a kind of yoga
pose, a delicious look on her face as she raised her head to the ceiling, expecting the sun. It also wore a dayglo pink bikini top over
its stone breasts. Kane couldn't help but laugh: he noticed signs of
it having spent at least part of its life outside. He had moved on to
the wall where the oil paintings hung by the time the safari couple
left for the savanna; Tweedy must have gotten tired of not smoking
and slipped out earlier. Ms. McKenzie caught sight of Kane as she
returned to the counter; she smiled hello but left him to peruse his
way down the row of paintings.

"Was the artist making a statement," Kane asked, nodding his
head toward the mermaid, "or did the town council make a stink
when that thing was out front?"

Ms. McKenzie laughed and started walking slowly toward
Kane. "I'm the artist," she said. "And the town council demanded
I clothe her. Something to do with the family nature of our tourist
industry." She shook her head. "How they determined breasts are
not family oriented, considering their use, I just don't know. Had
to bring her inside, though. Kids kept stealing the bikini. How did
you know she used to be outside?"

"Looks like a seagull had perched on her flipper after lunch one
day," he said, grinning. "Philistines."

"Oh gross," she laughed, coming to a halt a few paintings away
and waiting for Kane to draw closer. "Guess I better get a sponge."

Kane helped her laugh a little more, continuing his progress
down the row of paintings.

Don't let your face change!

Glancing at the next painting, Kane looked a little closer and
then shook his head and moved on. It was a seascape, a large men-
acing wave rising from a frothy sea beneath clouds churning in
the sky above. Each curl and rivulet of water had been painted in

exacting detail. It was not the anger of the movement, the raging violence it depicted, however, that shot a cold bolt down Kane's spine, momentarily blasting any thoughts of conversation from his mind. The writhing waves and twisting currents, when taken as a whole, composed the glaring visage of Cthulhu.

Careful not to let his face convey his suddenly keyed up instincts, Kane kept to the same slow pace with which he had traversed the rest of the oil painting wall. His eyes, however, ranging over the paintings with new interest, sought out any subtle indicators of a cultist's work. It wasn't long before he found a familiar cyclopean construction amid a ruined temple in the next painting.

"What about these paintings?" he asked. "Who painted these? Quite the local art scene you have here—some of these are damn good!"

"Thank you," she said. "But no, I'm the artist for these, too. Sadly the local art scene finds expression mostly at the shell-craft counter." She indicated the pile of crap on the desk behind her with a thumb hiked over her shoulder. "A couple times a year I hold a locals' day and people bring in their projects. It's fun."

Kane nodded his head and then took a few quick steps back to the camouflaged painting of Cthulhu. Its eyes were more noticeable to him now, following him as he moved into view, pregnant with malice. *You painted this, huh? Either the town is overrun with sensitives*, he thought, *or not.* He knew not to ask about Layla Odiome now; whatever was going on with the Mayor's wife, the mission had just changed. "There's something about this one," he said, stroking his chin. "I don't know what it is."

Keeping his eyes searching amongst the waves, he watched through his peripheral vision as all the blood drained from Ms. McKenzie's face. She ducked her head and hurried to his side. Only someone sensitive enough to receive a dream sending could pick up on the subtle character of the painting, could "feel" it, without knowing anything of Cthulhu beforehand. Just noticing the painting was a sign to any cultist that the viewer was ripe for recruiting. Something Kane was counting on.

Now start talking to me about oblivion, baby, he thought, *tell me about the release found in the primal. You've got this great barbecue out in the woods tonight, maybe I'd like to come along, murder a few people; it'll be great.*

"Haven't we met before?" she asked all but in a whisper.

"Have we?" he said. "I don't think so. I just got into town; taking a mini holiday to decompress. Stressful job, you know how it is."

"Yes, of course," she said, trying to meet his eye, hesitating, and then forcing herself. "Anything in the shop is, of course, yours."

Wait, what? "Uh, thanks," he said and then grinned. Sex was the cult's primary recruiting tool, particularly for potential sacrificial victims. Someone experiencing a visceral reaction to dread symbols, however, was usually given the sales pitch, urged to join and slowly inculcated into greater and greater expressions of brutality until finally being initiated into the cult's murderous rites. *Either way,* Kane thought, *it's an in.*

"I'd love to see more of your work," he said. "And your work-space, too, if that's not too private. When is the best light?"

"The best—oh, it's between 9:00 and 11:00, this time of year," she said hurriedly.

"Just missed it," he said. "How about I come by tomorrow morning about 8:30?"

"Of course," she said. "I shall await you."

CHAPTER 4

THE NIGHTMARE WITHIN

KIPPING HIS LUNCH, Kane spent the rest of the day casually walking around Odiome and not at all casually mapping infiltration and egress routes from his hotel to *Seascapes and Dreams*. After an early dinner and retrieving his pistol, Kane slipped from Lafayette Street down a residential avenue that ran parallel to Salem Avenue, where McKenzie's store was located. When reasonably sure he wasn't under anybody's eye, Kane ducked down a grassy alley between houses and settled in next to a central air conditioning plant and a tool shed, in easy view of *Seascapes and Dreams*.

Night had fallen and no one had come out to scream at Kane. It was nearly midnight when the lights above the now dark art gallery began to wink off, one by one. When the lamp hanging under the porch came to life, Kane pressed closer to the tool shed, watching with one eye. McKenzie came out with her hair under a hat, wrapped in a tweed coat that came to her knees, and a pair of tiny flats. She locked the art gallery's doors and then hurried off down the street, toward the bay. Kane watched her until she was out of sight and then went back up the grassy alley.

Circling a couple blocks so he could come down Salem Avenue on the left side, Kane knelt into a pool of shadow cast by the porch light and a column. After a casual look around him as he feigned tying his shoe, he ducked up the alley next to *Seascapes and Dreams. What do you want to bet there's an alarm down here,* Kane thought as he moved deeper into the alley, hand brushing along the windowsills, *just in case some local kids want to steal that bikini top again?* He hadn't noticed any video cameras when he'd been inside earlier but there had been a couple of little boxes that could have been old-fashioned motion sensors. He kept out of sight through the windows, therefore, when he pulled himself up between two of them, nearly doing a split with a foot on two different sills. The second story windowsills were much thinner, Kane found as he reached slowly up to find a handhold. It was just out of reach. Trying to cross those last two inches to get a grip, he pushed off with one foot—and lost his footing all together. He dangled for a moment by one hand, by three little fingertips, pawing at the air with the other hand, trying not to spin and wrench free from his precarious hold. Both hands now on the windowsill, Kane kicked against a lower window until he had a foot on top of its frame and then half climbed, half rolled up the second-story window until he had a foot on its sill and his hands on the roof's gutter. He took a moment to catch his breath.

This'll be hilarious, he thought, *if she has a camera hidden in the begonias.* The gutter wasn't strong enough to take his weight so Kane pushed off the top of the window, jumping out across the alley and onto the roof of the next house over. From their he leaped back to the roof of *Seascapes and Dreams,* hoping nobody in the next house had heard him. He crouched then and crept up the slope to the oversized turret.

It was more than an eccentric tearoom, as most turrets are, and nearly three times as large. Having windows that looked north, south, and east, Kane could see nothing of the turret's interior until he crossed over the roof's ridge and knelt near the southern-most window. Easels stood everywhere, brandishing paintings in various states of completion; the light of moon above and streetlights below made the lighter pigments shine, though the darker paints were deeper than shadows. There was a stool but no other furniture, save low shelves housing brushes and paints and thinners and all the accoutrements of a painter's profession. Kane could smell the cloying acidity of the room as he approached—and smiled grimly at it. A window had to be open.

You'd need ventilation in this room, he thought as he slowly swung the tall window out on its hinge. He stretched a long leg into the room, straining his trousers to step over a freestanding shelf full of crumpled paint tubes, like so much half-used toothpaste. Kane then stood breathing the fumes and letting his eyes adjust to the murkier light. The stairs going down were of the spiraling cast iron variety, their railing breaching the floor beyond three large closets that took up the west wall. Once he could see as well as he was going to, Kane began examining the contents of the turret.

The paintings were much the same as what he had seen earlier in the gallery below: quaint seascapes under sun and moon, frothing breakers on shell-strewn beaches, ships that hadn't sailed these waters in a hundred years slipping by barely visible in a misty distance. Nowhere in those works-in-progress did Kane see any dread symbols or motifs common to the mythos of The Great Old Ones or Cthulhu. Looking over his shoulder, he saw the closets had keyholes. *Just let those be locked,* he thought, *and my intuition isn't completely shot.*

They were locked, but the locks were original to the house and were designed to keep untrustworthy help at bay, not prevent the prying of a Venator on a stalk. Kane slipped his boot dagger between the lock plate and the opposite door, prying the old dry wood apart until he could slip the blade onto the ward's sloping surface and wiggle it free. The doors came apart with a satisfying pop. Kane stepped into the closet and pulled the doors almost closed behind him before grabbing the light cord that dangled in his face.

A monolith topped by a statuette of grotesque figuration, which gazed down with malice upon an orgy of blood and fire, of the naked and the raving, loomed enormously on the walk-in closet's far wall. Half-a-dozen paintings filled the room, some of sacrifice, some of dreams only half remembered by those who suffered them, some of long forgotten images of R'lyeh beneath the waves. The sacrificial paintings, though, drew Kane's attention most: the details of the victims' faces, their fear and pain evident, standing out beyond any other detail in the room. They were not the blurry imaginings of an insane mind trying to comprehend the unfathomable strangeness of The Great Old Ones. No, they were the product of an artist remembering an act witnessed firsthand. *So there's a cult in town after all*, Kane thought.

His first instinct was to set the house on fire but that would only warn the cultists in town, driving them further underground or out of town, to other places, to begin again. Kane took a deep breath and focused. Amid the depictions of horror, he found a ledger. Inside there was a two-column list, with the titles of paintings in one column and people's names in the other. He scanned through the list, a fingertip hovering above the page, and then froze: was there a sound below? He swatted at the dangling cord, killing the light, and then edged open the closet door. He stood listening for over a minute, knowing all the while that no matter where McKenzie had gone, she would return. He had to get moving. Finding his car keys, Kane bruised a fingertip activating a tiny flashlight and then returned to the ledger.

I'm guessing this is a list of people that she gave paintings to, he thought, *and the paintings' names in the next column.* He stroked his chin for a moment, reading the list of paintings and piecing the phonetic scribblings into words. He then clawed his smart phone out of his pocket and brought up the Odiome white pages: every recipient in the ledger was a local. He quickly snapped a photo of each name and its corresponding paintings. *Some of these titles are pretty explicit, too,* Kane thought. *Unless she didn't tell them the title, it's kind of hard to believe anyone would buy "Fhtagn Cthulhu Bloody Master's Rage." Hang* that *in the dinning room before a dinner party. Unless they're all in the cult,* he thought grimly. *That's Venator paranoia speaking,* he told himself. *But even the paranoid have their enemies. It could be she paints these things in response to the dream sendings she receives—or more likely thinks she receives—after a sacrifice; gives them to her little cultist buddies to keep their peckers hard until the next murder. She wants to know who has what, though, in case she needs to see it again, remember a particular nightmare she wants to work into another painting. There's one way to find out: there are ten names on the list—some with as few as three paintings and some with a dozen—and there are six hours between now and sunrise.*

In a flash of realization, Kane bolted from the closet and knelt near one window, gazing up at the sky. He sighed in relief, hanging his head: the stars weren't right for a sacrifice. *Wherever she went,* he thought, *it wasn't to a killing. Two days, at least.* He refastened the closet and let himself out through the window, this time dropping down to the porch roof before jumping down all together. He looked at the photos he'd taken of the ledger, comparing them to the addresses listed in the white pages. *If there is a sacrifice due in two days,* he thought, *the smart money is on McKenzie being there, gathering more inspiration for her goddamn art. If you keep her under surveillance, she's bound to lead you to some lonely spot in the surrounding hills where she and her playmates get down to business.* He walked another block, thinking back to North Carolina, to the look on Mr. Rush's face the day before Emily was slaughtered. He thought back to a darker night, ten years ago. *I just came from a blood bath,* he thought. *And I don't, strictly speaking, know these people are in the cult. Well, shithead, go find out.*

CHAPTER 5

NIGHT OF THE DAGGER

CHOOSING THE NAME on the list with the fewest number of paintings, Jed Stewart, Kane wound his way down to the wharf side of town, to a bungalow at the south end. Odiome's waning shellfish industry still employed a couple hundred people and they, by and large, housed close to their trade. Stewart's bungalow had seen better days, and may have been a low-rent vacation property at one time. All the lights were off but a bluish glow flickered and died, brightened and wavered through the front windows. Kane walked past the house and doubled back, up the two strips of concrete that passed for a driveway.

Edging around the corner of the house, Kane deliberately placed one foot and then the other, feeling the ground with his toes before committing his full weight. It was unlikely he would be heard, he knew, not with the din coming from the front room, but there was no benefit in taking an unnecessary risk. Coming to the miniature bay window, Kane passed one eye beyond the frame and saw an old TV, the size of an easy chair, squatting on one side of the room. Bruce Campbell stumbled around the screen, fighting with actors in makeup that wouldn't have passed muster in a high school play. On a couch opposite, an indistinguishable figure sat low, head barely above the cushions, occasionally raising a brown bottle to its mouth. Kane slipped back from the window and to the driveway.

Around back, Kane found a tiny, south-facing sun porch. The screen door was latched from the inside but the wood was old and the tolerance between door and frame was wide enough to see through. Kane pulled the dagger from his boot and passed its tip through the crack, lifting the hook from the eyelet. He then slowly opened the door, freezing every time the hinges—rusted from a life-time of bay moisture—squeaked. Slipping across the porch, which stank from bags of garbage that had never found their way to the curb, Kane took out his handkerchief and tried the backdoor. It opened. He passed quietly in.

The kitchen was as bad as the porch, only louder. Whoever was in the front room either really liked *Evil Dead* or had some sort of hearing problem. Kane came forward on his toes, feeling the boards beneath him flex with each step, swaying his weight onto his forward foot with a muscle-aching slowness. Once in the doorway between kitchen and living room, Kane waited a moment, looking at the man on the couch.

You don't know he's in the cult, he warned himself. *He could be a friend of McKenzie's. Got the picture for his birthday.* Kane didn't believe a word he told himself. A little assurance, though, was what he wanted. He licked dry lips and, almost in a whisper, said:

"Ph'nglui mglw'nafh Cthulhu, R'lyeh wgah'nagl fhtagn."

If Jed Stewart was in the cult, he might be surprised by his sudden visitor, but he'd talk first. Jed Stewart *was* in the cult, but he didn't want to talk—he spun off the couch and smashed the end of his beer bottle against corner of the TV, killing the picture and making a jagged weapon for himself. With a shout of, "Ai ai Cthulhu," he lunged at Kane, leaping over the couch and slashing wildly with his broken bottle.

Kane threw himself backwards, finding the wall behind him far too close, and raised his dagger just in time to deflect the jagged glass. Recovering in an instant, he kicked with everything he had, right into Jed Stewart's stomach; the younger man doubled over, heaving, and backpedaled until he came to rest against the couch, clutching his gut. Kane waded in, open hand outstretched, dagger just behind it.

"That's no way to great a fellow believer, now is it?" Kane growled, edging still closer.

"Cthulhu," Stewart panted and then shouted, "Cthulhu!"

Again the cultist lunged, his broken bottle swung in an arc to slash Kane's guard-hand aside, to cut an opening to his throat. But Kane's open hand wasn't there anymore; dropping it to one side, he raised his dagger to meet the attack, catching Stewart's wrist and taking a step forward, inside the man's reach. Stewart again recoiled and smashed into the couch, only this time it didn't pull him out of range. His wrist was slashed open and the bottle slipped from his weakened fingers; in the next second he gasped, bloody hand and unbloodied hand both swatting at the fist pressed to his chest. Kane had stabbed upward, just below the sternum, severing the diaphragm—making breathing impossible—and into the cultist's heart. The body that had been Jed Stewart slipped to the floor.

Kane stood on flexed knees for a moment, listening to the sound of his own heaving breath, eyes crawling over the little room bathed in the dead-air blue light from the TV. He then walked to the bay window and drew the curtains closed. Wiping his dagger off on the couch, he returned it to his boot and began searching the bungalow.

That Stewart knew the name Cthulhu put him in the cult, Kane assumed as he rifled drawers and stamped on floorboards looking for hidden compartments. But Stewart's unprovoked attack—in the face of someone who knew what only other cultists knew—baffled Kane. Unless he suspected a Venator was in town, Stewart shouldn't have reacted the way he had. *Maybe another Venator is in town,* he thought suddenly, standing up from where he looked behind the half-sized refrigerator. *Someone Helen didn't send. There are more than enough people out there who take up the war without knowing a thing about its history.* He shrugged and returned to searching.

It took only five minutes to find the false back to Stewart's only clothes closet, and behind it, a grotesque painting of an insane woman shaking the entrails from an infant held over her upturned mouth, a bonfire of green burning behind her. Kane felt the urge to burn it and the bungalow, to destroy it all as he would a statuette. If he did, though, he knew that would be the end of stalking in Odiome: the fire department would come, an investigation would show Steward had been stabbed, and the cult would be warned. *Five hours until dawn,* Kane thought, *and nine other names on the list.*

The longer he could keep it from being known that there had been a murder in Odiome, the longer he could continue hunting. So Kane dragged Stewart's body into the space behind the fake wall in his closet and refastened the false front. Fortunately, heart wounds bleed very little—no blood pressure in the arteries—and so there were few signs of a struggle. Kane left it at that, with the TV off, and slipped out the back. The next name up on the list had an apartment on the north side of town, a few blocks from an old boat factory. Kane was there in ten minutes.

And so the night progressed. In each case, Kane found a secret compartment containing ghoulish paintings: in a closet or beneath floorboards in a hallway or in a locked shed behind the house. Only four of the next eight people on the list were at home, however, and at least two of the missing showed signs of having left days before and most likely in a hurry. Un-emptied garbage under the sink, stinking to high hell, newspapers piling up on the front lawn, and clothes all over the bedroom indicated that at least a few had skipped town and not in a planned fashion. Kane wondered what it all meant but had little time to ponder. He knew he had to finish the list and then call Helen, once it was late enough in the morning. With this many murders in Odiome, he wouldn't be able to stay safely in town. She would have to arrange for another Venator to come down, a few days later perhaps, as well as put the word out about the names of those who'd fled. But before he came to that, there was the little matter of the last name on the list. Silas Moynahan.

CHAPTER 6

REVELATIONS OF DAGON

SILAS RENTED THE second floor above an ice cream parlor, just off Main Street. The building had two more floors rented out above his and a private entrance off to one side, between the ice cream parlor's old-time frosted glass front window and its antique store neighbor. The street door was open so the mailman could access the row of boxes on the wall just inside; five feet away there was another door with the words "Private Residences" in block lettering. Tourists were probably bumbling into that little airlock all the time. Kane slipped inside and pulled out a lockpick.

The treads of the stairs leading to the second-floor were clothed in little fabric swatches, stamped flat by fifty-years of wear but enough to aid Kane as he crept silently upward. Huddling next to Silas's door, hoping no one above would come down while he worked the lock—not impossible at 6:00 in the morning—Kane began with the deadbolt. He'd finessed the tumblers up out of the way and began turning with his other pick when he realized the bolt wasn't set. *Another one out of town,* he thought as he moved on to the knob. *Where the hell have these assholes gone?*

Kane froze in the next second. Acting on his ever-reliable hunch, and before inserting a pick into the lock, he took the doorknob in hand and twisted slowly. It turned. He dropped the picks into his jacket and pulled the dagger from his boot. Easing the door open, he didn't breathe as he slid inside, ears straining to hear past the fire alarm in his head.

Every cultist's apartment had smelled; they always do. If you're scrambling to lose your mind and devote the last ragged vestiges of your life to murdering people for the dead priest of strange beings, cleanliness drops on your list of priorities. Silas's apartment's stink, however, had a quality to it normally reserved for the cult's outdoor activities. It was there, faint but fresh: a sour metallic odor.

Kane stood with his back to the door for over a minute, letting his eyes adjust to the darkness. The outline of the doorway to his right slowly glowed into existence. He stood in a living room, the rear-most room of the apartment. The coffee table was missing two legs, the windows opening on the back alley were shrouded in thick curtains but by what little early-morning light seeped in below them, Kane could see a smashed television. Slipping away from the door in a fighter's crouch, he moved to the doorway forward.

A dark line meandered from the living room into the kitchen. The door beyond, to the bedroom, was open and enough light came through the front windows to illuminate a blood trail across the linoleum. At first, Kane thought he'd find a body at the other end of the building. As he crept on, however, he saw it was less blood than he'd originally thought, a spattering trail, a wound. At the kitchen's far end, he found the source.

From the spray pattern against the wall between the refrigerator and the bedroom door, Kane figured someone had been pushed into the corner and beaten, a blow breaking the guy's nose and then successive blows splattering blood on the dirty yellow wallpaper.

Kane stepped carefully over the blood trail, not wanting to leave his shoe print behind, and moved into the bedroom.

Bed unmade and closet open, the room did not otherwise appear to have been searched. Kane searched it. Above the closet, above a panel that had been cut out of the ceiling, Kane found three ritual knives, caked with old blood; the sort of gaudy nonsense some cults go in for, aping the aesthetics of what they saw in their dreams. He also found a statuette of Cthulhu.

Taking the strangely heavy sculpture to the window over the bed, Kane inspected it for authenticity. He needn't have bothered: he knew from the way he felt when he touched the stone that it was the real thing. The uneasiness, the sense of watchfulness the statuette evoked grew the longer Kane handled it; as if the statuette knew and looked back into Kane. Kane dropped it face down on the bed and was about to look into the space above the closet again when a noise came from the landing. Then the doorknob turned.

Kane slid across the bedroom and put his shoulder to the wall next to the doorjamb. He switched his dagger to his left hand and drew his pistol with his right. Anyone who had seen that particular statuette before, especially at a sacrifice, would feel something if it were handled, awakened, and might come to see why. A tiny click shouted in the small apartment, announcing the door to the hall had been shut—like the closing of an arena gate.

Kane felt the tension drop away, his muscles loosen to a supple readiness. Even the ever-present ringing in his ears quieted. His palm depressed the grip safety on his M1911A1, his thumb nestled against the other safety; he took in the positions of the furniture in the bedroom, knowing there was no better cover than the refrigerator on the other side of the wall. All he waited for was the sound of someone stepping onto the squeaky linoleum of the kitchen floor, and it would begin.

"Kane," a hoarse whisper grated the silence. "Kane, don't shoot me, boy."

"Hector?" Kane said and then inched around the doorjamb.

Hector Troy's muttonchoped face was leaning around the doorjamb on the other end of the kitchen, a heavy stainless steel Automag barely in view pointing downward. He straightened and put the .44 under his jacket—black leather, covered in unnecessary zippers and extra buttons—as Kane did the same with his .45. Hector was not quite Kane's height, nor weight; he had the trim muscularity of fast light heavyweight. His shoulder-length black hair had no gray in it, despite being the same age as Kane, though his skin was far more weathered; the scars of a motorcycle's kick starter on his boots gave a clue as to why. He normally wore sunglasses, but even without them his deep-set eyes were barely visible in the scant light.

"When the hell," Kane began but then thought Hector being there might explain the dead and missing cultists and changed his question, "have you been stalking in Odiome?"

"Nope, just got into town," Hector said and came sauntering through the tiny kitchen. He took in the blood trail and the smear against the wall without much interest, simply accumulating data. When he noticed the statuette laying on the bed, however, he strode forward into the bedroom, passed Kane, and flipped the hideous stone figure onto its back. He turned to Kane, a thick black eyebrow cocked high, and said, "The fuck is that doing here?"

"Surprise, surprise," Kane said, crossing his arms and leaning against the wall. "There *is* a cult in town."

Most Venators did not waste time with pleasantries, not with each other. There was never a reason to ask how someone's day was going, ask after kids or a job, to inquire as to health or happiness: they already knew the answers. There was only the war. And Hector was like every other Venator only more so. If Kane recognized that his own background and reasons for hunting the cult made him a rather typical Venator, if more successful than most, he nevertheless knew that Hector was far closer to the Venator ideal, the mythical wandering spirit of vengeance. Though he'd worked with Hector on three occasions, and usually crossed paths with him a couple times a year, he'd never asked why Hector had joined the war; it was a question Venators did not ask each other. He knew nothing of the man's past and little of what made him tick, other than the overwhelming desire to slay cultists. If there were cultists to kill, nothing else mattered to Hector, which is what made him so dangerous to the cult—and to other Venators. The only humanizing thing about the man, that Kane knew of, was that he and another pro—named Archie—had a thing for Helen, more than the usual crush most Venators developed for the historian.

"Yeah, I know there's a cult in town," Hector said. "But it ain't supposed to be this one."

"What other cult is there?" Kane said.

"Helen figured out what had been bothering her about this Odiome woman going nuts out in public," Hector said. "It was the picture in the newspaper. The woman's earrings: Innsmouth Jewelry."

Kane came away from the wall as if kicked. "Are you fucking kidding me?"

"No," Hector said. "Shit, would she ask me to drop a stalk I had going out near Buffalo if it weren't serious? Innsmouth Jewelry, Kane, which could mean The Followers of Dagon."

"Could mean," Kane said. "*Could.* I've seen specimens twice in ten years of stalking; neither time was it more than one piece and it was never connected with The Followers. Sometimes old cults come across an earring or ring. The cults and The Followers have always associated with each other."

"Really?" Hector said, arms akimbo. "Well shit, Kane, why don't you tell me a bit more about them? 'Cause I was thinking of hunting the motherfuckers and it sure would be helpful to know a little more."

Kane rolled his eyes and was about to fire back when all that he knew so far started to mesh with the one dangerous piece of information Hector had brought. "Jesus," he said quietly, absently tapping the tip of his dagger against the wall behind him.

"What?" Hector said.

"Normally Innsmouth Jewelry doesn't mean anything because Cthulhu Cults can't use it, right?" Kane said. "The stuff doesn't respond to the cults' sacrifices."

"But this broad going loco out in the streets says maybe the shit was working, driving her nuts," Hector finished the thought. "That's just what Helen thought."

"The last time The Followers of Dagon were seen was back in '36," Kane said.

"Yeah, at Innsmouth, Massachusetts," Hector said.

"Their MO is to takeover an entire town," Kane said. "To bring every single citizen into their cult and sacrifice anyone who resists. Then, they prey on travelers, the homeless, conducting their rites all but out in the open."

"This is just fascinating," Hector said.

"I'm getting to the point, goddamnit," Kane said. "They'll work with Cthulhu Cults because they need them, in the long run, but I don't think they'd allow one to operate in the same town."

Hector shrugged. "Maybe, maybe not," he said. "What difference does it make?"

"The difference is that this town *has* a Cthulhu Cult," Kane said. "Or did. I found a list of ten members, not counting the lady who made the list. I went through the list tonight. Only about half of them are still in town. Well, *were* still in town. I thought the missing ones had left and in a hurry. But maybe they were taken."

"Join or die?" Hector said.

"In each case," Kane said, "it looked as if the missing cultists had left in a hurry, packing only the bare essentials. It could have been a cover, though, so that if they were reported missing by their employers, the cops would have a plausible story waiting for them at each apartment."

"And then there's this dude," Hector said, pointing to the blood trail with a stubbled chin. "He had the cult's statuette—or more likely *she*—"

"No, it was he," Kane said. "Silas Moynahan."

"Male cult leaders are rare," Hector said. "And who else would be holding the statuette?"

"Yeah, but they do happen," Kane said. "And the leader may have given him the statuette before joining The Followers of Dagon, when they took over the town—shit."

"What?" Hector said.

"I think I met the leader," Kane said, rubbing the back of his neck. "There's a woman who owns an art gallery—packed with paintings bearing subtle Mythos imagery and dread symbols, by the way—who acted all kinds of uncomfortable when I pretended to feel the paintings but didn't outright call her on it. She said I could have anything in the store, or something to that effect."

Hector leered. "Did she now?" he said. "But your monkish ass didn't take her up on the offer, did you Kane?"

"Fuck you," Kane said.

"No, not me, boy," Hector said. "If you'd laid her right then and there, she'd have spilled the whole goddamn story: that Followers are in town, that her cult has been brought into the fold or killed off—on one of their ducky orange and yellow alters, if memory serves—and probably told you when and where the next sacrifice was. All for a quick bumping of uglies. But not Solomon Kane, no. Not him. He's gone monastic."

"I didn't know anything about Followers of Dagon being in

town, dick head," Kane said. "And there would have been time to take her up on her offer later."

"Except you've been going down her list," Hector said. "Killing off whoever The Followers hadn't gobbled up. They'll know something ain't right in crazy town, just as soon as they drop round to pick up another sacrifice and find he done already been knifed."

Kane shook his head, knowing Hector was right, though not granting the premise that he could have played McKenzie any other way. "Did Helen say anything else?" he asked.

"Not really," Hector said and threw back the sheets on the bed, picking up a pillow. "She said we need to be careful about finding the Innsmouth Jewelry, though. Find out who's wearing any and how many there are and wipe them out before the whole town is taken over."

"That's how they did it in '36," Kane said. "Before anyone had noticed, before a Venator passed through, they'd initiated the entire town of Innsmouth Massachusetts into The Followers of Dagon. A thousand-percent increase in missing persons in the surrounding towns; not a homeless person for miles. A death mill for Dagon and Cthulhu before it was finally stopped."

"Yeah," Hector said, taking the pillowcase off the pillow. "And afterward, the government claimed responsibility; said there was an infection that needed quarantining."

"Only it wasn't the government who burned down Innsmouth in '36," Kane said.

"Nope," Hector said, grinning wolfishly and stuffing the statuette of Cthulhu into the pillowcase.

"Some relative of yours, probably," Kane said.

"Ha! Could've been," Hector said. "The first bikers started after World War I, buying surplus Indians from the army." Hector's Indian Warrior was of a later vintage but every bit as recognizable. "And they didn't start traveling the country to make meth, like the fucks who call themselves bikers today. They had business. Business they'd learned about overseas; business they'd brought home; our business. So let's get down to it, boy."

The Followers of Dagon. Dagon was one of The Great Old Ones and like Cthulhu was strongly associated with the sea. Also like Cthulhu, his followers claimed to receive messages from Dagon in their dreams, though more specific than simple dream sendings. Quite why The Followers of Dagon chose to take over entire towns was not known but it had always been their modus oporendi

take over a town or small city, control the most influential families and determine who could and would be elected to positions of power, and then slowly convert every citizen until the town all but openly worshiped Dagon, sacrificing humans in rituals every bit as bloody as those of the Cthulhu Cults. The last known attempt to take over a town in the United States by a chapter of the Esoteric Order of Dagon happened in 1936 in the port town of Innsmouth, Massachusetts. Then, there had been war in the streets, as Venators from all over the country descended upon Innsmouth. The federal government had created a story of disease and quarantine to assuage the press, but the truth was far less neat. Where the jewelry had come from, which made The Followers' rituals possible, no one knew. Though the Venators of the time had gathered what they could from the slain, depositing it in the deep vault beneath Miskotonic University, the source had not been located, nor the leader or leaders of The Followers who had ordered the invasion of Innsmouth. Occasionally, Venators like Kane would come across a piece of the fabled Innsmouth Jewelry in the possession of an old and careful Cthulhu Cult, one that had gone unnoticed for a century or more. It was to them merely a memento, a sign that their cult had been used or promised something by The Followers of Dagon. The Followers needed the Cthulhu Cults. In the order of things as had been foretold for eons prior to recorded history, The

Great Old Ones awaited only the revival of Cthulhu, their priest, who by the greatness of his power would return them to life. The Followers of Dagon wished to hasten the day of their God's return by assisting the Cthulhu Cults in resurrecting Dread Cthulhu.

"Let's go take this cultist bitch," Hector said, "and then start stalking the pier side. The Followers in Innsmouth started by infiltrating the oldest fishing families. I'm betting they've done the same here, to build up a cadre of thugs. They'd need muscle to recruit—or otherwise—the Cthulhu Cult already in town."

"Maybe," Kane said, his lip between his teeth for a moment. "That's a good place to start but I don't think we should take the art dealer yet."

"What was her name?" Hector asked casually.

"Yeah right," Kane said.

"Shit, how many art galleries could there be in town?" Hector said, making an open-handed gesture in front of his crotch.

"Twelve," Kane said. "Good luck with that. But listen, no one will have found the bodies I dropped last night, not yet. We'll need to move quickly but Helen is right: the jewelry is the key. Somehow or other The Followers use it to commune with Dagon—or Cthulhu for all we know—and if we leave it out there floating around it'll find its way into the hands of someone who can use it, and then we're right back where we started."

"We gotta find The Followers before we can find their jewelry, beau," Hector said, swinging the pillowcase—now heavy with the statuette inside—over his shoulder.

"Yeah but we already know where one piece is," Kane said: "with Layla Odiome."

Hector reluctantly nodded.

"We've probably got at least a few hours before the alarm goes out about the dead cultists, official or otherwise," Kane said. "I'll try to get a line on where Mrs. Mayor Odiome buys her accessories.

If The Followers are running the old Innsmouth playbook, they'll have tried to take over the Mayor's office, to control the town. His wife would have been a good first step. Where are you going with *my* statuette?" he said, pointing.

"I'm'a break it up and dump it in the bay," Hector said. "I'm headed down there anyway to stalk out any locals already inducted. You go on and checkout the mayor-lady. That's a good idea. Keep you out of my hair."

"Yeah, I really don't want to be in there," Kane said, wrinkling his lip at Hector's greasy locks.

"Hey fuck you," Hector said with some heat. "It's a long ride from Arkham to Odiome, okay?"

"We should hook up later this afternoon, early tonight," Kane said. "See where we are. I'm at the flophouse next to the canal."

"Better move the fuck out of there, boy," Hector said. "Now that you've got a few homicides on your sheet here in fun-town. Oh and I noticed you still ain't ditched that Dodge POS you're driving around in."

"It's a Chrysler," Kane said, "and have you ditched your Indian Warrior?"

Hector slipped on his mirrored sunglasses, said two words to Kane, and then walked through the kitchen. With his hand on the doorway out, he leaned back and said, "We'll meet at sunset. There's a bar a couple blocks down from your flophouse, on the docks. If I'm not there, ask the waitress with an ass so round and tight it's got to be giving off sonar. She'll know where I am."

Kane snorted and said, "She in contact with Helen?"

Hector said the same two words as before and left. Kane stood thinking for a moment, giving Hector time to get clear of the building before he left, too. The question of how to learn where or from whom did Mrs. Odiome obtained a piece of Innsmouth Jewelry ran riot in Kane's mind. Hunting Cthulhu Cults was usually a lonely business conducted in out-of-the-way places, the desolate corners of the earth, where a dozen people barely able to keep their shattered minds within the bounds of poorly contrived cover identities killed and recruited and killed again in an ever-increasing orgy of blood. Their own madness was their goal and it proved a potent handicap when confronted not with unwary victims quietly going about their lives but with the relentless pursuit of the vengeful. The Followers of Dagon, however, were something else entirely. Murder was not their goal but their means; their ends lay in shadow.

"What could they want with an entire city?" Kane said to himself as he bent the slat of a venetian blind and saw Hector walking up the street.

The statuette of Cthulhu swung heavily at Hector's back as he walked. Though the hour was still early, people were going about their business: papers being delivered, cars being packed for the drive home, dogs walked. The statuette, though, was not unaware. Its influence permeated the air as it passed. Children began to cry, their mothers gathering them into a panicked embrace and rushing back into the hotel; dogs whined, tails between their legs, and cowered or pulled their owners off in the opposite direction; grown adults looked around as if expecting an attack, crossed the street as Hector approached, or stood ashen faced, incapable of moving under the weight of sudden and inexplicable dread. The very sounds of the street died, stifled beneath the unseen presence; nothing but a ringing in the ears, a single bell tolling; the weak sun dimmed and the air thinned to a wavering gasp: only the steady cadence of Hector's tread remained undaunted. And then he turned a corner, taking dread down another street, choking off life for another endless minute for another hundred people, and life swept in where he had passed, revived but not unchanged.

CHAPTER 7

CULTS WITHIN CULTS

KANE RETURNED TO Silas Moynahan's closet and pawed around in the crawlspace above until he located a pull cord, which released the false back panel. Inside, Kane found the dozen paintings listed in McKenzie's ledger; some were rolled, some in frames, all horrific. Kane closed up the compartment, locked the apartment on the way out, and used the alley behind the building to go a few blocks north before returning to the tourist-friendly streets of Odiome.

He thought of returning to the library, to again dig into Layla Odiome's past, but there was no time. Eliminating the remnants of the Cthulhu Cult in Odiome had put a clock on his stalk and Kane begrudged ever second lost. There was no time for a long and thorough investigation. *Luck is what I need,* he thought as he walked along, hands in his pockets and head down, eyes habitually taking in the crowd around him, *heaping truckloads of it.* A fundamental difference existed between the Cthulhu Cults and The Followers of Dagon, making each dangerous in its own way: organization.

The various Cthulhu Cults were more or less unaffiliated with one another, isolated groups of insane murderers slaughtering as often as possible and initiating new members from among society's various cast-offs and renegades; destroying one cult would not lead to the next—they didn't know one another. As such, Cthulhu Cults could—and did—exist anywhere, everywhere, and finding them was as much a matter of luck as diligence. A small cult, careful or simple enough to remain on civilization's outskirts, could go on murdering the forgotten and abused for decades, even centuries. Those whose leaders could not distinctively receive dream sendings, or were not savvy enough to interpret them, might have to do without a statuette of Cthulhu, but that wouldn't stop them from killing, even if they did not know the ritual words of sacrifice. New cults could form out of nowhere, too, without even a seed member from another organized cult: it only took a single look at a scrap from the *Necrnomicon* or other Mythos text and a whisper from Cthulhu's dead dreams could awaken the madness. Then nothing would satisfy the new believer except learning more and putting into practice the blasphemies uncovered. In this way, though the Cthulhu Cults might never coalesce around a single leader and rise to challenge the people of the world, to slaughter on a scale so large as to awaken Dread Cthulhu, they also could never be wholly wiped out. The dreams would always come to someone new.

The Followers of Dagon, however, were nothing if not organized. Those who fought against the resurgence of The Great Old Ones counted the centuries by when and where The Followers last returned, to again seize a town, to again begin sacrificing on a scale so enormous that it could sate the murderous need of Cthulhu, bringing back from death that which would return life to Dagon. Innsmouth was the last time. And not the last time. If the origin of the statuettes of Cthulhu was a subject of debate amongst Venators—simply a store of ancient art, created before the downfall of R'lyeh, or extraterrestrial and ever renewed from the depths of space—the jewelry indispensable to a Follower sacrifice was even more mysterious. Its purpose was guessed at but its source was unknown. Was it gathered or made? Did it call as a statuette might, to the sensitive or those doomed by artistic sensibility, or did the leadership of The Followers of Dagon control it inexorably? Again, unknown. But it was the organization of The Followers that made them dangerous. Though they could sacrifice on a scale that dwarfed even the most veracious Cthulhu Cult, The Followers practiced patience and prudence, staying hidden and safely away from those telltale signs that attracted Venators. They planned and stored resources, preparing decades in advance of an invasion. And when a target city or large town was determined, they would spend decades more to slowly and carefully recruit the Chief of Police, the leading citizens, heads of newspapers and industry, and—most importantly—the mayor.

But that's where this goes pear-shaped, Kane thought as he stood looking over a restaurant's posted menu to see in the reflection off the front window if anyone was tailing him. *If The Followers had designated Odiome as their next target, infiltrating the Mayor's family is a sure bet; particularly in a town like Odiome where the Mayor's family has been in charge for four-hundred years or some shit. But if that's the case, then they would never let his wife go bonkers out on Main Street. What the hell happened?*

The various options passed through Kane's mind, as did what little he knew of The Followers of Dagon. Even he—not the least solitary of the habitually individual Venators—had heard the few tales of Innsmouth, had read the diary of a survivor who, in his madness, had thought he was morphing into a higher order of being; an amphibian of sorts that could swim down to R'lyeh and revive Cthulhu by CPR, presumably. Venators called the morphed, "Frogboys." There was still some debate about whether it could actually happen. Some thought that morphing explained where the *real* Followers of Dagon were, under the ocean. Kane had no time to consider the debate, however. Whether The Followers of Dagon had actually invaded Odiome or Mrs. Mayor Layla had simply stumbled upon a pair of Innsmouth Jewelry earrings at a flee market, which had then driven her nuts, had to be determined. And it had to be determined before Kane's recent killings were discovered.

He fished his cell phone out of his pocket and brought up the Odiome City webpage. "There's one sure way of finding out," he said to himself as he dialed the Mayor's office. It took ten minutes to talk his way passed the switchboard to the Mayor's secretary, and then five minutes more to determine that Mayor Odiome was in the office but not available. That solved one problem: if the Mayor had been at home, taking care of his recently insane wife, it would have been much more difficult to see her. One thing complicated paying a visit to Layla Odiome, though: the Mayor always lunched at home.

Okay, Kane thought after he hung up, *so she throws a wingding out in public, the Mayor has to respond somehow. If he's already a Follower, he has her locked in the basement and fed more crazy-soup. If he's not, if The Followers tried to recruit her first, then he's a desperate man right now, trying get help for his wife's mental illness without ruining his political career. I assume the old boy has his eye on the Governorship. A mad wife might throw a monkey wrench into that. So, he pulls a Rochester and locks her in the attic, and then brings in a specialist from some psychiatric hospital to treat her. Should be a piece of cake to break into his mansion under the noses of his security and whatever mental health professionals he's hired.*

The Mayor's mansion was a monument to Victorian pretension. With enough turrets to make a castle jealous, the fish-scale shingles of a summer home, and huge meandering porches sporting carpenter-Gothic colonnades, Odiome Mansion bore the scars of generations of additions and "improvements" made by a family that had been touched by economic distress as infrequently as by good taste. Nevertheless, its sheer size was impressive, as were its grounds—enough land around it to make a decent farm—and sitting atop a hill that overlooked not only the town but the bay beyond, if it was ugly, at least it had a view of that which was not.

All Kane was thinking as he approached the citadel was that he still had to come up with some line he could use to talk his way inside. *No noticeable security*, he thought, *that's something at least: maybe the Mayor couldn't trust them not to go to the press. Hmm, the press.* As he came the porch, he quickly cinched up his tie and tried to smooth down his hair. He had a day's growth on his cheeks by now but there was no time for a shave; he'd have to play it as if he was deliberately scruffy. He knocked and after a few minutes the housekeeper answered.

"Good morning," Kane said, affecting a nasally sneer. "I'm afraid I've left my cards at the hotel," he said, patting his pockets, "but I am Mr. Clyde Markson, acquisitions agent for, er, Solomon, Kane, Hector, and Troy, Limited. I would like to see Mayor Odiome immediately."

"I am sorry, Señor," the housekeeper said, either impressed by or uncomprehending Kane's line of bullshit, if she wasn't simply too polite to notice it. "Señor Odiome is not at home. Perhaps the Mayor's Office?"

"This is not government business, if you please," Kane said, closing his eyes as if at a bad smell. "My business can be conducted with Mrs. Odiome as easily as with her husband. Gracious, possibly more so!

"She owns a pair of extremely rare earrings, you understand," Kane said, fluttering his voice in imitation of a haberdasher he'd once met in Manhattan (who'd refused to sell Kane a suit). "Part of a collection. I represent a client interested in assembling a complete set."

"I am sorry but la Señora is indisposed," the housekeeper assured him.

"No matter," Kane said, tossing his hand about as if it were only loosely attached to his wrist. "I'm sure Mr. Odiome will find the subject fascinating. I was led to believe he returns home for lunch."

"Well, yes, but—" the housekeeper began to protest.

"I'll wait," Kane said and walked all but through the housekeeper and into the hallway. "And I'll take tea as I do. Is this the parlor?"

With that, Kane entered the first room on the right and began to hum lightly to himself, strolling around the cluttered room with his hands behind his back, gazing interestedly at the porcelain figurines and glass balls and other needless effluvia indispensable to a useless room. Faced with what could have been breading better than her own and uncertain how to remove the intruder if he was not an honored guest, the housekeeper closed both the front door and the parlor door and went in search of two cups of tea—one for her unexpected quest and one to steady herself.

Kane listened to her quiet steps retreating to the back of the house before he crept out of the parlor. He left both the parlor and front doors open a crack, to give a ready explanation for his disappearance should the housekeeper return with the tea quicker than expected. He then trotted upstairs, betting even a Follower of Dagon wouldn't lock up his insane wife in a dank basement. *Not when their precious ocean can be seen from one of the turrets,* Kane thought.

Most of the mansion was conspicuous by its absences. There were a dozen or more rooms on the second floor but with the exception of the master bedroom, none were occupied. The Odiome's ten-year old son's room was still furnished but had clearly not been lived in since the boy went away to private school. As Kane ascended to the third floor, the first hint of occupation drifted lazily down the staircase to him: pipe smoke.

The hardwood floor would have been impossible to traverse quietly if not for the thick rug running its length. Kane kept to the center, carefully testing each step for moving boards, eyes watching the seams of doors for light, and ears trying to penetrate their own lonely ringing for the sounds of approach. At the north-east corner of the third floor there was a spiraling wrought iron staircase going up to the most prominent of the mansion's turrets. From behind the door closest to the staircase, Kane heard an inaccurate humming; the pipe smoke had grown distinct.

Sitting on his heels, making both knees pop, Kane brought his eye to the keyhole. The hardware must have been as old as most of the rest of the house and had a thick, straight-across barrel lock. Kane could see clearly into the room. In a chair near the eastern windows sat a man with a meerschaum pipe and a gauzy comb-over, studying something on an e-reader. The satchel under the desk nearby was of the heavy leather variety, with hinged arms at either end to hold it open if needs be and a stout lock to keep it shut otherwise. *Just like what a psychiatrist would have,* Kane thought: *a bag of goodies for the insane Mrs. Mayor. Well, Dr. Combover, there's not a pill or shot in this world that can help her now.*

Kane had to stifle a groan as he straightened reluctant knees; his back cracked loud enough that he worried the doctor might hear it. With the slowness of a man sneaking up on a proposal, Kane climbed the wrought-iron staircase.

The room at the top of the turret reminded Kane of McKenzie's studio. Paintings in various stages of completeness leaned against one wall, with two more on easels. In a long shelf opposite, under the south windows, books on painting, art, and the biographies of painters swept a colorful arc. The windows above were more colorful still, commanding a glorious view from south through east to north, overlooking all of Odiome and stretching across the slate-gray Atlantic to the newly risen sun. All that beauty—so unexpected it stopped Kane in his tracks—had no effect at all on Layla Odiome.

Kane stood in the tiny alcove at the top of the stairs and watched Mrs. Odiome for a moment, taking in the particulars of the room. It could have been simply that the Mayor's wife had a household staff to see to the cleaning, or that her much more expensive dwelling boasted better ventilation equipment, but there was no acrid smell of paint. More likely, though, it was explained by no paint-smeared palate laying about, no brushes sitting in thinner. Whatever painting had taken place in that turret hadn't happened recently. All this Kane saw and yet hardly noticed; it came in through the corners of his eyes. He focused instead upon the woman wrapped in a shawl, slowly rocking in a chair set before the east windows, watching the ocean.

The stiffness in his knees slipped away, his arms hung suddenly loose. The ringing in his ears, ever present when straining to hear something else, quieted as if it had moved into another room. Beneath the creak of the rocking chair's slow chant, in the pause at either end of its travel, Kane heard the quiet murmur of whispered words. He leaned forward as he crept into the room until he was bent nearly double. The soft rug of the third-floor hallways was gone but the mat put down to protect the floors from dripping paint muffled Kane's approach. He drew abreast of Layla Odiome but she took no notice of him, eyes locked on the ocean.

Kane had never met a sensitive before, someone capable of receiving the dream sendings of Cthulhu. He knew such people existed, that their appearance usually heralded the coming rise of an island door to R'Lyeh and the possible return of Cthulhu. Cultists could receive dream sendings, of course, but only after a sacrifice. To know the madness of Cthulhu's dreams, to see images of ancient torment and visions of the inevitable enslavement of mankind, to be pursued from restless sleep into the waking day by the unknowable strangeness of eternity without warning, without seeking it, must be an affliction, Kane thought, the most horrible affliction. Unless sought.

Kane slowly sat on the edge of a curving bench seat, under the east windows, and leaned his elbows on his knees. He watched as Layla rocked back and forth and mumbled to herself. Her waist-long café-au-lait hair fell over one shoulder in gentle waves. From the blankness of her stare and disarrangement of her clothes, Kane knew she had not dressed herself that morning. And yet, the luster of her hair showed that it had been brushed recently, and probably over several minutes. Someone had taken the time to sit with her, brushing her hair. She was certainly beautiful enough to elicit the tender devotions of a man the Mayor's age, but it was not her beauty nor her nearly catatonic mien that drew Kane's attention at that moment. Clearly visible with her hair to one side was an earring of a gold-like substance, an unnatural figure that swung in the motion of her rocking and bespoke the might and horror of Dagon.

At this close range, there could be no mistake. Kane ran a hand down his face, making a noise like sandpaper when he crossed his chin, and gazed at the tiny adornment pregnant with evil. The reputation of the flawless planning and implacable patience of The Followers of Dagon was not conveyed by Layla's total indifference to his presence. All the questions about how she could have come to wear Innsmouth Jewelry and whether she knew what they were returned to his mind. As he thought, however, her murmured words became recognizable in the stillness of the turret. She was speaking of the sea.

"Mrs. Odiome?" Kane said softly. She continued to rock and stare blankly through the window. "Mrs. Odiome? Layla," he said more firmly, "can you hear me, Layla?" She slowed and the sound left her moving lips. "Those are lovely earrings you're wearing," Kane said. "May I ask you about them?"

"From, from the sea," she whispered, eyes moving as if across a printed page, searching for a phrase she only half-remembered. "Down, down where . . ."

"Yes, the sea?" Kane prompted.

Kane heard the last three steps as Dr. Combover's head rose above the top riser and he emerged in the little alcove at the stairs' head. The man started when he saw Kane and snatched the pipe out of his mouth. He stamped up the remaining stairs and came to the edge of the alcove.

"What in the—who are you?" the doctor demanded in a high perturbed voice.

"I could ask you the same question," Kane said in his affected voice, adding outrage to his earlier flutter. "Barging in on people like this. Go away!"

"I'm, that is, no," the doctor said. "Listen here, Mrs. Odiome should not be disturbed. Now come away from there."

"Who are you to make demands of me?" Kane said indignantly and sprang to his feet. His five inches of extra height and sixty pounds more weight were not lost on the doctor, who took a step back and nearly fell down the stairs. "I am a guest in this house and I'm having a conversation with Mrs. Odiome."

"I'm her doctor," the doctor said, pulling down on his sweater vest, trying to regain some of the dignity. "Dr. Livermore. And she is my patient so—"

"The doctor?" Kane laughed and then strode to the smaller man's side and took his elbow. Pushing him into the alcove and then down the first few steps, Kane told Dr. Livermore, "I'm not in the habit of taking orders from the help. Good bye."

The alcove had a door, which Kane closed, but the key was missing. He didn't know how much time he would have before

Livermore could get the Mayor on the phone, but he guessed not much. Kane hurried back to Layla's side. She seemed not to have noticed the altercation. Her rocking had returned to its previous pace, as had her mumbling. Without the time to slowly draw her back to consciousness, and not knowing if she had been medicated into insensibility, Kane chose to use extraordinary methods.

In a whisper close to her ear, barely louder than her own murmured words, Kane said, "Ph'nglui mglw'nafh Cthulhu . . ."

". . . R'lyeh wgah'nagl fhtagn," Mrs. Odiome completed and then turned tremblingly to Kane, a fully conscious intelligence now alive in her terrified eyes. "What's happening? What are those voices and where is that place?"

"It's alright, Layla," he said. "It'll be okay, I'm just going to—"

The alcove door flew open and slammed against the wall. A man in a police uniform—with the word *Chief* preceding his name on a plate above his pocket—stormed into the room, hand on his holstered pistol. With him came an older gentleman in a flawless gray suit of worsted wool; his hair and eyes were nearly of the same color. Looking over their shoulders from the alcove, Dr. Livermore's absent chin trembled in a mix of fear and anger.

"Step away from Mrs. Odiome," the Police Chief ordered, pointing with his free hand.

At the same time, Mayor Odiome demanded, "Who are you and what are you doing in my house?"

Kane straightened, smiled a little cockeyed grin, and, with much more composure than he felt—while carrying a gun and a dagger used in half-a-dozen recent murders—asked with a laugh, "Excuse me?" After another silent chuckle, Kane extended his hand and said in his normal voice, "Mayor Odiome?"

Stepping around the Police Chief, who was about to repeat his order, Mayor Odiome ignored Kane's hand and said, "Yes, now who are you and what are you doing in my house, bothering my wife?"

"I'm not bothering anyone," Kane said amicably. "I'm here because the housekeeper let me in. I've come on business."

The Mayor quickly crossed the room to his wife and placed a hand on her shoulder, leaning down to whisper a question. She had returned to her rocking and mumbling and took no notice of him.

"What are you talking about?" the Mayor then demanded. "I've never met you before in my life: we don't have any business."

"We could," Kane said brightly. "I've come about those earrings of your wife's. They are a part of an ancient collection and I represent a client who is trying to assemble a complete set. Pay a fortune for them."

"They're not for sale," Mayor Odiome said incredulously.

"Mayor, if I may remind you—" Dr. Livermore began to say.

"Be quiet, Dr. Livermore!" the Mayor shouted, causing his wife to jump; he bent and whispered his apologies.

"Mr. Mayor," the Police Chief said, "much as I hate to say it, this is exactly why I was against your dismissing your protection detail. Anyone can just walk in here." To Kane he said, "I don't know how far you thought you'd get with that bull about earrings, mister, but I'll tell you where it'll get you: right down into my jail."

"Oh, nice tourist-friendly town you have here, Mayor," Kane said. "A man has a look around, makes an offer on something, and they throw him in jail."

"We welcome tourists here, sir," Mayor Odiome said, straightening. "Not muckraking reporters."

"Now come along with me," the Police Chief said, extending his free hand toward Kane. "You can take the tour of our town jail."

Kane pulled his arm out of the Chief's hand—wondered how many deputies were downstairs, if it came to fighting his way out— and said, "You lay a hand on me again and I'll sue this town, you, and his Honor the Mayor. You think the tourist trade is suffering now, with the economy and your wife's visions showing up in the paper," Kane said to the Mayor, "you just wait until they run a headline about how the acquisitions agent for Solomon, Kane, Hector, and Troy Limited was arrested for making an offer on a pair of goddamn earrings!"

The Mayor cast a quick troubled look at the Police Chief but said nothing. The Police Chief licked his lips and said in a vicious quiet, "You may think you'll hide behind the housekeeper letting you in but I think she'll have a different story for the State Prosecutor come the trial."

"It doesn't matter what she tells anyone now," Kane said, stepping closer to the Police Chief so he could look down at the man. "It only matters how it reads in the papers."

"Wait, wait," Mayor Odiome said, stepping nearly between the two larger men. "I am willing to believe that this is just a misunderstanding, Mister, er—"

"Markson," Kane said, certain they'd already heard it from the housekeeper.

"Mr. Markson," the Mayor went on hurriedly. "Manners differ and I can appreciate a difficult client. However, my wife is unwell— at the moment. *At the moment*, my wife is unwell. So if you would be so kind as to leave, perhaps we can pick this up at another time."

"Certainly," Kane said, eyes never leaving the Police Chief. "Perhaps, if they aren't for sale, you could tell me where your wife bought them?"

"She didn't, she," the Mayor said, touching his forehead and talking fast, "she, they were a gift from the new jeweler in town; something to do with a custom from his home country."

"The jeweler have a name?" Kane asked.

"Mr.—Christ—Mr., er, Mr. Ashurbanipal," the Mayor said. "Now, please."

Kane slipped past and went for the stairs. His was on the top step when the Police Chief spoke out.

"You got yourself a first-rate line of bullshit, Mister Acquisitions Agent," he said quietly, "and the Mayor may find it expedient to let it slip by but I'll tell you this: I want you out of my town before nightfall."

"You couldn't pay me to stay in this fly stain you call a town," Kane growled and then left.

CHAPTER 8

THE THREE
OLDEST FAMILIES

W ITH A SENSATION between his shoulder blades as if the Police Chief was pointing a pistol at him the whole way back, Kane returned to the flophouse and packed up his caved-in suitcase. He packed his pistol and dagger, switching them to the concealed compartment in the trunk of the Cutlass before driving off. It was even money that the Police Chief or one of his eager-beaver deputies would pull him over just for the hell of it. *You never know what frisking someone's car will turn up, after all,* Kane thought as he drove north and out of town.

He kept to the speed limit while driving the winding road for about a mile, watching his rear-view mirror for pursuit. When reasonably certain no one was watching, he pulled off the road and down a shallow gully between scrub-covered hills. There, he camouflaged his car with a bit of foliage and opened the trunk.

The dark suit and black turtleneck sweater still smelled like a campfire. Kane climbed into them and loaded his pockets with extra magazines for his M1911A1. He put his dagger back in his boot, too, before digging into the little compartment for a small, curiously heavy bag. He slipped it into his hip pocket and then closed the trunk. It was almost ten hours until sunset. Kane sat on the ground with his back to a front tire. Sat, thought, and watched the sun drop behind the western hills.

For his return to Odiome, Kane walked down to the shore. The rocky coast that lined the bay became treacherous as night fell and Kane had to pick his way slowly and carefully as he came to the north end of town. A large and seemingly abandoned factory marked the beginning of the Odiome waterfront; a derelict from a time when Odiome dabbled in the luxury yacht business. Kane passed it by, glad it wasn't a house full of nosy neighbors, and made his way down the pier to the bar close to the flophouse that Hector had indicated.

The local crowd filled the stools and high tables nearest the bar, watching the row of flat-screen televisions above the mirror and shouting abuse at *The Patriots'* opponent. The bar was as old as the rest of the pier-side quarter of Odiome, with scarred wood-work covered in years of polished grime and neglected gaslight-style lamps bolted to the partitions between booths. They couldn't com-pete with the light from the televisions and so the booths sat in murky shadow. Kane took one farther back but not all the way in the corner—couldn't see the door that far away—and waited for Hector.

Hector's sonar-assed waitress had brought Kane a scotch neat and come to check on it twice before Hector appeared. He flung the door open so hard it smacked against the exterior wall, drawing a moment's consideration from the sports fans. He then walked in wearing mirrored sunglasses, despite it being nighttime, and scanned the bar as he took them off. It took him only a second to spot Kane and when he noticed the dark suit streaked in what might be dirt, Hector swore openly and stomped over.

"The fuck did you do, boy?" Hector said.

"Sit down," Kane growled. After Hector's waitress brought him a beer, Kane related everything that had happened at the Odiome Mansion.

"Cat-O-tonic, huh?" Hector said when Kane had finished.

"Yeah," Kane said, rolling his eyes. "Very nearly."

"And the Police Chief just happened to stop by?" Hector went on. "I don't buy that. He and the Mayor are probably in on it. Keeping an eye on her while the Innsmouth earrings turn the mayor-lady's brains to mush."

"I don't think so," Kane said. "For one, they would never have let me leave. Secondly, the Mayor seemed genuinely concerned about Layla: would a cultist—or a Follower? It sounded like the Police Chief had come by to rate the Mayor about dropping his protection detail. Why would the Mayor get rid of his bodyguards? Because he couldn't trust them not to go to the press, which is what they thought I was. A Follower would have just brought in his own people and been done."

"Maybe," Hector said and then reached into his jacket's outside pocket. "Speaking of Followers."

He dropped a rolled up wad of greasy handkerchief on the table, smelling of motor oil. Pulling back one corner, Kane saw what was inside: fingers. Half-a-dozen human fingers lay heaped together in a macabre imitation of cocktail sausages. Each finger, however, was encircled by a ring of curious gold-colored metal, intricately engraved with a motif of the sea.

"Found some of the frogboys," Hector said.

Kane looked up fast and gulped, "What?"

"I'm kidding," Hector laughed. "None of them had morphed. I don't even believe that story of them changing into amphibians."

"Because tales of the supernatural are just superstitious nonsense, right?" Kane said. "What happened?"

"What do you think?" Hector said. "I stalked the pier side, down by the clammers' boats. Picked up on the first one, figured out who he was, and checked out his family. More than half the folks in that first boy's family had rings. All of them looked a little, I don't know, intense about shit. I asked around and they are one of the three oldest families in town. It's the Innsmouth playbook all over again, Kane: control the economy, control the Mayor's office. Hell, I figure they must be trying to take control of the tourist trade, too, though I can't figure how."

Kane snapped his fingers, "Maybe that's why they targeted Layla," he said. "The Mayor said the new jeweler in town—Ashurbanipal—gave Layla the earrings as some sort of tradition from his home country. If Ashurbanipal is the source of the Innsmouth Jewelry, he could have given her some so she'd go nuts, start raving in the streets, killing the tourist industry. He must have known that the Mayor couldn't send his wife to an insane asylum because it would hurt his chances when he runs for Governor. Two birds with one stone: drive down tourism—to make the fishing trade more important—and then get a foothold in the Mayor's office."

"Smart, I guess," Hector said, rubbing his neck. "But I don't see how that allows him to control the Mayor or the town government."

"Maybe once she's fully under control?" Kane said lamely.

"You've got it all worked out," Hector said and killed his beer. "Listen, I'm going to go back and finish up on those three families once it's dark enough, late enough for them to be home. You going to stalk this Ashurbanipal fellah?"

"Yeah only keep it down when you go in on those Followers," Kane said. "It didn't sound like the Police Chief had heard about my killing the Cthulhu Cultists last night: a massacre takes place down at the pier and I think he might just catch wind. We still don't know where the hoard of Innsmouth Jewelry is yet and it'll be a hell of a lot harder to locate if the Police Chief calls in State Troopers because of what looks to him like a gang war."

"Then you'd better work quick, boy," Hector said and stood up. "Because I've got the trail and I ain't letting it go cold. Those fucks won't escape me. I'll call you when I run out of bodies, let you know how loud it got."

Hector stuffed the wad of fingers back in his jacket and left, paying no heed to Kane's hissed imprecations. Kane sat fuming for a few minutes and finished his drink. He'd worked with, or at least near, Hector on a couple of occasions. If Hector was thought of as one of the best, it had nothing to do with his discretion or investigative abilities; it had to do with his knack for survival. A thirty-to-one gunfight wouldn't phase Hector at all, nor the thought of facing the entire New Hampshire State Police. That it would sink any chance of finding the source of the Innsmouth Jewelry wouldn't bother him at all, Kane knew. He left a few bills for the waitress and headed out.

CHAPTER 9

DREAMS WITHIN DREAMS

ASHURBANIPAL HAD A jewelry store on the north side of town, at the end of the merchant district. Kane had taken his time reaching the alleyway across the street, using alleyways and keeping out from under streetlamps. He knew from an ad in the Yellow Pages that the store stayed open until 9:00. 9:00 had just passed when a little man with a big paunch waddled out, fiddling with a large keyring. Dressed in a three-piece suit and carrying a satchel, the man Kane assumed was Ashurbanipal stood thumbing through keys until he found the one he wanted. Pulling a rolling metal gate from its housing above the front door, Ashurbanipal locked it to the sidewalk, picked up his satchel, and headed east in a splay-footed stroll. Kane watched him, waiting for the right moment to pick up the tail, when someone across the street left a darkened doorway and hurried after Ashurbanipal.

Who in the hell is that? Kane thought. *Is there another Venator stalking in Odiome? Whoever he is, he has no trade skills to speak of.* Kane shook his head as he watched the man come too close to Ashurbanipal and then slow down, fruitlessly trying to huddle against the brick wall for cover, and then stride out again to come too close. Kane moved stealthily down the opposite side of the street, avoiding the light of streetlamps and keeping an eye on both Ashurbanipal and his inept tail. *Could be his security*, Kane thought, *but the guy seems too nervous.*

Kane increased his speed until he drew even with the tail. The tail wore a pea coat that had never shipped out on an ocean voyage, designer jeans, and expensive name-brand shoes. He did not wear a hat over his perfectly sculpted hair. The hands he had jammed into his coat pockets did not seem to be holding a pistol or knife; the knuckles showed through the fabric. Kane passed the man in the pea coat to get a look at his face, and to get to the next corner before Ashurbanipal. *Whoa, whoa, whoa,* Kane thought as he came to an abrupt halt. Nearly opposite Ashurbanipal, Kane watched as the rotund little man passed an alleyway and raised his left hand to his chest, pointing at himself with a cocked thumb. As Ashurbanipal walked on, Kane saw three forms move closer to the mouth of the alleyway. *Pea Coat, you are about to get jumped,* Kane thought.

Stepping quickly onto the asphalt and under the light of a streetlamp, Kane looked straight into the alley as the three figures closed in. They halted and stared back, the light from above illuminating their eyes if not their features. Pea Coat looked sidelong at Kane, hesitating at the sight of a strange man standing in the middle of the street, and then ducked his head and plowed after Ashurbanipal, never having noticed the ambush. Unwilling to jump someone with a witness staring at them out in the open, whoever was in the alley allowed Pea Coat to pass. Once Pea Coat turned the corner after Ashurbanipal, Kane walked into the alley of the would-be ambushers.

With the streetlight behind him, Kane's eyes began to adjust to the darkness and he saw there were three of them, the one farthest back standing up out of a crouch. He knew they were locals as much from their worn clothes covered in the seagoing scars of fishermen as from the smell of the wharf that hung in the air. It was when the faint light caught their hands, however, that he knew exactly what they were: each of the three wore a ring of gold that was not gold, graven with images of the sea and madness.

"Three frogboys hiding in an alley," Kane said. "I'm sure there's a joke in there somewhere."

"What did you call us?" the foremost Follower screamed, spittle evident in his voice.

"Say, any of you fellah's actually started to morph?" Kane asked. "Everyone wonders if it's actually true, so is it extra webbing between the toes, you grow gills or somethi—"

The Follower cried out in rage and leaped at Kane, thrusting with a kitchen knife. Kane caught the knife wrist and swung the cultist against the wall; he curled the fingers of his free hand at the middle joint and drove a knuckle punch into the Follower's back, just below the belt on the sciatic nerve bundle. Gasping as if he'd had the wind knocked out of him, the cultist collapsed to the ground. The other two drew knives of their own and advanced more cautiously, agreeing to attack simultaneously with a quick nod. Kane smiled and held out his hands as if welcoming them. They charged. With a crescent kick arcing across his body, Kane diverted the left attacker into the right one's path before taking him around the neck with one arm and seizing his knife hand with the other. Faced with his comrade struggling between him and his target, the third Follower hesitated before stabbing wildly at Kane's face: arching his back violently, Kane lifted his human shield and twisted him to receive the stab in the head; the cultist's strangled cry was only the barest bark of fear before the blade blasted through one rolling eye and into his brain. Kane tossed the body aside and snatched the dagger out of his boot. Stunned at having killed his companion and suddenly finding himself unarmed—his knife having ripped from his hand as his comrade fell—the last standing Follower lost the only moment he would get to defend himself. Kane drove the tip of his shoe into the cultist's xiphoid process, a bony protrusion at the bottom of the sternum; the shock of the blow paralyzed his diaphragm, making breathing impossible. Kane then plunged his dagger into the Follower's heart.

"I guess," Kane said between gasps of exertion, "we're going—to have to move—a little faster—on this one."

Kane grabbed the first would-be ambusher by the head as he tried to rise and pressed his chin to his chest before giving the head a quick sideways twist, snapping the Follower's neck. With his own head hanging wearily and arms akimbo, Kane wanted a minute to catch his breath but knew, as things now stood, he had not even the luxury of time to breathe. After a resigned sigh, he bent to each body and cut off their ring fingers. He then wrapped the corrupting Innsmouth rings in a handkerchief, stuffed them into his pocket, and left the alley at a run.

At the next corner, the street became suddenly crowded. People milled about between storefronts, sat at outdoor seating in front of restaurants, and even danced down the sidewalk to the competing music drifting out of jazz venues: what passed for nightlife in Odiome was in full swing. Kane looked at the mass of people—and hiding spots—and knew finding Ashurbanipal in that mess was next to impossible. He swore as he caught his breath. *Should have let them have that jackass and kept on Ashurbanipal,* he said to himself, knowing there had never been a chance of his letting that happen. *Wait, wait, Pea Coat saw me and nearly dropped one down his pant leg. He knew his tail was blown. He wouldn't keep following Ashurbanipal. He'd get under cover as quick as he could, no matter how bad his trade skills are. It's only been about a minute and a half, two minutes. Where'd you go, jackass?*

Looking around, he saw a pool hall called *Bill's Billiards.*

Shaking his head at the name, Kane trotted over to the place and went in. Though the name implied the sort of atmosphere found in most pool halls, being an Odiome establishment it draped itself in the finery of a mansion's billiard room. A huge cigar counter took up one wall opposite the hall master's, with his rack of cues and display case of a hundred different things that couldn't possibly help anyone play the game. Light was provided solely by lamps hanging under stained glass above the tables, leaving much of the far wall in darkness. There, as if mesmerized by a painting of a pink-jacketed hunter doting on a brain-addled terrier, Pea Coat kept his back to the room and an eye over his shoulder.

Kane, knowing the three dead Followers laying in an alley up the street had whittled down the few hours he could have safely spent in town to mere minutes, pushed through the circles of tourists and grabbed Pea Coat by the collar. Protesting at first and then turning white, Pea Coat became as eager to leave the pool hall as Kane. Once out the back, Kane spun the man around and pushed him far enough into the alley that the light from a lamppost fell across his face—and hands.

"Okay, take it easy, take it easy," Pea Coat said.

Kane looked him over carefully: no rings, no earrings, no sign of belonging to one of the three oldest families of fishermen; the pea coat was merely attire and not professional equipment. He was no Follower of Dagon. Kane dropped his hand from the man's collar. Pea Coat fumbled a few phrases, not making any sense. Kane quieted him with a reassuring clap on the shoulder.

"Calm down," he said. "What's your name?"

"I'm, uh," Pea Coat hesitated.

"You can tell me or you can tell the police," Kane said. "Along with why you were stalking Mr. Ashurbanipal."

"Whoa whoa whoa—stalking?" Pea Coat said. "I wasn't stalking anybody."

"Name," Kane said.

"I'm Mike," he said. "Mike Nichols. I work up at the Fairmont Hotel, I'm the sommelier."

"And a lousy Venator," Kane said.

"A what now?" Mike said.

Kane looked at the confusion on Mike's face and then burst out laughing. This did not help Mike's nerves at all.

"Sorry," Kane said, wiping an eye. "Sorry. You just happened to be tailing Ashurbanipal? For what, some personal beef? Ashurbanipal?"

"Yeah, I guess I, yeah," Mike said, slumping at the shoulders, certain he was the butt of a joke but not getting it.

"Here, pal, one last test and then you spill your guts," Kane said and straightened Mike up with the hand on his shoulder. "Look me in the eyes: Ph'nglui mglw'nafh Cthulhu—" Kane paused for Mike's reaction; Mike squinted in incomprehension. "—R'lyeh wgah'nagl fhtagn? No? So no ring and no reaction to the chant. No cultist and no Venator. What in the hell are you doing following Ashurbanipal, then?"

"Cultist?" Mike whispered. He licked his lips, nodding. "You're, you're here about them?"

The laugh dropped out of Kane's demeanor like a bomb off a fighter plane. He guided Mike away from the back door of the billiard hall, stepping into the shadow of a corner and brought their heads closer together. Matching the other man's hushed tone, he said, "Here about who?"

"Hey, look man, I don't know anything about ventilators but I guess I know plenty about some freaky cult here in town," Mike said.

"Venators," Kane said.

"What?" Mike asked.

"Venators, not ventilators," Kane said. "Well, *When-Ah-Tors*, really. No hard Vs in Latin." Mike slowly shook his head. "So it's *Way Wick Toos*, not Vay Vick Tuss, you know? Didn't you have AP in high school? Never mind, doesn't matter. What's this about a cult in Odiome? You tell me what you know and I'll tell you their name. First, though, why were you following Ashurbanipal?"

"Listen, it's," Mike began, swallowing in a dry throat, "it's complicated. I was following him because, because I think he did something to my girlfriend."

"Who's your girlfriend?" Kane asked.

The color came back to Mike's face in a blush that shot from his collar to his hair line. "It doesn't matter who, does it?" he said. "I shouldn't have got her involved, it's just that I didn't, I thought it would—fuck, man, fuck."

"You dog," Kane said and chuckled again. "It's Layla, isn't it? Layla Odiome." Kane's grin died in the next instant when Mike's ashamed eyes met his; and Kane knew the younger man's shame hadn't come from having stepped out with another man's wife. "What the fuck happened, Mike?"

"Look, yes okay, it's Layla," Mike said. "She married the Mayor but that was when she was younger and, you know, taken in by his charm and money and power and all that. Then we met and, I don't know. We weren't looking for this to happen but it did. I wanted her to leave him, for us to run away together. I can find work anywhere there are restaurants, you know? I could support her while she paints—we could have been happy."

Mike was on the verge of tears but Kane couldn't afford to stand there and be a pal to the distraught young man. He said, "But something bad happened. Tell me what."

"She'd accepted some earrings recently," Mike said, looking at his feet. "From this guy Ashurbanipal. He's the new jeweler in town, a really natty dresser, rich. She started wearing them all the time, talking about them, and then dropping out of conversations, like she was daydreaming about—I don't know. I got jealous. There, I said it. I got jealous. I thought she was taken in by his phony foreigner routine and I wanted to show her he was just a salesman with a schtick. So I followed him."

"Where?" Kane asked.

"At first I just watched him, you know?" Mike said. "I was trying to work up the nerve to go and talk to him, tell him off. Tell him not to give her any more presents. I sounded so ridiculous in my head, though, that I never did. But then, a couple weeks back, I saw that he wasn't headed back to his apartment but down toward the waterfront. I thought, this is it; he's going down to find one of the hookers that work the pier and the shady bars. So I followed him. He didn't go to the pier, though. He went to the Pleasurecraft building."

"What's that?" Kane asked.

"It's an old factory on the water," Mike said. "Pleasurecraft used to be a big name in luxury yachts; handmade and all that. It folded after the crash in '29. No one has ever taken over the building. It's a wreck but a picturesque wreck. Kids sneak in there sometimes to screw but otherwise it's empty.

"Anyway, I followed Ashurbanipal and he went in there. I'm still thinking at this point that he's up to something nasty. I kneel down at this broken board on the side of the factory and look in. Man, I don't think you'd believe what I saw in there."

"A ceremony involving a few priests in robes of yellow and orange," Kane said, "chanting in a tongue that doesn't sound human, over an alter draped in a cloth with a heavy fish motif, and ending with a bound victim—usually a woman or boy—being sacrificed with a long dagger with an intricately figured handle."

"Or maybe you would believe it," Mike said.

"You saw them kill somebody?" Kane asked. "And you didn't contact the police, the FBI?"

"Well, I didn't actually see them kill the dude," Mike said quickly.

"Look, there were all these people jumping around—naked!—and screaming and everything, and the two guys in the robes, one with a chalice and the other with the big knife, and then some other guys drag this *other* dude over toward the whatever-it-was."

"The altar?" Kane offered.

"Yeah, I guess," Mike said. "And that dude was struggling and screaming and I didn't know what was going on but, honestly, I didn't think they were going to kill him."

"What the hell did you think they were going to do to him?" Kane said, a little heat entering his voice.

"I don't know, I don't know," Mike said. "I thought, you know, they'd—I don't know. But not kill him." Mike hung his head before continuing in a more subdued voice. "I got out of there. That's all I needed to see, anyway. I told Layla I had seen something she'd want to know about and—"

"Fuck," Kane shouted and walked two steps away; Mike froze, all the color draining back out of his face. "You asshole. You thought you'd sneak Layla down there the next night to watch the sacrifice, so she'd see what a freak-show Ashurbanipal is. Right?" Mike nodded dumbly, tears in his eyes. "Only she never had a thing for Ashurbanipal. She was spacing out because of the earrings. Everyone at that sacrifice was wearing either a ring or a pair of earrings or, maybe, a tiara of the same metal. The priests, they had tiaras? Big-ass head pieces in a strange gold, covered in oceanic pictographs?"

"Y-yeah," Mike said.

"Priest of the Esoteric Order of Dagon," Kane said. "The Followers of Dagon. The jewelry allows them to listen in on the dreams of Dagon in his dead slumber. During a sacrifice, though, the Followers sacrifice to Cthulhu. Human sacrifice is supposed to hasten the day of Cthulhu's return as well as bring dream sendings to the Followers, guiding them toward his resurrection. They need to revive Cthulhu because only Cthulhu can revive their dead god."

Mike was now shaking visibly. "Shit," Kane said. "Listen, the particulars don't matter to you. Just by wearing those earrings near the sacrifice, Layla was tuned in to the whispered dreams of Cthulhu; a big, bad creature under the sea. You two didn't watch the sacrifice all the way to the end, though, did you?"

"N-no, sir," Mike said through a tear-choked throat. "They killed a woman, started to cut her open right in front of us. Layla started to rock back and forth and I thought it was shock so I dragged her away and back to her house but she never spoke except to whisper and I was really scared that she'd been traumatized and—"

"Okay Mike, easy, easy," Kane said and put a hand on the other man's shoulder. "This is a lot to take in all at once. You brought Layla home? That's good. But also not so much. Because she didn't see the end of the sacrifice, the ceremony was not completed for her. She's still tuned in to Cthulhu's dreams. That's why she's been acting so strangely."

Kane paced back and forth for a moment, stroking his chin and thinking through everything that he'd been told over the years about Dagon and The Followers. Most of what the Venators knew of Follower rituals was second hand or came out of one of the Mythos texts. He knew Cthulhu rites first hand and could use their peculiarities against them. Against Followers of Dagon? The information gap was enormous.

Mike sniffed, wiped his nose on his sleeve, and said, "What was it you said earlier? About Venators? You thought I was one. You're one, aren't you? A Venator. That's someone who stops these crazy sons of bitches?"

"Yeah," Kane said with a sigh. "Something like that."

"Well, if it means stopping those bastards who hurt Layla," Mike said, stepping away from the wall, "sign me up. I'll help."

Kane smiled sadly. "I know you would. That's how it starts.

They hurt someone you love, take away everything that matters in your life, and you're left with two choices: to kill yourself with grief or kill them with whatever comes to hand." Kane shook his head. "There's no signing up. There are no Venators, in a sense. It's not an organized group. Not in the United States, not anymore. Among the families and friends of those who die in the sacrifices, a few always want to know more; who did it and why. They begin to look into things, starting with the sacrifice site, tracking people who may have taken part; they come upon dread symbols from a long-dead language in the ramblings of a cultist; they trace that back to one of the ancient texts, the *Necronomicon* or the *Unausspre-chlichen Kulten*; they learn of the horrifying limitations of man's perceptions of the universe, of time and history; they discover that they've been dreaming their whole lives and that waking life is a nightmare. And with the signs still fresh in their minds, they get lucky: they come upon an active cult. And they wipe it out. I'm not going to go into the whole history of the Venators, which dates back to ancient Rome, or the goal of the cults, which is to end the world. You haven't lost enough, Mike, not yet and hopefully not ever. I don't know if Layla can be saved or not but you still have your life. Leave dealing with the cults to me.

"Now, you said the Pleasurecraft building?" Kane asked. Mike nodded slowly. "And it's on the waterfront?"

"Yeah," Mike said quietly. "North edge of town."

Kane smiled when he realized he had passed it on his way back into Odiome. "Okay, Mike. Thanks. You leave it to me. For now, you can't go home. You didn't see it but Ashurbanipal had signaled some Followers to jump you; that's why I had to walk out into the street instead of stalking Ashurbanipal. I need you to keep out of the way, okay? And you can't go home because they may know who you are and where home is. So go to a hotel for the rest of the night. Stay awake in the bar, drink coffee, and keep your eyes open. You see anyone come in wearing a ring like this," Kane said and pulled out and opened his bloody handkerchief of fingers and rings, "you get the hell out. Got it?"

Mike covered his mouth to keep from vomiting, nodding his head vigorously. Kane tried to soften the blow a bit with soothing words but he knew it was better for everyone if Mike was freaked out enough to stay out of sight. After sending off Mike—and tailing him a few blocks to make sure he wasn't followed—Kane weaved his way north as well as east, heading for the edge of town before starting his infiltration toward the Pleasurecraft building. Along the way, he called Hector.

"Hector, where are you?" Kane said without preamble.

"At a little place just south of town," Hector said casually. Just as Kane was about to tell him what he'd learned, a shotgun blast punched through the phone. "I'm just about done," Hector said. "Looked like these folks was set to head out, do a little following."

"I know and I know where," Kane said. "There's an old factory on the north side of town, on the water, called the Pleasurecraft building. That's where they've been holding the sacrifices. Ashurbanipal was on his way earlier. We need to move quickly. Meet me at the south-west corner of the building. Do you have anything else with you? All I brought was my pistol."

"No can do, Kane," Hector said and the sound of his heavy boots passing through long grass rose to the phone as he walked. "I'm headed out."

"You're what?" Kane said and stopped short.

"Back to Arkham," Hector said. "Something I need to check on."

"Hector, the Temple to Dagon is a fucking factory," Kane said. "It isn't a one man job. And with the three dead Followers I left in an alley fifteen minutes ago—to say nothing of the family you just slaughtered—the city PD are going to be all over the place."

"Just firebomb the temple, shit," Hector said, grunting as he threw a leg over his Indian.

"Hector," Kane shouted, "this something you need to check on up in Arkham, it doesn't happen to be Archie hitting town, does it? Jesus, we have a full-blown invasion—an attempt by The Followers of Dagon to remake Innsmouth—now isn't exactly the time for you to go pining over Helen."

"Hey, Sol," Hector said with a sigh. "I've always liked you, man, and I hate most other Venators, but you got a big mouth. I'm taking the rings I've gathered from the *two* families I dropped tonight back up to Arkham; I'll melt them there. You let me know how things shake out at the Temple. If I don't hear from you in a couple days, I'll come back and burn this whole fucking city to the ground. Good luck. Oh, and fuck you."

Kane stood fuming at his disconnected phone for a moment before turning it off and heading east.

CHAPTER 10

THE TEMPLE OF DAGON

A LARGE LOT SURROUNDED the Pleasurecraft building, overgrown with weeds and decades of random trash. Three stories tall and as long and wide as a football field, the factory's only windows ran in a series just under the roof overhang. Through them, a faint yellow light illuminated rust-red girders and open space; the interior was a single giant room. Its nearest neighbor was a small food processing plant that froze and packaged local shellfish, some thirty meters away. The moon was rising full and bright, lighting those meters as if they were in *Giant's Stadium*. Kane crouched at the corner of the food processing plant, pistol in hand, and surveyed the long blank wall of the factory.

Time and sun had burned the paint off the walls but they still stood. In places, boards had been pulled off or broken enough to sway in the land-breeze, their creaking like a mournful insect hum. As Kane waited for sentries to peek out of the high windows or come walking around the far corners of the building, chanted words grew in volume until they could not be mistaken. He felt the slowing of his heart and the loosening of his muscles, and then dashed toward the factory, crossing the open lot made white as snow by the moon's light.

Keeping so low to the ground that he used his empty hand as much as his feet to run, Kane quickly searched for a broken board with enough of a breach to see through. He found it about half-way down the wall, just as the chanting within had grown loud enough to distinguish the words. Dropping to his stomach, he inched the board aside and peered into the darkened interior.

After the blazing full moon, the factory floor was as murky as a swamp to Kane's dazzled eyes. The only light came from two enormous candelabras off to the left. They were set atop a makeshift altar fashioned out of two fifty-five gallon drums and a door. Draped in the orange and yellow of Dagon, the altar cloths were streaked with a grimy rust-colored crust. Kane took it in unconsciously, the accouterments of horror holding less fascination for him than those gathered before them. In the flickering light off the altar, ranged between the factory walls, stood dozens upon dozens of Followers of Dagon.

Kane had never before seen the rites of the Esoteric Order of Dagon: they differed dramatically from those of a Cthulhu Cult. Their numbers were greater—and Kane keenly felt how little ammunition he'd brought, stuffed into every pocket—but it was their control, the Followers' apparent calm that startled him. A Cthulhu Cult would have already descended into madness, with wild dancing and howls of lust and fear. The Followers, however, stood swaying to the droning chant, breathing noticeably even in the scant light. Most were unclothed, though some wore the orange and yellow sash of a supplicant of the order. When the candlelight caught them in their movement, a star of gold-that-is-not-gold flashed from every hand or swung from every ear. Innsmouth Jewelery. Kane licked his dry lips, knowing this was merely the calm before the storm.

Distracted by the deep ranks of Followers, Kane did not at first notice the muffled cries of protest coming from deeper within the factory. Everything beyond the altar, farther to the left, was obscured by the candelabras' glow. With the solemnity of a funeral and the joy of a wedding, four men entered the sphere of moving light. Two were clothed in the flowing robes of High Priests of Dagon, one of which carried a long dagger with a figured hilt. The other was Ashurbanipal. The calm, man-about-town expression had dropped from his mien. The intensity of his features as he led the Followers in chant bespoke a total capitulation to madness. But even he was no more than a single datum in the instant calculation of Kane's mind: the other two men had come forth carrying a girl not older than twelve, bound at wrist and ankle and gagged.

"No, no," Kane grunted as he clawed at the board, desperately prying open a few precious inches.

Thrusting his arm through the narrow hole, the jagged wood crumpling his sleeve and drawing long red gashes up his forearm, Kane shot the cultist carrying the girl's feet. The report of the heavy .45 echoed between the distant walls, momentarily silencing the cultists in communal incomprehension. In the next second, though, Kane blew a hole through the head of the High Priest wielding the sacrificial dagger and the world inside the factor exploded in a cacophony of shrieks and demands for death. Kane fired again and again, emptying his pistol and telling with every round. The falling High Priest had knocked over one of the candelabras, further darkening the factory, so that the muzzle flash of Kane's pistol revealed him to the assembly. Those closest to him charged en masse.

Bare feet pounded concrete a second before hands grabbed at Kane's arm. He nearly lost his pistol as he wrenched free and away from the wall. An arm followed his out through the hole and strained, tearing its flesh on the jagged board, its hatred beating in its pulsating veins. Kicking backward and trying to rise while his hands were busy finding a fresh magazine, Kane watched the white-bathed wall as it buckled under the beating fists of the cultists within. They screamed as they threw themselves against the wall, their meaning unmistakable though they spoke no words. Kane stumbled to his feet just as the wall gave way. A dozen naked and enraged Followers, outstretched hands bloody from where their fingernails had torn off in the wooden wall, launched themselves at Kane. He fired his pistol empty, taking a backward step between each shot and replacing his magazine with the speed of thought. Then, though the shouts of rage continued within, no one else dared to the breach. It took Kane the span of a heartbeat to consider what could be done. *They'll kill her*, he thought. *If they think they have a second to spare, they'll kill her.* Kane charged the opening in the factory wall and threw himself through it, rolling out of the bar of light the moon made and into the darkness beyond.

Returning fire from the cultists followed him as he scrambled for cover behind one of the many three-story steel girders. Ashurbanipal, huddling behind the makeshift altar, swiped at the remaining candelabra, darkening that side of the factory floor. Kane tried to return fire at the nearest muzzle flash but his shots only brought three shrieking Followers charging out of the blackness: he shot at them wildly, guided by the flickering gold on their hands and ears, as sparks hissed menacingly from rifle bullets glancing off the narrow steel girder. Kane dived onto his stomach and crawled a few feet away before rising and making a dash for another girder: he landed in a heap behind it—upon a quietly raging cultists. They struggled for the pistol before Kane drew his dagger and stabbed blindly into flesh until he could wrench himself free and run farther into darkness, to another thin strip of cover, to reload, to keep fighting, to keep all attention on himself and away from the girl.

"No, no, stop firing," Ashurbanipal cried to his guards.

Another cultist, on Kane's side of the beam of light, had crept through the blackness, hands out, hoping to come upon his hated prey by luck alone: his luck held. Without warning for either, the Follower's hands bumped into the back of Kane's neck. The cultist screamed and seized Kane's throat: Kane jabbed his pistol over his shoulder until the muzzle found meat. He squeezed the trigger, ejected the Follower into eternity, and then made a dive to his right, as fire from the armed cultists near Ashurbanipal aimed at his muzzle flash. Kane crawled for a second and then rose to his feet and dashed for another steel girder. He had to still his frantic breathing to keep the sound from reaching whoever else lurked in that blackness.

"Cease fire, damn you," Ashurbanipal screamed. "You'll only hit one of the devout. All of you, my children, be still your righteous anger. No one enter that beam of light. Those of you with guns, hold your fire and wait. Carver?"

The girl, pinned to the ground by her remaining captor, managed to reach her gag with her bound hands, or else wormed her way free of it. She cried out, "Help!"

"Silence her!" Ashurbanipal commanded. "It is an honor to be given to Dread Cthulhu, child. To feed his dreams and bring about the blessed day."

"The Blessed Day," The Followers intoned throughout the factory.

Kane fell to his left, surprised to hear a voice mere feet away and, fired instinctively. The choked off words announced a hit but Kane never heard it, running for the next piece of cover.

"Carver, where are you, damn it?" Ashurbanipal demanded. After a mumbled answer, Ashurbanipal continued. "You still have the lantern? Good. Take it and climb one of these girders, all the way to the top. Do not light the lantern until you are there. You others who are armed, await the lighting of the lantern and then kill this intruder."

Yeah, Carver, climb up one of these girders, Kane thought as he quietly reloaded his pistol. *I promise not to shoot you.*

"And Carver, use the side of the girder opposite the beam of light," Ashurbanipal said.

Shit.

"Well now, Venator," Ashurbanipal said, "you have committed a great sacrilege by interfering here. Yes, I know exactly what you are, filth. And you shall be justly rewarded: if you are merely wounded during the barrage to come, I will see that you suffer so long and loudly that it might wake Dread Cthulhu from his slumbers. Fool that you are, you've trapped yourself. The only entrance is here by the altar; that massive door behind you is chained and padlocked. Unless you care to try escaping through that bright hole in the wall. Would you like to? Children, kill anyone who approaches the light. There, Venator, there fool, you are welcome to try."

Kane fired a shot at Ashurbanipal's voice and was rewarded with only the hollow tolling of lead hitting steel drum. *Keep their attention, damn it,* he thought. *You don't get her, you sons of bitches, you will not take this girl.* Kane could hear the clump-pause-clump as Carver climbed the far side of one of the support girders. It was only a matter of time before he reached the ceiling and lit the entire factory floor. Hiding then would be impossible. Even a single lantern would provide enough light to shoot by and he had counted no less than five rifles seeking him amid the darkness. Alive or dead, Ashurbanipal would then be at his leisure to finish the sacrifice of the girl and then to move on. The Followers were far too careful to stay in a town they suspected a Venator had investigated. Ashurbanipal and all the Innsmouth Jewelery would then disappear from Odiome, to arise again in some other town, to enslave another cadre of the insane, and labor at murder until they brought about the return of Cthulhu.

"Find the dagger," Ashurbanipal ordered a Follower crouching near to him.

Like hell, Kane thought. Looking around, not knowing how many people were left in the factory, which were armed, where the girl was—or how long it would take for Carver to light up the place and lay him bear to his enemies and death—Kane came to the only conclusion he could. He needed an advantage and he needed it in the next few seconds. Readying himself for the plunge, he took a slow deep breath and then sprang away from the girder, running. Some vagary of light floating down from the high windows caught him for an instant and shots screamed by from two sides. Flinging himself to the ground, sparks exploded where bullets met steel gird-ers. Crawling like mad, Kane ran head-first into the front wall of the factory. He rolled to one side, groaning, as bullets plowed into the ancient wood of the huge double sliding doors.

Pawing his way down the wall, Kane found the edge of one door and tried to yank it open. Nothing doing. Bracing himself against a nearby girder, he pushed and strained with everything he had only to open the door a scant inch before the chain binding the outside handles checked his progress with an ominous clang. But with the full moon still low in the sky, blazing white light like a beacon at sea, that one inch of searing light blasted into the fac-tory, blinding the Followers. Shots sang out wildly, as if attacking the door. Kane leaped to his left, landing hard on his shoulder, took aim at the lock and burst it with one shot. Quickly crawling to the door's interior edge—under the cover of blackness made impenetrable by contrast—he threw the sliding door completely open and the deluge of moonlight revealed the entire factory floor.

The shadow of the corner where he stood was all the protection Kane had and all that he needed; he was invisible next to so bright a light. He could see the two dozen Followers—and Ashurbani-pal—shielding their eyes and running blindly for cover; he could see the girl where she lay pressed to the ground by one armed cult-ists, trying to hide his eyes with the crook of his arm. Kane made the flash decision to shoot him last; better the girl be kept on the ground and out of his line of fire. Then he shot as fast as he could while still aiming.

Kane crouched and weaved in the shadow of the factory's corner, firing with impunity: first the armed Followers, then the crazed and naked chanters who charged him or the door or the broken wall; all came under the wrath of the Venator. With all he had labored to create, with all he had orchestrated in devotion to murder now falling like wheat before the scythe, Ashurbanipal charged headlong into the light of the moon, arms shaking with rage, mouth straining wide in an endless scream—until the center of his face stove in and the back of his head burst out in a shower of blood. In the next instant, Kane had to throw his last magazine into his pistol quicker than thought: the Follower who held the girl was about to execute her, raising the heavy candelabra like a mace with which to cave in her head. Kane shot him through the heart. *Well, I guess Carver gets to be last,* he thought before blowing the shocked climber from the factory's ceiling.

The sudden silence of the—almost—empty factory, punctuated only by the moans of the dying and the ringing in Kane's ears, held a menace all its own. Kane dashed forward, keenly aware that he had only five rounds left in his pistol. He scrambled over the heaps of bodies, sparing Ashurbanipal's corpse a kick as he neared the altar, and then dropped to his knees behind the girl.

"It's alright, you're okay, you're okay," Kane said, his voice cracking despite feeling his usual battle-calm. He used his boot dagger to cut the cords binding the girl's wrists and ankles. Though hesitating for a second, she chose Kane as a friend in the next instant and launched herself into his arms. He needed longer than she did to come to his senses and do what had to be done.

CHAPTER 11

NO END OF MADNESS

WITH THE FOLLOWERS in Odiome wiped out, and the gunfight sure to bring the police before long, Kane scoured the Pleasurecraft factory as fast as weary limbs could move. He wanted the girl—Lindsey—to wait outside but he could see by her expression that she would refuse to be left alone, even for a moment. She seemed strangely unmoved by Kane's cutting the fingers off of the Followers, when the rings wouldn't slide off easily. *I guess she's seen enough tonight not to be shocked by much ever again*, he thought. He gathered all the Innsmouth Jewelry from the Followers—pausing for only a second when he came to Selma McKenzie—including two twisted tiaras from the High Priests, and then despoiled Ashurbanipal. As important as all the jewelry present at the sacrifice was, more important still was the set of keys Ashurbanipal had in his pocket. With his pistol in one hand and Lindsey holding the other, Kane slipped through the hole The Followers had made in the wall and headed off toward Ashurbanipal's store. In the distance, police sirens filled the night.

At Odiome Mansion, the Mayor stalked back and forth in his office, eyes unable to find interest in anything except the phone. Dressed in a bathrobe over pajamas and smoking a cigarette—a habit thirty-years quit until the week before—he looked as though the night had already been less than easy when the screams started. He ran to the office door and flung it open in time to see his young wife leaping down the stairs with the housekeeper and Dr. Livermore hot in pursuit.

Layla had tears streaming from her eyes and blubbered unintelligibly as she ran from room to room. Mayor Odiome took up the chase, adding his ineffectual restraint to that of the other two, who from physical weakness or tenderness of feeling could not bring Layla to a halt. She broke free of their encircling arms and ran down the hall to the conservatory, her voice overflowing into sobs. The conservatory had been a later addition to the house and, as such, its double doors were wide and heavy, having led onto the terrace long ago. Layla tugged and strained to open them as the other three tried to coax her fingers from the handles and sooth her hysteria. Nothing availed to calm her, though, until she pulled open the heavy glass doors and came face to face with Solomon Kane.

"Evening," Kane said, grinning. He still had Lindsey by the hand; she looked interestedly at the others but not alarmed. Over her shoulder she carried a burlap sack. Kane scratched the side of his unshaven face with the checkered grip of his pistol. "How about we all step outside, take in the night air on the patio?"

Layla's lower lip still trembled but her weeping and mumbling had abruptly ceased. As if half in fright and half at command, she stumbled through the pots and planters thick with flowers. The housekeeper kept a hold of her mistress's arm as she went, opening the door to the patio and guiding Mrs. Odiome to a padded deck chair. Mayor Odiome looked as if he would gladly have charged Kane and risked a shot in the face, but went along with his wife, not willing to be separated from her. Dr. Livermore cowerd behind his employer.

"You are no doubt responsible for the murder spree at Leviathan Terrace," Mayor Odiome said, spinning on his heel when he stood beside his wife. "Murder and arson, I should say."

"Is that the little village the fisherman use, just south of town?" Kane asked. "No, that wasn't me. Friend of mine. Well, not *friend*, exactly. Lindsey, here hand me that," he asked and took the burlap sack the young girl carried. "Can you run over to that garden shed and see if you can find a sledgehammer? If there isn't one, any big piece of metal should do." Lindsey nodded and ran across the flood-lit lawn. When Kane returned his attention to the inmates of Odiome Manor, ashen faces stared back.

The Mayor watched Lindsey approach the shed and heave open the door before he swallowed in a suddenly dry throat, wondering for what purpose the madman before him had requested a sledgehammer, and asked, "What is it you intend to do?"

Kane replied lightly, "I intend cure your wife."

"How?" The Mayor asked, shocked back to his usual voice.

"The earrings," Kane said and grinned.

"What? This again?" The Mayor shouted as the color flooded back into his cheeks.

"No, Mayor, I'm not saying I'll cure her *for* the earrings," Kane said, "not as payment. I'm saying the earrings are to blame."

"Nonsense," The Mayor said. "Why would you say something so preposterous? What is it you're really after?"

"Well, it's not to steal your wife's earrings—I've got more than enough," Kane said and dumped the contents of his burlap bag onto one of the far flagstones of the patio. The cascade of jewelry filled the night with its gold-like color and yet made it darker, as if the strange substance devoured the light. Kane knelt next to the pile of jewelry and picked through it. "Rings, earrings," he said. "These tiaras are wild. I wouldn't suggest trying one on, though."

Looking first at the mound of unsettling jewelry, and then to Layla's earrings, and then back to Kane, Mayor Odiome said, "I don't understand."

Kane came to his feet with a sigh, saying, "Yeah, I know. I could tell you the whole story now and I think you still wouldn't understand. No one can. I know more than most and even I can't understand. Comprehension of this level of horror is beyond human capacity.

"The story goes that in the depths of pre-history, the earth—and most of the surrounding cosmos—was ruled not by humans but by beings later called The Great Old Ones. I know, it sounds like some made-up science fiction religion but it isn't. The Great Old Ones existed on many planets, and in many times, simultaneously. Earth, however, being a minor planet in a solar system of no great significance, was given to the High Priest of their worship, a creature called Cthulhu. For reasons surpassing understanding, The Great Old Ones died, along with Cthulhu. Only, for beings so far beyond the pale, death is not final; and in eons to come, even Death may die. Since that time, Man—who had been the slaves and sacrificial victims of Cthulhu—has, of course, recovered, and moved on, and forgotten. But not all Mankind. Some, infected by the madness of The Great Old Ones, want to resurrect Cthulhu. They believe that at an appointed time, Cthulhu will return and through his might and through slaughter unimaginable, recall The Great Old Ones to life. Down through the ages until modern times—to this very night—both the direct worshipers of Cthulhu and the followers of this or that Great Old One have tried to hasten Cthulhu's return by sacrificing people. That's where your town comes in, Mayor. You *have* noticed the 1000% increase in missing persons, right?"

"Wait a moment, are you saying that the rash of disappearances our town has suffered, as well as the murders from earlier tonight, were carried out by people who believe this, this bizarre history you've just told?" Mayor Odiome said, incredulity contorting his face. "Madness. Madness is too weak a word for it. I thought, for a moment, that you were telling us that *you* believed it."

"Oh, I do," Kane said. "And you will to."

As Lindsey returned with a five-pound sledge, Dr. Livermore leaned cautiously forward and into the Mayor's peripheral vision; they shared an anxious look before returning their wide eyes to Kane's doings. Kane handed his pistol to Lindsey, telling her to hold it by the slide, not the grip; "I don't think those boys'll try to rush me, not while I'm wielding this," he said as he brandished the sledgehammer. He then knelt and began pounding the tiaras into smaller, collapsed bundles. The strange metal endured the punishment far more resiliently than real gold would have done. It took everything Kane had to bend the tiaras, the stone underneath chipping and cracking with every swing. Layla responded to the slow pounding rhythm of the hammer, wincing as if struck.

"As hard as it is to believe," Kane said, turning the tiara in his hand and selecting his next place to strike, "what I've told you—or something close to it—is true. And cults teeming with believers are everywhere, killing endlessly in preparation for the return of their dead gods. If you go down to the Pleasurecrafts building, you'll find what's left of the cult that had tried to conquer Odiome.

"Conquer, Mayor," Kane said, tossing the first tiara—now a mangled wreck—onto the heap of earrings and rings and then taking up the second tiara. "And they almost succeeded. You see these rings? Or these earrings? We call them Innsmouth Jewelry. When worn by a cultist during a sacrifice, it attunes the wearer with the dreams of Cthulhu. The cultists hope for the total capitulation to horror that madness brings; the dreams are the method.

Ashurbanipal—the new jeweler in town, and also High Priest of The Followers of Dagon—gave your wife those earrings in order to induct her into the cult, slowly bringing her under his control. Through her, they would have gained access—and eventually control of—your son. Once he, as Mayor and cultist, was in charge of the town, further resistance would be impossible."

"Just a moment," The Mayor said. "Are you actually suggesting my wife attended a human sacrifice?"

"The insistence of magic rings you accept without argument," Dr. Livermore mumbled, tossing up his hands, "but Layla attending a séance gone wild you refute?"

Kane, now finished pounding the second tiara into a smaller package, dropped it on the pile of Innsmouth Jewelry and stood up. Ignoring Dr. Livermore, he said, "She wandered too close to a sacrifice a couple weeks ago. Doesn't matter how. The sacrifice plugged her into Cthulhu's dreams, which is why she's been nuts ever since. She's agitated tonight because everyone else wearing the jewelry is dead. By destroying them—and her earrings, too—we should be able to break her free of Cthulhu's dreams."

Kane threw the sledgehammer to one side and then took his pistol back from Lindsey. Walking slowly forward, he came and stood on the opposite side of Layla from Mayor Odiome. Leaning down a little, hard eyes locked on the now shaking Mayor, Kane said in a soft, gentle voice, "I'm going to take off these earrings now, Layla. Just hold still and this will all be over soon." She began to weep silently as the first earring was slipped from her flesh; at the second she began to breathe as if the wind had been knocked out of her. Mayor Odiome reached for Kane's hand as if he would interfere but he hesitated, not certain which was the best course of action. Kane gave him no time to consider, striding back to the heap of Innsmouth Jewelry and dropping Layla's earrings onto the pile. *If this doesn't work*, Kane asked himself, *are you going to put that poor woman out of her misery?*

He turned back to the others and withdrew a small but heavy waterproof pouch from his jacket pocket. He held it up for them to see before pouring its contents, a fine powder, over the Innsmouth Jewelry. "This is thermite," he said. "It takes some pretty intense heat to get it going so we have to use a magnesium fire-starter as a fuse. Don't look straight at it; it'll blind you. Brighter than the sun."

Sticking a rod of magnesium the size of a candy bar into the thermite, Kane then lit a waterproof match by striking it against the grip of his pistol and set it atop the magnesium. It took several seconds for the magnesium to catch. When it did, the patio flared into a sputtering while light, angry and loud. When the thermite finally caught, it burned so hot that even fifteen feet away the others could feel it. Kane stood with his back to the blaze, shielding Lindsey's eyes with one hand while the other was at his side, loosely holding his pistol. He watched Layla. *Come on, god damn it, come on.* The point of critical mass could not have been guessed if Layla had not been there. Shooting to her feet and shrieking like someone coming out of a dead sleep to a bedroom intruder, Layla covered her mouth and looked around frightened and confused. Seeing her husband next to her, aghast with apprehension, she threw herself into his arms, nearly knocking him down. Both wept openly, in the passing of fear, in relief.

The thermite burned down as Mayor and Mrs. Odiome whispered words of returning to one another. It was not until a violent hiss coughed at the other end of the patio that they turned to the others. Kane had used a garden hose to cool the now unrecognizable lump of what had been Innsmouth Jewelry. Once it ceased to steam, Kane kicked the lump back into the burlap sack.

"What he said is true," Layla said, whirling back to her husband and gripping the front of his bathrobe. "The whispering, the endless nightmare. But, but I saw you," she said, looking over her shoulder at Kane.

"Me?" Kane asked, surprised.

"Yes, in the factory," Layla said, turning toward him but unwilling to release contact with The Mayor. "As if floating above it all, I saw you save this little girl. You faced all of those people, all of those crazed murderous people alone, to stop the sacrifice. I saw it all."

Dr. Livermore, recovered from the first fright of an armed man ordering him about, could contain himself no longer. Rising to his feet and straightening his tweet jacket, he said, "I'm sorry, Mayor Odiome, but I must speak. If Mrs. Odiome's hysteria has finally passed, no one could be happier than I. I should say that it is likely that this pyrotechnic display has merely triggered the positive effects of the medication I prescribed but never mind. What's important now, though—my god, you can't believe this nonsense!" he said, exasperated by the expressions on both Mayor and Mrs. Odiome. "You have already heard from your Chief of Police that a dozen people were murdered at Leviathan Terrace. Now we hear that this man has killed god only knows how many more."

"To save me," Lindsey shouted indignantly, arms akimbo.

"So she says," Dr. Livermore said. "But, Mayor, even if that is true, this man's motivations are, are—well—the product of a diseased mind, sir." In a whisper, which everyone could hear, he said, "He's a mass murderer, for chrissake, suffering from a psychosis." Straightening his narrow shoulders, Dr. Livermore took a dignified step forward and addressed Kane directly: "Come now, sir, give me the gun. We can then go inside and talk further."

"Sit down, doc," Kane said, suppressing a chuckle. "I'm not going to shoot you but I will knock your block off if I have to."

"Dr. Livermore, do sit down," Mayor Odiome said, shooing him with one hand. To Kane, he said, "I don't know what to believe. All I know is that Layla has returned. The earrings were destroyed and Layla returned. I cannot thank you enough, sir. Though you ask me to believe the impossible—and to overlook a massacre, it would seem—you have cured my wife and I feel I owe you more than I can possibly express; my life is not enough, though I would have gladly given it."

"Yeah," Kane said softly and the pain that swept through him at the sight of a man whose wife came back was obvious to all present. "I don't want your life. And I'm not asking you to believe anything. Just see Lindsey gets home okay. And keep your eyes open. It's not likely The Followers of Dagon—the cult—will ever return to Odiome. But if people start going missing again, it could be a Cthulhu Cult returning to find their lost artifacts. If that happens, I—or someone like me—will be back."

Kane left Odiome on foot, slipping through the police cordon and finding his Cutlass. After stowing the soggy lump of what remained of the Innsmouth Jewelry in the trunk, he took off, heading west toward Arkham, Massachusetts. Once far enough away from Odiome that his phone wouldn't use local cell towers, he called Helen.

Kane's description of events was not without certain editorializing when it came to Hector but he was constantly distracted as he spoke and Helen eventually asked him why.

"What's wrong, Sol?" she said. "It sounds to me that things couldn't have gone better."

"Yeah, I guess," Kane said. "The girl is with The Mayor, and Layla seems to be out of the woods. I don't know. Though no one got out of that factory alive, and though I think I recovered all of the Innsmouth Jewelry from Ashurbanipal's store, my gut tells me that this is a failed stalk. No, listen: I don't know why I feel that way but I do. Somewhere, someone accomplished what they'd set out to do. And we better figure out what."

BOOK 2
THE DOOR TO R'LYEH

CHAPTER 1

THE DISAPPEARANCE OF DR. PLEMBY

I T WAS ONLY April but the sweltering heat of summer gripped Louisiana with all the hatred of an angry god. Another night of thunderstorms had driven the sun from the sky as Solomon Kane drove down Interstate 10, over Lake Pontchartrain, toward New Orleans. Clouds thick as smoke churned darkly over the expanse of the lake, its waters seeming to feed on the floating night and grow in obscurity. The lights of The Big Easy, huddled between those two black horizons, took on the aspect of vigilance.

Kane had the ragtop down on his '93 Cutlass in a vain attempt to eke some respite from the hot, heavy atmosphere. The wind that blew through his salt-and-pepper hair, however, was as soggy as a bar towel and smelled a little worse. Whatever the storm off the coast had picked up in Texas, had died before it hit the ground in Louisiana. Looking down at the car's gauges, Kane wondered if the tank had enough left to get him across the lake.

Past an enormous circular church—like a small arena—Kane had to drive all the way down to the Holiday Inn before he could find a gas station. The Cutlass coughed itself dead about twenty feet from the entrance—just as the sky opened and started vomiting warm rain. Kane jumped out and tried to keep as much of the car's forward momentum as he could, pushing toward the gas station. To his surprise, a couple guys from a truck on the other side of the pumps ran over to help. He knew enough Spanish to say thanks and then offered them a few bucks but they wouldn't take it. He put it in the gas tank and asked the attendant where the cheapest motel in town was. Back the other way.

At the motel, the clerk—who drew most of his business from the hour-at-a-time crowd—did his best to look disapprovingly at Kane's suit. It may have once been called blue but it was hard to tell now and so wrinkled it looked as if Kane kept it balled up and stuffed in the couch when he wasn't wearing it. He took a ground-floor room at the back, paid in cash, and made a suggestion to the clerk which only a contortionist could accomplish.

The stale smelling room had all the charm of a subway platform and was about as clean. Whatever the usual clientele expected, the management expected worse: everything was chained to something else: the lamp to the table, the telephone to the bed, and the TV to the wall with a chain so thick it must have been left over from mooring a ship. There was enough slack in it, though, for Kane to swivel the TV around and unscrew the back panel. Into the plastic shell, he put a .45 automatic pistol and half-a-dozen loaded magazines. Once he reassembled the TV, Kane unpacked his suitcase and left.

"Considering New Orleans' reputation," Kane said to himself as he crammed his six-foot-three frame into the Cutlass, "I probably ought to keep the gun on me. Too bad out-of-State plates attract cops."

Though he wanted dinner, Kane drove past the French Quarter with its tourist traps—and some of the best restaurants in the South—and headed to a five-star hotel a few minutes from Tulane University. Built in the old French style of the city's past, the hotel was a new resident, constructed after Hurricane Katrina. The revolving door led Kane into a long-awaited moment's pleasure: air conditioning. He almost wished he wasn't working. Marble floors and polished-brass everything, a soaring ceiling and bellhops in uniform let the newly-arrived know just what they were overpaying for. For the second time that night Kane was sneered at by a desk clerk. The man looked like a shaved ferret.

"Can I help you?" the clerk said acidicaly.

"Dr. Plemby," Kane said. "Is he in?"

"No, no of course not," the clerk said, his voice rising along with his eyebrows. His usual servility with guests appeared with a fringe of unease. "I would have called immediately."

"I better go check," Kane said, thinking: *this is never going to work.* "Room number?"

"Don't you," the clerk began to say but hesitated. "May I see your badge please?"

Kane shook his head. "No badge."

"Then I don't understand," the clerk said, not sure if he should climb back on his high horse or hide under the desk.

"There's nothing to understand," Kane said. "I'm looking for Dr. Plemby and I want to go up and see if he's in: what's his room number?"

"But don't you know that he was declared missing?" the clerk said.

"It hasn't been made public," Kane said, thinking: *right?*

"It was on the news this evening," the clerk said.

Crap.

"Who are you, if I might ask?" the clerk said.

"I'm someone who's looking for Dr. Plemby," Kane said but before he could ask again for the room number the clerk cut him off.

"I'm sorry but if you are not a part of the investigation, I'm afraid I can't allow you upstairs," the clerk said.

"Oh, I'm a part of the investigation, Sunshine," Kane said. "Just not the police investigation. His university hired me to look into his disappearance. They usually recommend your hotel to visiting professors—at least they did," he added significantly.

"Ah," the clerk said. "I don't know what you expect to do up there that the police couldn't but his room number was, or is, 813. He is booked through the end of the week, though the police have forbidden us to enter or disturb his room in any way."

"He may have come back," Kane said. "I'll go check."

Against the clerk's mumbled rebukes, Kane walked to the elevator and went up to the 8th floor. The carpeting was a sunny pink and yellow, striped with a recent vacuuming, and thick enough to muffle the sound of Kane's footsteps. As he drew near the door to 813, crossed with yellow police tape attached to the jamb, Kane noticed the door was ajar. He crept close enough to put his ear to the opening, pressed his body to the corridor wall, and cursed himself for leaving his pistol safely hidden back at his motel. I *should be safely hidden back at my motel.*

A heavy muffled object fell inside the room and someone swore under his breath. The various possible identities of whoever was in the room argued in Kane's mind: *could be a cop so leave, could be a cultist so go in and kill him, could be a reporter so go in and bluff, could be the cleaning staff so back off, could be Elvis wrestling a degenerate Esquimaux so why don't you hesitate here until they come out and see you?*

"It's like you don't want to be found, Dr. P," said whoever was inside.

Kane pushed away from the wall and laughed. He could hear

the man inside spin toward the door. Kane ducked under the police tape and walked slowly in, closing the door completely behind him. Across the room, a man in his late thirties and dressed in a new suit tailored to his weightlifter's build was reaching under his jacket at the small of his back.

"Easy, Archie," Kane said. "What the hell did you do to this room?"

"Solomon Kane," Archie said. He didn't change his posture or remove his hand from whatever it held at the small of his back. "How'd you get here?"

"Helen called me," Kane said as he looked around. The drawers of the wardrobe and desk were piled in one corner of the room as if thrown there, the sheets were in a pile under the coffee table, the paintings were torn from their frames, and the carpet had been pulled away from the baseboard. "I was nearby."

Archie didn't move. "Bullshit," he said as Kane knelt next to the bed.

"Call her and ask," Kane said, peering into the drawer holes of the night table; the drawers themselves nowhere to be seen.

Archie snorted and then took his hand out from behind his back: it didn't hold a pistol. "I'll pass," he said. "She seems to think Venators ought to get along."

"Imagine that," Kane said, grinning up at Archie for a moment.

"Yeah well, I get along with most of the fellahs just fine," Archie said. "It's the ones that run with that prick Hector that I'm a little wary of. I heard about the stalk you two ran up in Odiome," he added.

"That I ran," Kane said, standing up. "Hector skipped town before the big finale. Seemed real urgent that he get up to Arkham and see Helen. I think you may have been up there about that time, right?"

Archie colored and looked at his feet for a moment. Licking

his lips, he shrugged and said, "Okay, so maybe he's not your best friend either. Anyway, I'm all for working a stalk together but I don't even know if there's a stalk going on."

"What have you got so far?" Kane asked.

"Let's see," Archie said, taking a notepad from his jacket pocket and flipping through it. "Dr. Plemby, geologist and consultant for BP—must love that guy around here—was conducting a survey of the Gulf, using a combination of satellites and drone-based sonar to search for new oil fields."

"They're now using Predator Drones to find oil?" Kane asked

"Apparently," Archie said.

"There's irony in there somewhere," Kane mumbled, inspecting the slits someone had cut in the mattress.

"Anyway," Archie continued, "he sent a report to BP saying he thinks he found a natural tunnel on the seabed that leads down to a huge supply of oil and that the tunnel is capped off by only a thin layer of rock. The tunnel exit is located at 28°44′12″North 88°23′13″West. This is all in his report, see? But the thing is, the report was intercepted; email hack."

"Why?" Kane asked, taking out his notepad and writing down the coordinates.

"Don't know," Archie said. "But how it was hacked tipped off Helen so she gave me a call."

"The cult?" Kane asked.

"*A* cult," Archie said. "Or, at least, that's what she suspects. There's no way they could have been monitoring Dr. P just for shits and giggles, right? So she thinks they were tipped off."

"A dream sending," Kane said. "A dream sending, something on the sea floor, and now the doctor goes missing. Great."

"Looks that way," Archie said. "But that's all there is. He dropped off the face of the earth a couple days after he sent the intercepted email. For all we know, he's holed up with a hooker and a bottle of hooch."

"Maybe," Kane said with a sigh. "But if so, why was his room torn to pieces? You can't tell me the police did this. Did you?"

"No way," Archie said. "I didn't think of that, why it was tossed. And what were they looking for?"

"Was Dr. Plemby working with anyone down here?" Kane asked. Archie shrugged. "Wonder how many companies around the Gulf operate Predator Drones with airborne sonar."

"Not many, I'm guessing," Archie said. "Too late to call them now. You eat yet?"

"No and I'm starving," Kane said, dropping the edge of the carpet he was peering under and brushing his hands.

"I know a place," Archie said.

They checked the hallway and then took the elevator down. As they passed through the echoing lobby, Kane saw Archie visibly stop himself from looking to their right, at a collection of chairs and couches guests could use while waiting or for a quick lunch. Though they were in the middle of the blank hours of a New Orleans' night—between the end of dinner at 9:00 and when people head out at 11:00 for an evening at the clubs—a man was sitting by himself, half concealed by a potted palm.

"Easy," Kane whispered through unmoving lips.

Once outside, they went right; Kane's car was parked a block away, in the other direction.

"Could be a cop," Kane said. "The clerk didn't like my looks."

"He's following us, whoever he is," Archie said. "You keep on, let him follow you for a block or two while I get around behind him; once I'm on him, breeze on out of here. You got my number? Good. Call me tomorrow morning."

Archie waited until they passed the edge of the building, when the shadow beyond a hanging balcony light would obscure them from the trailing man, and then ducked right and down an alley. As Kane fought to maintain the same unhurried pace, he could almost feel the trailing man's eyes on his back. *For a big man,* he thought, *Archie has some dynamite trade skills; can't even hear him run down that ally.* The trailing man wasn't so good: once Archie had disappeared, the trailer pressed forward, perhaps worried that Kane would give him the slip, too. Kane let him close in for a couple blocks before he turned a corner and slid under someone's porch.

Well, if it is a cop, Kane thought, *and he's got better eyes than his tailing suggests, I'm going to have a fun time explaining hiding under this porch.*

Footsteps hurried to the corner of the house and then pounded to a halt, stuttering in uncertainty on the sidewalk a yard from where Kane crouched. He could see the man's legs as he turned to look up and down the street. His trousers were neither new nor old, same as his shoes but the shoes had an odd stain around the seam where the leather met the rubber sole, almost as if they were corroding. His knees bent and he weaved back and forth, trying to make out whatever moved farther down the road.

"I lost him, shit," the man said in a reedy voice. It took a second but Kane realized the trailing man was talking into a cell phone. "I know, god damn it. I know! They ain't cops, whoever they are. Cops wouldn't run off like that."

That means you're not a cop, Kane said to himself. Still in a low crouch, he slowly shifted his weight to one foot and slid the other soundlessly forward. *And maybe you'll have something to say if properly motivated.* He slid forward as he listened, the tip of his shoe just shy of the line thrown by a porch light from across the street. A slow inch farther and he'd be out in the open.

"Naw, naw, he's gone, too," the trailer said. "Shit, just—no—just get up here."

A car gunned its engine and then swung around the corner,

screeching to the curb. Two doors slammed and more legs joined the trailing man. Kane tried to recoil from the edge of the porch, to get deeper into its shadow but he was off balance and nearly fell. To keep from making any noise, he had to throw a hand back to catch himself. Like a kid playing *Twister*, he hung in a strained contortion trying not to collapse, as the three unknown men huddled three feet away.

"What did you see?" a deeper voice demanded.

"Nothing," the reedy voice answered. "That's the problem. I come around the corner and—bam—nothing."

"He must have doubled back between the houses," the deeper voice said. "Go check."

"Naw, naw, don't bother with that," the reedy voice said, one of the pairs of legs taking a step away before stopping. "If he's out among the houses, you ain't going to see nothing. He's long gone by now."

"You lost them both," the deeper voice said menacingly.

"Hold on, hold on," the reedy voice gushed. "Listen, we know who they are now. Are you listening to me? That's what we were told to do. Figure out who they are and what they's up to. They's Venators, man, no doubt."

"Supposition," the deeper voice said.

"Sup-a-what?" the reedy voice said. "Listen, we know they ain't cops because they spotted the tail and went poof; we know they interested in Dr. Plemby because they searched his room: now who the only kind of folk do both those things? Venators, gotta be."

"He's probably right," a third voice timidly offered.

"Shut up," the deeper voice growled.

A keyring fell into the uncut grass just beyond the opening to the space under the porch. Kane felt the flush drain out of his face, his trembling muscles smooth, and the ringing in his ears quiet along with his straining breath. He found his balance and poised on bent legs, like a defensive tackle before the hike of the ball. A hand followed the keys and rooted among the grass; a poorly shaved chin dipped into view, below the floorboards of the porch.

"The hell they go?" the deeper voice grunted.

Kane curled the fingers of his free hand at the first knuckle, holding them just within the slanting line of light and shadow, aimed at where a throat should be.

"There you are," the deeper voice said. He stood up and the keys came tinkling out of the grass. "I'm not the one you got to worry about, fool. You'll have to explain it to the lady. Let's go."

The three returned to the car, which spun in a quick u-turn before racing away in the direction it had come. Kane sat down heavily on the dirt below the porch and took a few deep breaths, the battle-calm leaving and the muscle-shake returning.. On hands and knees, he crawled out and only straightened up fully once he had slipped between two houses.

Well that was fun, he thought. *Wonder what the chances are that they're watching the Cutlass.*

CHAPTER 2

SOLUTIONS, PROBLEMS, AND MARGARITAVILLE

I T TOOK KANE a half-hour to get back to his car and another half to ensure it wasn't watched. Driving around to see if he was tailed again and not taking an obvious route back to his motel ate up much of what remained of the night. By the time he was back in his room, he'd given up on dinner and lay down fully clothed, satisfied that at least he had his pistol on him now.

By 9:00 the next morning, Kane was drinking coffee next to a gut-truck and searching the New Orleans business directory on his phone. Ten minutes later he had the address of the only business in Louisiana that offered airborne sonar from a drone: *Aerialgraph Solutions, Inc.* They were south of the city so, past starving, Kane hit a chain pancake house of international pretension before heading out. While he waited for his second cup of coffee and previously-frozen sausages, he called Archie: no answer.

That's not good, he thought. *If he was tailing the guy that tailed us, he must have seen them call off the search and leave. It would have been hard, if not impossible, to follow their car on foot; if he's in trouble, he had a hell of a time getting into it. Maybe he's still sleeping or left his phone turned off.*

Out of habit, Kane didn't leave a message. After inhaling his breakfast, Kane drove south to a small town near Lake Salvador, where *Aerialgraph Solutions* was located. The building could have been that of a prosperous dentist or honest lawyer. The only feature that set it apart from its neighbors was the enormous antenna tower scraping the sky in its backyard. Inside, the dentist-office feel returned with the receptionist sitting behind a sliding glass partition. Kane leaned on the counter and rapped a knuckle against the glass.

The partition slid aside and a woman with blue hair and an affronted expression said, "May I help you?"

"Sal Manning," Kane said. "BP. I've come about Dr. Plemby and would like to speak to whoever he worked with a few days ago."

"Oh, oh of course, of course," she said, standing up quickly and then sitting back down and grabbing her phone. In a voice that betrayed none of her physical agitation, she said into the phone, "Mr. Brice? Mr. Brice there's a gentleman here from BP asking about Dr. Plemby. Yes, I will." She replaced the receiver, patted her hair, stood up, sat down, and said to Kane, "Mr. Brice will be right out," about a second and a half before a glad-hander in a polo shirt and black-dyed hair came barreling out of the back offices, a little red in the face.

"Good morning, good morning, I'm Mike Brice, CEO around here at *Aerialgraph Solution*, sir, good to meet you," Mike Brice said.

"This is Mr. Manning, sir," the receptionist said.

"Pleasure to meet you, sir," Brice said, shaking Kane's hand as if he was trying to take it off the arm. Then he froze. "Well, no, not a pleasure exactly because of poor Dr. Plemby, you know, I just meant—"

"Mr. Brice," Kane said, sensing his advantage and meaning to make full use of it. He yanked his hand free and said, "My time is very limited. While the local police are conducting their investigation—they have spoken to you, correct?"

"No, no sir," Brice said. "We didn't even know Dr. Plemby was missing until we saw it on the news this morning."

"That's the kind of professionalism I've come to expect from the authorities down here," Kane said with exasperation, "which is why I've been sent to conduct the company's own internal investigation into Dr. Plemby's whereabouts. I'll call the police myself, as soon as we're done: your statements need to be taken before any more time passes. But first, I'd like to know if the doctor gave any indication as to what his next step would be in his research. I understand he found an interesting geological feature at, let me see," he said, pulling out his notebook with Archie's coordinates written down, "yes, at 28°44'12"North 88°23'13"West. Can you remember the conversation?"

"Perfectly, sir, perfectly," Brice said, for some reason shaking his head in the negative. "Dr. Plemby spent the day in our command room—would you like to see it? No? Okay. That's where we fly the drones from, even though they're launched down at Port Fourchon. After we conducted a second pass of the location you mentioned—"

"Which was when?" Kane interrupted.

"Which was, uh," Brice stammered and looked to his receptionist.

"Three days ago on the 17th," she said, a clipboard in each hand.

"Right, the 17th," Brice said, again shaking his head. "After the second pass, he had us make a video clip of the sonar and visual record and then he asked us for a recommendation of a boat that could take him out to look at the spot up close, something with a towed sonar array and, if possible, submersibles. I told him to give Jake Hastings a call, a good friend of mine with that kind of gear."

"And where can I find this Jake Hastings?" Kane asked.

"Oh, uh, he's out at, well, you can take this road here," Brice began, pointing out the window.

"Here you are, sir," the receptionist said, handing a slip of paper through the partition.

Kane took it and said, "Thank you. Now, I'm going to go talk with Jake Hastings but I want to thank you for your help. I will probably have to return to go over it again and the police will want to take your statements, too. Stay available."

"Yes, sir," the other two said in unison.

Kane headed for the door but turned back with his hand on the knob. "You don't happen to have that video clip handy, do you?" he asked. After a furious few minutes digging it up and nearly demolishing the receptionist's desk, Mr. Brice handed Kane a DVD on which was Dr. Plemby's sonar sweep.

Jake Hastings was the captain and owner of *The Naughtylass*, a sixty-five-foot research vessel that looked more like a yacht. It had a very sophisticated towed sonar array, which could accurately create topographical maps of the ocean floor, as well as unmanned submersibles that could dive to a depth of over two miles to take video and still pictures. A freelancer of sorts, Hastings was affiliated with several universities and was in-demand by small companies that needed the level of technology their larger competitors could bring to bear but that they could not afford for more than a day or so at a time. The building at the end of his private pier—hurricane proof, on concrete pylons—could have passed for a crab shack or bait store, if the umbrella'd tables, loud t-shirts for sale, and unbroken stream of Jimmy Buffet songs were relied upon. Kane walked from a wide spot in the road where he'd left the Cutlass, rethinking his approach along the way.

The Naughtylass was at moorings at the end of the pier, long deep-sea fishing poles lined up to attention along her stern. At one of the tables on the building's wrap-around, wood-grained deck (actually made of indestructible recycled material), a man in flip flops, with a white stripe down his nose, sat holding a frosted glass and swinging his foot to a song about margaritas.

"You made it," the man said, pushing his cap up by the brim with one finger and tilting his head forward to see over his sunglasses. "Wondered if you'd get here before I set out for some fishing."

"Who were you expecting, Mr. Hastings?" Kane asked, a sudden keen sense told him that lying to *this* man was the same as telling him the truth, except for the consequences. He'd know.

"Not that question," Hastings said before taking a long pull from his margarita and wincing a little at the brain freeze. "What can I do for you?"

"I just came from *Aerialgraph Solutions*," Kane said. "I'm looking into the disappearance of Dr. Plemby and they said he may have come to you for a look at some kind of terrain feature he found on the sea floor."

Hastings said nothing. The angle of his head didn't let on what he was looking at; his eyes could have been ranging over the emerald green waters of the Gulf or staring down at the strange, unkempt man walking up the stairs to his deck. Kane had felt the heat with every step from his car and looked back at the retracted top of his Cutlass, realizing that the seats would be unbearable by the time he got back. Hastings chuckled.

"Kinda hot for a Yankee," he said, though from his accent he was not a native, either. "Especially in *that* suit."

"Brother, it's hell in here," Kane said. "But the shirt underneath looks even worse."

Hastings laughed with his head back and patted his thighs. "Woo-eee, I bet," he said. "Come on inside, it's air conditioned."

They went inside. The surf-shop atmosphere died on the threshold: the reason the inside was air conditioned instead of left open to the cool breeze off the water was that the computers inside needed both temperature and humidity control. *Cape Canaveral has nothing on this place,* Kane thought. There were standard desktop computers, laptops a-plenty, radar and radio suites, gear Kane couldn't begin to theorize about alongside satellite communication equipment and what looked like a control station for Hastings' submersibles, if someone wanted to pilot them from shore. Hastings took a seat at one of the computers and swiveled around to face Kane, not offering him a seat.

"So, you're not a reporter and you're not a cop," Hastings said. "Mind telling me who you are?"

"I could be a reporter," Kane said.

"Not with that suit," Hastings said with a smile. Kane shrugged. "Or the gun."

"You've got good eyes, Mr. Hastings," Kane said. "Navy man?"

Hastings nodded as if at an unnecessary question. "P.I.?" he asked.

"I have no credentials whatsoever," Kane said. "Not in this state. I am looking for Dr. Plemby, though. Truth be told, I don't think he's alive anymore. As for the piece," he said, patting it through his jacket, "I didn't have it on me last night and almost regretted it." Hastings grunted after a moment of silence. "Did Dr. Plemby come to you, Mr. Hastings, about three days ago and ask to go out to 28°44'12"North 88°23'13"West?"

Hastings laughed a quick, silent laugh. "Didn't even need a cue card," he said. "Okay, you're looking for him. I'll tell you, I wasn't sure what to expect. A man called me two days ago and asked about Plemby. He sounded like a cop and said he'd drop by but no cop ever showed up. Funny thing: that night, someone broke in here."

He hiked a thumb over his shoulder and Kane saw a broken window, a window that had been burned out with a blow torch. Hastings had patched it with a bolted-on piece of Plexiglas.

"Acetylene torch," Hastings said.

"And you know I'm not with whoever did that," Kane said.

"Because you wouldn't come around later to ask questions," Hastings said. "No, I guess I know that. I figured it was corporate espionage. But the joke's on them if it was: Plemby didn't find a pre-drilled hole down to oil riches."

"Mind if I sit down?" Kane asked. Hastings nodded toward a chair opposite him. "Why don't you start at the top?"

Hastings got up and walked over to a little table by the window with a small refrigerator underneath. From it he pulled a blender's pitcher half-filled with a pale-green liquid. He held it up and Kane nodded. Hastings filled two glasses from a stack in the fridge, brought one to Kane, kept one for himself, and sat down.

"Well, it's like this," Hastings said with a sigh and a sip. "Three days ago, Dr. Plemby called me and said he'd pay any amount of money if I could take him out to look at a little offshore property. I had nothing on but a vague idea about fishing so I agreed, provided he stopped for tequila on the way here. He did. We headed out. He told me along the way that he had found something interesting on the Gulf floor while surveying for BP.

"Did you know he was an archeologist?" Hastings asked with a chuckle. Kane shook his head, no. "Yeah, as well as being a geologist, Plemby had a doctorate in archeology; and probably a few other things he hadn't mentioned. Well, I think he had *started* looking for something for BP—that's what they'd paid him to do, after all—but he wound up finding something for himself.

"Did you know that there are stone roads on nearly every island in the Caribbean?" Hastings asked. Kane nodded his head. "Oh, you know that one? Stone roads that lead right out into the water and, for some, go out a good long way. Some of them go for miles. Rising sea levels," he said with a roll of his eyes. "There are also remnants of stone buildings underwater, very similar to what are found among Incan and Aztec ruins. Similar in construction, I should say."

"But different in the gods they depict," Kane said. "Different in their artistry."

"You know something after all, Mr. John Doe," Hastings said.

"Not enough," Kane said. "And Plemby found something along those lines? A building, perhaps?"

"Yahtzee," Hastings said and finished his margarita. "We had gone out to the coordinates he gave me and used the array to build a topographical map. That was easy. It indicated what he thought it would."

"Which was what?" Kane asked.

"That there was evidence of an undersea, underground tunnel," Hastings said, "with a cap over it of some sort. Thing was, he couldn't make out with airborne sonar how deep the tunnel was or what was the nature of the cap. The towed array didn't do much better. So, we dropped my little friend," he said with a smile. "My little buddy the MRV. Remote controlled diving camera, he is. He went down and took a look at the spot and what he saw hasn't left my dreams since."

Hastings rose and poured himself another margarita, finishing the pitcher. He sighed at the empty pitcher and returned to his seat, carefully sipping his drink.

"In nearly 10,000 feet of water," he said, "we found a door. This thing must have been twenty, thirty feet tall and nearly as wide. It looked all wrong, too."

"As if the rules of geometry didn't apply to it," Kane said, setting aside his drink, no evidence of it having taken effect.

"Exactly," Hastings said, a look of fear replacing the puzzlement of a moment before. "It shouldn't have looked that way, not even with the distortion of the water."

"And there were figures graven upon the door," Kane said.

"Horrible," Hastings whispered. He put back his drink in one gulp. "I've been on undersea explorations before. I've seen dead bodies, I've seen skeletons of kids in ancient wrecks, but this? No way, man. This was *wrong*. You know?"

"Yes," Kane said. "I know." Hastings' eyes had blanked and he wasn't seeing the room anymore. Kane let him take a moment before he spoke. "And Dr. Plemby?"

"Oh, he thought it was the greatest thing ever," Hastings said. "Christ, he shouted and jumped for joy while my little friend took the video. We came back, I made him a DVD, and he left. Two days ago, I receive a call saying he'd gone missing and nothing surprised me less in forty-seven years on this very fucked-up planet. The guy telling me this—who said he's a cop—asked pretty much what you asked, only more insistent, and I told him pretty much the same as I've told you. He said he'd come down. What he didn't tell me was that he'd cut through my window with an acetylene torch."

"What did they take?" Kane asked.

"You see," Hastings said, "I keep a copy of everything I record for a client. Every once in a while, a client will come back, even years later, and say he lost everything and do I please, please, have a copy. I do. Well, I did. When I came in, the morning after, I found the window burned out and everything from this year wiped from the computer. I'm a big dummy, you see; I can't guess within a nanosecond that the creepy undersea door had something to do with it.

"You'll like this part, though," Hastings said and the sweat stood out on his face. "Plemby? My last client. I hadn't taken anyone else out because it's Spring Break and all the professors are on vacation. So, the data from Plemby's trip was still on the MRV and in the towed array's computer. I still have everything he filmed."

Kane felt himself lean forward, licking his lips like a starving man before a luau pig. Hastings didn't seem offended by his interest. He merely reached into the cargo pocket of his shorts and pulled out a DVD.

"Take it," he said.

Kane did and then walked to a computer beside Hastings, popped the DVD in the drive, and opened the MRV's video file. Hastings turned away, refusing to watch as the remote-controlled swimmer plunged to a door that led to madness. One look was all Kane needed to recognize the blasphemous carvings upon the door, depictions of the greatest catastrophe mankind had ever suffered in the unrecorded past, a prediction of man's fate.

The vast size of the monstrous doors could not be captured entirely by the MRV, nor truly compassed by the human mind that watched. The slime-draped blocks of its construction created angels beyond the geometry of man; whether the graven portal lay flat or nearly vertical was impossible to judge, as it changed from glance to glance. Every inch of the massive edifice was covered in bas relief depicting only madness knew what: eons of human enslavement, the hideous rites to the Great Old Ones, or purposes beyond man's imagination of pain, none could know. None save It that slept dead and dreaming beneath. Staring from a point central to the lintel, hovering in the illusion of its inhuman form, the stone portrayed a creature of dragon shape and proportion, though sitting upon a simple throne as a man might, vestigial wings flaring to either side, its fore-claws upon its hind knees giving the impression of contemplation; but it was the intent upon its many-tentacled face, the set of its squid-like head and the stabbing knowledge of its many eyes, that bespoke malice: Dread Cthulhu's image surmounted the door.

Kane turned off the DVD, stood, and stepped behind Hastings. "After he returned with you," Kane said, "did he mention what his next move was?"

"He only said he needed to talk to someone who might recognize the markings on the doors," Hastings whispered, losing control of his voice, unable to meet Kane's eyes. "I don't know who. A friend at Tulane, I think."

"Hastings, thanks," Kane said and took the DVD and went to the door. "But listen: don't tell anyone else. Especially, don't tell anyone that you have this recording. In your shoes, I'd erase it. If they ever find out you possess a copy, it might not be your window that gets burned. Oh, and keep an eye on the news over the next few days. Something will happen and, yes, it is related. Good luck."

Hastings tried to return the wish but knowing that the horrid door had been shown again in his presence seemed to overwhelm him and he struggled to keep from breaking down into tears. Kane left. The car seat was like fire. He didn't feel a thing.

The pier with Hastings' boat at its end was the farthest point of a long man-made finger of land, pointing south into the gulf. Only fifty-yards wide, docking for boats was its stock in trade with only a few buildings to break up the endless flat of the Gulf and the enormity of the sky. About halfway back to the interstate, Kane came to the strip of stores and a restaurant that serviced the boaters by selling tackle, bait, marine supply, and booze. The parking lot held barely enough pickups for each store to have one person minding the till; the place looked deserted otherwise. That is, until Kane passed the southernmost building.

From the back of the bait shop came a Cadillac revving so high Kane could hear it over the sound of his own screaming tires. It had four men inside, one obviously armed with a shotgun. Kane was already passed it when the Cadillac hit the road, screeching to a halt blocking both lanes behind him. Turning quickly, Kane saw another car—an old Ford LTD station wagon—plow across the parking lot from behind the northern-most shop and block the road ahead.

It was only a flash of thought, an instant in which the mind does not know time, in which Kane saw the standoff, saw himself bring the Cutlass to a halt in the middle of the road, nowhere to go, the Gulf to either side, as impossible to go back to Hastings' concrete bunker as it was to blast through the roadblock and make for New Orleans; stopped between the two carloads of men, he would wait while they converged on him—all avenues of escape cut off—and then open fire; he could shoot back, maybe take a few with him, but that would be the end of Solomon Kane: stopped on a strip of rock, captured and killed by the cult at last. *Fuck you.*

Kane stamped on the accelerator and took the wheel with his left hand, levering himself up so his head and shoulders were above the windscreen. Drawing his 1911, he fired shot after shot into the Ford, the first taking the driver through the head, the next sent after the frantic passenger who tried to grab the wheel, the next through the rear door where the men in the back were hunching over, trying to crawl under their seats, and then three more generally into the car. Kane fired and fired while trying to keep his own car on the road, steering and holding himself upright with the same arm and shooting with the other. The Ford, without a driver, was still in motion and crossed the road, rolling into the gulf, clearing enough space behind it on the road for Kane to squeak by. He'd never outrun the Cadillac, he knew, but he had one more card to play: he'd purposely left one round unfired in his pistol. Dropping into his seat, he threw his right arm over the back and took careful aim at the Cadillac. Inside, disbelieving faces pressed to the windows as the driver tried to wrestle the shifter into reverse—not fast enough. Kane fired his last shot at the ground about three feet from Cadillac, just behind the rear tire: the round impacted the asphalt road and ricocheted upward, hitting the car's gas tank, which burst immediately into flame.

Unlike in the movies, the exploding gas tank didn't flip the car into the air as if fired from a mortar but it did scare the hell out of the cultists inside, who jumped out and scrambled away, forgetting to fire at Kane. Kane hit 110 inside a minute and then held the steering wheel steady with his knee as he fed a fresh magazine into his 1911. He then fished his cell phone out of his pocket and called Hastings.

"If you want to keep on living, Hastings," he shouted over the roar of engine, tires, and flying wind, "then you'll get into that boat of yours double quick. The guys who did Plemby are on this floating highway and I think you're next. Good luck."

Kane didn't wait for an answer and Hastings didn't make one; only the sound of a door slamming and feet pounding down a deck came through the phone before Kane hung up.

CHAPTER 3

WEIRD TALES

THE ARCHEOLOGY DEPARTMENT at Tulane University had one of the nicer buildings on campus, one that hadn't gone under water during Katrina. Finding it had been the easy part; finding out who if any of the professors had talked to Plemby took nearly the whole afternoon. Finally, a grad student remembered seeing Plemby hovering around outside of Dr. DuBois's classroom a couple days ago. No one seemed to have heard of Dr. Plemby's disappearance. Kane found Dr. DuBois in her office, grading papers, drinking espresso (with a smell so wonderful, the exhausted Venator nearly asked for a cup), and being generally not what he had expected.

The room was as dark as most rooms stuffed with books seem to be. Kane knew the *Indiana Jones* image of archeology couldn't possibly be real and yet Dr. DuBois' office was doing its best. Carved wooden masks with fantastic faces and painted symbols hung in one corner of the room, ascending to the twelve-foot ceilings; more masks huddled below them on the floor as if deep in discussion.

Rock samples, bones, primitive instruments, and the tools used in their unearthing lay heaped together on an antique tiger-maple table pushed under the window. The walls were one continuous bookcase from either side of the door all the way around the room, even encircling the window. Dr. DuBois's massive oak desk needed every ounce of its strength to support all the papers, books, and computers she had scattered atop it. She looked up slowly from what she was reading, clearly expecting a student.

"Oh, I'm sorry," she said, taking reading glasses off a nose far too young to need them. She wasn't yet thirty by her looks and Kane thought for a moment he'd found Dr. DuBois's TA. "Can I help you?"

"I hope so," Kane said. "I'm looking for Dr. DuBois."

"I can't help you there," the woman said with a smile. "You've already found her."

Kane smiled and stepped into the room. She continued smiling back until he closed the door, then it wavered a little. It dropped off her face all together when he said, "I want to talk to you about a Dr. Plemby."

Dr. DuBois twisted in her seat and put the foot she had curled under her onto the floor, feeling around for her shoe. She swallowed a couple times and took a quick sip of her espresso. "Dr. Plemby?" she said, her voice shaking. "Dr. Plemby, I—"

"Talked to him two days ago," Kane interrupted. "And on the news this morning, you saw that he had been kidnapped and maybe you're a little scared. You should be, but not because of me."

Kane took out the DVD Hastings had given him and held it up. Without ceremony, he walked behind her desk and opened the DVD drive on her laptop. Dr. DuBois pushed her chair as far away as it would go and began to get up, making inarticulate but unmistakable noises of distress.

"Take it easy, doc," Kane said, holding up his hands. "I'm going to show you something you've probably already seen and then I want you to tell me what you told Dr. Plemby about it."

Kane played the MRV's visual recording of Dr. Plemby's undersea doors. The recording was over an hour long and began with the descent. Kane advanced the recording until the MRV found the massive temple. Again the camera wavered as the impossibility of the temple's construction hove into view. The bas relief of madness and torture, the corruption of the mind and debasement of the flesh, squirmed as if alive on the irreconcilable edifice. Kane let the video play until the MRV caught a glimpse through the murky green water of the depiction of Cthulhu. There he paused the recording and looked back at Dr. DuBois, seeing recognition ashen her face.

"Why did he come to you?" Kane asked lightly, as if it had just occurred to him. "Maybe that's a good place to start."

"Who, who are you?" DuBois asked. Kane only smiled back. "And why are you interested in what Dr. Plemby found?"

"What did he find?" Kane asked.

She turned to the computer and watched as the huge ancient-beyond-ancient doors wavered in the incomprehension of her mind. She watched fascinated as the madness of all that the door foretold corroded her belief in the universe, her surety of reality, her hope in the promise of man.

"So," he said, "why did Dr. Plemby choose to come to you with this? What makes you so special and what can you tell me about that door?"

"Archeology isn't as big a community as you might think," she said.

"I know it isn't," Kane said. "So imagine my surprise when an unknown like you is suddenly consulted on a door covered in the bizarre bas relief of the Cthulhu Cult."

If he was expecting her to jump, he wasn't disappointed. Her jaw began to shake as she looked from screen to man and back again.

"You've heard that word before, haven't you?" he asked.

She nodded quickly. "Yes," she whispered. "And you have a strangely good pronunciation of it." Kane smiled again. "I do know something about it, but only a little. Everyone in archeology has heard something. Cults, strange artifacts, rare books that are always surrounded with murder and disappearances. It wasn't you, was it?" she said, her eyes suddenly filling with tears. "You didn't take my father, did you?"

"Your father?" Kane said, startled. "Easy now, I haven't taken anyone. Who's your father?"

She blinked rapidly and the terror that had contorted her face relaxed. Kane's raised hands and obvious discomfort at her tears did not coincide with her ideas of a kidnapper. No kidnapper would care if she cried. She brushed the tears from her cheeks and took a deep breath, composing herself as if she'd just walked into the room to discuss a project with a fellow professor. Only the quiver in her voice remained of her disquiet.

"Dr. Plemby!" Kane said and snapped his fingers. "He was your father? I did some background on him before I came down," he said, pulling his notepad out of his jacket. "All I found said he has two daughters—one in Connecticut and one on Long Island—and a son down in Miami."

"Those are the children he had with his wife," Dr. DuBois said, wiping her eyes. "He met my mother at a conference here in New Orleans, many years ago. The rest is private, their business."

"Sure," Kane said. "And, surprise surprise, of all his kids it's you who goes into the family business, so to speak." Kane smiled at the hitch only he could have heard in his voice. "And to have a PhD at your age, I'm guessing you're good at what you do. As good as him. So he wasn't coming to get your opinion of it, he came to show off for his little girl."

"Not exactly," she said and rifled the papers on her desk until she uncovered a box of tissues and blew her nose. "My focus is on local archeology and anthropology. I study the indigenous people and early waves of immigrants to this area. So, as you might expect, I've heard a lot of strange stories."

"I bet," Kane said and sat on the edge of her desk.

Dr. DuBois licked her lips and took another sip of her espresso with a shaking hand. "What little dad knew about, about—"

"Cthulhu," Kane prompted.

"Yes," she said, "about Cthulhu, he heard from me. He was a geologist first and so hadn't heard many of the legends, the campfire stories archeologists tell out on digs. He knew I would be able to tell if those doors belonged to the Mythos."

"How?" Kane asked.

"Because of a story I know a little bit about," she said. "I was even going to do my dissertation about it but could never find enough information."

"And this story is what?" Kane pressed.

"In November of 1907," Dr. DuBois said, "the New Orleans police were called out by local 'squatters,' as they were called—supposedly descendants of Lafitte's men—because there were a lot of disappearances in the lagoon country and strange noises at night. So convincing were these appeals for help that an Inspector Legrasse took twenty men out into the swamps and discovered what he called an orgy of violence: people, mostly from the islands, dancing madly about a statuette—who sacrificed captives in the name of Cthulhu. Legrasse and his men killed or captured most of the cultists and he took the statuette. He later brought it to a prestigious meeting of notable archeologists, where the name of Cthulhu was attached to it. Little more is known about the cult Legrasse destroyed or how many statuettes exist and how many cults are out there sacrificing people to them. The statuette went missing years later, from the police warehouse, but a picture was taken of it at the conference of the American Archaeological Society, where Legrasse had taken it and learned what he could of Cthulhu. I studied that photo and tried to locate more of the artwork as a grad student but never could find any."

"No, you couldn't," Kane said. "We're rather careful about that kind of thing."

"We're?" she asked breathlessly.

"There's more to that story," he said. "A lot more. There are many cults, many active cults, scattered around the globe. And their dark sacrifices to idols of Cthulhu are just their happy way of passing the time. You see, their real goal is to bring back their dead priest. It's complicated but it goes something like this: the earth was once ruled by creatures from somewhere else, known by the cults as The Great Old Ones. They were creatures of bizarre power and held mankind in thrall before history was recorded. But a time came when their mighty city of R'lyeh sank beneath the waves and The Great Old Ones returned to the dark stars from which they came. But in R'lyeh, their dread priest Cthulhu lies dead and dreaming. When the stars are in the correct configuration, R'lyeh is supposed to rise again and the faithful can open the doors, revive Cthulhu through human sacrifice, and then he will call back to life—and back to earth—The Great Old Ones. As you might guess, this would be bad for us humans. But some humans don't think it's so bad. They want it to happen because they've either been tainted by what we call dream sendings from Cthulhu or they're just nuts all on their own. And they've tried.

"Here's a little story for *you*," Kane said. "In early 1925, an undersea earthquake shot a large island to the surface of the Pacific Ocean, east of New Zealand. A trading vessel was in the area and inadvertently intercepted an armed schooner racing for the new island. On the island were doors just like these," Kane said, hiking his thumb over his shoulder at the computer image of what Dr. Plemby had found. "The armed schooner was full of cultists trying to get to the island, to open those doors. It isn't entirely clear what happened, the only survivor of the trading ship had a very shaky tale to tell. But it does seem that the doors were opened but that insufficient sacrifices were made to draw out Cthulhu. If the cultists had sacrificed enough, well, you get the idea."

"Oh my god," Dr. DuBois said. "That sounds just like another story I know from the Gulf—but it's not possible."

"What story?" Kane asked.

"In 1815," she said, "there was a minor earthquake in the Gulf of Mexico and a small island surfaced off the coast of Louisiana. They say a group of locals tried to sail out to it, armed to the teeth, but this was January, 1815, and the last battle of the War of 1812 was about to take place. The locals were caught by naval ships and sunk, thinking they were an attacking force."

"Hadn't heard that one before," Kane said and then stood up: "which is why we didn't know about a door here!"

"But it doesn't make any sense," she said. "If those are doors to the sunken city of R'lyeh, how could they be here in the Gulf of Mexico and lead to the same city as the doors you say surfaced in the middle of the Pacific Ocean?"

"Because Euclidian geometry doesn't govern the work of Cthulhu or The Great Old Ones," Kane said absently, thinking of what the local cult could do with the information they had stolen from Hastings.

"That's impossible," Dr. DuBois said flatly. "Geometry is not something you can ignore."

"Hmm? Dr. DuBois, Euclidian geometry was considered the only kind of geometry until the 19th century," Kane said. "But there are others. There are even laws of physics that simply do not apply to creatures like Cthulhu. What seems like a huge distance separating Louisiana from New Zealand is just a fold in space to The Great Old Ones.

"I thought maybe those doors," he said, looking at the computer, "were from something else, a Temple to Dagon long sunk, but if an island has ever risen beneath it, those are definitely doors to R'lyeh. How could we have never heard of these before?"

"We?" she said. "Who's we—oh my god, I know what you are. You're a Venator, aren't you?"

"Hey now," Kane said, looking up and smiling. "Where'd you hear that word?"

"Archeology is a small community," she said. "Campfire stories. Scary campfire stories about people who've learned of the cults and hunt them down. Venators. Who are you?"

"Solomon Kane," he said. "You can look that name up later and have a good scare. Yes, I'm a Venator and that's a good thing, as New Orleans has a funny way of attracting these cults. It just occurred to me that they took your father the day after, or maybe even hours after, he came to you with that video. If you had ever researched the statuette of Cthulhu that Legrasse took from the cult back in 1907, then the cult may have put you on their radar, kept tabs, monitored your computer, and then when Dr. Plemby came in with his video, they snapped it up and took him to find out all he knew."

Kane looked out the window at the darkening night. Turning back, he saw guilt crushing Dr. DuBois, squeezing the very air from her lungs. *Good going, jerk,* he told himself.

"Shit, sorry," he said. "Hey, it's not your fault. It isn't. You couldn't possibly have known and it's their fault anyway, they're the ones running around doing these things. They had a go at me this morning." He put a hand on her shoulder and looked into her eyes. "I'm sorry about your dad and if he's still alive, I'm going to find him. But right now, you need to keep it together because we need to get out of here. Fast."

She nodded but then shook her head, "Why? Why do I need to get out of here?"

"Because the cult knows who you are," he said. "And because I played this DVD on your computer just now. Chances are that's how they discovered your dad, too. Didn't he play his DVD on here?" She nodded, the guilt returning to cloud her face. "Okay, let's think this through. If they have agents in the university, they have to be either in a technical position or a position of administrative power so that they could monitor your computer. Is there anyone around here with a wild reputation, connected with the occult? More than just Mrs. So and So claims she's Wiccan. Ever been invited out to the woods by someone just a little too insistent?"

"No, no, I don't think so," she said. "Wait a second, Dr. Scratock's wife is said to have some very strange artwork in their house. And come to think of it, I guess it does sound like Cthulhu cult work: the bizarre sea motif, scenes of sacrifice, odd perspective lines."

"That's the one," Kane said. "She's our gal. The odd perspective lines are the clincher. They're not actually odd at all, it's just that humans don't possess the visual organs to make sense of them. She ever seem overly friendly to you, invite you to racy parties?"

"Oh that's so creepy," she said. "Yes, she tried to get me to come to a meeting she was holding at her house about, quote, the Esoteric Aesthetic of Virgin Defilement in Pre-Christian Yucatan. I told her I had the flu."

Kane laughed. "Nice," he said. "Alright, I'm convinced. I'm going to go pay her a visit but first we need to get you out of here."

"Me?" she said, standing up.

"Yup," he said and reached into a back pocket and pulled out a fold of cash. "Here, that's about a thousand dollars. You need to go buy some food and then hole up at a motel for the next few days. Don't use your bank card, your credit card, your cell phone—in fact, leave it here, it can be traced even when turned off. Don't call anyone you know from the motel. Just sit tight and watch the news. If you hear of a massacre, it's safe to come out." Dr. DuBois reeled a bit but caught herself against the desk. "Easy," he said. "Alright, we go out this way and then move to lose the tail, if we pick one up."

"This can't be happening," she said and threw a leg out the window.

"I know, it's a hoot, right?" he said. "Oh, you don't happen to know where Mrs. Scratock lives, do you?"

CHAPTER 4

BETTER RUN THROUGH
THE JUNGLE

T
HE GARDEN DISTRICT of New Orleans would have
looked picturesque in the daytime, its sweeping live oaks,
dripping with Spanish moss, and late Victorian architecture
coalescing into an image both wild and refined, natural and artistic,
a green tunnel of tree limbs leading to the stately organization of
history preserved as houses. At night, as grey clouds boiled across
the sky as if called to blot out the stars, the concealment of the trees
and the creaking of the houses in the rising wind all crawled with
potential ambush as Kane stole from shadow to shadow, approaching the Scratock mansion.

If word has reached her of the failed attack down by Hastings'
place, Kane thought, *she may be waiting for you. And what's this? A*
sentry in a car, watching the road: did you really think I'd drive up
to the front door?

A dark sedan, indistinguishable as to make and model, sat in the obscurity beneath a live oak. The approach to it wasn't easy, Kane found. The Garden District was the wealthiest part of town, and the Scratock's street not the least wealthy part of the district; every house on the block had security systems including motion detectors and heat sensors. If Kane tried to use the houses for cover, he'd likely activate an alarm. Forced to keep to the sidewalk, Kane crept slowly forward, never stepping into the weak rays of light peeking through the curtained windows around him.

Nearer the sedan, Kane could just make out the license plate: it was out of state, Vermont. He dropped to the ground and crawled another tree forward. *Now would be the perfect time for someone to walk by with a dog,* he thought. Rising in a pushup, he passed one eye far enough around the trunk of the tree to get a look at the driver. *He's big, damn. Shooting him is going to make too much noise but that is one big goddamn neck to break.* Kane knocked his head against the tree a moment later and thought, *idiot.* He reached down to his ankle and drew the long, thin stiletto dagger from his boot sheath.

Rolling onto his back, he dropped into the gutter and crawled using his feet and his shoulder blades. Passing the driver's door, he moved to the rear passenger's door and slowly—enough that it made his muscles ache—sat up and pulled his legs under him. *Don't look in the side-view mirror, pal,* he thought, *this'll just take a second.* He debated for a moment whether to open the door with his right and stab with his left or open with his left and slash with his right, when up ahead, a car turned onto the street.

Kane kept his head below the level of the window as headlights strafed him and the sedan. He fastened his eyes on the side-view mirror, trying to will the driver not to look into it. As the passing car's headlights flooded the sedan's interior, Kane could make out the driver's features.

Kane chuckled then and waited until the passing car was out

of sight before tapping on the window—and then Archie almost shot him. Both took a second to glare at the other as their pulses returned to normal. Kane sheathed his stiletto as a sign of good faith and Archie reached back and unlocked the rear door. Kane slipped in, careful not to let the door slam.

"What the hell are you doing here?" Archie whispered harshly.

"The same thing you're doing, probably," Kane said. "Oh, and thanks for answering your phone this morning."

Archie barked a quiet laugh and dug into the glove compartment before holding up a smart phone with a bullet protruding from its smashed screen.

"Saved by the ghost of Steve Jobs," Kane said.

"Yeah, I guess," Archie said. "But I think the windshield of the last car I had also slowed the bullet down a bit. That sucker had my name on it."

"What happened?" Kane asked.

Archie told him how, after separating at the hotel, he had seen a car following the guy who had been tailing them. Archie had quickly stolen a car to follow it. He'd apparently been just down the street when Kane had his fun hiding under the porch. Tailing the car had led him to a lonely road-side bar out in bayou country. Given the way the driver had yelled at the other men as he'd dropped them off along the way, Archie figured the driver was the better target. At the bar, the driver had met a woman who obviously didn't belong there—from her clothes—and yet demanded respect from everyone present.

"I must have been seen, though," Archie said, "because as I'm watching the place through the windows, some geezer with a revolver takes a shot at me from behind a cigarette machine."

"Aren't those things illegal?" Kane asked.

"Because that's the important part of the story," Archie said.

He'd had to get out of there fast, but Archie had picked up the license plate number of the most expensive car in the dirt parking lot, a Mercedes. Calling Helen, she had traced it for Archie and he wound up outside the residence of Dr. and Mrs. Scratock.

In his turn, Kane told Archie all he had learned from Hastings and Dr. DuBois.

"Okay, you win," Archie said sulkily.

Kane laughed grimly. "Not yet."

"So you think they grabbed Dr. Plemby because he knew too much?" Archie asked.

"Maybe," Kane said. "Or maybe they were afraid he'd tell what he knew, put it in a paper in a scholarly journal."

"Then why not grab his daughter, too?" Archie asked.

"Probably because they wanted her to do more research," Kane said. "By leaving Plemby out there looking around, he had found the exact location of doors to R'lyeh. They grabbed him up before he could tell too many people but maybe they're hoping his daughter will find out more, which means they learn more because they're monitoring her computer. Once she turns dangerous, though: whack."

"You squirreled her away?" Archie asked.

"She's safe," Kane said. "For now. Whoa, whoa, here we go, here we go—get down!"

The front door of the Scratocks' opened and a woman dressed in a wraparound dress and a twenties-style turban walked out to a Mercedes SLK Roadster parked in the driveway. In seconds, the little red roadster was flying down the avenue. Archie's stolen Audi was game to follow and soon the two cars were burning through stop lights on their way south, out of the city.

It was nearly an hour through increasingly overgrown country, along twisting single-lane roads with the headlights off—to avoid alerting Mrs. Scratock of the two Venators tailing her—before the Mercedes swerved without warning down a dirt trail. Archie and Kane nearly skidded past it on the lightless road.

"Wait, wait," Kane said: "Stop here."

Archie pulled the Audi onto what passed for a shoulder on the two-hundred year old road and shut off the engine. With the windows down, they could hear Scratock's car in the distance as it came to a halt and its engine died. The Venators shared a look and strained in the darkness but could hear no more. *Ready?* Kane silently asked Archie. The huge man nodded and they both slipped out of the car.

Pistols in hand, they crossed the tree line into the soggy forest. They kept the dirt trail Scratock had used to their left, a dark space without trees, shaded by the endless centuries of growth and death and re-growth. The sounds of insects surrounded them and overhead the flapping of fleshy wings froze them with its suddenness. They pressed on, convinced that every sodden step they took splashed audibly through the trees to their enemies ahead. Another noise slashed the night to their right and both fell back against a furrowed cypress tree, pointing their pistols blindly into the darkness.

Nothing happened and then a slithering sloppiness slouched away.

"Kane?" Archie whispered through clenched teeth. "Are there alligators in the swamp?"

Kane took a few audible breaths and then growled back, "Why can't you just be quiet?"

Then they heard it. In the distance, unclear yet distinct, without form but repetitious, unknowable but primal in frightening effect: the two men felt their already pounding hearts race in response to the beating in the distance. Music as of drums, voices shouting or chanting or shrieking in pain or ecstasy, seeped through the vine-draped woods. Though they could not see each other's eyes, cloaked from the light of the moon by the canopies between them and the sky, the two Venators exchanged a look.

Kane knelt and took a handful of muddy swamp dirt and smeared his face with it, blotting out his pale skin, paler now than ever. Archie followed suit and then both smeared the foul-smelling muck on their white shirts as well, knowing that premature discovery could lead to their deaths, or worse.

Again they moved through the woods, now senseless to the wildlife around them, ignoring the road, never looking for a sliver of sky: all the guide they needed was the beat and screams of the cultist orgy ahead. The ululations keening amid the galleries of cypress trees broke beyond the normal vocalizations of mankind and bordered upon the animal or the unearthly. Louder and louder the bombastic screaming grew and with it, the searing orange light of fire.

The Venators kept their feet below the water of the swamp, never raising them too far for fear of the noise it would make, despite the cover the orgy's screams undoubtedly gave them. From the sounds ahead, there could have been a hundred raving cultists and without surprise Kane and Archie had no hope. Several minutes passed achingly until they came to the edge of a small islet deep within the swamp.

Here, on a relatively flat and dry acre of land, a half-circle of fire clawed frantically at the sky. Around the fire, a half-dozen scaffolds leaned in ramshackle disorder at the islet's edge. Between the fire and the scaffolds, several dozen people threw themselves into rhythmic convulsions. Unclothed, some filthy, some scarred, all crazed and most drenched in blood, the cultists had bound sacrificial victims to the scaffolding. Two were clearly dead, their innards having been torn from their chests; another was insensible, despair driving away consciousness; another tried to plead for mercy but his screams drown amid the unholy din of his captors. The last victim, haggard and filthy but alive and taking in the hellish scene before him with either shocked quiet or scientific aplomb, was Dr. Plemby.

Dimly seen past the half-circle of fire, at the islet's center, was a granite monolith some eight-feet high. Upon the squared top of the monolith resided a small, weirdly wrought statuette, which seemed to brood over the atrocities committed for its approval. At its feet, pressed naked to the monolith with raised hands, Mrs. Scratock held a knife of simple, cruel design. By far the most blood-covered of the nightmarish horde, she led them with her example of brutality.

As Kane and Archie crouched at the islet's edge, surveying the scene, Scratock turned to the wild congregation and they joined her in chanting:

"Ph'nglui mglw'nafh Cthulhu R'lyeh wgah'nagl fhtagn."

Again and again the sounds unnatural to the voice of man where screamed at the sky, the fire, and the squatting figure of the statuette. Kane glanced at Archie and saw that the ceremonial fire had a rival in the heat of vengeance that burned in the Venator's eyes. They both readied several magazines between their fingers for rapid reloading, took aim behind cypress stumps several yards apart, and opened fire.

The first shots were lost in the mad chanting of the cult, and bloody bodies flailing on the ground drew no special notice on that islet. When Kane had quickly shot dead three revelers to clear a path to the monolith, his next shot took Scratock between her gore-covered breasts, smashing her life out against the granite pillar; she smeared her way to the ground, lifeless. Their leader dead, the cult turned upon its attackers—and more than thirty charged two.

The two, however, were armed and had faced overwhelming odds since the reality of mankind's precarious position in the universe had been revealed to them; they flinched not at all. The distance from the fire to those who fired was not far, but the Venators did not miss. Again and again their pistols roared and down fell madness with every shot. It was not a hunt, it was not a battle, it was a firing squad. In no more time than it took for each man to empty three magazines, the islet was wiped clean of the cult in a torrent of blood.

The ringing in their ears seemed piercing, overwhelming as jet engines, in the sudden quiet. With shaking legs and wary eyes, the two Venators walked onto the islet and stalked through the heaps of bodies, alert for anyone feigning death. Convinced, and hearing the weak pleas from one of the would-be sacrifices, Kane drew his knife and cut the bonds of those who still lived, Archie covering him. Dr. Plemby was the last cut from the scaffolds and he thanked his two rescuers with a soundless nodding of his head. Two days without water had stolen his strength but hadn't broken his spirit. Unsteadily, he left the scene of slaughter and walked with the others back to Archie's car. Before they left, however, Kane approached the monolith, took down the horrid statuette—a wave of scrutiny washed over Kane's thoughts as he held it—and then smashed it against the granite again and again until it was unrecognizable. Picking up the pieces, he cast them into the waters of the swamp, scattering the remains as they made their slow way back to civilization.

CHAPTER 5

THE DOORS TO R'LYEH

THEY DROPPED THE two unknown men at a roadhouse an hour outside of New Orleans. Though in need
of medical attention, they knew their rescuers could not
be questioned by the police and promised to wait before calling
an ambulance. Circling the city in a wide arc, Kane, Archie, and
Dr. Plemby stopped at an all-night diner, ordering from a window
because their muddy clothes precluded entry. Sitting at picnic
tables, drinking cold beer and munching crawfish, they said little,
laughing absently at nothing except the vagaries of fate that brought
them together, out of the clutches of so fell an enemy.

Dr. Plemby asked them who they were and how they had found
him. They gave him an abbreviated version of their story and, surprisingly, it seemed to satisfy him. Having seen the cult in action,
little would shock the geologist for the rest of his days.

"What I wonder," Plemby said, somewhat sleepily on his second
beer, "is what did they hope to gain by knowing the location of

those doors? How on earth could it help them, in whatever it is they do when not kidnapping and murdering?"

"Knowing where the doors are?" Archie said around a mouthful of crawfish. "Well, if they know where the doors are, next time the stars are right, they can be ready for the island to rise. If it does, they can open the doors, make the necessary sacrifices and poof—Cthulhu walks the earth again. Finding the doors is really the hardest part."

"Cthulhu also sends the locations to those sensitive enough to receive his dreams," Kane said. "Usually artists."

"Even though he's dead?" Plemby asked.

"Yup," Kane said. "That's what the chant means: 'In his house at R'lyeh dead Cthulhu waits dreaming.' They want to be ready for when his time of waiting is over."

"I'm not so sure," Archie said, a look of horror driving even the flush of alcohol from his face. He pointed through the window of the diner at a TV hanging from the ceiling. He jumped from his seat and ran to the window, shouting inside, "Hey! Hey! What's going on there?"

The waitress, trying to look disapprovingly at the mud-covered gentleman, said as if to a slow child, "Terrorists is what's going on. Terrorists stole an offshore oil rig. About an hour ago. They're towing it someplace. It's a drilling rig so people think they may try to drill into the oil field and let it out into the water like BP did. On purpose, though."

"Fuck, fuck, fuck!" Kane shouted.

"They don't mean to wait for Cthulhu to be ready to leave his house at R'lyeh," Dr. Plemby said. "By the devil, they mean to drill through his door and drag him out by the tentacles!"

Kane and Archie ran flat out to their car, all weariness dropping from their bodies, but halted at the hood as Dr. Plemby caught up. They exchanged a bewildered look.

"How in the hell are we going to get out there?" Kane said.

Archie squinted up at the sky, hands balling into fists, jaw muscles bulging until they stood out like cords.

"We could fly!" Dr. Plemby said.

"We?" Archie growled.

"Not unless you have a helicopter in your back pocket," Kane said.

"Oh yes, of course," Dr. Plemby said, biting his thumb. "Where can we get a helicopter?"

"Hastings!" Kane shouted and clawed his cell phone out of his jacket. "Hastings, come on, Hastings. Hastings! You're still alive, fantastic: where are you? Out at sea is just the place to be, buddy. Listen, we need a ride and we needed it about an hour ago. You had a bad feeling about that terrorist thing, too, huh? Okay, how do we get to you?"

Using the Audi's GPS and Hastings' access to topography satellites, Kane and the others wound there way as far south as they could go by road to a place where Hastings could take a rubber dinghy out to pick them up from the shore. The satellites he could call upon also allowed Hastings to take accurate bearings of where the hijacked drilling rig was. A semisubmersible offshore platform, the rig was designed for open-water oil drilling and could be moved from location to location by tugboat. Once in place, the rig would be secured to the seafloor by cables and could then begin accurate drilling. How the cultists planned to drill, no one knew. They didn't need to be accurate, particularly; all they needed was to open the doors to R'lyeh and then their sacrifices would awaken Cthulhu from his undead slumber, calling him forth to the world's demise.

Once aboard *The Naughtylass*, Hastings pushed the ship full throttle. Kane and Archie reloaded their emptied magazines from an ammo can Archie had taken from his car trunk. Dr. Plemby found a spear gun Hastings kept for when he went scuba diving in shark-filled waters. On the foredeck, the three watched as the dark bulk of the drilling rig colored the murky distance. Coastguard boats surrounded it, they knew, and helicopters with searchlights swept its towers and jutting platforms: how they would board the rig unseen, or at all, they could not yet guess.

"Kane," Archie said, pausing in his reloading. "You ever stop to think: man, we have got the most screwed up job in the world?"

"Not really," Kane mumbled, filling his pockets with loose rounds.

"I mean," Archie said, resting his huge hands in his lap, sitting cross-legged, "I mean, what we do is, what we do is we hunt down weirdos who try to end the world through magic and then we kill them—it ain't normal!"

"Roger that," Kane said and settled back on his elbows. "It ain't. Hey Doc, is that the only weapon Hastings has on board?"

"Afraid so," Dr. Plemby said. He brandished the spear gun in one hand and an extra spear in the other. "I've got five of these extra spears, though. I don't know how much use I'll be with them but I hope to take out at least *one* of those bastards!"

"Uh-huh," Kane nodded. "You know, you should probably stay onboard the ship."

"Not a chance," Plemby said. "No, no, I'm coming. I haven't heard much of Cthulhu over the years but if even 1% of the .001% of what I have heard is true, I'd rather be eaten in the first moments of his horrid reign than have madness and terror haunt me into a heart attack somewhere else. *He* at least I'm sure I can hit: big as a skyscraper, right?"

"That's what they say," Kane said.

"But how the hell do they know?" Archie mumbled returning to the task at hand.

After a few minutes, as the mass of the drill rig became a shadow over the water in the distance, Archie asked, "Hey, is it true there were Followers of Dagon up at Odiome?"

"Yup," Kane said, eyes fixed ahead.

"Innsmouth Jewelry," Archie whispered. Then, more loudly, "I've never tangled with the Followers."

"Yeah, me either," Kane said. "I wonder what brought them out, what was worth risking all that Innsmouth Jewelry."

"Does it, did it really control peoples' minds?" Archie asked.

Looking over, Kane noticed a faint blush coloring the huge Venator's cheeks. Careful not to sound more than casual, he said, "Yeah, but you'd have to wear it during a sacrifice."

"They must have been organized as hell," Archie said, "to take over a whole town. Do you think this oil rig is more of their work?"

"I don't know," Kane said. "I can't see The Followers agreeing to drill through a door to R'Lyeh. With their bizarre belief that they can eventually transform into amphibians, wouldn't they just wait until they could swim down to the door?"

"Yeah," Archie laughed. "Seems sort of sacrilegious, from their point of view. The Followers', I mean."

"Yeah," Kane said. "Which means this bunch on the rig is liable to be a bit more impatient than The Followers and more determined than your average swamp cult. Wish we'd had time to get some better weapons."

"And ten other guys," Archie said.

The Coastguard challenged Hastings as *The Naughtylass* approached but was out of range to intercept, not expecting anyone to race toward the rig from deeper into the Gulf. Helicopters swooped down on them to see what was going on; Kane waved back, as did Dr. Plemby. The radio crackled with warnings and commands to change course; Hastings did not respond.

Instead he shouted down from the bridge, "If you want to stop them from drilling the doors, taking out the tugboat that's dragging the rig should do the trick."

Kane looked over the people and gear he had on hand and quickly issued a few orders.

The Naughtylass veered toward the rig at full throttle. The four huge legs of the rig rode through the waves of the Gulf leaving four distinct wakes behind them; *The Naughtylass* kept at least one leg between it and the tug at all times in an attempt at concealment. With the Coastguard filling the airwaves with news of her appearance, though, the cultists aboard the rig and tug would soon discover her. Tiny flashes smote the darkness from one of the rig's rear-facing platforms, a hundred feet in the air. A second later, the water around *The Naughtylass* snapped and spat, and a few rounds punctured her forward deck. Kane, Archie, and Plemby dove for the stanchion rail and fled rearward. Hastings kept his cool and brought his ship as close to the rig's pylons as he dared, pitching wildly as he plowed through the wakes and overtook the towed, floating building. Once underneath the rig, the firing stopped but it was very dark and Hastings had to guess how close they were to the pylons by the bucking of his prow. Nearly nosing into the forward-most pylon, Hastings swerved *The Naughtylass* around it at the last moment and dashed for the tug. Gunfire erupted from its stern as soon as *The Naughtylass* was clear.

Immediately, Kane and Archie lifted and tossed the rubber dinghy overboard, Plemby holding its rope so it wouldn't disappear. All three then leapt in and started the engine. In seconds they were outpacing *The Naughtylass*, weaving back and forth as those who fired from the tug shifted to the new, and seemingly more urgent, target. Plemby took the tiller, crouching in the rear of the little boat; Kane and Archie huddled at the bow, trying to aim while every second the dinghy jumped another three feet up or down over waves. Fortunately, the cultists firing at them had nearly as difficult a time. Unfortunately, they had better luck and a few rounds scored on the dinghy's side. Slowly, their boat was sinking.

Anticipating the next jump of the rubber dinghy, Kane squeezed off a round—and missed. He cursed; there was no telling how many cultists would be onboard, how well-armed they were, or how they were situated. He couldn't afford to waste a shot. He fired again. Again he missed. Archie gave him a baleful look but wouldn't risk a shot himself. *Alright you son of a,* Kane thought and let a shot fly from instinct. The firing from the tug abated momentarily before increasing to a fevered pitch. The dinghy drew within thirty feet of the tug. From the lower angle their crouching afforded them, Kane and Archie looked up at the cultists on the stern of the tug, silhouetted against the sky: from where they stood, the cultists looked down into a pool of ink—until two eyes of fire winked in the blackness and their screams joined the sound of engines, helicopters, and rushing water.

Plemby threw the tiller to one side and the dinghy drove against the side of the tug. Kane grabbed a rubber bumper hanging from the tug's side and lashed the dinghy's mooring line to it. Immediately, four cultists leaned over the side and filled the little boat with fire, some shooting with a pistol in each hand. Archie returned fire in a wild arc—screaming even as he took shots in the shoulder, leg, and abdomen—killing two. Plemby nearly fell overboard as he reeled away from the fire but managed to launch one of his spears, taking the cultist nearest him through the throat—he'd never been luckier in his life. Kane, though encumbered with tying their boat to the tug, managed to squeeze off a round, dropping the fourth attacker. The dinghy, however, was fatally damaged and was soon below the water.

Kane threw an arm over the gunwale of the tug, using it for cover, and swept his eyes across the deck. Shots exploded from behind a pile of ropes and from the cabin doorway: a few rounds sailed overhead, a few thudded against the gunwale, reverberating against Kane's chest. He shot back twice. The firing stopped.

Plemby tossed his spear gun into the tug and then clung to its side with one hand, trying to keep Archie from going under with the other. Kane reached down and together he and the geologist managed to drag the enormous Venator onboard. He was losing blood fast and could offer little help, his strength fading. Kane pressed a pistol into the hand of the wheezing doctor and then charged the cabin. The moment he was fully in front of the door, he slid like a baseball player passed it: a hail of shots sailed over him and into the night.

Still lying prone and using the door for cover, Kane thrust his arm into the tug's darkened cabin and fired where he remembered the shots had come from; more shots were returned and Kane moved from flash to flash, stone-faced and deliberate even when the wood of the deck snapped and splintered from rounds blasting home an inch from his chin. A moment to write, a second to live; the cabin was quiet.

Kane scrambled to his feet and swatted around the doorjamb until he found the light switch. The glaring electric bulbs buzzed at four more dead or dying cultists—and a large first-aid kit on the wall. Kane tossed it back to Plemby with a remark that it was time to pretend he was the other kind of doctor. Kane then switched off the light and plunged into the darkness of the tug.

At the back of the room, a tiny cramped stairway led up to the tug's conning tower. Kane paused and listened. It was unthinkable that no one waited above, pointing a gun down the stairs. Bending over without taking his eyes off the dark stairwell, Kane removed his shoes and socks. Silently, he placed one foot upon the metal stair and tested it for creaking. It held firm and he began his soundless, spiraling ascent. After a dozen steps had passed with the agony of hot coals, Kane heard a sniff and a mutter. Someone was around the sharp turn of the staircase. Kane's mind raced, wondering how he could possible fire accurately without taking a round in the face.

Simply sticking his hand around and firing blindly was not a good idea: if the cultist had any sense, he would be at one side or the other, using the steel walls for cover. *If he had any sense,* Kane thought, *he wouldn't have joined a cult that wants to revive a bunch of dead gods to eat all mankind.* Kane knew that as soon as his head came around the corner, the cultist would fire at it. Looking around in the murky light from above, Kane could see there were handrails on either side of the stairway. Kane smirked and then slowly put a foot on the inside handrail, raising himself until he had to hunch, bracing his back against the ceiling. Leaning until his muscles vibrated with the strain, Kane tried to keep his head pressed against the ceiling as he inched his way up and around the stairwell, walking the handrail like a tightrope. A few agonizing moments later, his eye passed far enough forward that he could see the conning tower's top. There, crouching behind an overturned table, a man was pointing a pistol at the stairway, staring fixedly at the lowest point he could see. At the highest point, Kane was all but invisible. He knew he had only one shot: he swung his right arm around and into position, the other man saw him and aimed in answer, but too late: Kane shot first.

The tug suddenly rocked to a halt as Plemby was bandaging the last of Archie's wounds. The giant man was still conscious but he looked ashen and had begun to shiver. A moment later, Kane came running out of the tug's cabin, shoes in hand.

"You stopped the boat," Plemby said unnecessarily.

"And you stopped the bleeding," Kane said after a quick examination of Archie's wounds. "Good job, doc. I radioed Hastings, inside; he's coming to get us."

In less than a minute, *The Naughtylass* roared out from amid the oil rig's pylons and came alongside the tug. The tug's rubber skirt kept the collision from damaging either boat. Jumping down from the bridge, Hastings held the two craft together as Kane and Plemby lifted Archie and carried him over, falling to the deck under the strain a second after they were home free.

Ten minutes later, Hastings had them cruising toward Mexico. Archie had passed out after Kane had given him a bag of blood expanders from the extensive medical supplies Hastings kept on board. Kane then returned to the bridge and gratefully accepted a cup of coffee from Dr. Plemby. After reassuring the others that Archie would make it (and that he'd taken worse in years past), Kane asked about coastguard pursuit.

"No sign of them on surface radar or from the towed sonar array," Hastings said, again checking his equipment. "It's weird but they didn't give chase for even a minute. Not even one measly helicopter!"

"Oh, I don't know that it's all that weird," Plemby said, smiling to himself. "It just so happens that we are in international waters. Aha! And always were, although just barely. Since that rig and the tug had been hijacked, that made the cultists pirates and piracy laws haven't been altered in this country since before it was a country. Most other places, too. And killing pirates is hardly a crime. I don't think we'll have to worry too much about the law catching up with us."

"Well, what the hell?" Hastings said. "Should I turn us around, then? We're still closer to Texas than Mexico, and that guy downstairs needs a doctor asap. And not your kind, Plemby."

"Mexico is still best," Kane said, both hands wrapped around his warm cup of coffee. "They'd figure out who Archie is in an American hospital. He'd end up in jail. As far as the authorities are concerned, we're both mass murderers."

"Me, too!" Plemby said. "I killed one with my spear," he added to Hastings with equal parts horror and pride. "But why worry about what happened in the swamp?" he asked Kane. "You had to kill those lunatics to save me." Kane gave him a wink. "Oh," Plemby said knowingly. "Not your first cult, I take it. That's right, you two are Venators."

"What's that, exactly?" Hastings asked.

"Too long a story for right now," Kane said. "Maybe tomorrow."

"But you'll be gone tomorrow," Plemby said sadly. "Won't you?"

Kane smiled warmly but didn't answer.

"So, uh, what will happen now?" Hastings asked.

"I figure the coastguard will mop up the rig in due time," Kane said. "It's not going anywhere without the tug pulling it. Then, the government will cook up a nice lie about what happened. In a few months, maybe, someone will stumble upon the cult we wiped out, in the swamp, and find a hair of mine or something, for DNA testing, and another few dozen bodies will be added to my warrant. It ain't a good life but it is exciting."

"We saved the world today," Plemby said soberly. "And it doesn't count for a damn thing, does it?"

"Only to the world," Kane said. "Not the people on it at the moment, not as far as they know."

"And yet you keep going," Hastings said. "Why would anyone choose such a thankless—no, scratch that, I don't think I want to know. Better question: how can I help?"

"Yes, me too," Plemby said. "We're in this now, together."

"You two are not in this," Kane said and set aside his cup. "Listen, you can and should go back to your lives. The government will probably keep it all quite if they can. You'll be okay with them. The cult that knew you is either dead or will be soon. Leave any survivors to me. You don't have to take up this life."

"That may be," Plemby said. "But I still want to help."

"You can," Kane said: "Keep your eyes open."

BOOK 3

FIFTY SHADES
OF KANE

CHAPTER 1

THE ONE THAT GOT AWAY

WHOEVER HAD JAMMED himself into the crawl-space must have finally reloaded because double-aught buck suddenly came raining down like an angry hail on the burning tractor Hector Troy hid behind. The night was alive with fires and firing guns. The trees creeping up from the Mississippi stood stock still, shocked at the carnage under their boughs. The river passed as a whisper of cold emptiness, haunting and calling and strangely peaceful as it underlie the cries of the dying.

A body fell heavily behind a tree to Hector's right, the thick man's grunt coughed between the shot-gunner's barrage. The would-be flanker hadn't gone far enough, though, and couldn't take a shot, couldn't see Hector; he scrambled on knees and elbows, edging around the tree. Taking two breaths in time with the shooting above him, on the third, Hector pushed with his legs and shot up the side of the tractor far enough to stretch an arm over it and shoot. He knew he took his man through the kidney, disabling him at least, just as he knew he'd burned his arm clear through to the bone while pointing over the burning tractor. He swore furiously as he dropped to the ground—a second before the shot-gunner's next blast—hovering his left hand near his now ruined right arm. From beyond the glow of the burning machine, farther away from the front of the house, a figure dodged from tree to tree and then ran straight for Hector.

"You silly son of a bitch, what the hell have you started here?" Solomon Kane shouted as he landed in a heap next to Hector. "And where's our man with the idol?"

"Don't know," Hector spat through clenched teeth. He tried to peal his burned leather jacket away from his wound but nearly passed out as pain washed over him. "Could've been in the church."

"What church?" Kane said. He dropped the magazine from his .45 and patted the pockets of his suit jacket until he found a fresh one.

"You see that big burning pile of waste up by the road?" Hector said.

"Fantastic," Kane said. "Just stay down."

The shot-gunner had run dry again but Kane didn't charge the house. He waited, picking through the sounds of the fire's breathing and the whisper of the river, listening for the shot-gunner's reloading—the sliding-metal-hanger sound of each shell being shoved into the magazine—as it rang as distinctly as a bell on a hilltop. Reloaded and still angry, the shot-gunner rose to begin blasting the tractor again: ready for his next attack, though, Kane sent a round at the window a split second before the shot-gunner appeared. The clatter of a shotgun on a wooden floor above and the breathless heave of a man with the wind knocked out of him, tripped out of the window and down to the two Venators.

"How many more are there?" Kane asked.

"Beats the hell out of me," Hector said. "Maybe one more, I don't know. If there is, he's wounded."

"Our man?" Kane asked.

"No, this guy's bigger," Hector said.

"Of course he is," Kane sighed. He shook his head as if away from a bug and then darted around the flaming farm equipment and to the side of the house.

Hector leaned forward and got a strong whiff of his leather jacket being cooked by the burning tractor. The extra straps and buckles and things on his jacket had always been about fashion, about living up to and enjoying the persona of the lone biker, grizzled, dangerous, reckless and free. The buckles and straps were now a convenient way to fashion a sling for his burned arm. Clenching his jaw but unable to keep gasps of pain from rising with each movement, Hector bound his arm to his chest. He wiped his face, the dirt and blood making his eyes run as much as the tears of pain, swatted at the ground until he found his pistol, and then heaved unsteadily to his feet. He walked around the tractor, killed the man he'd wounded earlier, and then went into the ancient frame house.

Kane was in the back room, tearing dried and dusty doors off of cabinets and stamping holes in the floorboards. Hector looked around in the wavering fire light coming in through the glassless windows: the house was a faded picture of the turn of the last century, with homemade furniture rotted to fragments, paint or stain or even dirt forgotten in the long passage of time. Dust clung to everything, even the walls running with riverside moisture. Kane came into the front room rubbing the butt of his pistol against his head.

"So what the fuck happened, Hector?" Kane said as if he didn't care what the answer was. "Where's our man?"

"What's this 'our' business?" Hector said. "I took up the stalk of this son of a bitch when Tweedle-dumbass and Tweedle-dipshit blew the stalk out near Shenandoah. Those idiots! First they let this guy, Levi, escape their ambush and make off with the idol, and then they lose him and he comes clear across Iowa."

"They were always idiots," Kane said impatiently. "The two of them together don't have half a brain but that's not what I'm talking about. When Helen called me she said you'd picked him up headed toward Burlington. Instead, I hear on the police scanner that all hell is breaking loose in some podunk place called Muskaloosa, show up to find you've burned down half the damn town, killed all their cops, and—by the look of it—lost the mark."

"I got made!" Hector shouted back. "Levi was never headed to Burlington, it was a feint. He was always headed here and you can see why. The whole fucking town was corrupted; every damn one of them was in the cult, even the cops. Which is how I got made, if you hadn't figured that out. Once they tagged me, they went straight to their guns, Kane. And they weren't the only ones: there were grandmothers and granddads, barbers and who-the-fuck-all else after me the second I hit Main Street Muskaloosa."

Kane threw up his hands and paced back and forth a few times. "Funny how something always comes up in your stalks that makes wiping out a town the only option," he said.

"Oh, is the Salem Slaughterer going to tell me how a Venator should stalk?" Hector said. "They were all in the cult and any damn one of them would have sacrificed his own mother to Cthulhu and bathed in her blood. What the hell difference does it make how loud a noise I make putting down those animals?"

"The difference is," Kane said, shoving his stubbled face an inch from Hector's handlebar mustache, "that if you'd done the job right we'd have this Levi character—and the fucking idol. It doesn't matter how many cults you destroy if you don't find and break the idol: that's Venator 101. The damn thing will just call some poor slob of an artist or other sensitive type to wherever it's buried or hidden and he'll think he's the luckiest duck on the pond—until the cult finds him and the ugly-ass idol watches as they roast the sensitive young lad over an open fire."

"Not my first time, Kane," Hector said. "You seem to forget I was stalking crazies when you were still pretending to be a mild-mannered family man."

"Twenty years, Hector," Kane said.

"That's right!" Hector shouted.

"Twenty years and you haven't learned a damn thing," Kane said wearily. "Least of all to keep your eye on the ball, to never forget the mission."

As they glared at one another, Hector felt the heat seep away from his heart, growing cold as the shock from his wound made itself known. Getting angry had kept him on his feet and he half thought that *that* had been Kane's only purpose in balling him out. Then he heard the sirens in the distance.

"That'll be fire and police coming down from Davenport," Kane said, looking out the front window. "Which means we're going to have a hell of a time searching the burned-out remains of the church."

"What about the last guy in here?" Hector said, hastily putting his pistol in his belt before he dropped it. His left hand was going numb.

"Dead," Kane said. "Looks like you caught him in the lung. He ran but he was already done. On the kitchen floor. Shotgun didn't have the idol on or near him and there's no place to hide anything quickly. Did you ever see Levi? Actually *see* him?"

"I'm not sure," Hector said.

"What about this church?" Kane asked. "Did they have a ceremony under way?"

"Yeah, screaming girl all trussed up for The Great Old Ones, dagger to her throat," Hector said. "She didn't make it."

"Really?" Kane all but shouted.

"Was before I torched the place," Hector said, unable to shovel heat into his voice anymore. "Fuck you, Kane, I tried to get in there. Fifty to one and you're going to ride me for it?"

"Could you see the altar?" Kane asked, ignoring him.

"No idol," Hector said.

"I don't like that," Kane said. "If a cult like this—unfavored, near a river and not the sea, no idol of their own—if they had a chance to sacrifice to an idol they wouldn't let a Shoggoth stop them—they would have slit their own throats rather than miss the opportunity. Maybe the idol never made it this far. Maybe Levi dropped it off along the way."

"Oh, man, don't say that," Hector said and then sat down on the floor.

Kane came over and hauled him back to his feet. "No you don't," he said. "You're bad enough as it is. What's hurt? Beside that well-done flipper?"

"Shot through the bicep," Hector said. "Not bad. Fire sealed it. Fuck, man, I think I'm going to puke," he said as if admitting he had forgotten his dry-cleaning receipt.

"Where's your bike?" Kane asked. "Not that you can drive it."

"In the church," Hector said.

CHAPTER 2

ON THE TRAIL

KANE DROVE THE twisting country road—which couldn't seem to keep parallel to the Skunk River—with an all too familiar exhaustion. It had taken what was left of the night to sneak Hector across the Mississippi and to a pet hospital with a vet who liked the sound of hundred-dollar bills unfolding almost as much as he liked the sound a cork coming out of a bottle of bourbon. Leaving Hector in those shaky if broadly capable hands, Kane took away what little information he had gathered. Oliver Levi, thirty-five, one-time meth maker and dealer turned Cthulhu Cult grand poobah, Sacrificer-in-Chief on the Missouri River, who escaped his cult's destruction when two west coast Venators attacked their special cave. Unfortunately, the west coast Venators had the sort of reputation you hope the other guy has and Levi managed not only to escape but to take his cult's small idol of Cthulhu with him. The west coast Venators were able to learn Levi's name and pass it on to Helen; with it, she was able to hack into his credit card's online tracker and guide Hector onto Levi's trail.

The card had been used to buy gas at a station on Rt. 34 heading toward Burlington. Hector, on a hunch, questioned the desk clerk at a hotel Levi had used for a few hours and discovered that he'd sold his credit card to a dealer and that he'd asked about the best road north. The rest was bloody history. The last place Levi had stopped before Muskaloosa was a small, one-road town south of Big Hollow Creek Recreation Area called New Masyaf.

Kane was shaken out of his fugue state by the Cutlass's palpitating engine. "Come on, girl," he said, alternately revving and idling the engine until it ran something closer to normal. *Ever since Louisiana you haven't run right*, he thought. *Bog water clogging things up.* "Too bad I can't feed you some of their gumbo," he mumbled: "that'd clear you out."

New Masyaf didn't give itself away in the distance, like most towns did in Iowa. Not out in prairie country, the rolling hills of south-east Iowa gently pealed to either side of the road after it left the Skunk River behind and there, nestled amidst some of the densest trees in the state, was the lightly populated mile-and-a-half called New Maysaf. The town's attitude to strangers could be interpreted by the first thing to greet a newcomer—the gas station—and the last thing you'd see in the rearview mirror—the one-cop police station: "keep moving, or else."

For all its small-town insularity, New Maysaf did cater to a particular group of outsiders. The town's livelihood depended upon hog farmers, with their small but very efficient operations up in the hills. The pork buyers and restaurant-chain representatives of the country would frequently come out to inspect this or that farm, do a little taste testing. When they did, they stayed at the local *Doze Inn* hotel. A couple bars, a repair shop, sporting goods store, and supermarket serviced the needs of the farmers.

Kane pulled into the gas station and under the V-shaped pavilion covering the pumps. He wondered how the outside edges sloping up higher than the center helped: was it because of tornadoes, to deliberately let rain soak customers, or simply left over from the '50s? Then he looked at the pumps and realized it was option three—they looked like sad little space men with arm akimbo. He unfolded himself from the Cutlass, decided he was a damn fool for riding with the top down as soon as he felt his burned neck touch the collar of his wrinkled suit, and walked around to gas up the car. He put forty bucks of regular in the tank and remembered when gas had been under a dollar-a-gallon. Maybe that's why he was shaking his head; or maybe it was because of the kid gyrating to whatever his earbuds blasted so loud Kane could hear it outside the plywood hutch where he sat.

Kane walked over to the hutch and dropped two twenties on the scarred and doodled counter. He took a closer look at the kid: nineteen or twenty-five or thirty, in a baseball cap angled to two o'clock, wearing an Iowa State basketball jersey and jeans three sizes too big. *He looks like he tried three different lockers after gym class today and never found the right one.* The kid leaned briefly out the front of his hutch to see the meter on the pump and then opened the register and dropped in the money.

"You need a receipt, mister?" he squawked in a voice that jarred Kane with its polite earnestness.

"Yeah," Kane said. He stuffed the noisy printout into a pocket containing similarly unneeded receipts and then fished out another twenty-dollar bill and dropped it on the counter.

The kid looked at it and then, a little guardedly, said, "Sorry, mister, if you want smokes you have to go into the store." He jerked a thumb over his shoulder indicating a side of the garage that looked like a subway restroom through the grimy window.

"I'm not buying cigarettes," Kane said. "I'm buying something far more precious than that: I'm buying time. Your time. There's twenty dollars, just for thinking about it. You ever seen this fellah?"

he asked, raising his smart phone with a photo of Oliver Levi on it that he'd transferred from Hector's phone.

The kid looked down at the twenty, licked his lips, and then up at Kane. "I don't know that I'm supposed to talk about the customers, mister," he said.

Kane smiled, thinking the kid looked like someone who could be talked out of anything he was supposed to do or not. "This fellah here isn't going to have time to make a complaint," Kane said. "Either I find him or the cops do. I know he passed through this town because of his credit card. Take another look at him."

The kid glanced all of a half-second and then licked his lips again and took a couple steps in place, not sure if he wanted to sit on his stool or stand. He pulled his earbuds out and turned off his MP3 player. "Cops, huh?" he asked. "Why not just let them get him and then ask *them*?"

Cagey little rooster, ain't you? "Because if I get to him first, I get paid," Kane lied. "This customer has something that doesn't belong to him," *or to any human being*, "and I aim to get it back."

"Oh, I get it," the kid said, nodding and smiling now. "Bounty hunter, eh?"

"Nope, much worse than that," Kane said. "Insurance."

The kid laughed and said, "That explains the money. No bounty hunter would ever drop cash like that. I'll tell you what, twenty dollars buys a lot in this town—but thirty would buy you more."

He looked down at the twenty and then grinned up at Kane.

"Thirty more?" Kane asked. The kid nodded. Kane dropped two twenties on the counter. "I've only got twenties so there's forty more. Spill."

"Sure, I remember him," the kid said, scooping up the money and jamming it into his pockets, almost debagging himself. "Twitchy cuss with a worse Yankee accent than yours. Shouted at me to fill the tank for him."

"What was he driving?" Kane asked, already knowing what the west coast Venators and Hector had said.

"A BMW M6 convertible, midnight blue," the kid said without missing a beat. "Beautiful, mister, just beautiful. I hated to see an ugly little creep like him in it; like seeing a nice girl on the arm of some greasy geezer with money."

Kane laughed and then said, "Gear head, huh?"

The kid shrugged. "Ain't much else to do around here but read the car magazines," he said. "Car like that'd be noticed anyway: mostly pickups come through town."

"When was this?" Kane asked, knowing what the answer should be.

"Yesterday," the kid said. "Wait, no, the day before, just before my shift ends at four. He went down to the *Doze Inn*. Didn't have much choice if he wanted to sleep around here: it's the only hotel there is, unless you go back down to Burlington."

"Thanks, kid," Kane said. He climbed back under the wheel of the Cutlass.

"Hey, you never told me your name," the kid yelled over the angry sound of the Cutlass starting.

"Philo Vance," Kane shouted back.

"Philo?" the kid asked incredulously.

"I had cruel parents," Kane said.

"Sounds like it," the kid said. "Almost as bad as that rattling throttle body. I'm Greg and I hope you get that little cuss."

"Thanks, Greg," Kane said as he pulled away. "Me, too."

CHAPTER 3

BRAZEN TALK

THE *DOZE INN* looked like every other *Doze Inn* in the world constructed after 1995, only greyer in color and the attached restaurant was subcontracted to the diner that had been demolished to make way for the hotel. The parking lot was mostly empty with the only vehicle not a pickup or SUV being a patched and badly painted—but obviously well-loved—'98 Firebird. It's one eye peered around the back corner, looking surprised to see another old-timer wheezing into a front-of-the building parking space, as Kane's Cutlass rolled in.

What I should do is take four or five hours and sleep, Kane told himself as he fetched his caved-in suitcase from the trunk. *I ought to eat a good meal, have a drink, call one of the numbers in the want ads,* he thought as he pushed through the revolving door into the lobby, *rent an apartment, meet a nice—*

"Hello, welcome to *Doze Inn*," the chipper round face behind the reception desk said. "May I help you?"

"I sure hope so," Kane said, dropping his suitcase, which

promptly fell over. He dug his fake ID out of his trousers' back pocket, the one with the button down flap that he never used, and held it where the receptionist could see.

She wrinkled the flesh between her plucked-clean eyebrows and said, *"Alliance Insurance, Inc.?* Are you the HPD man? I thought we were with *Wakefield and Knob?"*

HPD stood for Hotel Protective Department, the arm of a security or insurance company that looked after hotels. Everything from counterfeiters and thieves to suppliers who skimmed to pimps setting up shop, if it was a problem, HPD handled it.

"No, ma'am," Kane said. "Not my division. I need a room for the night and for you to take a look at this photo." He held up his phone and the picture of Oliver Levi.

The receptionist, Betty by her name tag, peered at the phone as her hands moved automatically over her keyboard, pre-registering her new guest. "Oh, I know him," she said, glancing at her computer screen for a moment. "He's the one with the car, right?"

"That's him," Kane said. "Oliver Levi."

"Sure, that's the name," she said. "Can I see your ID again? And a credit card? He only stayed with us over night. Seemed the business-trip type. Funny that he stayed here, though, huh? Is he trying to make an insurance claim or something? Wish my company was as responsive as yours, mister, uh, Mr. Vance."

Kane gave up trying to answer any of her questions when she hit three and simply waited for her to wind down. It came sooner than he thought when a door with a frosted glass window banged open despite the pneumatic closer and a tall man with more than his share of belly stamped his way across the lobby and down a corridor with a sign that said "pool" on it. Betty dipped her head and her flow of speech shut off as if from a tap. She finished with her entering Kane's forged information and held a receipt for him to sign.

Kane nodded at the corridor and whispered, "Boss?" Betty nodded, keeping one eye peeled for him. "I'd like to ask you a few things about Mr. Levi's stay here, if I could."

"I'm sorry," Betty whispered. "Mr. Norton is very strict. He'd yell if he thought I was chatting while on duty."

"Well, I won't ask when your shift ends," he said kindly and not too flirtatiously; Betty worked up a blush and breathed a little giggle that most hotel receptionists lose after the first week of passes. "Think it'd be safe if I called down from my room? You could say you had a bear of a guest."

"Honestly, I don't know how much I could tell you," she said. "But I'll call your room just as soon as I'm off the desk, if you like."

"I would," Kane said.

He took his electronic key, had to bend all the way over to get a hold of his squashed suitcase, and gave Betty only a small, pleasant smile before walking to the elevator. Once inside his room, he threw his suitcase on the bed—to keep from falling onto it himself—threw back the lid, and pulled out six loaded magazines for his M1911A1. He took the gun from the middle of his back and then turned to look for the TV, his usual hiding place.

"A goddamn flat screen?" Kane said to the wall-mounted television. "You got to be kidding me."

Without the option of opening the TV's shell and stashing his weaponry inside, Kane spun in a slow circle trying to think of a new hiding spot. Under the bed, in the medicine cabinet (there wasn't one, just a mirror), in the toilet tank, taped to the bottom of the toilet tank, in the air conditioning vent: every place he could think of had been in at least a dozen movies and even more books. He stuffed the extra magazines back in his suitcase and left it where it was.

Jamming the pistol back into his belt, he mumbled to himself, "I hope the one cop in this town doesn't decide to pat down the new guy. You know, you could shave your face; might make you look less like a meth dealer."

He looked longingly into the bathroom at the clean and inviting shower and then left the room and went down to the restaurant.

Somehow I don't think Betty is the type of girl to have learned all that much about Mr. Oliver Levi, Kane thought to himself as he took a seat at the bar. It was that quiet hour in most bars and restaurants between the lunch crowd and the early bird specials, even in a town as small as New Masyaf. The sun still glowed on the curving glass of the enclosed patio seating, lined with fake plants to conceal the heaters they'd need on full blast come winter. The place tried for the wood-paneling class and rich red-leather ambiance of an eastern-establishment hotel but the materials were all strictly off-the-shelf. The bottles behind the bar were the real thing though, and Kane eyed each one fondly as his mind worked the problems of the stalk.

So Levi moves through town, only stays one night, but why even stay that long? He could have pushed through to Muskaloosa. Particularly with a couple of Venators on his ass. Why stop here? The simple answer is he'd been running for two days, part of that on foot, and was too tired to run anymore. Simple is usually correct but something feels wrong about this town. Towns like this shouldn't exist; small to the point where you can't go near the place without all five-hundred inhabitants knowing who you are; small enough that if you sneeze at one end of town, the guy at the other end calls you up to say bless you. You're on the run, you're part of a murderous cult, which was just wiped off the face of the earth after years of killing people in a cave by the river; Venators, angry people who just want you dead, and cops, in all likelihood, are after you: why in the hell would you go to a place so small and rural that your flashy car would make you remembered for years to come?

"Because someone *is* following you," he said aloud and then took a deep breath. "Someone not a Venator. Someone you *want* to follow you but you don't dare contact. You leave signs like bread-crumbs for him to follow so when you ditch the idol, he knows where to pick it up. Smart."

"What's that you said, mister?" the waitress said, appearing from the kitchen all at once. A tall, underfed woman with four kids and a fussy husband using the skin under her eyes as hammocks. Her costume—tight black jeans and a skin-hugging black t-shirt with the word "Brazen" emblazoned on it as if the hotel's restaurant was world famous—fit the ambiance they were trying to create but it didn't fit her. She looked like she'd worn a collared dress and an apron until the diner had been bought out, and missed them both.

"Just thinking something through," Kane said.

"You should have thought of putting up the top on that car of yours," she said, cracking a very small smile made out of rawhide, nodding at his forehead.

"Oh, am I tanned and gorgeous now?" Kane said, raising his face for inspection.

"I'll give you the tanned part," she said. He laughed in just the right way to let her know he was teasing, not flirting, and so she helped him laugh about it for a second before asking, "Get you anything?"

"Rye neat, please," he said. "And a question."

"Is it my turn now?" she said, taking the bottle of *Old Overholt* from in front of the mirror without looking at it, fetching a glass from below the bar the same way. "Don't know how much help I can be to an insurance man."

"The grapevine they got around here puts the internet to shame," Kane said. "This is an easy one, though. When's the night shift come on?"

She shot up straight and if she ever had lips it was impossible to tell at that moment. She carefully set the glass down in front of Kane and gave him her answer with two cold eyes.

He held up his hands, shaking his head, and said, "I read my bible every night."

She laughed in spite of herself and said, "No, you *don't.*"

"No, I don't," Kane agreed, slowly dropping his hands, feigning a worry that she might hit him. "I'm from a wicked eastern city and I've been around long enough to know that there are b-girls in every hotel from the cheapest seaside motel or slum SRO on up to the most expensive five-star resorts, from fifty-dollars and a line of coke up to fifty-grand an hour. Not what I'm looking for. You know the man I'm trying to page?"

"Not personally," she said, crossing her arms but looking less hostile.

"I figure maybe he came down for a drink the night before last," Kane said. "Maybe he got to talking with the bartender—as I hear people sometimes do—and maybe he let something slip that would put me wise. Or maybe he left with someone? This isn't a nice or righteous fellah we're talking about, you know?"

"I *don't* know," she said. "And I'm going to keep it that way. I'm the night shift, mister. And he didn't come in for a drink. No, don't reach for your roll: I'm sure you have plenty to spend but he didn't come in. From what I heard tell, he could barely drag himself up to his room."

"Thanks," Kane said and tasted his drink.

A moment passed with her staring at him and Kane, staring back, peeled away the years and saw the feisty woman waking up in the back of her eyes, who had probably always wanted to leave town. She finally laughed silently to herself and said, "You know all that about whores, do you?"

Kane simply smiled mischievously and drained his drink.

She laughed again and said, "I don't believe for a minute you know anything about no fifty-grand an hour escort."

"Hell, I can't think of anything between the sheets worth fifty-grand," he said and they laughed together.

"You look like you've seen a lot of miles, mister," she said, letting her eyes travel across his face, his shoulders and down his arms. "But you still have a good build on you. I don't think you'd have trouble finding company tonight if you had a mind—down at one of the local bars, you understand."

He winked his understanding. "Local bar, huh?" he said, feeling the stubble on his chin with the palm of his hand. "Could my man have gone down there?"

"How would I know?" she said. "He doesn't even need to pass the front desk to get out. Closest bar is only a five minute walk, over on Waters Street. If you do go down there and find some trouble, do yourself a favor and bring her in through the pool door."

"Yeah, I heard Mr. Norton is a bit of a prude, putting it low," he said.

She looked at the ceiling a moment and shrugged in such a way that left no doubt in Kane's mind about how much she knew of Mr. Norton, prude or otherwise.

"He wasn't always," she said. "His daughter, you see. Had a couple years of business schooling at the community college, came back and works for the one ad agency we have in town, *Sutters and Kyle*, and went a bit wild," she said, ending in a whisper. "Lives on her own; goes up to the farm, they say. I'm all for having fun, and I'm a sinner like every woman since the first, but there's a limit."

"The farm?" Kane said. He must have pointed at the word like a dog on a hunt; the waitress stepped back a step, suddenly feeling the conversation had turned serious.

"That's just what they call it," she said.

"Call what?" Kane pressed, hearing the edge in his voice but unable to suppress it.

"Well, it's not a real farm," she said. "Or, at least, I don't suppose it is. One of those hippie communes they had back in the '60s, is my guess. There are other ideas about it. People live up there. Not sure what they do but there are some crazy stories. Townies don't visit but they say some of the younger men from the farms roundabout will go by when they feel the need for a spree. There are nastier stories about the girls that go visiting."

"Anyone ever disappear out there?" Kane said.

"Some," she said quietly, sparing a glance at the empty restaurant. Her crossed arms were tighter around her thin chest and she was tapping her foot.

"Any of them ever turn up?" Kane asked.

"Some come back," she said. "Not in good shape. Usually don't stay. I only know of one that went to a hospital."

"Any of them turn up dead?" Kane said as if she hadn't spoken.

"Dead? Heaven's no!" she said. "Why would you ask something like that? They come back in bad shape, like I said, but no one's died. At least, I haven't heard of anything like that and I've lived her for thirty-eight years."

"But some have disappeared and never turned up?" Kane said.

"Well, they've just never come back, that's all," she said. "They'll come back. Norton's daughter, Barbra, comes and goes as she pleases. Everybody knows. It's why he's so cross all the time."

"Sounds like just the place to go if you don't want to be bothered with a lot of questions," Kane said and then thought: *or want to drop something off that no one will find.*

CHAPTER 4

STORIES FROM THE FARM

KANE ORDERED ANOTHER drink and pork chops with peas and baked potato and nearly forgot he was a Venator. The pork was so fresh, it could have been munching acorns that morning. Nothing from the supermarket would make the grade ever again, he knew. With his tank topped off and enough of a glow on that he couldn't feel his sunburn, sleep didn't seem as pressing as it had when he'd rolled in an hour earlier. He looked at himself in the mirror behind the bar and thought he ought to invest in one clean and pressed suit for times like these but knew it was too late and he wouldn't. He smoothed his hair, caught the bartender laughing at him in an admiring sort of way, and returned to the lobby.

He asked Betty if Norton was in with a pointing finger and significant look. She nodded as if he were asking about flamethrowers. Kane rapped on the manager's frosted glass window and was a nanosecond away from opening the door when a voice called gruffly to come in.

180

The office didn't have the airy luxuriance of an executive's court but rather the cramped appearance of a den outgrown by its resident animal. The animal in this case was a Norton: over six feet, hard in the shoulders and arms but soft around the middle, hair missing in a wide streak over his head like dust wiped off a bowling ball, chewing his teeth until something strayed close enough to bite.

"Yes, can I help you?" Norton said, daring whoever opened the door. "Oh, it's you. The *insurance* man."

"Yes, Mr. Norton, I'm Mr. Vance," Kane said, holding out his hand.

Norton took it but only because it gave him a chance to squeeze something. He motioned to the chair across from his desk. Kane took it and surreptitiously wiped his hand on his knee.

"I was wondering if you'd take the time to ask *me* what you've been asking every other member of my staff," Norton said.

"Only two, so far," Kane said. "The desk girl just to make sure I had the right place—I confirmed he stayed here before I arrived—and the bar tender, just to pass the time. I'm sorry if that upset you, Mr. Norton." Norton snorted, as if no mistake could be made if he were ever upset by something. "But I've been up for two days and change, and thought I should get a good meal in me before I got down to business."

"And what business is that?" Norton asked.

"Tracking a fellah named Levi," Kane said and held up his phone.

"Yeah, a smart mouth Yankee with a flash car," Norton said. "He was here; he left. What's your connection?"

Kane let a moment interrupt them, silence slipping in like a secretary with a file. "The man's a thief, Mr. Norton, and he has something I'd like to recover. He may have taken it with him when he left or he may have stashed it, passed it off to some other party. No, I'm not saying it's here in your hotel, take it easy. But there is a connection to you and it might not be easy to hear."

Norton took his elbows off his desk and did a fair job keeping his scowl in place. Kane had swept an eye over the walls and desk as he'd come in, and seen a picture on the wall of Norton as a young man with his wife and their little daughter; on the opposite wall, another photograph of the child looking older and mischievous; again, on his desk, the daughter appearing there as a teenager, but the mother was missing. The last picture of Norton's daughter was of a coolly leering woman in her early twenties, with far too much experience—or what she thought looked like experience—sharpening treacherous eyes.

"Well, let me hear it then," Norton said thickly.

"My man was on his way to Burlington," Kane said. "Then he swerves off the trail and heads up into pork country, up to your little town. Why? Going up to Davenport? Probably, but why the back roads? Why, if he didn't want to be recognized or remembered, go through a small town where—after an hour and a half—I'm known to everybody?

"We know rather a lot about Levi, including his known associates."

Norton made the motion of a man cursing and dropped his head to one side, looking into the wastepaper basket, but didn't make a sound.

"I guess it's not a surprise to you that your daughter's name came up," Kane said.

"No, Mr. Vance, I'm not surprised," Norton said quietly. He shot a wary look at Kane and a weary one at his desk drawer. The bottle won, as it usually does, and he opened the drawer and took out most of a fifth of scotch and two glasses. He poured a stiff drink into each of them and put the bottle away. He held his glass under his nose as if talking to the scotch. "My daughter went a bit wild, in high school, and after her mother died—when poor Barbra was only eighteen—she, I don't know, she took the brakes off. I'm no saint, and her mother wasn't either and we got up to plenty at that age, too, but Jesus. I didn't expect her to be a nun. We call her Barbie," he said and smiled. "She was always beautiful. See her there? She grew up beautiful, too, as not every beautiful child does. And so, yeah, the boys couldn't get enough of her and sure she liked the attention. But it was normal. After her mother passed, though, she seemed to throw herself into it, into that attention. As if, maybe, it was easier than thinking about what she'd lost. I don't know. Half the time I think I'm just making excuses for her. She went away to school for a couple years, and there were stories. She came back and went to work at the ad agency but didn't settle down. She goes up to the farm now."

"That's the second time I've heard about this farm," Kane said. "Where is it?"

"I couldn't tell you, mister," Norton said. "Back a bit. I've never been there and if half the stories are true I'd be sick to my stomach if I ever did."

"What's wrong with the place?" Kane asked.

"Wrong?" Norton said incredulously. "The people up there, that's what's wrong. Hell, we don't even know who they are. The hills up there are honeycombed with trails. Back in prohibition days, they'd bring corn up there, for the distillers; there are cabins and camps all over. Most are falling down or already collapsed, but a few remain. And some of them are sprawling affairs; they should be condemned. Trouble is, it's all private property. Can't just go snooping, or I can't. And Constable Morris, our town constable, won't go up there. Not by himself."

"What are they doing up there?" Kane asked.

"Sodom and Gomorrah," Norton said and took his bottle back out and refilled his glass. "We had a local girl go up there, about two three years ago. No one sees her for, I don't know, six months or so and then she comes walking into town one day late, barefoot, barely clothed, and makes her way to her father's store (he runs the sporting goods store). She tells a story about what they all do up there. We're not just talking wild sex parties, either. She tries to tell what happened to her but always breaks down. Sick stuff. They take her off to the hospital up in Davenport. I guess the doctors got it out of her eventually, what was going on up there, but when the State Police go up to ask the owners about it, nothing's going on but a lot of people living like hippies and talking free love. And there's my Barbie front and center, putting rumors to rest.

"At first, I was worried that they were doing stuff to her, too, but she comes and goes as she pleases. Later I found out it was worse. She's the one who brought Mr. Carpenter's daughter up there in the first place. Jesus!" he cried and put back his second drink in a gulp.

"So, no, Mr. Vance," he said tiredly. "I'm not at all surprised a thief on the run from you and the police, who looked like a meth dealer to me in that fancy car, would know my daughter. He seems just the type to take a few restful hours up at that farm of theirs."

"But you don't know where it is?" Kane pressed. Norton shook his head. "Okay. Listen, Mr. Norton, I want to thank you for talking to me. I don't see any reason to involve your daughter in my investigation and her name won't appear."

"Thank you," Norton mumbled.

"But if I could talk to her, I might get a line on Levi," Kane said.

"If you're hoping I can set up a meeting, you're out of luck," Norton said. "I haven't seen her in a week and whenever I do see her all I get is a sneer or maybe some mocking laughter."

"That's alright," Kane said. "Just point me in the right direction. She has an apartment, you said?"

"I ought to have gone to Jim White," Norton said, staring at but not seeing the desk. "Gone to Jim White, our mayor, and have her apartment over the agency's storefront condemned or something. But that wouldn't have done any good: she wouldn't have moved back home. She would have moved out there. Jesus, if I thought she was happy—but, hell, all she looks is mean."

Kane lifted himself slowly out of his chair and walked softly to the door, leaving Norton staring back into memory, trying to remember a sweet little girl. As his hand touched the knob, Norton stood up.

"Oh, Mr. Vance," he said. "Listen, I don't know how she connects to all this, and I hope she doesn't, but maybe you coming around will be a wakeup call for her. She shrugged off those State Police, I know, but maybe now, if you say she's in trouble for harboring a fugitive or something, she'll wake up and see all she has to lose. She's probably down at the agency, now, but if she isn't you can find her tonight at McCain's Truck Repair, it's a shop on Main Street. The place is practically a night club after hours. Gambling. Not that we could afford the scandal of shutting it down: if those prissy pork buyers from back east were to hear of it, they may go somewhere more honest for their heirloom swine. Jesus, how I hate this town sometimes."

CHAPTER 5

TOP

K ANE WENT UP to his room to take a nap but napping never happened. Despite lying on the bed and feeling not only the last fifty or sixty hours sitting on his chest, to say nothing of the good meal mingling chummily with a few drinks in his stomach, his mind wouldn't give unconsciousness its due. *Wild sex parties, out of the way place, State Police handled, girls recruited: a cult. They may not have an idol, though—or didn't before Levi blew through town. Even with an idol to call those susceptible to Cthulhu's dreams, the cult's orgies are always the prime recruiting tool. And you, poor Mr. Norton, have I got bad news for you: if your sweet little Barbie is doing the recruiting and talking the police away, then chances are she's also the one who uses the knife come sacrifice time. Happy Father's Day.*

It was not yet five o'clock, and Barbie was probably still at her office, but Kane chose to wait until night fell before heading out. If the cult was still recruiting, and they were disconnected enough up in the woods that they didn't hear too much about Venators, Kane thought he might just talk an invitation out of Barbie Norton. Or, if they were paranoid because of Hector's massacre in Muskaloosa, the right hint might send her running for the farm to rally the troops. Either way, he'd find the club house.

At nine, he changed into his dark suit and turtleneck. Though he'd washed it three times in Mexico, the month before, it still smelled vaguely of the Louisiana swamp. *Good thing this whole town has a slight odor of pig shit about it; I'll smell like mountain lilac in comparison.* He put a couple extra magazines in various pockets, decided to risk carrying his .45 in a shoulder holster, and headed to McCain's Truck Repair.

New Masyaf had curiously few streetlights on Main Street and none on the half-dozen side streets. It suited Kane perfectly as he kept out of sight. McCain's was on the edge of town and had its own junkyard attached, piled with old pickups and farm equipment that couldn't have been used within fifty miles of New Masyaf (there wasn't an inch of space flat enough for corn farming). Kane stood at the corner of a dark building purporting to be a feed importer and watched the repair shop for a few minutes, listening. The building was in perfect repair, fresh paint, clean for an auto repair joint, and—by the signage—didn't go out of its way to attract new business. It didn't have to. In a town as small as New Masyaf, there was only the one truck repair shop. And no one else would get a permit to open a competitor.

After a few minutes, Kane could hear a thumping noise coming from the back of the building. At first he thought one of the mechanics must still be there, working late on a cranky crankshaft. Then he realized it was music. He sucked his teeth, regretted not having earplugs, and walked down the wide alley between the garage and the next building over, to the repair bay entrance.

The heavy steel door wasn't locked and Kane would have fallen through it in surprise if the blast of music charging from the opening hadn't set him back on his heels. It was nearly as dark inside as out but not as clean. Whatever polish the shop had was kept up front: in back, they did the work. Five stalls with pneumatic lifts lined the right wall, various engines in varying stages of disassembly lay scattered about, the back wall was a series of garage doors, all closed, with the other two walls lined with tool cabinets. Green and red lights on a string circled the ceiling, as if stolen off of last year's Christmas tree. About two-dozen people stood around or danced; one cat with headphones was engrossed with his DJ equipment in a corner, occasionally looking up to see if anyone cared. From a gaggle of greasers throwing dice on a homemade craps table, a thick-necked local tough who looked like an inflated version of Greg the Gasman came sauntering over, holding up a hand.

"This is a private establishment," he said, moving into Kane's line of march.

"You're stretching the word establishment pretty far," Kane said. "There's little enough to do in your one-pig town, they ought to make this place legal, put it out front; maybe people would visit."

"You got it wrong, mister," the tough said. "This ain't a club. It's private in that everyone here knows each other. It's a party. A private party."

"Perfect," Kane said. "I love parties and making new friends. And I can already see the first one I'm going to make."

Across the room, standing with a champagne flute in her hand (the bottle sticking out of an enormous engine's cylinder, surrounded by ice packs), ignoring a young man dressed in a tuxedo (minus the shirt) and short spiked hair, was Barbie Norton. From the neck to her waist she looked like any well-dressed office hotshot—but she would have had to keep her legs under the desk to maintain the illusion. Her skirt looked like a very good French dinner: expensive in price and tiny in portion. She stared back at Kane giving him the look Mr. Norton had described earlier.

"Her?" the tough asked with a snort. "Figures, but nix. Or do I have to call my brothers over here?"

"It's alright," Kane said. "I think I can handle her myself."

His shoulder was heavier than the tough's so he brushed past and walked straight through the few couples bouncing around in the center of the cement floor. The kid in the tuxedo stopped his impassioned appeal to Barbie when Kane came within earshot. He looked Kane up and down as if a Martian had walked in.

"Look, someone new," Barbie said as cute as she could over the barrage of thumping bass. "Did you come to bring your daughter home?" She flashed him a challenging, but not discouraging, smile.

The cults often used kink as a recruiting tool. Anyone who could be dared into going a little bit further, anyone who could be lured with a new excitement, was white meat for a cult. The trick to coming off as a potential joiner, Kane knew, was to seem either malleable to perversion or already psychopathic and in need of release. Either one would suit the cult. And if, when brought to a sacrifice, a potential inductee lost his nerve, he'd become the next sacrifice. All Kane needed to know was what would get him an invitation.

She's young for a cult leader, Kane thought. *A little reverse psychology might work, make her look less "sophisticated" until she gets mad enough to show me just how far she'll go.*

"Daddy issues, huh?" he asked, stepping close enough to her so she had to look up at him.

"Oh, I love optimists," she said and took a sip of champagne.

"That explains him," Kane said, pointing his chin at the tuxedo.

"Who the fuck is this guy?" Tuxedo asked. "Hey, what the fuck are you doing in my garage?"

"Pipe down, Justin Bieber," Kane said calmly, not taking his eyes off Barbie. "The adults are talking."

That one split the uprights, he thought, watching her reaction. *Chachi here must know the score: go right for the confrontation, impress her, and she'll drop that napkin she's using as a skirt. But if you get pushed around by anyone—and that would include talking with any-thing approaching manners—then you're not "man enough," she won't think you have the nerve to take watching a sacrifice. Honey, if you only knew.*

"Barbie, you know this punk?" the tough from the door asked, bringing over two similarly clad gorillas.

She turned bored eyes on the three additions and then returned to Kane. Smiling her one mischievous smile, she said, "Never seen him before in my life—can you think of anything sadder than that?"

"You want to walk outside before we pound you," the tough said, "or do you want to start in here, near all these fun toys?"

One of the tough's gorilla brothers took a five-foot long torque wrench off of an engine block so greasy it looked burnt and tapped it against his hand.

Kane smiled at the gorilla and said nothing until the tough smiled too and glanced over his shoulder at the torque wrench—giving Kane the split second he wanted. He kicked the tough in the stomach, just below where the last ribs meet the sternum, knock-ing the wind out of the tough and bending him double. Using his momentum, Kane followed it up by smashing his other knee into the tough's nose; the tough was out before he slipped to the floor. The gorilla without the huge wrench stepped forward and swung a sweeping right hook. It looked to be a very heavy hand traveling like a freight train, only a little slower: Kane slapped the hand so it missed him and turned the gorilla to face his wrench-wielding brother. Pushing them together, Kane swiped the champagne bottle out of the engine cylinder and when the first gorilla untangled himself and turned around, he got Kane's champagne bottle across the jaw. The one with the wrench looked down at his two broth-ers, wide-eyed, and then up at Kane with hate burning through his alcoholic buzz. He brandished the wrench between them—so

Kane took a quick step forward and slapped the heavy top of the wrench back into the gorilla's face. The gorilla reeled to one side, recovered a second later, and then charged with his head down only to have Kane bash him across the face with the champagne bottle, breaking his nose; his bloody face hit the ground with a soggy smack. Out of nowhere, as Kane looked at the three unconscious brothers, Tuxedo came in with a quick left cross. Kane took the punch and then slowly turned on the boy and shook his head incredulously, saying, "What are you *doing?*" Tuxedo broke for a side door and disappeared.

Kane dropped the champagne bottle near the tough and brushed off his hands. Barbie glowed with excitement. Though she carefully controlled her face to keep up her one mischievous look, her mouth forgot what it was doing every other second and she'd start smiling. She almost got the scowling leer to stick when Kane took a step toward her. Then she pulled a gun out of her purse.

"I think they've had enough," she said breathlessly.

Kane didn't pay attention to the gun—a small, pocket automatic—and stepped closer to her. Barbie reluctantly backed away, her eyes never leaving Kane, until his left hand came up fast and her gun when skittering off under a truck. He acted as if he hadn't notice it or didn't care. The heave of her chest showed how much *she* cared.

Alright sister, he thought, *given the bad luck cults in Iowa have had lately, aren't I just the type to bring into the fold? How about a little fun as a reward—say, up at the farm.*

"A little bird told me this was where the freaks frolicked," Kane said, looking around at astonished faces, speaking only loud enough for Barbie to hear. "Looks like the options must be pretty limited in this one-pig town, if *this* is the best you can do."

All she did was giggle and bite her lip, waiting. *Okay,* Kane thought, *reverse psychology isn't working all that well. A dim-witted cult leader, maybe? That can't be it.*

"I'm not leaving with you," she said, stepping to within an inch of Kane, her skin flushing.

Who is playing whom here? If she wants . . .

"Yes, you are," he said, having to take her by the upper arm to cover the question in his voice. He dragged her out of the garage and it took all the force of opening a package of tissues.

CHAPTER 6

WANTING IT BADLY

I N THE ALLEY, with the door closed, holding the thumping bass in, Barbie slipped from Kane's hand and put her back to the opposite wall, her face glowing with expectation.

"Okay, okay, hold on," she laughed. "I'm not really into men beating the hell out of each other, but you handled them so casually—dripping with scorn—it was awesome. I am *never* letting them live it down. But the thing is, I'm more D/s than S&M, you know? If I take you back to my place, how much are you going to have to hurt me to get off?"

What the fuck kind of question is that? Kane thought. *She can't be the cult leader. God damn it. The cult leaders are all sadists; she'd never let me hurt her in some kinky-sex way, let alone request it. She should be offering me one of her followers, a sacrifice, a chance to do some real damage. But she must be in the cult in some capacity—she talked the law away from the farm that one time a member got loose. She's just the recruiter, maybe? That's it, she's looking for sick fucks, guys who are already into torture and murder, so the transition to cultist is smoother, more likely to succeed. That means if you don't pass her little test, she won't bring you up to the farm. Wonderful.*

All the while, as Kane thought through this newest wrinkle in the business of cult slaying, Barbie squirmed provocatively against the wall, as if being made to wait for an answer was a huge turn on.

"You'll find out," Kane said and reached for her arm again.

Barbie held up her hands, though, becoming more serious. "Whoa, hold on," she said. "Look, you are very hot—and I admit you're tapping my kink just right—but we need to, you know, get a few things straight? I have a professional job so no bruises on my face, or arms below the elbow, or legs below the knee. Though, if you know how to slap me right," she said with an affected sigh, "you'll own me. Oh, and no scat or water sports: yuck, not my thing. Cool?"

Jesus, I wish Hector was here, Kane thought. *I thought she was talking about sex at first but now it sounds like kickboxing, or surfing. Water sports? I don't even . . .*

"I don't respond well to orders, Barbie," he said, flashing a grin that usually worked with normal women.

Her eyes rolled as if she'd just tasted something delicious and she moaned. Stepping closer to Kane and looking up at him like a naughty child, she said, "Please? I'll follow your every command. Oh! I almost forgot: my safe word is sushi."

Commands, Kane thought. *Commands? Oh, it's one of those domination things. That must be what the "D" in D/s means. So, I don't have to beat the crap out of her, just boss her around? How the hell does anyone get off from being talked down to?*

Barbie was getting a little bored with the long silences. She came up on her toes, trying to kiss Kane's frowning lips.

"Don't put that filthy mouth of yours on me," he said, tugging her head back by her hair in a flash of inspiration. *She liked that? So calling names is a compliment; a shove is a caress. Easy. It'll be easy. Fuck, I don't think I can do this.*

"What do you want me to do with it?" she asked, pressing against Kane so her throat was constricted by having her head pulled backwards.

"Use it to tell me if you live around here," Kane said, "or up on one of those revolting pig farms."

She laughed, a calculated breathless laugh, and said, "I live down the street."

"Show me," he said.

He pushed her toward the sidewalk, keeping his hand on the small of her back. Though Kane shoved her forward whenever she slowed, he felt like he was speeding out of control to her apartment. To get to the cult—and the idol—he had to get past the recruiter. To get past the Barbie, though, would take something Kane had never before done on a stalk. Or off a stalk, for that matter. *Well, Sol, how bad do you want it? How bad do you want to stop them? You made a promise and the next victim of the cult won't give a damn about your morals or your squeamishness. Because she'll be dead. Like . . .*

"The strong silent type, huh?" Barbie said under her breath. "Going to tell me your name?"

"It's sir, to you," Kane said absently.

"Of course; yes, sir," Barbie said, slowing against Kane's hand as they drew abreast of the ad agency, below her apartment, *Sutters and Kyle* in bold font on the plate-glass window. "This is it, but I'm not sure I should let you in. You started playing back at the club, before we'd even had a chance to talk. I should walk away; you might be too rough with me. I'm sorry, am I spoiling the mood?" Her provoking leer had returned, giving the lie to most of what she'd said.

How bad do you want it?

Kane took her by the hair and spun her to face the plate-glass window. He pushed her against it and set his elbow against her spine, as a fulcrum, and pulled downward. Barbie's head went back and she came up on her toes, pinned between the cold glass and the strong arm. Kane slid his other hand between her thighs and into her skirt, finding a place for his forefinger and another for his thumb. Barbie swatted the air beside her as if trying to keep her balance, her breath quivering along her lip.

"I'll take care of the mood," Kane whispered into her ear. "You just shut up and do what you're told."

Her apartment was small and modern and didn't look like it fit rural Iowa. It had a bed, though—and a kitchen counter and a bathtub and a front window overlooking the street and a floor—and that's all it needed. The sex Barbie wanted wasn't tough to understand, it was a kind of game. She wanted to be ordered around, resist a little, be induced to please, disparaged verbally all the while but praised in the diminutive from time to time, particularly when she was out of breath. The slaps and the choking, the spanking and throwing her around was done playfully, at first. As the night progressed, though, Kane could see that she wanted more vigor, actual pain, no matter what she'd said on the street. It inflicted its own special kind of exhaustion on him, the effort to suppress how he thought a man should behave, to suppress how he wanted to touch a woman. And every time he felt a sting on his palm or touched the back of her throat or heard actual distress in her voice, the deep place where he packed in his shame burst anew and welled into his eyes. But he had to play the game, he told himself, he had to push her face into the sheets or the floor, cover her eyes with his foot, until he could wipe the tears out of his own. He couldn't fathom how he maintained an erection through the ordeal; only his decade-long abstinence and pent up animal response could explain how he remained capably aloft despite the loathing he felt. Ten years since the last time. Ten years since his wife was murdered at the foot of a twisted and grotesque statuette of Cthulhu.

"Where the hell do you think you're going?" he said the next morning as Barbie untangled herself from the sheets and stumbled sleepily off to the bathroom. His voice didn't sound very convincing to him.

She rolled bleary but pleased eyes at him before disappearing into the bathroom. She didn't shut the door and he could hear her peeing. "Is that your way of saying you want a morning fuck?" she called through the open door.

Looking at the apartment with the early sun coming through the front windows in dusty columns, Kane could see just how young the place looked. A few posters of heartthrobs wouldn't have been out of place. It was trying to be grown up with the aping quality of a clip-on tie.

"Not if you're going to talk like a whore," he said.

"Ha, you love it," she said. The toilet flushed and in a second she was in the doorway, arms akimbo. She looked over her naked body appraisingly. Holding up an arm, she discovered three deep bruises in the shapes of fingers. "Oh, that's a good one! I guess I'm not going sleeveless today."

She skipped to the bed and jumped in, leaning over to kiss him. He pushed her into the pillows and she clicked her tongue. "All business with you, Solomon Kane," she said dropping her voice on his name. He had waited until she was about to orgasm before telling it to her, thinking that if she recognized the infamous name it would shock her out of the moment. All she did was scream it as she came. "Solomon, ha! Who named you that?"

"The dog catcher," Kane said. "Who do you think?"

"I really enjoyed last night," she said, shaking her head and looking out the window. "You really know how to play. Do you ever stop, though? It's nice to talk like normal people afterwards. *And* you didn't want to cuddle at all last night. I like a good cuddle after a man beats my ass raw."

"Maybe I don't want it to end," he said, thinking: *for crying out loud, don't talk her into another round, I can't take it.*

"Aww, that's kind of sweet," she said. "I have to go to work, though."

"Screw that, take the day off," he said, grabbing her arm as she slid out of bed.

She tried to pry off his fingers, saying, "Easy, easy, no bruises down there. I have to go to work, I need the money." She broke free and scampered to the bathroom door again. "Want to join me in the shower? Maybe I can relieve a bit of your tension."

"Go," he said and leaned back and closed his eyes. She shrugged and closed the door.

After waiting until the water was running and he could hear her feet squeaking on the tub floor, Kane rose and went to her desk. None of the drawers were locked but there was nothing of any interest: a little paper and most of it nonsense, jewelry, some old photos, one drawer full of bank statements, another full of student loan receipts. He rummaged through the heaps of clothes on the floor until he found her phone: it was locked. He looked under the bed and in the closets before he heard the shower turn off. Slowly and silently, he got back into bed. He looked as if he hadn't moved by the time she came out.

He watched her get dressed and she seemed to like that. She asked him to choose between this and that, to instruct her; he played his part and she liked that, too. Once clothed and ready to go, she looked at him still naked as a Jaybird, sprawled across her double bed, feet hanging over the edge as always.

"Are you going to stay here?" she said. "Look through my things?"

The idea seemed to please her but Kane couldn't be sure. "When will you be done with work?" he asked.

"By five," she said.

"I'll probably go back to the hotel," he said.

"Should I call you when I'm done?" she asked.

"No," he said flatly.

She turned on her pleading eyes and pouted, saying, "Will you come by for me after five?"

"Maybe," he said. "Got any friends?"

She laughed. "Oh, I see," she said. "Maybe. Who says I'm willing to share?"

"Your willingness isn't really at issue, is it?" he said, grinning cruelly.

Her breathing quickened and her eyes lidded; then she shook her head to clear it and said, "We'll see, we'll see: stop turning me on, I have to go to work. I hope I see you later. Bye."

She left and Kane waited a few minutes to be sure she hadn't forgotten anything and had to come back, and then he rifled her things again. Her office was only downstairs but she had all but consented to him searching so he made it as thorough a search as possible. Nothing. He found a small bag of pot in the back of a cabinet, very poorly hidden amid some ancient and useless spices but nothing of value, nothing that would indicate where the farm was located. And certainly nothing that looked even vaguely related to the cult.

CHAPTER 7

THE USES OF PAIN

KANE CLIMBED INTO his clothes and walked back to the *Doze Inn*. He showered, scrubbing with unusual vigor, and took three times as long brushing his teeth. He looked at himself in the mirror when he began to shave but decided he'd take a bad shave and turned his back. Leaning against the counter, listening to the hot water run in the sink and looking down at the little plastic razor, he forced himself to think through everything he'd done the night before again and again.

So what if you didn't like it, he thought. *You're acting like a fucking kid, here. Put it behind you. This life is about doing whatever it takes to find these bastards and wipe them out. You get on Hector's case whenever you see him but the truth is* he's a Venator. A real Venator: *ruthless, relentless, implacable, un-phased by what must be done. This girl has a free pass to the farm; and if Levi did stash the idol anywhere around here, that's where it'll be. You have to use her to get to the farm. Do it and quit your fucking crying.*

He turned around and finished shaving.

Dressed again in his wrinkled blue suit, again wearing his gun (which Barbie had not seen because he'd held her face down on the floor while hiding it under the mattress last night), Kane took a to-go cup of coffee from the restaurant after eyeing the bottles behind the bar with naked yearning. He walked out to what passed for a garden at the *Doze Inn* and called Helen. It was his habit never to talk on the phone in a hotel room; too many of the rooms were bugged.

He asked her what she knew about New Masyaf, about a place known only as "the farm" that had drawn some State Police attention a few years back. Helen had very little. Iowa was not known as a hotbed of cult activity; the Midwest generally wasn't. She told Kane she'd look up the police incident but not to hold his breath.

"What has you convinced Levi cached the idol in New Masyaf?" she asked in that interrogatory way all professors develop after dealing with lying undergrads for too long.

"I admit it's a hunch but it's a strong one," Kane said. "This town just isn't right. It isn't right that Levi went through here— went out of his way to pass through. He would have been more anonymous on the highway."

"You're imputing a lot of knowledge to him," Helen said. "Not everyone you stalk is a criminal mastermind, Kane. He may have thought getting off the main highway was smart, even if it wasn't. 'Never attribute to malice what can be explained by stupidity,' I believe is the quotation."

"Even without Levi passing through, things are far from normal around here," he said.

"Maybe," she said lightly. "But the statuette is still in the wind. That should be priority one."

"I know you're right," he said. He'd come to a little stone bench and kicked it idly. "I have a bead on the farm, though, so I want to take a run at it. One more day, or night really. The crime scene and arson folks are probably still all over the church Hector burned down. Will you hear if they find anything?"

"Of course," she said. "Something as disturbing as a Cthulhu statuette will be brought to a university. I'll hear; you know that. What's this bead you have?"

"A wild child," he said and then heaved a sigh. "Some young woman who is free to go to and from the farm. She's the one who talked the State Police away that one time. Daughter of the hotel owner."

"You're hoping to follow her up there?" Helen asked. "How do you know when she's next due for a visit?"

"I don't," Kane said. "I tried scaring her into it last night but she didn't recognize my name."

"That was risky," Helen said. "Is she the recruiter?"

"That's what I'm thinking," Kane said.

"Well, I normally wouldn't bring this up to you, but that could be your way in," Helen said. "Get yourself recruited and she'll take you herself. I'm sorry, maybe I shouldn't have said that."

"It's okay," Kane said. He sat down on the bench.

"Sex has always been their main recruiting tool," Helen said brightly as if to usher them out of an uncomfortable topic and onto an academic one. "Even for those cults that do not possess a statuette—or I should say, especially for those cults that don't possess one—sex is their main attraction. First it lures in the reckless and the abused, then it's used in their conditioning. It's horrible the uses something so intimate, so—honestly—pleasurable can be put to. From the Manson Family to child soldiers to most of the world's religions, control of sexual intercourse is the first and most powerful tool. Sleep deprivation and the control and ritualizing of food consumption come next, of course."

"Yeah," Kane said softly.

"Oh my, I'm sorry, Sol," she said. "This can't be an easy subject for you. Not that I don't think it would be healthy for you to try talk about it. A life without intimacy is very difficult to live. Of course, I am sensitive to what the loss of your wife and children must have done to you."

"I know you know," Kane said. "Get back on the horse, is that it?"

She laughed lightly, thankful he didn't hang up in her face. "Well, not a horse, no," she said and they both laughed. "But in that area. I suppose being a Venator and finding a girlfriend are not easily compatible."

"It's going to take you all day to work up to suggesting I shag this girl in order to convince her to take me up to the farm," Kane said.

"I, no, I said it would work, it's true, but, really," she said, oscillating between motives. "I don't suggest it. Perhaps I can find someone nearby who would be better suited. Send him to help out."

"*There's* a phone call every Venator dreams of," Kane said. "But they'd be a day late."

"Oh, would they?" she said. "Well, well, Mr. Kane, you are full of surprises. I didn't think you had it in you, I admit it—I mean, I didn't think you were ready! Oh god, I sounded horrible just then, didn't I?"

"You're fine," he said. "It was what needed to be done. I can't say I enjoyed myself but it was the right call."

"No invite, though?" she asked.

"Not yet," he said. "But I've got another shot at it tonight. We'll see."

"Pace yourself," she said with a chuckle.

"Funny," he said. "Hey, what's a 'D/s' anyway? And how does it differ from BDSM?"

"What!" Helen coughed and Kane could hear coffee spilling on a desk. "What did you—Jesus, Sol, what the hell kind of sex did you have?"

"The kind that makes me want to take myself to the police station," he said. "Or shoot myself."

"Oh, god, I'm sorry," she said. "That's not something to just jump into, after all. And was this, god, was this your first time since—"

She said no more when she could hear Kane try to suck air through clenched teeth. The pavement around the garden dissolved before his eyes and Kane felt he couldn't open his lungs enough to draw a breath.

"Sol? Sol!" Helen called through the phone; he had it pressed to his forehead.

Grunting to get air, he said hoarsely, "Just a second, okay?" He dropped his phone on the stone bench next to him and put his head in his hands. And for the first time in ten years, he wept.

He wept with the image of his wife lying on a muddy patch of ground with her throat cut, skin streaked with blood flickering in the firelight, as vivid in his mind at that moment as it had been when he'd first stumbled into the clearing ten years ago. He saw her roll onto her side in bed, the pale blue sheets they had, in their first house, translucent around her with the moon streaming through the window. He could smell her hair. And he could hear Barbie's throaty grunt as he twisted her harder, plead as he went deeper, beg.

He wanted to thrust away all memory, to blank his mind; he tried to see the flowers of the garden, to feel the hard concrete of the bench; he felt trapped in pain, unable to escape shame. He pawed blindly at the bench next to him and found his phone. Smashing it against his head, he pushed "Helen" through a throat nearly shut.

"Sol!" she said. "Sol, listen to me: I want you to call a cab and go to the airport. There's a small airport about thirty miles away. I'll have a ticket waiting for you. Come back to Arkham."

"No," he hissed and felt the memories slow. "I'm fine."

"Yes, you sound wonderful," she said. "Come back to Arkham,

Sol. We don't need to locate the farm this way, if at all. I'll contact a couple Venators in Wyoming, Rangers; they'll comb the county around there and find anything there is. You need to come home. I mean, here, to Arkham. This isn't good for you."

"I'm fine," he said and his voice was steady. "It's just pain. And I've gone through much worse than this. Every time I smash an idol or wipe out a cult, that night I dream of Meghan. I wake up with her tombstone on my chest and I shake for an hour and it hurts. I think of Becky and Michael all the next day and I have to drive and drive and drive. That's pain.

"I've killed I don't know how many of these cultists, Helen. Plenty of them were women. But even if vengeance is part of why I'm out here, I have never hated any of them as much as I hated that girl last night."

"Sol, it isn't the same thing to her," Helen said. "Whatever you did, it didn't mean to her what it means to you. To her it's a game, it's satisfaction."

"I know that," Kane said and coughed. "But if you smack a woman across the face, you still smacked her: doesn't matter who you hit or why, you hit a woman—you did it. Doesn't matter if she saw it as a game, I'm now a man who has raised his hand to a woman. She said I was a great top; I don't feel on top. All I feel is wrong. Every second of that night, all I felt was wrong."

"Sol," she whispered. "Shh, it's okay. Come back, please."

"It's just pain, Helen," he said and heaved a shuddering sigh. He discovered that his coffee had turned cold but drank it off anyway. "And I don't want to have gone through last night—and have to live knowing I did that to a woman, however willing—and have it be for nothing. I hope to hell she's the high priestess of this cult: I'll shoot her through the liver and be able to sleep by tomorrow night."

"Father's Day," Helen said absently. Clearing her throat, she continued, "You're one of the best I've ever worked with, Sol, and I don't want to lose you. Are you sure?"

"Yes," he said and shook his head trying not to see Becky and Michael. "I told her she needs to bring a friend tonight. I'm hoping either she volunteers to take me up to the farm or I can worm its location out of her, make her feel less—I don't know what word they'd use—*whatever* than me and take me up to the farm to prove she's more, whatever that word is."

"Might work," she said. "Sol, I'm just going to say this: I don't think you're dealing with a cult. I think if you do make it up to the farm, you're going to find a meth lab and junkies. I don't think it's worth putting yourself through this another night."

"I'll let you know how it turns out," he said.

"Please do," she said resignedly. "Take care of yourself, Solomon Kane."

"I will," he said. "One of the best? Hmph!"

They shared a laugh and hung up.

CHAPTER 8

CLIMAX
AND CONSEQUENCES

ACROSS THE STREET from *Sutters and Kyle*, Kane watched through the windows as someone in a polo shirt and tight chinos gave Barbie a chuck on the chin before walking out to his Escalade. She rolled her eyes and then sat staring at her phone. Kane walked across the street and went inside. He played as he thought he should, impatient, demanding, demeaning, eventually making her close the office early and then dragged her up to her apartment.

Inside, much the same game played out as the night before, this time themed around her failing to provide a third partner. She reveled in her disobedience, admitting her fault and promising to suffer whatever punishment he thought fit. Kane suggested she take him to the farm.

Barbie stepped back and looked guardedly into his face. "How do you know about that?" she asked.

He took her cheeks in one squeezing hand and drew her closer. "I told you yesterday, I'm an insurance investigator," he said. "You need to pay attention. I had most of the day to pull information out of the yokels around here. Think it took long to find out about the one interesting place in this shit hole? You should have told me about it."

"They're pretty crazy out there," she said, trying to draw his thumb into her mouth. He pushed her against the wall. "I can't just bring every good lay I find up to the farm."

She wanted a smack, he knew: he raised his hand and then let it fall to a pat on her cheek. *I've got your number now.* "Really?" he said. "You're going to tell me where it is and then take me there so I can enjoy some of its finer delicacies; maybe watch you between another woman's legs."

"That does sound fun," she conceded. "But, no. I'm not going to tell you," she breathed and the defiance was exhilarating but not for itself: she expected to be proven wrong.

"We'll see about that," Kane said.

The night was a grinding ordeal. Unlike the night before, Kane couldn't arouse himself, not even for a second. He had to keep Barbie constantly occupied with one task or another—orders, debasement, manual stimulation—to distract her from his impotence. He used every object in the apartment that would fit inside her as a dildo, at one time or another. Face down on the floor, head pulled back by her hair until her vertebrae popped like cracked knuckles, gasping as his other hand wormed its way between her legs, she began grinding against his hand, on the brink of climax—and he dropped her and stood up. She moaned her disappointment and then tried to finish herself off, pawing for a vibrator in her nightstand: Kane picked her up and pinned her to the bed, face up.

"Tell me," he said quietly.

"No," she said through clenched teeth and he could see how

much she wanted to yield already, that she was spoiling her own good time by not submitting. She tried to grind against him but he kept himself too far above her.

"Then we start again," he said.

And again they started, and again she seemed within seconds of climaxing, and again Kane hauled her to her feet and pinned her arms behind her back, not getting her off or allowing her to finish alone. She wavered between anger and forced meekness and almost screamed that she wouldn't tell him.

And they started again, this time with her vibrator. He had seen her climax many times the night before—too many times to too many things that made him feel sick—so he knew exactly how close she was, no matter how she tried to fool him or rush headlong into it. He threw the toy into a corner and kept her immobile with a common wrestling hold. She squirmed and for the first time he heard her plead for real.

"The farm," he said.

"Please, baby," she said. "I'm not supposed to. Fuck! I'll take you tomorrow, just let me cum."

"Not good enough," he said. "You're a whore. What's your word worth? Where?"

She described the roads and said she'd take him tonight, if only he'd let her climax. He dropped her to the floor and let her crawl after the toy. He put a foot on her head, pinning her down as she finished, and then ordered her to get dressed. He splashed water on his face in the bathroom as she put her clothes back on and gushed praise at him in the voice of a teenager who just received her first car. The best play she'd had in forever.

It was after nine by the time they left and the streets were again in near darkness. They walked the three blocks to the *Doze Inn* and took Kane's Cutlass. She broke out laughing when she saw the car:

"*This* is your convertible? I hope I'm classy enough for it." They got in and started driving.

Even with her description of the roads they had to take, roads that were barely dirt tracks before they reached the halfway mark, Kane would never have found the place without her guiding him. One of the few densely wooded areas in Iowa, the roads were forgotten by time and the shacks and camps that had once housed moonshiners now stared darkly through the moonlit trees, gaping at the rare foolishness of a trespasser.

At a bluff overlooking a shallow gorge, Barbie pointed through the trees; in the distance Kane could see lights. He pulled to the side of the dirt road and took a long, searching look.

"Well?" she said. "You said you wouldn't fuck me because you wanted to save it all up for the fun little things we have up at the farm. So let's go!"

"Haven't you learned yet to keep your mouth shut, yet?" he said. *This is going to feel so good,* he thought. "But now I'm thinking I shouldn't go in too randy. And I'm thinking you're wearing too many clothes. Come back here."

He got out of the car and went around to the trunk.

"You are always so full of surprises," she said as she joined him and looked into the trunk. "Wait, there's nothing in there."

"There is now," he said and tossed her in. He slammed the lid shut and took the keys out of the lock.

Dimly from the back of the car he could hear her shouting, "No, no, I don't like confinement play: let me out! Sushi! Sushi! Sushi, goddamn it!" she repeated, her safe word.

Kane took his pistol from the glove compartment and strapped it on, filling his pockets with the extra magazines. "Two reasons you're locked in the trunk," he told the backseat. "One, in case you were planning on leading me into an ambush up there and, two, on the wildly off chance that Helen is right and all I'll find is a meth lab and a few junkies. There's antifreeze in there if you get thirsty."

He set off cross-country toward the lights of the farm. The trees were thick in spots but with night having fallen heavily about them, the light from the various farm buildings kept Kane from losing his way. Finding the Cutlass on the way back would be a different story. *You've got to live through it for going back to matter: don't get ahead of yourself.*

As he closed in, the buildings became distinct. "Farm" was clearly an honorific; nothing but weeds and trees grew anywhere on the place. There were no power lines; a haggard generator could be heard squealing in a shed. There was a large building with two stories and a sagging roof, with lights on in the first floor, but no observable movement. There was also a long low building like a bunk house on the far side of the clearing, a couple obvious out-houses, and what looked like a barn. The barn put out more light than any of the other buildings. It also put out the droning noise of chanting.

Kane kept low to the grown, using one hand as much as his feet as he moved along, pistol pointed out in front of him, and moved to the main house. Peering around the edge of the windows, he could see inside. Filth pervaded the interior, beyond the casual un-cleanliness of a bachelor; it was as if someone was trying to create a swamp. Finding no one, Kane moved on, down the wall to the corner of the house where he could see the barn. Its two wide front doors had a smaller entrance cut out of it and through this open entrance he could see a setup not unlike a church. He crept closer, staying out of the wedge of light stabbing from the door.

At the side of the cut-out entrance, Kane saw clearly that there were two rows of slapped-together pews, neither varnished nor painted, nor clean. The floor was well-worn, hard-packed dirt. Lights hung from the rafters in no conceivable pattern and shone down on twenty or so long-haired persons of no perceivable hygiene. At the front of the barn was a podium, and at the podium was a thin man of average height with a great red beard sticking out all over and stringy dirty hair. He wore jeans, no shoes, and a kind of vest cut out of an old shirt. He was talking to the others after they stopped their chanting.

"Though you all have now devoted yourselves to Jesus," he said, "and have prayed for his return with many star-ships filled with his sacred virgins, not all of you have truly cast the false beliefs of your former lives into the great black void of hell above. How can you embrace the alien intelligence of Jesus, know the love like a spear of our father's great wrath, unless you vomit your unlovely minds into the stars? Jessica, stand forth."

At this a woman who was probably in her late teens or early twenties but looked on the raw edge of middle age from dissipation, starvation, and uncounted abuse, tried to climb over the pew behind her and run screaming for the door. Strong hands from two overall-ed men plucked her off her feet and carried her crying and pleading to the podium. She huddled on the ground begging to be forgiven.

"But to whom do you pray, Jessica?" the bearded man asked mildly. "Your god? Yahweh? A false idea planted by those who hate alien kind. Buddha? Delusions of grandeur and an excuse to forget the might of Jesus's star-ship armada. No, you must be cleansed. Yes, yes, you must. Emma, remove my trousers. Terrance, you will join me in forcing sin from Jessica's body."

Kane shot the bearded man through the liver. Terrance didn't even get his zipper down before his head exploded in a red mist. Kane stepped into the doorway, the only escape, and chaos filled the room. Every man there rushed him in one mass, raving, savage, sunk below the threshold of humanity by the brutality of their lives; the inflicting of pain had cauterized their perceptions of reality. And they fell like wheat before the scythe. Kane fired his first magazine empty, reloaded, and shot the second one empty. The women huddling between the pews did not cry out after the last shot echoed into the rafters. Chaos, striking down the last inhuman wretch, turned its back upon the scene and stalked into the woods, leaving the dead, the victims, and Kane.

Kane slowly wound his way up the aisle between the pews, watched by the dozen or so women, each a portrait of long suffering and hopelessness, each waiting for whatever was to be done with them. He kept his eyes straight ahead, fastened on the still-living bearded man. Behind the podium, staring as if fascinated by his life dribbling out of his skin, the bearded man waited. He mumbled something about Jesus but Kane hardly heard him.

"You've inflicted terror and pain for what?" Kane asked quietly, incredulously. "All this, for nothing? Because you're insane? A life without knowledge of mercy is not a human life," he said and then shot the bearded man through the head.

He turned and finally forced himself to look at the women. Their tormentors lying broken and motionless around them, they seemed not to comprehend what had happened. A wave of despair crashed over Kane as the enormity of what was necessary to heal them overwhelmed him. He was a slayer, a killer, a hunter, a Venator and knew nothing of healing: not himself for his past and not them for their lives. And the reality of his helplessness struck him as motionless as the dead. He found voice and action only when Barbie stepped into the doorway.

She looked at the dead, lying with the same mad hatred on their faces that last contorted them in life; she saw the near headless bearded man stain the far wall; she saw the huddled mass of women, many of whom she had brought to the farm. She dropped to her knees as all her strength fell into the earth.

"What, what, how did this, what happened?" she screamed, crying on the verge of hysteria.

"What happened?" Kane said, his voice rising to a shout. "What happened! Look around you! What the hell do you think happened to all the women you lured up here? Look at them! What did you think these insane bastards were doing?"

"No, no," she cried. "No, they said they'd moved on. They told me they'd stayed for a while and then moved on. I thought they were high all the time, not, oh my god. I'm sorry, I'm so sorry, I can't believe this, it can't be true."

The utter hysterics she descended into was so wretched that those among the abused that could still shed tears joined her in weeping. Kane looked around and found the woman called Jessica. He helped her to her feet. She looked confused but functional. After a short effort to convince her he wasn't going to kill anyone else, he told her he would send help and that she should try to get the rest of the women into the big house and get some food into them, if she could find anything fit to eat. She seemed to understand and gathered the women together. The older ones seemed tired but willing to do as they were told; the young wouldn't be left alone. Though it made Kane's skin crawl, he lifted Barbie by the shoulders and marched her down the dirt road back to the Cutlass.

They drove a few miles before she stopped crying uncontrollably and then a few more before she could speak.

"It was never like that when I went up there, you have to believe me," she said. Kane watched his headlights as they passed between the two lines of trees, fifty feet ahead of them. "I didn't know, I swear. You know what I'm into, you know it's just play. When I took a friend up to the farm, it was just like that with those guys. Trevor was silly about Jesus being an astronaut or something but he was harmless. I haven't been up there in a while. I guess the meth finally got to them. I read about Waco in school. Please Solomon, I didn't know."

"You didn't know," he said. "You convinced people you called friends that they could find a swell time back up in the woods in a house full of strangers playing a sex game where someone is never in control—and you left them there!" She burst into tears again. "Sure with some punk who feeds pigs for a living and has to put up with his father balling him out every day, a little sex play is just for gags, just a way to put aside your real lives, sure. But *you* know the lingo, *you* know the rules, *you're* willing to say, 'that's too much, this is what I like.' You brought those girls up here without them knowing a damn thing and then left them and never looked back. You don't take a hell of a lot of responsibility for your own actions: who are you to put them in that position and then not take responsibility for it?"

He had to stop himself. She could barely hear him anyway and he knew he was taking out on her the disgust he felt in himself. Intellectually he knew there was nothing inherently wrong with how Barbie wanted to live her life, just as there was nothing wrong with him not wanting to live that way. But pushing himself into a situation that repulsed him had not been kind to an already over-strained mind.

"Fuck all this," he said after a disgusted sigh. "Talking about what you did and didn't do won't help a damn. Shut up and listen," he said firmly but not harshly. After a minute, she quieted. "I'm taking you back to your father. You don't have to like him and you don't have to live with him but he's the only man in town who will believe you without a bunch of questions. He'll be able to pull the locals together and come up here and help those women. *You are going to do that.*" She nodded. "Good. You can run off and do what-ever the hell you want afterwards but for today, you help clean up what you helped create, however unknowingly. Not caring enough to find out is not an excuse."

They drove back to town without another word to each other, though when they hit Main Street, Kane called Helen.

"Yeah, I'm fine," he told the phone. "Turns out you were more right than wrong. There was a cult but not our sort. Some asshole who thought Jesus was an alien, and that gave him the right to set up some kind of Serbian rape camp. Yeah, he's dead, along with his little helpers. I'm headed back to town now to roust the locals, get those women some help. The girl, Barbie, says she didn't know what was going on out there; I guess I believe her. Turns out she's exactly who she said she is. In a funny sort of way, she's the only honest person in this town. I guess I'll drop in on our friend, afterward, see how he's doing. We'll have to wait for the crime scene people to work out who died in that church and around town before we'll know if Levi is among them. I'll call you in a couple days. Me, too. Take care, Helen."

In the parking lot of the *Doze Inn*, Barbie got out of the car and stood looking at Kane but not meeting his eye.

"I'm going to help clean this up," she said. "We'll have a dozen people up there in an hour, I promise. But I need you to believe I didn't know this would happen. What we just saw up there isn't kink, isn't about control or boundaries; there is no submission without consent; without consent there's only crime. I just need you to believe I never meant for anything like this to happen."

"Sure, I believe you," Kane said wearily. "But it was probably only luck that those nutjobs up there didn't keep you on the farm, too. You don't get lucky like that twice in one lifetime. Now get out of here and be quick about getting assistance up to those women. And forget the name of Solomon Kane."

BOOK 4

THE MIGOU OF CALIBOGUE SOUND

CHAPTER 1

TO LIVE AND DIE ON
DUNSANY ISLE

H E SLAMMED AGAINST trees hard enough to knock the wind from his lungs as he barreled through the darkness beneath a shadowed sky. Nothing mattered, not his lungs burning for air that he could not draw, not the impenetrable obscurity around him, nor the blood running from his hair into his mouth, nothing mattered: he drove himself toward the sound of her screams. The trees parted without warning; grass blades swayed in an un-felt current across a tiny glade. He lunged first in one direction and then another, but the sound of her screams echoed between every tree. Rising from the long grass, dark man-shaped shadows swooped in to surround him, laughing or gibbering to themselves. He raised his pistol but the hammer fell on an empty chamber; he took it by the barrel as a club and charged the nearest shadow. He moved through mud, his arm an unbearable weight; his blow against the shadow's skull was no more than a tap. He pushed with everything he had, knowing his energy remained, feeling its potential but unable to bring it to bear. He had to get past them, to reach the screaming, to reach her. The shadow took the gun away from him, and then took the arm. He staggered to one side, warmth gushing unseen down his right side. Throwing himself between shadows, he ran for the tree line. The shadows followed. He opened his mouth to cry out but he could only cough; could only hear her; could only feel the shadows stripping his flesh, pulling him back, every step forward bringing him no closer to her.

Kane awoke pounding the steering wheel with his left hand, lungs refusing to open without a fight. He fought. He breathed. Night was around him and for a moment he thought he remained in the forest of his nightmare. Then he remembered. He'd been working nonstop for days, had fallen asleep while driving once too often, and decided to pull over for a couple hours of much-needed rest. He'd taken a fire access road—little more than a dirt trail—off of 278, near Moss Creek South Carolina, and pulled over. *I guess that's enough sleep for now*, he told himself and ran his left hand over his face. Looking down at his right, he had to exert an effort to lift the hand: it worked as well as the other. He gripped the steering wheel with it, his left finding its way into his wrinkled blue suit to the scar tissue on his shoulder that he could feel even through the fabric of his shirt. Kane then turned the ignition key and the Cutlass growled angrily to life. With the top down, so the cool night air could help keep him awake, Solomon Kane made his way back to 278 east, toward Hilton Head.

The dream and the blasphemy of what it counterfeited did not want to go quietly into his subconscious; it clawed at his deliberate motions, distracted him from the passing miles. The last thing Kane wanted was to think of that night.

"As I walk down the highway all I do is sing this song," he sang, his voice much deeper than Robert Plant's as he covered Zeppelin's

Out on the Tiles. "And a train that's passin' my way helps the rhythm move along. There is no doubt about the words are clear, the voice is strong, is oh so strong."

There was no train, of course, and the radio in the Cutlass didn't work—having taken a bullet a seven months earlier—but that wasn't the point. Kane sang all the way to the bridge to Hilton Head, turning off just before it and driving down the county road that led, after another hour, to another bridge and Dunsany Island. By that time the sun had come up and he didn't need to sing anymore.

Dunsany Island was the ugly younger sister to the opulent Hilton Head. Harder to get to without an airport, what Dunsany Island lacked in convenience it made up for in small-town charm. Or so its microscopic tourism campaign said. Out in the middle of Calibogue Sound, the island boasted beaches on the Atlantic, fishing on the sound, forest hiking trails, and a Main Street that was as wholesome as any family could want. *I need to hide the .45 as soon as possible,* Kane thought as he crossed the bridge: *a town like this, owning its own island, is probably a Fourth Reich when it comes to civil liberties.*

Victor Armwell, Kane thought as he drove the oak-lined county road draped with Spanish moss on his way to Main Street USA, *boy was he poorly named. Fifty-eight, murdered presumably in his own house at 75 Altair Street, Dunsany Island. What an island! All a family vacation needs and closer than the Bahamas: beaches, fishing, local crafts, and—oh, let's not forget—a two-thousand percent increase in homicides in the last three months. I wonder if anyone else has been murdered in this charming little town since Helen shot me the tip thirty-six hours ago.*

Altair Street was one of many winding, live-oak lined streets that snaked their way from Main Street back into the brooding woods of Dunsany Island. It was close to the bridge from mainland

South Carolina, too, so Kane went directly to Armwell's. Each house's lot looked like a photograph out of a real estate agent's wet dream: ancient trees draped in picturesque Spanish moss, wide lawns, and deep porches. Not a house on the island was more than thirty-years old—that being when Regan allowed the island off the protected list—but the architects who peopled the pristine, undisturbed lushness of Dunsany Island had earned every cent making the houses appear as century-plus antiques. The porches surrounding Victor Armwell's house even had cozy swings hanging from the ceiling.

Kane parked on the street and unfolded his six-foot-three-inch frame from the Cutlass, cracking in so many places he had a momentary vision of this being the end. *Forty-three for christsake,* he thought, *I sound like a stroll through the woods on a Fall day.* With a sideways glance at the neighbors—a hundred feet away on either side and across the street—Kane walked boldly to the front door. No answer. *What I don't know about Vic Armwell I could just about fit on this porch,* he thought. *No next of kin was listed online, nor a marriage certificate; not discoverable by the quick search Helen had time for, anyway. Let's have a look around,* he thought and followed the porch around the side of the house.

Blinds where pulled down and curtains were drawn at every window. Trying the service entrance, Kane found it locked. The detached garage had a car in it but the door wouldn't budge. Coming back to the front yard, Kane looked for movement at either of the neighbors' windows. *Lucky left,* he thought as he saw a curtain fall at the next house over. He went around the hedge, rather than pushing through it, and up onto the neighbor's porch.

"Good morning, ma'am," Kane said when an older woman straight out of a cookie-dough commercial cracked the door almost wide enough for the chain to straighten out. "My name is Karl

Leifson and I'm with Alliance Insurance. Would you mind if I ask you a few questions about Mr. Armwell?"

"Mr. Armwell?" the woman said hesitantly in a voice like a loose fan belt. "Who did you say you was with?"

"Alliance Insurance, ma'am," Kane said. "Adjuster. I understand Mr. Armwell passed."

"You have a card, Mr. Leifson?" she asked.

"Of course, where are my manners?" Kane said. He took a card from his wallet—slowly enough to make sure it said 'Karl Leifson' on it—and passed it through the sliver of open space Mrs. Whosis kept making smaller. "Here you are."

She read it and bit her lip and then said, "Is that your car?"

Kane looked over his shoulder, suddenly feeling a bit uneasy. *If it turns out Hector is right about my needing to get rid of the Cutlass, I'll never live it down,* he thought, *provided I live at all.* "Yes, ma'am, that's my car. Is it in the way?"

She told him to hold on a second and shut the door firmly. Kane could hear what must have been half a dozen deadbolts shot into place. Stepping back in surprise, he saw the curtain on the far window pull back and Mrs. Whosis press a pair of binoculars against the glass.

"The fuck?" Kane mumbled to himself.

After a moment, the door shook with all the bolts and chains being taken off and then opened wide enough to see the lady of the house.

"Oh, you're from out of state," she said with a broad smile. "I'm Mrs. Winchester, pleasure to meet you." She held out her hand after rubbing it on her apron.

"And you, Mrs. Winchester," Kane said.

"Poor Mr. Armwell," she said. "I don't know how much I can tell you. He was killed."

"Homicide," Kane said. "Yes, I'd heard that. Naturally I'll stop by the police station—"

"Sheriff's office," she corrected.

"Sheriff's office, yes," Kane said, "to get the full details but I thought it best to contact the next of kin first. Unfortunately, our records are a bit vague on that point. Would you happen to know if Mr. Armwell's family is reachable?"

"Oh, I don't think Mr. Armwell had anybody, poor soul," she said. "We'd been neighbors for nearly thirty years but I'm afraid we never did socialize much. My Howard used to pass the time of day with him, my husband did. He's been gone ten years now and, shoot, I guess you could say I'm not what you'd call a socialite." *And how,* Kane thought. "You might ask Mr. Munch."

"Mr. Munch?" Kane asked.

"Yes, Cecil Munch who owns the malt shop on Main Street," she said slowly, as if expecting Kane to write it down. "It's a real, old-time malt shop. The tourists love it," she said, smiling proudly. "He owns next door; Mr. Armwell only rented."

"Thanks very much, Mrs. Winchester," Kane said, taking a step back. "You've been very helpful."

With a crawling feeling going up his spine as if Mrs. Winchester was about to pull an implement with her name on it at any moment, Kane walked briskly back to the Cutlass and then drove down to Main Street. *I guess old Vic Armwell getting iced next door did a number on the old lady's nerves,* he thought. *But binoculars? And what the hell does my being out of state have to do with anything?*

CHAPTER 2

A CONFERENCE BEHIND THE FINEST CONFECTIONERIES ON THE EASTERN SEABOARD

M AIN STREET DUNSANY Island was a fantasy world of anachronisms: part nineteenth-century London, part western revival, and part 1950s TV set, its shops catered to well-financed sentimentality. *Munch's Malt Shop* was near where Main Street hit the beach and as Kane parked the Cutlass, he saw the sun glittering on the gray-green Atlantic. 9:30 in the morning and it was already getting hot.

Kane went through the screen door of the shop, setting a bell on a spiral spring above it tinkling, and into the coolness of several ceiling fans wafting about the scent of fresh-baked everything. Not really a malt shop in the traditional sense, *Munch's* was a variety of eateries all rolled into one. The antique soda fountain along the back wall had an espresso machine crammed in beside it; flanking either side of the seating area were an ice cream counter with a few dozen flavors as well as frozen yogurt and gelato, and across from it was a bakery counter with pies, breads, cupcakes, and confections of every sort. A ten-foot wooden menu swinging from the ceiling announced that the kitchen's fare ran from omelets to burgers to short ribs. You weren't getting out of *Munch's* without a meal.

When the bell above the door rang, every face behind the counters—two young women at either side and three more ahead—turned frightened expressions on Kane. A second passed as they exchanged glances and head-shakes with one another and then collectively sighed with relief. The breakfast crowd of tourists—loud shirts and fat thighs shouting over screaming children—didn't seem to notice. Kane walked around the tables to where the soda fountain met the bakery counter, waved over the cagiest looking attendant, and asked if Munch was around. She shared another uncomfortable expression with her fellow workers and then, without a word, went into the back.

Cecil Munch was a frisky jasper in the costume of a western bank teller, who jittered around like he was standing barefoot on hot stand. He had the eyes of a ferret and a chin like a piece of dented crown molding. Coming out of the back room, he took one look at Kane's wrinkled suit and three-days of beard and he wasn't happy.

"Something I can help you with?" Munch asked in a voice about three octaves higher than Mrs. Winchester's fan belt. His left eyebrow was cocked so high it nearly met his receding hairline.

"Yes, Mr. Munch," Kane shouted as if he was hard of hearing. "I'd like to ask you a few questions about Victor Armwell, who was murd—"

"Yes, yes, of course, of course," Munch said, lunging to take Kane by the arm and—with surprising strength—hurry him through the counters toward the door marked 'Private.' "Glad you stopped by, a real pleasure, golly it is. Please, let's use my office. Oh boy, what a great crowd of guests we have today, Margaret," he said to the woman who had brought him out, his back to Kane, shielding him from the crowd. "What a bunch, oh boy. Oh and this one, the cutest of them all," he said to a girl not more than three who bawled at the harshness of life over a bib spattered with unappreciated grits. Munch scampered over and leaned his hands on his knees and said to her, "You know what makes breakfast better? Peach cobbler!" The girl quit her crying, whether she knew what cobbler was or not, but looked as if she held more tears in readiness if cobbler did not in fact make breakfast better. "Margaret! That peach cobbler done baking? Good, good: a portion for everyone who wants one—on the house. But especially for this little angel."

Munch backed out of the seating area and to the door, corralling Kane with his backward-stretched arms, and into the hallway to his office. Once out of sight, he turned on Kane, caught between fury and fear.

"Are you crazy?" he squeaked. "You want to kill the town? You don't go mentioning our—blast it—*difficulties* with the tourists sitting right there enjoying the finest confectioneries on the eastern seaboard."

"Thought I might have a private word with you, Munch," Kane said.

Munch made a noise like a sick horse and led the way to his office. He closed the door tight and waved Kane to a chair. Even the office looked like a set from a Dickens' novel. Munch crashed into his plush leather seat and wiped his expansive forehead with a red handkerchief.

"Armwell," Kane said.

"What about him?" Munch said. "And who are you?" Kane handed him another of his business cards. "Insurance?"

"That's right," Kane said. "Whenever we get a sudden death

like Armwell's, we like to look into things. Especially in a small town like Dunsany Island. Small-town sheriffs and coroners find it easier to be nice to relatives by calling suicides unsolved murders, on account of insurance not paying out for suicides. Care to tell me about how Armwell got dead?"

"Huh, it weren't no suicide," Munch said sulkily. "We don't have no need of suicides around these parts, Mr., uh, Mr. Leifson. We got murders enough."

"So I've heard," Kane said. He grinned like death across the desk.

"Now see here," Munch said. "There's no way you could think a man with a hatchet through his head did it himself? What's your angle?"

"My angle is that something isn't right in this town and Alliance wants to know what before it shells out life insurance on so many people," Kane said. "We've seen wacky suicide cults before."

"Something ain't right, mister," Munch said. "But it ain't suicide. Listen, if it gets out what's going on here it could sink the town. Will you keep it to yourself?"

"Of course," Kane said. "It's in our best interest to make sure you can continue to pay your premiums."

"Well, I guess that does make sense," Munch said. With a big sigh, he continued. "People have been going crazy. Killing each other left and right. Hardly a day goes by. It started about three months ago when Tucker Masterson was found brained on his front porch. Next day, Fisher Anderson was hanging from a tree in his back yard, beaten like a piñata. And now," he threw up his hands helplessly, "it's day in, day out. I'm sure someone was probably killed last night that we haven't heard nothing about yet."

"Kind of a dangerous place for tourists, don't you think?" Kane said.

"No no no, don't say that," Munch said quickly. "Never been a tourist killed. Not the last three months or ever. Only town folks been killed. And done the killing. That's how we've been able to keep it quiet."

"Surprised the town folk stay, bad as it is," Kane said.

"Well what in the hell can we do?" Munch said. "Our businesses are here, our lives. I've lived here for thirty-two years, Mr. Leifson. I'm too old to go off somewheres else. And certainly not because people are losing their blessed minds."

"What's causing it?" Kane asked.

"No one knows," Munch sighed. "We had a couple smart gals come down from the university to test the water and whatnot. That weren't no good; it's fine. I could've told them that! Hell, if it'd been the water, wouldn't the tourists go nuts, too?"

"Not if it takes drinking it for thirty-two years," Kane said.

"Huh, never thought of that," Munch said. "Well, butt your platinum brain against this then: they tested the water, the air, even all the food in my storeroom and came up with a heaping pile of bupkis. Nothing in the way of organisms causing the madness."

Kane grunted and pulled at his lip for a moment. "None of this explains anything specific about Armwell," he said. "Any idea why someone would want to take a hatchet to him?"

"None that I know of," Munch said. "He always lost at cards gracefully. And before you ask, we wagered matchsticks. Haven't had a game in two months. No one wants to be nowhere outside after dark, I can tell you. Those that do go out, go armed fit for war. I tell them to stay the hell away from the beach and off of Main Street. Tourists don't need to see any of that nonsense."

"Armwell," Kane reminded him. "I'll need to talk to his next of kin. He have one?"

"You're the insurance," Munch said. "Don't you know?"

"I don't know," Kane said. "Why I'm asking."

"He has a daughter down in San Antonio," Munch said. "Married a ophthalmologist."

"Address?" Kane said.

"Don't know it," Munch said.

"It'll be somewhere in his house," Kane said. "You've got a key?"

"I can't just let you into the man's house," Munch said. "You'd need a warrant."

Kane fixed him with his stare and nodded slowly, saying, "I can get a warrant. I can have my company file for one with a state judge—up in Colombia."

"Whoa now, okay," Munch said, shooting forward. "No need to get hot at me. Let me just find it." Munch pulled out a huge ring of keys and found the one to 75 Altair Street. "There you go. Though I don't know what the Sheriff will say to me, if he finds out. Shouldn't you talk with him about it?"

"I will," Kane said, standing up. "Thanks for the key. I'll bring it back as soon as I'm done."

CHAPTER 3

THE NEXT AMITYVILLE

BACK IN THE sweet-smelling splendor of *Munch's Malt Shop*, Kane's first sight coming through the door was a man about six-five and two-hundred-seventy pounds, straining the fabric of a sheriff's uniform. The gold star above his left breast pocket said he was the Sheriff; the mirrored sunglasses and well-brushed Stetson hat said he took it seriously. He leaned his elbow on the top of the pastry case, smiling at all the tourists enjoying their breakfasts. His sunglasses took in the crowd but Kane could see the Sheriff's baby-blue eye straining around the side, looking in his direction. *Great*, Kane thought.

"Sheriff," he said, coming abreast and looking—not without interest—at the pastry case.

"Mr. Leifson," the Sheriff said.

"Quite the grapevine you have on Dunsany Island," Kane said, handing him a business card as if it was a reflex.

The Sheriff nodded. "Yup, we do," he said, moving his jaw as if he missed his lump of chaw. "Don't think less of Mrs. Winchester, though; she doesn't think any less of you. I expect she thought it a kindness to make me aware of an insurance man taking a tour of our town."

"Saves me the trouble of finding your office," Kane said.

"I live to serve," the Sheriff said. "Lovely day outside. How about we go and enjoy it?"

"Be happy to," Kane said.

They walked out and down Main Street, moving as slow as well-fed lions, sticking to the shade under the over-hanging second floor balconies. The Sheriff offered his hand.

"Sheriff Jackson," he said.

Kane took it and wondered for the thousandth time why some people think squeezing a hand until it cracks is a friendly way to greet someone. *Maybe he isn't being friendly*, he told himself.

"How's Munch this morning?" Jackson asked, watching the street and the people as they passed, smiling and nodding at proffered hellos.

"He told me about the *difficulties*, as he put it, your town has been having these past three months," Kane said. "Sounds like a hell of a mystery. Particularly how you've managed to keep it out of the national news. I expected to see the FBI flying around in helicopters."

Jackson nodded. "Not much of a mystery at all, Mr. Leifson," he said. "We have the murderers in custody for nearly every case."

Kane stopped short. The Sheriff took a couple leisurely steps and then circled back to Kane.

"You've made arrests?" Kane asked. "How about Mr. Armwell's killer?"

The Sheriff sucked his teeth and looked over the street for a moment. "Been sixty-two killings this year," he said quietly. "Up until three months ago, we hadn't had one. Normally we get one or maybe three a year. My jurisdiction stretches across the sound to a roadhouse near the bridge; get most of my customers there. Then, something happened. I don't have all the answers, Mr. Leifson, but I do have most of the guilty parties. Fifty-nine of them, to be exact. I can't tell you why all of a sudden people couldn't live and let live but they didn't get any smarter for losing their minds. In most cases, they weren't very bright about how they did their killings. A smart feller like you might say that we've kept the FBI out of here to protect the tourism; only, tourists never been killed. The truth is, though, that I didn't call them in because I never needed them."

"Doesn't sound like you did, Sheriff," Kane said. "And my man Armwell?"

"Don't have his killer yet," the Sheriff said. "Matter of time. Whoever done it wiped off the handle of the hatchet but didn't swab the bottom of it. It's one of those multi-use hatchets with a nail puller on the one end and when the owned last used it, he—plop—put a dandy of a thumb print on the butt end. We'll have him as soon as the State Police send me the name. They don't know it's for murder, of course, but they'll send me the name.

"So, as you can see, we have everything under control," he said, leaning significantly toward Kane.

"You call sixty-two killings in three months under control?" Kane said.

The Sheriff chewed his jaw for a moment before saying. "Don't see how that concerns Alliance Insurance," he said coldly.

"Something is not right on this island," Kane said. "Something is causing this rash of murders. And if Alliance is going to be on the hook for life insurance payouts, we have a right to investigate."

"Interfering with a police investigation is a serious crime, Mr. Leifson," Sheriff Jackson said.

"I don't intend to step on anyone's toes," Kane said.

"I have very big toes," the Sheriff said. "It only takes one misstep for me to haul a body in."

"It only takes one phone call to a national newspaper for Dunsany Island to become the next Amityville," Kane said.

The Sheriff took off his sunglasses and stepped close enough that his belly touched Kane's. "That a fact?" he asked. "Don't misunderstand me, Mr. Leifson, I wouldn't turn away help, if that's what you're offering. If you can assist us in determining the cause behind this sudden rash of homicides—assuming there is one—nothing would make me happier. Only, keep me informed of where you go and what you do."

"I'll do that," Kane said, stepping back and exerting an effort not to brush off his stomach.

"Right now would be a good place to start," Sheriff Jackson said.

"I'm headed back to Armwell's place," Kane said. "You're done with it?"

The Sheriff nodded. "You find anything interesting-like," he said, "you let me know."

Kane nodded back and asked, "Now that were on the same side, were any of the bodies moved?"

It took a minute before the Sheriff could bring himself to answer. "Yup," he said. "Four or five of them, in fact. Mostly it just made finding the murderer that much easier."

"And the murderers?" Kane asked. "Have any of them given you an idea of how or why they did what they did?"

"You mean are they copping insanity pleas?" Sheriff Jackson said. "A couple have. The others seem as bewildered as the rest of us."

"Can I talk to them?" Kane asked.

The Sheriff shook his head slowly. "I'm not ready to do that," he said. "But if you want to talk to someone who has represented a few of them, talk to Mike Blanchet. He's a lawyer in town. Doesn't know much about criminal law but times are tough and most don't have a hell of a lot of choice."

Kane said he would and asked where he could find Mike Blanchet; Sheriff Jackson pointed across and down Main Street. *Naturally.* Kane then went back to the Cutlass and drove off toward Altair Street. Sitting under the cool shade of a live-oak in front of Armwell's house, he called Helen.

Voice mail, he thought, *perfect.* "Hey Helen, it's Sol," he said. "Dunsany Island is supposedly in the grips of End-Times-like crazy. Had a nice chummy chat with the Sheriff. He said they've had sixty-two murders in the past ninety days and—get this—he's made arrests on all but three of them. Bullshit. At a murder-and-a-half per day, he'd have to solve each one within hours. So, I'm thinking the Sheriff is either in on the killings and covering up for the cult or he's orchestrating the whole thing as the cult's leader. They've kept the national press out, like you said, but it seems to be good old fashion business interest behind that. And a strangely high level of cunning: they haven't targeted any tourists. That's a little restrained for your average cult but who knows, maybe they're getting smarter—there's a scary thought. I'm going to take a run at a lawyer who defended a few of the so-called murderers, see if there's anything to their stories. Supposedly the town had a team from a local university check their water, air, and food: can you hack the findings? Also, can you get the names of everyone Sheriff Jackson has arrested? I'd like to know if they're related in some way. If he's pinning murders on them, maybe there's a rhyme or reason behind who he's picking. Thanks, Helen."

Hanging up, Kane used the key that Munch gave him to enter Armwell's house and frisk it. It looked like whoever killed Armwell had started beating him in the kitchen, at the back of the house. Nothing had been taken: TV, computer, cash taped to the bottom of a drawer in Armwell's bedroom were all left. Nothing of interest jumped out at Kane otherwise. *Not that I expected it to,* he thought, *victims are not usually selected for any special reason unless it's that they won't be missed. Maybe Armwell qualifies that way but laying siege to an entire town is not MO for the cult, not unless they have one sophisticated leader laying a-whole-lotta faith in the business sector's need to keep bad news quiet.*

Leaving, Kane drove down to the beach and found a motel. Taking his suitcase out of the trunk, he thought, *Well, Sheriff Jackson, I guess you'll be searching my car and room as soon as I'm safely inside Mike Blanchet, esq.'s office. Better hide the .45.* His favorite hiding place—unscrewing the back of the TV and stuffing the pistol inside—felt just a little too obvious in the motel room's sparse décor. *I'm not hiding it in the toilet trap,* he told himself as he screwed the TV back together, *never again.* After that, he took a few minutes to shave and comb his hair, eyed the bed with longing, and walked out into the ninety-degree weather.

CHAPTER 4

AS IF IN A DREAM

THE BEACH WAS thoroughly peopled. Colorful umbrellas and plastic pails looked as carefree as the screaming children racing around sandcastles and roughhousing in the ocean. Parents chased little ones who'd escaped from their trunks or sent dour teens up to the innumerable beachfront stalls for hotdogs and ice cream. Summer was in full swing on Dunsany Island—but the man in the wrinkled blue suit, sweating his way up Main Street, didn't look as if he saw much of it. He had murder on his mind.

The law offices of Michael Blanchet seemed more like an interior-decorator's parlor than a lawyer's sanctum. Airy and white, with pillows all over the couches and chairs, and a stink like six new cars juiced into the air conditioning, it looked as phony as his secretary's smile. The Sheriff's name worked like a key and in less than two minutes Kane was sitting on one side of a mile-and-a-half of executive desk, across from the very tan Mike Blanchet, who wore white duck trousers and a polo shirt. Mike had beamed the encouraging smile of a used car salesman when Kane first came in;

but when the door shut and Kane asked about the killers Mike had been ordered to represent, the man sagged back into his chair, the mail-order charm returned to sender.

"I'm surprised Jackson would talk to you about that," Mike said slowly.

"Insurance," Kane said.

"Not the town's," Mike said, his face turning as white as his trousers.

"Nope," Kane said. "Life, for a number of the victims. I'm still surprised the state hasn't pushed in. How come they haven't snatched up jurisdiction, forced everybody off the island?"

"They don't know how bad it is," Mike said. He bit his thumb nail, breathing heavily, and Kane could smell it now: bourbon.

Now there's an idea that might make you talk, Kane thought. "It's a hell of a hot day," he said. "Don't suppose you have a drop of anything wet on hand."

Mike smiled hesitantly and then dove for his bottom drawer. "You know what?" he said, pushing files aside to get at a bottle of something promising and a couple glasses. "When I went to Stanford, I did it at least in part to thumb my nose at my dad. He had a practice in Savannah and would come home lit almost every night. I mean stumbling! I never understood, thought maybe he was into something shady, and swore I'd never be like that." He held up the bottle and, when Kane nodded his approval, poured them both a brimful glass. "But then the nice, loyal, salt-of-the-earth people of Dunsany Island started murdering each other and, brother, I've needed a drink sometimes like I need air."

"From what I've heard around town," Kane said, tasting his drink, "it's practically a war zone out there. People patrolling at night, armed to the teeth."

"Won't do any good," Mike said. "Hasn't, anyway."

"Any of these murderers ever tell you why they did it?" Kane asked.

"Oh yeah," Mike said and then killed his drink. "Guess?"

"The devil made me do it," Kane said.

Mike held up the bourbon bottle like he was awarding a trophy, then poured himself another drink. "You got it," he said. "Not exactly, but yeah, they didn't have any real explanation. Most, when the Sheriff put them in front of old Markaway, just folded; I mean like a cheap—uh," he hesitated, looking at Kane's suit, "you know. They admitted it and didn't fight. They did it! They all admitted it. Said they were crazy."

"You didn't try an insanity defense?" Kane asked.

"I thought of it at first," Mike said. "Believe me, I did. But after ten of them, after fifteen? Shit, I'm just hanging on like everyone else, mister."

"But if there was no motive," Kane prompted.

Mike swallowed his drink and sat staring at the bottle. "There was," he said quietly.

"For all sixty-two murders?" Kane asked.

"For the fifty or so that we have people locked up for, yeah," Mike said. "Listen, here's the last one: Sumpter Meyer, they call him Sump. Early thirties, not very bright—never was—but a heart as big as all outdoors. They say he tried so hard on the high school football team that he was a hair's breadth away from a scholarship to USC. Married Glenda Ford, now Meyer, not long after she got back from the Navy. They had a couple of kids; he bowls; she bowls better; they work a booth down on the beach. A week ago, Sump waited in the bushes outside of Cleetus Thornton's house until Cleet's wife went to bed and then Sump kicked in a window and shot Cleet in the head with a twelve-gauge and then ran home. They brought me in and the first thing Sump told me was that he did it. I asked him why. He told me he didn't know but that it won't take a jury too long to figure it out. Seems Sump had a condition with his, uh, with his testicles. His sperm had more left feet than he did. He and Glenda couldn't afford the treatment with test tubes and artificial insemination so they just kept at it. And then one day she was pregnant. Three years later, she wants another; they try; it takes a while; and then she's pregnant again."

"Cleetus?" Kane said.

"Yahtzee," Mike said and poured his fourth. "Seems when she was in high school, she and Cleet were sweethearts. Cleet even got her pregnant back then and she had gone down to Savannah to have it taken care of. So, when she wasn't getting anywhere with Sump, she asked Cleet to step in. Sump never knew until their youngest was three and Cleet said something quietly to Glenda, not knowing Sump was bending down below the bar trying to unfuck a tap hose. They didn't speak for two years after that and then, when they finally did, it was mutually agreed—without saying a word, you understand—that all involved would never admit it had happened.

"So, Sump had a motive, in a sense," Mike said. "A motive that any jury in the world would buy. You could easily believe it built up inside of him until, one day—a crazy day in a crazy town where people were just killing each other left and right—he decided it was his turn."

"Only he says he doesn't remember," Kane said.

"More or less," Mike said. "He says he remembers but that it was as if he was dreaming. I was thinking of a sleepwalking defense of sorts, but a whole town's worth? Doesn't make sense."

"Can't be environmental because it doesn't affect the tourists," Kane sighed. "Very weird. How many people knew of this motive?"

"Aw, beats the hell out of me," Mike said and Kane noticed he was losing his TV accent with each drink. "Sump said it weren't nobody but him and Cleet and Glenda that knew. Maybe Cleet's wife? I don't know. You think it could have been someone else?"

"It'd have to be one hell of an operation," Kane said. "And you'd need plenty of people to pull it off. There are drugs that could create a sleep-like state, open the victim to hypnosis."

"Hell, Sump was hardly there on the best of days," Mike mumbled.

"Was the motive mentioned at his trial?" Kane asked.

"Naw, he pleaded guilty," Mike said. "His wife said she wouldn't visit him in jail if he didn't. Jail, ha! What jail? We only had three cells at the Sheriff's office. Jackson set up an honest-to-god prison camp behind the station—using tents and barbed wire. He has rickety towers with volunteer guards in them watching the camp. It's madness. Only a matter of time before one of them volunteers loses his marbles and opens up with a shotgun on the prisoners. None of them have had a fair trial, you know. None of it'll stick."

"How do you mean?" Kane asked.

"Not enough jurors," Mike said and stifled a belch. "All bench trials, only a judge. Markaway made junior judges out of three of the other lawyers in town; all real estate guys; two of them were retired. They do all the trials between them. Take two three days. I have another in, shit, twenty minutes. That all you need to know?"

Kane said it was, thanked Mike, and headed out. *This is the damndest thing I've ever seen,* he thought while crossing the street and heading for the malt shop. *A Cthulhu Cult might try to cover their sacrifices by planting the bodies elsewhere, even hanging the killings on a biker gang or something, but this is sophisticated as hell. Sol, baby, if these fuckers are getting smarter, wiping them out is going to get a lot harder.*

CHAPTER 5

DON'T FORGET
THE MINCEMEAT

U NDER THE OVERHANGING porches and second floors of Main Street's shops it was a bit cooler, though packed with people trying to keep off the smoking asphalt. As Kane drew nearer to *Munch's Malt Shop*, he saw a few people peering through the windows who, by their dress, must have been locals. They gently waved away a couple with two small children strapped to their chests that tried to go into the shop. Kane quickened his pace.

Not bothering with the undoubtedly well-meaning locals, Kane pushed through and found the shop had become a sort of theater in the round. The servers at each of the three counters watched with pale faces as the eight tables of tourists continued eating, seemingly unaware of the lone man at a table near the door who had a dreamy look on his face as he ate a slice of apple pie. He heaved an erotic sigh after every bite, eyes rolling back in his head, whispering something inaudible under the spinning fans.

Kane sidled over to the pastry counter and leaned back to watch. The man was over six feet and built like a linebacker except for his face, which was curiously round and fleshy. *Used to be obese,* Kane thought, *and then worked his ass off to build that physique, lose the fat, but it never reached his head.*

"Margaret," the man moaned loudly. Kane couldn't help himself and chuckled as he looked around: a father at a table busy with hotdogs spared a moment from his chili-covered five-year old to scowl at the pie-eating man. Margaret all but ran from behind the counter, trying to appear busy without giving the impression of hysteria Kane could see at the back of her eyes. She didn't move quite fast enough for the pie eater. Angrily, he shouted, "Margaret!"

"I'm here, I'm here, Mr. Wicket," she said, reaching his table.

"I want," he said, still staring lustily at his plate. "I want another slice of apple pie."

"Right away, Mr. Wicket," she said with a shaking voice.

"And," he said as she tried to turned away, "and a slice of the blueberry. And the key lime, and the Boston cream, and cherry and rhubarb and don't heat them up just bring them to me. Got that?"

"Yes, Mr. Wicket," she said. Kane could see over her shoulder as she scribbled on her notepad and doubted she—or anyone else— could have read what she drew there. "Right away."

"And, and, to drink," Mr. Wicket said and then paused to lick his plate, pressing his face to it with sounds usually reserved for more intimate occasions.

"Chocolate shake?" Margaret suggested, all but in tears.

"Yes," he moaned. "Oh god yes. Chocolate shake."

"This is just creepy," Kane said. Margaret's eyes nearly shot out of her head; she turned and ran to the pie section of the confectionery counter and three other servers rushed over to help her with all the pie.

Mr. Wicket stared at the servers as they worked, becoming

more and more agitated. Margaret hissed for the others to keep working and then hurried back with four slices of various pies. Mr. Wicket fell to with gusto, forgoing his spoon and jamming first one and then another slice of pie into his slowly masticating mouth. *A zoo full of hyenas at lunch couldn't make as much noise as little Georgie Porgie here,* Kane thought. *I guess I can understand why the girls are upset. Damn but I could go for a slice of that rhubarb.*

The bell above the door rang and Sheriff Jackson walked calmly in, his plastic crowd-pleasing smile vibrant under his mirrored shades. He nodded neighborly to Kane and then slid past Mr. Wicket and addressed himself to the various tourists. A few questions were asked of him but mostly he did the talking, the gist of which was that Mr. Wicket suffered from a kind of imaginary hypoglycemia and if his blood sugar dropped too low he went a bit batty. Nothing to worry about.

"There's one, there's one missing, Margaret," Mr. Wicket said suddenly as she squeezed a piece of blueberry onto his little table. He was conscientious about every syllable of her name: Mar-gar-et. "One's missing, Margaret, which one is missing?"

"I don't know, Mr. Wicket," she said. "Those are the ones you asked for. I'll go check, if that's okay."

"One's missing," Mr. Wicket said. "It's missing, it's missing, Margaret."

Sheriff Jackson turned slowly to face the cluttered table and its agitated occupant. His hand rested almost unnoticed on his pistol.

"Mincemeat," Kane said under his breath with a cough.

Margaret looked over her shoulder frantically.

"It's missing, it's missing, it's missing, my pie," Mr. Wicket said as he stuffed his mouth and moaned and shouted all at once. "My pie, Margaret, my pie, my pie, it's missing."

"Mincemeat," Kane growled at her back and then mouthed the word twice at the petrified servers hugging each other behind the pie case. One understood suddenly and grabbed the whole pie, rushing over and handing it to Margaret. Margaret half placed, half tossed the entire mincemeat pie onto the collection of empty plates in front of Mr. Wicket.

"My pie," he whispered, cherries dropping from his cheeks, all but in tears. "My pie came. It's time for dessert, Bobby. You can have a slice of pie." With a sweep of his hand, he sent the plates on one side of the table to a crashing death against the wall. Sheriff Jackson had his pistol out before the first shard of crockery hit the floor. Mr. Wicket took up his spoon and daintily scooped up the most tender portion of mincemeat at the center of the pie. He placed it between his lips and his reaction was of relief.

He swayed in his seat, slapping his hands slowly against his mouth, spoon forgotten, and then heaved to his feet. His stomach was a near perfect half-sphere protruding from his chest. He stumbled to the door and out. Kane, casting a grin at the Sheriff, followed him. Mr. Wicket stumbled down the street, singing under his breath, until he reached a bench and fell onto it. Kane and the Sheriff and many of the local bystanders drew near and looked at the—seemingly—most recent person to lapse into madness.

Mr. Wicket's gibbering trickled to a standstill when his swaying stopped. His eyes blinked to a semblance of clarity, he leaned to one side and vomited in four body-contorting heaves, emptying chewed pies onto the sidewalk. People jumped back from the gastronomic fireworks. Kane circled into the street and then to the other side of Mr. Wicket, patting him on the back; the Sheriff looked at him like *he'd* gone mad.

"Totally worth it," Mr. Wicket said between gasps as he sat back and slapped his face clean of vomit. "Totally, totally worth it. Finally. *Finally!*" he shouted, smiling like a marathon winner, and then noticed the people around him.

Kane looked up at the Sheriff—still holding his pistol—and said, "If that doesn't say, 'Best pie in town,' nothing does."

He left the crowd and made his way back to the malt shop. Pushing through seekers of the best confectioneries on the eastern seaboard—as well as seekers of gossip—Kane patted Margaret on the shoulder and asked if Munch was in back. She wrinkled her face scornfully at the name and said yes and that he probably had the door locked and barred. Kane gave her a wink and headed back.

Kane gave Munch the all clear and then heard a bookcase being slid away from the door. Once inside he recounted the one-man pie-eating contest and reassured the businessman that no one was lost during the festivities. Kane remarked on how funny it was, though Munch didn't see it, and about how it seemed that Mr. Wicket was living his dream, finally eating a slice of every pie in the shop. He wondered aloud if anyone else in town was living their dreams.

"Hell, it's World War Three out there," Munch said, digging through his desk drawer for a bottle. "People are acting like there's no tomorrow."

"Like who?" Kane asked.

Munch didn't know specifics beyond a couple rumors of wild sex and one ninety year-old charging onto a high school football team's summer camp—in full pads—trying to score a touchdown. Almost made it, too. Munch told him to try the woman who ran the local paper, Laura Swift. He gave Kane directions—on Main Street—and Kane left.

On his way to the beauty salon (the paper was part time and Laura made her money as owner of the only beauty salon on Dunsany Island), Helen called.

"Helen, you are not going to believe this island," Kane said. "All I'll say is that pie was involved. Lots of pie."

"Having a good time, are we?" she said, not happy. "Enjoy yourself, by all means. While you were leaving your voicemail, I was on the phone with Sheriff Jackson pretending to be Vice President Helen Grady, Alliance Insurance. Infuriating man."

"I told you I was using the insurance cover," Kane said a little confused. "Didn't I?"

"Oh, you told me," she said. "You failed to mention the Mount Rushmore sized *ass* I would have to talk to for twenty solid minutes trying to keep your cover from being blown. I've dealt with small town Napoleons before but Sheriff Jackson takes the—"

"Pie?" Kane said.

"Why are you going on about pie?" she said sharply. Kane took a few minutes to tell her. "That is weird, I'll grant you," she said.

"Doesn't sound like a cult to me," Kane said. "Any Professor-Emeritus-of-Ethnology-and-Archeology-sized insights you'd like to lay on me?"

"There are other things in the universe than Cthulhu, Kane," she said. "And man is perfectly capable of inflicting evil upon man. You've seen that recently," she added softly.

A minute passed with nothing but street noise going through the phone before Kane said, "Yeah." He cleared his throat before he went on. "Okay, that's true but could this be a new wrinkle? Has Cthulhu ever sent dreams to a town—this is a seaside town, after all—dreams that make people seek out their greatest desires? Sure sounded like a dream with that pie guy; like he'd been denying himself for a long time and it was killing him."

"Nothing like that comes to mind," Helen said. "I'll look into it but that doesn't sound familiar at all. Not for Cthulhu, at least."

"Maybe they learned to focus his dreams?" Kane said. "I'm reaching here."

"Yes, you are," she said. "But we have to be open to the idea that a new tactic has arisen."

"So to speak," Kane said.

She laughed, "Yes, poor choice of words. The next time a door to R'lyeh is due to rise is in three months."

"What?" Kane shouted.

"Plenty of time," Helen said soothingly. "I'll get you there. Of course, you'll have to wait in line: there are about a hundred Venators on standby already. In the meantime, we need more data. Find this newspaper-hairdresser and see what she knows about odd behavior. I'm going to dig into the island's history to see if there was ever an incident like this before. I looked for mass murder earlier but not dream fulfillment." She sighed heavily. "God, does that ever say something horrible about mankind."

"What does?" Kane asked.

"That, if we're right, the greatest dream of a significant portion of the population is to kill someone they don't like," she said. "Take care of yourself, Sol. Against the cults, you are almost charmed. This is something different."

"I'll take care," Kane said. "Thanks, Helen. Oh, and tell Hector he's a big baby."

She laughed, promised not to, and they hung up. Kane went down the street and found the beauty salon.

CHAPTER 6

OF INK AND PAPER AND PIPE TOBACCO

THE RECEPTIONIST MADE a point of looking Kane up and down after he asked for Laura Swift, and then asked him if another hairdresser would do. When he said no, she asked him if a receptionist would. He shook his head and she directed him around the corner to the back stairs. Apparently the *Dunsany Observer* had its offices concurrent with Laura Swift's kitchen.

Kane rapped a knuckle against the carved shingle hanging next to Laura Swift's second floor back door. Looking in through the screen, he saw most of a woman in jeans and a tank top protruding from what he assumed was an industrial-sized photocopier.

"Wow, you got here fast," she said as she pulled her head and shoulders out of the machine, a black smudge running down one cheek and a screwdriver in her hand. She waved him in.

"Always been lucky that way," Kane said, opening the door and stepping in.

Laura Swift tossed her screwdriver onto an open newspaper on the kitchen table and wiped her forehead with the back of her hand. When Kane was across the table from her, she tilted her head to one side and said, "You know, you don't look like a printer repair guy."

"Just as well," Kane said with a shrug. "Don't want to get people's hopes up. I'm Karl Leifson."

She took his proffered hand, matched his grin, and said, "Laura. Alliance Insurance, right?"

"I love small towns," he said.

She laughed and said, "I bet. What can I do for you?"

"I've been around town asking about what Munch calls your *difficulties*," Kane said.

"I heard," she said, losing the grin. "I'm surprised people have talked to you."

"It's my cheery smile," he said. "I'm a bit curious, though, about what your paper has said these last few months. The impression I got from Munch and Jackson was that they'd tie an anchor to anyone who made too much noise and drag it out into Calibogue Sound."

She put her hands on her hips and nearly took her lower lip off biting it. "I guess it doesn't make me much of a newspaper woman, does it?"

"I didn't say that," Kane said softly.

"You might as well," she said. "I've been saying it to myself ever since Munch's goddamn *difficulties* began. You should see what the town council's minutes look like: makes the transcripts of the Nixon tapes look like full disclosure. But I," she said and couldn't meet Kane's eye.

"But you care about the town, too," he said.

"And we don't know what's going on or why people keep killing each other," she said. "Maybe if I really cared I'd start shouting from the rooftops. That'd be the end, Mr. Leifson."

"Ka—er, excuse me—Karl," he said. *Idiot!*

"Kay-Karl?" she teased. "I'm sorry, I guess I'd be more broken up about my lack of character if I wasn't afraid of someone breaking in my back door with a hatchet, each night."

"Like they did to Armwell?" Kane said. "And I don't think you lack character, Ms Swift: you're the only person I've met so far who's even questioned what she's doing."

"It's Laura, I told you," she said. "You want coffee?"

"In this heat?" Kane said and pulled at his collar.

She laughed and said, "Iced tea?"

"Please," he said. She motioned to a seat and he took it. As she went to the refrigerator for the tea, he said, "I've talked to Jackson and some others about the murderers, about their motivations and excuses. Munch said you'd know more than he would about town rumors and such."

"Ha, that's nearly as rich as his best-confectionery-whatever crap," she said and brought two tall glasses over to the table. She sat. "What he meant was he wasn't willing to tell all that he knows, Kay-Karl. You can count on it. But I'll tell you whatever I can. I won't ask you to keep it quiet and not let the world know what's going on here—and scare all the tourists away and destroy the town—because the lord knows I can't decide which way would be better. But ask the questions."

"Thanks, Laura," Kane said. "There was one case in particular I was wondering about: Sumpter Meyer's."

"Killed Cleet, Cleetus Thornton," she said soberly.

"You know why?" Kane asked.

"Because he went as crazy as the fifty other maniacs," she said.

"He had an honest-to-god motive," Kane said. "I was wondering how many other murderers had one and if anyone knew Sump's."

"Oh, I see," she said. "I heard there was a falling out between them for a while but never heard why. A few people said one or the other of them said something about the others' wife. Maybe more than that. But they patched it up and so the rumor died."

"Who would know the truth about it?" Kane asked.

"Besides the two of them?" she said. "Their wives, I guess. Some said they had a brawl outside of the roadhouse, once. I think it was—hold on—Jack Tower? Yes, Jack Tower broke it up. You could ask him; he might have heard what it was about."

"What sort of man is Jack Tower?" he asked.

"Oh just like most of them on the island," she said. "Only time he comes in to the salon to get his hair cut is when his wife is visiting her folks on the mainland, and he wants to get an eyeful of Birdie. She's my receptionist. Bet she tried to take a bite out of you."

"Had to keep my back to the wall the whole time," he said.

"I bet," she said and took a slow sip from her glass. "Jack owns a boat engine repair shop on the sound. Can't miss it."

"Thanks," Kane said. "The other thing was people going a bit peculiar. Not violently peculiar, like the murderers, but people acting like there's no tomorrow, to quote the esteemed Cecil Munch."

"Oh, you heard about Cathy and Hilde out on the beach, huh?" she said, blushing faintly.

"No but it sounds like I'd enjoy it," he said. "They couldn't be the only ones."

"Nope, they aren't," she said and her knee began to bounce under the table. "People have been cutting loose ever since the craziness set in. I figure it's a natural reaction: you don't know if tonight is your last night so you throw caution to the wind."

"Makes sense," he said. "What else, though? I just saw Bobby Wicket eat fifteen pies down at Munch's."

"You didn't!" she said. "Oh my, the old Bobby breaks loose at last. He was a very stout boy when we were in school and then, after starting college, he tried and tried to slim down until—after he came back from what must have been a hellish two years on Wall Street—he buffed out the way he is now. I guess he'd had enough. Or *hadn't* had enough."

"Cathy wanted Hilde and Bobby wanted pie," Kane said. "Anybody else try to get something they always wanted?"

Laura's blush returned deeper than ever and she looked at her hands. After a second, she glanced over her shoulder at the printer. "I don't even remember ordering it," she said. "Wiped out my savings. Bought what amounts to a hundred years worth of paper and ink, a fancy typesetting program for my brand new laptop. Ten years of savings—in this economy—gone in one night I hardly remember."

"Do you remember any of it?" Kane asked, leaning in.

"Well, I, I guess I do," she said. "I must have been drinking. Too much wine. It all seemed to happen in a haze. You have to understand, Karl, I've wanted to make *The Dunsany Observer* into a real-life newspaper since I was a little girl and my grandfather ran it on a manual press. That's right: he had an antique press that you operated by turning a crank. I still remember the smell of it, of the ink and paper—and his pipe tobacco. If I could make *The Dunsany Observer* into a subscription-based paper, I would die a happy woman."

"And one night, less than three months ago," Kane said, "you did everything in your power, everything you could think of, to make that dream come true."

She sat very still for a moment, peering into Kane's eyes as if reading his mind. "You," she said and then took a quick pull from her glass. "You're saying you think the same sort of hazy experience is behind these murders? That's, that's—"

"Insane?" Kane said. "I know. But so are these murders. None of it makes sense. Your description, though, of what you felt, matches Sump's almost word-for-word." He shrugged. "Doesn't tell us what's causing it, though, does it? We still don't know if it's a biological agent or radiation or hypnosis or aliens or what."

"I vote for aliens," she said. "Then I can turn my paper into a supermarket checkout rag."

Kane patted her hand and then stood up. "No, I don't think you could, not even if you tried." She smiled at that. He finished his iced tea and walked to the door; she held it open as he walked out onto the landing. "Thanks for the names," he said. "I'm going to go talk to them, see if they have any similarly hazy stories."

She nodded but waited for him to take a couple steps down before saying, "You going to tell me what they say, afterward?"

"Sure," Kane said, pausing on the stairs. "Over dinner?"

"Where are you staying?" she asked.

"*The Golden View,*" he said.

She rolled her eyes. "Nice place if you like salmonella. Come back here when you're through pestering people. I'll cook you a real southern supper."

"I look forward to it," he said. As he reached the Cutlass, across the street from Laura's salon, he looked back and saw her wave from her second story landing. He waved back, sat on the burning upholstery, and quietly sang, "I'm so glad I'm living and gonna tell the world I am; I got me a fine woman and she says that I'm her man; One thing that I know for sure, gonna give her the loving like nobody-nobody, nobody-nobody can."

CHAPTER 7

REVELATIONS
OF CTHULHU

THE REST OF the day Kane spent tracking down local after local who had confessed undying love for his mailman or sold everything to buy a shrimp boat or enrolled in Clown College or went to church naked or any of a hundred other things that people admit they've dreamed of doing after enough booze. In each case, they reported lightheadedness during the experience and difficulty remembering their thoughts, though their actions were as clear as if they'd been wide awake. Six o'clock found Kane sweating nearly through his suit jacket and walking back to *The Golden View*. The westering sun rippled amongst the swaying tree-tops, stretching fingers of crimson across the rolling Atlantic. Kane watched the waves and for a moment wanted to forget his tiredness, his mission, his life, and sit in the sand and listen to the salty water run up the beach. But he knew what lay under those waves, what ancient implacable being lay dead and dreaming, awaiting an ocean of blood sacrificed in its name to bring about the re-subjugation of mankind. He turned his head back to the sidewalk and his mind back to the mission. Too late.

He had his key in the door and the door open before he thought to look down the row of parked cars for anything suspicious. He hadn't stepped a foot onto the thin carpet before he knew the dark room was occupied. He froze and the lamp by the bed flared to life.

"Good evening, Mr. Leifson," Sheriff Jackson said from where he sat in the room's only chair, across from the door. A deputy sat on the bed near the lamp and another leaned against the wall next to the door, his arms loose at his sides. "Don't let the air conditioning out, boy: step inside, let's wag the chin a while."

Oh hell, they've got that squeal-like-a-pig look in their eyes, Kane thought. He didn't move. The Sheriff nodded minutely and the deputy to Kane's right took him sharply by the wrist, yanking him a step forward. Kane had thirty pounds on him, though, and only took the one step; he put his shoulder against the door to keep it open and pressed against the wall opposite the grabby deputy.

"Sheriff," Kane said.

"I said come in, boy," the Sheriff repeated, voice like a wood rasp.

Not moving, Kane said, "I've found out a few things you may find interesting."

"And I've found out a few interesting things about you, whoever you are," the Sheriff said. He left his chair like an Olympic skier setting off downhill, overturning the chair in the process. He stepped as close to Kane as he had that morning, belly to belly. "I first called that cockamamie number on your business card and talked to a rude Yankee woman, but it didn't satisfy me. So I had one of the boys go on the com-puter and wouldn't you know what they discovered through their internet? Alliance Insurance doesn't exist. They checked every insurance association in the country: there is no such company as Alliance Insurance."

"Guess that means I'm out of a job," Kane said.

"No, boy," the Sheriff said. "It means you a lying son-bitch and probably a reporter—or worse. You know what lying to an officer of the law is?"

"Charming?" Kane suggested.

"On Dunsany Island," the Sheriff said, "it's a hanging offense."

The deputy to Kane's right jumped behind him as if at a cue and tried to pin his arms. Kane had been waiting for the punch line, though, and brought his foot up to catch the deputy's knee: the deputy double over, hitting his chin against Kane's shoulder. The Sheriff reached for Kane's throat with both hands, roaring like a bear; Kane deflected them with a sweeping left arm, trying to keep the charging Sheriff between him and the other deputy across the room—who'd pulled his pistol. Kane quickly learned the Sheriff's bulk was comprised of far less fat than he'd thought. Smashed against the open door, Kane took elbow shots from the Sheriff, trying to hold the enraged man as a rodeo rider tries to hang on to a bull. All the while the first deputy alternated between screaming about his knee and trying to wrap his arms around Kane's. The second deputy kept shouting for the others to clear him a shot, weaving back and forth trying to draw a bead on Kane's head. The Sheriff threw himself sideways, his shoulder striking the doorjamb, and Kane spilled out onto the sidewalk, nearly smashing his face into a metal pole that held up the balcony above—but as his hands had clawed their way off of the Sheriff, he'd taken the man's handcuffs with him. The Sheriff spun around, nearly trampling his own deputy, and threw a savage right cross at Kane; Kane smacked the incoming fist to one side and slapped the handcuffs securely around the Sheriff's wrist; on the return stroke, he secured the other end of the handcuffs to the pole. Dodging the Sheriff's left hook, Kane was in front of the door—the second deputy saw him and let fly a wild shot that rang off the pole. Kane cursed and ducked to one side of the doorway. The Sheriff, yanking madly at his imprisoned arm, kicked Kane in the chest and sent him sprawling. The first deputy crawled out of the doorway and tried to handcuff Kane: Kane broke the deputy's nose with a quick jab, took his pair of handcuffs, and then pushed him back inside by the face and pulled the door shut. He stood, barely dodging a left from the Sheriff, and then grabbed the proffered wrist—snapping the deputy's handcuffs around it and then to the doorknob. Kane, out of breath and dizzy, stumbled back a few paces and looked at Sheriff Jackson. The man struggled like Samson chained between Philistine pillars, his right wrist handcuffed to the steel pole and his left to the doorknob. He cursed and sputtered, nearly apoplectic with anger, as Kane relieved him of his pistol and extra magazines. As he turned to run back to Main Street, Kane could hear the second deputy pulling on the door and the Sheriff screaming for him to both stop tearing off his arm and to catch up to the suspect.

Too many killings over the past months, too inexplicably committed, drove the locals from the street, hearing the madness in the irate Sheriff's screams. Kane jammed his stolen pistol into his hip pocket and the magazines into his jacket and avoided the questioning eyes of the tourists he passed. *Great, just great,* he thought: *I can guess what the Sheriff's dream must have been: a prison camp, you prick. And now my .45 is going to live in the back of that shitty motel TV for the rest of eternity.* He growled curses at himself and fate and the foolishness of getting attached to objects. Then he went to his car.

"Screw them, they're not taking my Cutlass," he said and got in.

He tore over to Laura's, hoping he could stash his car somewhere inconspicuous behind her building while he tried to find the source of the compelling dreams. He ran up the exterior stairs to her kitchen door and found it locked. He was about to pound on it when he heard sirens coming down Main Street. Fishing his lock picks out of his wallet, Kane turned the deadbolt first and heard a yelp inside. Thinking some new danger lurked on the other side of the door, threatening Laura, Kane kicked it in, breaking the jamb near the knob, and lunged into the kitchen, pistol in hand, throwing the door closed behind him. There, across the kitchen, using the refrigerator for cover, Laura held a shotgun leveled at Kane.

"Whoa, whoa, whoa, easy: I'm not a local, remember," he said, pointing his pistol at the ceiling and taking his finger off the trigger.

"I know exactly who you are," she whispered, shaking so much the barrel vibrated against the fore-grip slide. "You're Solomon Kane."

Kane blinked a few times rapidly, opened his mouth to respond but found nothing immediately available in his head. "Okay, I wasn't expecting that," he managed to say. She started breathing heavier, getting more excited by the second and still holding the shotgun on him. "Easy now; yes, I am Solomon Kane and I'm guessing you've read some pretty horrifying things about that name."

"I saw your car," she said. "I half worried you were some kind of psycho, here because of the murders, so I did an internet search with the make and model. Nothing came up so I added 'mass murder' to the search and there was a picture of you."

"Better than Facebook, huh?" he said but she didn't even register the lame attempt at humor. "Can I maybe explain something?"

"You killed all those people," she said.

"Easy, take it easy, everything's fine," he said. "I'm just going to put this pistol on the table, very, very slowly. You're the only one armed, totally in control. Okay?"

"Get out," she said.

"Okay, not quite that in control," he said.

She bounced up and down on knees that were growing weak, trying to stay standing or trying to work up the nerve to pull the trigger.

"Laura, please listen to me," he said. "You don't know the whole story yet. Which group did you read about?" She didn't respond. "Alright, it doesn't really change anything. I did kill those people but not because I was nuts like the folks here on your cozy little island. The people I killed were part of a cult, or several cults actually. They capture people, usually drag them out into the woods, and then kill them in the name of their dark god Cthulhu. Have you ever heard that name?"

"No," she whispered and didn't seem at all comforted.

"Good," he said. "Safer that way. You can look most of this up online. I can see your laptop open there on the counter. Type it in: C-T-H-U-L-H-U."

"I'm not taking my eyes off you," she said.

"That's going to make this harder," he said. "These cults, they hunt down people and sacrifice them; I hunt down the cults and put an end to it, and them. That's why I'm here, Laura. We thought a cult had set up shop on Dunsany Island."

"We?" she said. "Who's we?"

"I'm what's called a Venator," he said.

"What's that?" she said.

"Are you going to believe anything I say?" he asked, trying to grin.

"No," she said.

"Then we're not getting anywhere," he said. "Would a crazy-as-hell mass murdering asshole do any of the things I've done today? Does that make any sense? Could he put dreams in your head? In the heads of everyone in town? Come on, Laura. Wouldn't I have just shot you when I came in, when you didn't have the nerve to shoot me, because you weren't sure—and still aren't—and kinda because, uh, you still have the safety on, on your Mossberg."

She looked down and then quickly back up, almost hysterical at having taken her eyes off Kane, never having seen the safety.

"Fooled ya," he said. "Whoa whoa whoa, sorry, sorry! The safety really is on; it's that thing on top, just push it forward. Or you could not; I wish you wouldn't."

"Now's not really the time for jokes, you know," she said, a tear sliding down one cheek. She dropped the shotgun from her shoulder, keeping it in her hands at her thighs. "I don't think I can shoot you. But if you try to come closer, I sure as hell will try!"

"I'm not coming any closer," Kane said, shaking his head. "I'm just going to sit down right here, is that okay?"

"Yes," she snapped.

He pulled a chair back and settled slowly into it. "Take my pistol, if you want."

She did and stuck it in the waistband of her jeans. She then brought the laptop to the table and said, "Okay, talk!"

He didn't say anything and waited. She typed in Cthulhu and tried to read a little of what was available while still keeping an eye on him. After a minute, the strain of her face suddenly lifted into paleness. She looked up.

"Wild, isn't it?" Kane asked.

"There are people really doing that?" she said. He nodded. She asked, "And you hunt them down? You're a—what did you call yourself—a Venator? What's a Venator?"

"Venator is simply Latin for hunter," Kane said. "The first Venators were Roman. You see, in the Classical Age, Cthulhu was just one of many gods worshiped, even though he isn't technically a god but a priest of a group of gods collectively known as The Great Old Ones, who used to rule earth and enslaved humanity. Scroll down, you'll see it. The Romans were funny about other people's gods. They would allow the people they conquered to continue to worship their own gods provided they also worshiped Rome's gods. In some instances, though, they would deem a foreign god—or his worship—dangerous and would outlaw it. But, they didn't want

the foreign god to become angry with Rome so they would perform its rites and worship in private, just to appease it. Cthulhu
was one such god. Cthulhu requires human sacrifice, and when
the stars are in proper alignment, if enough are killed in his name,
a door to his sunken city of R'leyh will open and he will come
forth and call The Great Old Ones from their slumber to retake
earth and enslave mankind. Rome, obviously, wasn't keen on the
idea and only performed enough sacrifices to keep Cthulhu from
sleeping too restlessly, sending dreams out to his minions to stir up
trouble. Problem was, after Constantine decided to do an end run
around his political opponents by converting the Roman Empire
to Christianity—thus stripping his rivals of their influential positions as High Priest of this and that cult, Jupiter, Dis, whatever—all
the worship of foreign gods came to a halt. Cthulhu, no longer
appeased and his cults no longer hunted and controlled by the
Praetorian Guard (who, by the way, were first established not as
the Emperor's bodyguards but as cult hunters and monster slayers),
grew restless and his cults began to form again. With Rome weakened and Constantine ruling the Empire from Constantinople,
Cthulhu cults flourished in Italy and Gaul. After the sacking of
Rome by the Vandals, Visigoths, and finally the Ostrogoths, the
last remnant of the Praetorian Guard was forced underground and
became the first Venators, hunters of Cthulhu's cults. Since then,
pretty much anyone who discovers the existence of the Cthulhu
cults and decides taken up arms against them, and against the
annihilation of mankind they wish to bring about, will eventually
run into the Venators. We're not a tight organization, not anymore; attempts to make it so always fail. We're mostly just people
who've, who've," Kane swallowed as the dream he had while driving
returned for a flashing second, "who've lost loved ones to the cults.
It's not exactly a healthy way to deal with grief, Laura, I'll grant
you. But we do what we can. I've been doing it for about ten years

now. My fingerprints have ended up at a lot of crime scenes. But I stand by what I've done."

Laura had laid the shotgun down on the kitchen counter and was scrolling through web pages. "Jesus," she whispered. Looking up, she said, "I can't believe this. Or I wouldn't if it weren't for the busloads of crazy that Dunsany Island has had for the past three months. You know the FBI website says that you Venators are the cult."

"I'd heard that," Kane said.

"They also say you may be a militant Irish Catholic organization waging private war against a hedonistic sect of Protestant West Indians," she read, looking confused.

Kane took a moment to process that. "Okay, a bit out there," he said. "Obviously they've never met Hector. Hector, a fellow Venator, is about the most hedonistic person I know."

"I guess you never get afraid anymore," she said sourly. "You joke at everything!"

"Sorry," he said. "Yes, I get afraid."

She sat down and crossed her arms. Evening was falling and the kitchen was growing darker. "I don't know how much more of this I can take," she said, her voice breaking. Kane made to stand up, to walk over and comfort her, but she snapped, "Sit down!" He did. "My friends, my parents, their parents. It's only a matter of time before my friends' kids start with the crazy."

"Wait a second," Kane said. "Ages, fucking ages!" He wrestled his cell phone out of his pocket, ignoring Laura hastily grabbing her shotgun, and called Helen. "Helen, ages. No, no, listen, the ages of the murderers, do you have them on a spreadsheet yet? Don't be offended, it just means I know you; not that your absurdly organized and predictable. Okay, okay—look, this is not the time. Their ages: nobody under thirty, right? Ha ha, knew it! That's our first bracket. It means something. Disappearances—shit, you know what? I'll do the research here. I beat up the Sheriff—who is out of his gourd by the way—and am on the run. Yes, again. Can you do your thing? Not that I think he'll call for State Police help. Thanks. I'll call later tonight. I will. Bye."

Kane left his seat and began pacing. After a minute, he saw Laura following his every step with the muzzle of her shotgun. "Listen, sister," he said, "lay off with the gun, will you? You're not going to shoot me and we both know it. Thirty years old: I think that means that whatever's causing the dreams and craziness was here thirty years ago. Or arrived thirty years ago. No, that can't be it. Left thirty years ago? You're kind of an authority on weird stuff around here: have there been any odd disappearances over the years? Maybe about thirty years ago someone vanished after going nuts?"

Laura dropped her shotgun on the kitchen table with a thud. "Shit," she said. "Yes, there was. There used to be a priest who lived in the old church, the mission church out in the woods. It was here from when the Spanish tried to settle the island in the sixteenth century. He refurbished it and held mass, although there was only one other Catholic lady in town and she eventually moved to San Francisco to live with her son's family. The whole town loved him! Even though we weren't Catholic, he was one of our favorites. He'd talk to everyone, very nice. I remember his face, his whiskers. He was so kind. It was sad, though, because before he went away . . . away . . . he went, oh, he went a little crazy." She looked up at Kane. Kane nodded his head, grinning ear to ear, and then pulled his chair over and sat down. "Father Kilpatrick—don't say anything funny about his name! He said he'd been visited by an angel, at the beginning. Then, later on, he just said visitor, instead of angel. And then he was gone. No one knew when or where to."

"And he live out at this old Spanish mission church?" Kane asked.

"Yes," she said.

"Think you can find it in the dark?" he asked.

"Jesus but you do ask a lot of people, don't you?" she breathed.

"Only everything," he said.

She nodded.

CHAPTER 8

THE MISSION

THE SUN LIT the sky in strips of red, yet underneath the canopies of ancient trees night had already fallen. Kane and Laura ran through the forest toward Dunsany Island's southwestern shore, and toward the nearly forgotten Spanish mission church. Twice, as they crossed local roads or trails, they could hear the roar of Sheriff's vehicles and the shriek of sirens. And everywhere around them, the ubiquitous insects thrummed their primordial call to count time with generations and the coming of death.

The rolling terrain must have kept the developers at bay, when Dunsany Island was made safe for investment. To the conquistadors who built the mission with enslaved native labor, the rippling land was a natural bulwark. Rising out of a nature-torn trench, the mud-brick building with its arched gate and low roof was green with moss and dark with abandonment. Whatever restoration Friar Kilpatrick had accomplished thirty years before had been undone: nature had taken possession of the walls, flora owned the fountain, and the nave was a roost for birds.

With the Sheriff's pistol in hand and his shoulder to the wall, Kane peered around the broken gate arch at the tiny grounds within. Behind him, Laura covered the nearly extinct trail, down which the Sheriff's men might come if they guessed rightly. Seeing no movement except the swaying of ropey strands of moss shifting in the rising breeze, Kane motioned them forward and crept slowly around the silent fountain and into the church.

Along the naked wooden beams overhead, scores of birds sat motionlessly and nearly silent, a faint cooing fluttering down without apparent source. The tread of each step sounded indecent to the trespassers as they scrapped their way, breathing through their mouths, the dense air smelling of rot too thick for nostrils. At the building's far end there was a podium. Circling it, gun pointed as if expecting to find some hideous thing huddled there, Kane slowly traversed the darkest part of the building. Nothing. If ever a bible had sat upon the podium's top, it was long gone: a layer of dust an inch thick and turning to mud covered nearly everything. Surveying the building, as their eyes adjusted to the darkness, Laura saw a hatch in the floor, to one side of the nave. Kane trotted back to the entrance and found a candle near a statue of Mary. Coming back, Laura opened the hatch as Kane lit his candle and then led them below.

"Why would there be an underground room in the mission?" she whispered, staying close, though nearly walking backward to keep her shotgun pointed at the entrance stairwell, steep as a ladder.

"Natural air conditioning, being underground," Kane said. "Down here it would be cool enough in summer and warm enough in winter."

"But the smell," she said.

"Yeah, something reeks down here," he said.

The candle's faint light could not reach both mud walls at the same time and only strained a few feet ahead. When finally they reached the far wall, they found a cot and rough shelves cut out of the earth, containing several books. They also found a desk upon which lay a curious cylinder connected to a few metal boxes by old, cloth-covered wires.

"Did Father Kilpatrick live down here?" Laura said. "How awful. I wonder why he chose this."

"Vow of some sort, perhaps," Kane said. "Hey, you see that?"

Kane took a quick step toward the head of the cot and found a switch attached to a small junction box. Flipping it, four light bulbs snapped to life around the room. Laura caught a shout in her throat and tossed a momentarily angry look at Kane.

"I guess he must have had power run out to the old mission during his refurbishment days," Kane said. "Although, maybe it had something to do with that evil looking contraption on the table. And look at this."

He took a book from off of the thin and crumbling pillow at the head of the cot. It was a simple diary written in a spidery hand. Kane handed Laura the candle and gently opened the book, thumbing through the years, past half-filled pages, until he came to days that took page after page to record. Where the church's repaired roof took a paragraph, four pages were devoted to something Kilpatrick called the Migou.

"The Migou returned today," Kane read. "And have told me the time for my journey has arrived at last. It will take several days to prepare me for our trip but I shall feel no pain, despite the loss of my earthly body; the machine they instructed me to assemble will see to that. And the reward! Oh, the reward is more than god could grant. I shall be immortal on their world, blessed with a body such as theirs, one that obeys the commands of will, subject to thought, not imposing cruel animalism upon the exalted mind. Such is their mode of travel that a fragile human body could not survive. My mind safely freed from such weak flesh, I shall travel with them, to Iukkoth."

"That is the craziest, most, I don't even know," Laura said. "Let's get out of here; we can read it upstairs."

"Just a second," Kane said, flipping to the last written page. "The Migou have come and say now is the time. I shall go with them to Iukkoth, to Yuggoth, and there amid their glory and knowledge I shall meet Nyarlathotep and the bounds of the universe shall be lifted from me forever."

The lights went out.

"Kane, Kane, Kane," Laura repeated quietly as a violet glow grew and swirled in the corner near the table. She tore her eyes away from the radiating mist and looked at Kane. Sweat beaded on his forehead and his eyes might as well have been shut for all they seemed to perceive. His mouth moved with inaudible words, he almost swayed in his delirium. "Kane, oh god no, Kane," she said, shaking him lightly by the arm. "Please, don't dream, don't let it get you."

The swirling violet mist coalesced with a crack like lightning into a convoluted ellipsoid, segmented with pyramidal rings of a fungus-like substance from which fleshy wings stretched raggedly; its head bristled with a multitude of antennae and sensory organs for which no human language had a name. It spoke, or made itself known through a mode beyond speech, and Laura knew it commanded.

She backed away as Kane turned slowly toward her—and then blasted shot after shot at the monstrosity in the corner. But the 00 pellets seemed to have no effect, passing harmlessly through and burying themselves in the mud wall behind the thing. She looked in horror at her weapon's uselessness but continued to fire until Kane suddenly swiped her shotgun out her hands and sent it clattering into a far corner. She threw herself away from him, back against the mud wall.

"Kane, please, please think about what you're doing," she said, struggling to keep calm. "Wake up, don't listen to what it's saying."

In a sleepwalker's shuffle, Kane crossed the rough floor, passed the creature in violet who whispered darkly, coming at last to the master junction box on the wall. In the glow of the whisperer in the dark, Laura could see wires rise from the box through the ceiling, bringing in the electricity that powered the room's lights. Kane dropped his pistol as he came to a halt and then grasped the wire that ran from the junction box to the bizarre objects on the table.

He mumbled to himself as he rotated with tiny steps to face her: "Standing in the noonday sun trying to flag a ride; People go and people come, see my rider right by my side; It's a total disgrace, they set the pace, it might be a race, the best thing I can do is run."

Kane ran one hand down the wire to the metal box on the table, where the wire split into two, the positive wire going in one side of the box and the negative going in the other. He wrapped his fingers around the positive and jerked it out; something inside the box popped. Holding the positive wire firmly, he pulled the box off the negative wire with his other hand and dropped it forgotten to the floor.

Laura said, "No, no, no, no," as waves of unspoken words came from the whisperer in the dark, telling her 'dream, dream, dream.' "I'm not one of them, Kane! I'm not one of them!"

He took two shuffling steps toward her and held up the wires, pregnant with hundreds of volts of electricity—and then tossed them over his shoulder at the creature. The wires came into contact with the bulging, misshapen flesh of the glowing thing and instantly it shot rigid, screaming like a steam whistle, its wings vibrating the air with impotent motions of escape, filling the room with the noxious reek of its cooking substance. Kane stumbled forward as if kicked but made no attempt to leave; Laura grabbed him by the arm and dragged him up the stairs, desperate to flee. In a last impulse of existence, the Migue exploded, drowning the basement in darkness.

Compared to the stench below, the fetid air of the moldering church was cleanliness incarnate. A second explosion below announced the overload of the panel as Laura stumbled under the burden of keeping Kane on his feet. They both crashed onto a pew, and the jar seemed to bring Kane around.

"Hey, what?" he said, shaking his head and rubbing his eyes. "What the hell happened?"

"You scared the shit out of me, that's what happened," she shouted and punched him in the arm.

"Ow!" he shouted back.

They snarled at each other for a minute, the scant light inside the church not illuminating much.

"What happened?" she repeated. "You started sleepwalking. You knocked my shotgun out of my hand and then—I thought—you were going to electrocute me. But you electrocuted the, oh my god, the monster. There are monsters in the world."

"Oh, that's right," Kane said as if remembering. "Of course, stupid thing."

"This makes sense to you?" she asked.

"Kind of," Kane said. "It made me dream, made me try to achieve that one thing I want more than anything in the world."

"Scaring the shit out of me is what you want more than anything else?" she said. "Mission accomplished."

"Heh, no," he said and rubbed his neck. "Killing things like that. It—or I should say he—he didn't realize what my dream was, what anyone's dream was. He had probably forgotten what dreams are. I think, I don't know."

"What?" she said, more calm now, guessing much of it herself. "You don't mean . . ."

"Oh, it definitely was Father Kilpatrick," Kane said. "What was left of him. He went, like he said in his diary, to Iukkoth or wherever and he had to leave his body behind. So they changed him into that thing downstairs, which, by his diary, is a Migou. I guess he did what he said he would, flew off to Iukkoth and his mind was detached from his physical being. The only thing is, maybe he became homesick, after thirty years. He came back and looked up everyone he ever knew. But he wasn't Kilpatrick anymore: what is a human if the mind is divorced from the urges, the lust and the fear, perpetrated by the flesh? Controlling it is one thing; not knowing it is another. If he really did see the secrets of the universe revealed, maybe it was too much for human consciousness to handle. From what I felt in the basement down there, I don't know. Maybe he never meant to hurt anyone; maybe he wanted to know what it was like to be human again; maybe he wanted his old town to find as much happiness as he did but didn't realize dreams must be tempered with reality, where action is concerned; or maybe his coming here was an attack, a way to torture him devised by Nyarlathotep. That's a name not unknown to the Venators; it appears in many Mythos texts, the *Unaussprechlichen Kulten*, the *Necronomicon*."

"That was poor Father Kilpatrick," Laura said quietly. "Touching our dreams, only our dreams weren't worthy."

"Something like that," Kane said. "Although, since he never made anyone but locals dream, until me, my guess is he was visiting only the people he knew in life. He probably heard me reciting his words and reached out to me, probing my dreams trying to determine who I was."

"And your dream was to kill him?" she said.

"Not exactly," Kane said. "Not him specifically. Just things like him, I guess. Not you. I just met you. And if any thoughts of you entered my head, Laura, I can assure you, the ones concerned with doing things to you didn't involve murder."

She leaned a little closer but said nothing.

"All in a day's work," Kane said with a heavy sigh. "Now I have to swim across Calibogue Sound and walk down to Georgia, to escape the still-dreaming Sheriff Jackson. Fantastic."

"Not this minute you don't," she said.

BOOK 5

THE
NAKED TRUTH

CHAPTER 1

ONE LUCKY OLD COOT

I 95 WAS NOTHING but the sound of tires, a rhythmic heartbeat of segmented asphalt tapping south and west. Despite the
strange smell that greeted them crossing into Delaware, Kane
had left the top down. It had given him and Hector a good excuse
not to talk, trying not to breathe the stink more than necessary.
Hector had taken the Amtrak down to Trenton, where Kane had
picked him up as a special favor to Helen. This was to be Hector's
first time back in the saddle since Iowa, since the stalk that had
ended with a gunshot wound and a badly burned arm. With his
motorcycle an exploded wreck in an Iowa junk yard, he had to ride
shotgun the whole way to Maryland.

"No way for a man to travel," Hector mumbled into the clean
air of Maryland. "Not to start a stalk."

Here it comes, Kane thought. *An hour and a half without a
complaint, you must be boiling over.* "Surprised you haven't bought
a new bike," he said.

"Shit," Hector spat out the side of the car. "It may have been past time to trade in that beauty, get it off my MO, but I ain't going to just dump her like it was nothing, move on without a mourning period. Surprised you ain't still puttering around in the Cutlass POS."

"Lost her on my last stalk," Kane said. "Probably towed off the island by now."

"Yeah, I guess I heard that," Hector said. "Didn't you lose your piece, too?"

Kane glared at Hector as the other man's smile lifted itself up into his mustache. Despite the rough treatment of late, Hector looked the same as ever (except for the obviously burned arm). His long hair blowing about in the speed of the car had no gray in it, despite his forty-some years; neither did his mustache and mutton chops; he wore his biker's regalia straight out of a Roger Corman film—topped with ancient, chipped mirrored shades—with a uniform's precision.

"You look like Mad Max with the arm missing off of your jacket," Kane said, motioning with his chin at Hector's bare right arm. The sleeve had been burned off below the bicep.

"This is my jacket," Hector said.

"What's left of it," Kane said. "Why not get that off your MO, too, and buy a new one?"

"This is my jacket," Hector repeated louder.

People who live on the road, Kane thought as he shook his head, *on the move, no homes and little to call their own, no regularity, no roots, the only place they belong is in their clothes.*

"Is that a new tattoo?" he asked.

Hector beamed a toothy grin and held his forearm closer. "Not exactly," he said, pointing out ridges and ripples in the pulpy mass of burned flesh, congealed like pink lava and stained by cave painters. "I had one here that got messed up by the fire; a cute little Mexican girl, a really beauty, too. Didn't look like much once the puss stopped," he said, searching among the piled flesh for some sign of the former picture. "So I had Gus turn what was left into this."

"Yeah?" Kane said. "But what's it, you know, what's it supposed to be?"

"It's a '68 Impala," Hector barked. Kane peered at the forearm and nearly hit the guard rail along the inner median of the road, squinting at the black and blue ink. Hector sighed and put his hand behind his head, inverting his forearm as if he was about to lay back for a nap.

"Ooooh, there it is," Kane said. "I see it now."

"It's perfectly clear," Hector said.

"Right," Kane said. "You invent a story for why it's upside down? Something to tell the barflies when you kick back on your stool, one bare arm cocked behind your head?"

"I know what I'm going to tell you," Hector said. "It starts with fuck and ends with you. Why the hell should I make anything up? I'm not a pathological liar like some people: I don't need to tell the locals stories during *my* stalks."

"Sure, you just burn their whole fucking town down," Kane shouted.

"Like you've never burned down a town before," Hector shot back.

"Not to flush out people I only *suspected* to be in the cult, you crazy shit," Kane said. "And how old was the one kid up in Odiome?"

"That little bastard was more than half crazy from the Innsmouth jewelry they had him wearing," Hector shouted angrily. "Don't give me that crap. That little fucker came at me with a hatchet: what would you have done?"

They glared at each other for a minute before Kane said, "Did you bring a briefing from Helen or what?"

Hector stared straight through the windshield until Kane wondered if he would refuse to share what info Helen had found. Then he said, "Dr. Richard Grendel. Professor, Gradonfield College, Maryland."

"Never heard of it," Kane said.

"No surprise there," Hector said. "Even for a college boy like you; although 'boy' is maybe pushing it—pops. Gradonfield is a tiny, third-tier liberal arts college, for the most part, but it has a respected economics program. And for the last four five years, a suddenly thriving archeology program."

"Dr. Richard," Kane said.

"The old coot's been too lucky," Hector said. "Once in a life-time an antiquarian might find an important text, important to us. Or a statue or jewel or something. This son-bitch? He's found a dozen. He came back from Greenland with a *Liber-Damnatus*—intact; from Thailand, a Cthulhu idol the size of a beer keg; from Hungry, a few chapters of *The Tarsioid Psalms*—printed on human skin. Any one of those would make a career. He never comes back empty handed. He's like the King Midas of creepy human-sacrificing cult memorabilia."

"Kinda out in the open, isn't he?" Kane said. "To be active in the cult, I mean. Why draw that much attention?"

"Hiding in plain sight," Hector said. "And who says he's only collected the stuff he's given to museums or written about? He could have storehouses full of who knows what."

"*Could* have," Kane said. "He *could* be hiding in plain sight. Remember the 'could' part. We don't need to go in and burn his house down, first thing. What else?"

"We *could* burn his house down," Hector said. "The other thing is that kids have been going missing from the college. That's not huge news; every year, at every college, a few kids fall off the map. Usually it's drugs or prostitution, running away to join the circus so they don't have to tell mommy and daddy they blew twenty-grand on booze and weed. But at least five in the last three years have made Helen wonder. They were all scholarship kids or kids with little or no family."

"So they wouldn't be missed," Kane said. "And let me guess: they all had classes with Dr. Richard Grendel."

"Burning down his house sounds pretty good about now, don't it?" Hector said.

Kane stepped on the gas and pushed the '94 Camaro convertible a little faster toward Gradonfield, its college, and Dr. Richard Grendel.

CHAPTER 2

DRESSED FOR
THE OCCASION

DRIVING UP COLLEGE Avenue, with its two-hundred year old white oaks lining the way and vine-draped brick buildings' stately columns soaring three stories into the air, the living history of the college implied a traditionalism that the students who walked the grounds seemed to violently contradict. Nearly every student who walked from the classroom buildings at the avenue's head down to the quads and shops leading to the cul-de-sac where the avenue ended was entirely nude.

Kane slowed down as he noticed the first knot of naked students strolling along, deep in conversation, the only fabric about them the straps of their book bags. Ever endangered by the uncanny, his right hand slipped down to the space between his seat and the gear shift, fingers encircling a Mk23 pistol. Hector needed a double take before he realized it wasn't his imagination, slipping his sunglasses off his nose as a smile spread across his face.

"What in the hell is going on around here?" he said throatily. "Oh, my, god—would you look at her? I don't see how you can be an atheist, Kane, when something *that* heavenly is walking around and—"

"Look to your left," Kane said.

"Why—holy Jesus!" Hector said, throwing up his arms defensively. "Now that's just nasty. That is the hairiest mother fu—that boy must weigh fifty pounds more when he gets out of the shower. I'm looking this way; much better this way. Hey, pull over a sec, I want to ask this beautiful young woman what's going on."

"We attract enough unwanted attention with your Mel Gibson wardrobe, Hector," he said. "We don't need a story floating around the sorority house about a creepy old man in a one-armed leather jacket catcalling on College Ave."

"Who's catcalling?" Hector demanded. "You don't think all these folks walking around nekkit is worth a moment's consideration? I've learned in my twenty years of stalking not to pass by anything out-of-the-way weird."

Classes having dismissed for the period, a cloud of mostly nude students wafted from each doorway. At a crosswalk, Kane had to yield to the sauntering pedestrians. Hector was not about to pass up the opportunity.

"Excuse me, miss?" he said to a group on the sidewalk. Kane's forehead nearly struck the steering wheel as he slumped at the shoulders. "Miss, can I ask you something?"

"Yes?" a tall woman said with the luxuriant condescension of youth, looking out from her circle of friends as if from an impregnable turret.

"I'm just going to ask," Hector said. "Why's e'erbody nekkit?"

"Why are you clothed?" she said without missing a beat.

Hector sat back in his seat as if he'd received the word of god. He then tried to undo his belt, but Kane slapped his hands away.

"You are not taking off your clothes," he told Hector. To the woman, Kane said, "There's no town ordinance against it?"

She smiled at Kane and walked over to lean on the Camaro's door. "The town council had been taken over by students once in the late '60s. They passed a law that said student club dress codes could not be held in violation of town ordinances. They pretended the motion was to protect their Civil War reenactment club; but when it was passed, they formed a nudist club. Tricky, huh? And the rest is history. A guy from the Libertarian Club found the ordinance in an old newspaper article, and revived the nudist club."

"Must be the biggest club on campus," Kane said, looking around.

"Everyone's welcome to join," she said, tucking a strand of hair behind her ear. "Even visitors."

Hector looked Kane up and down disbelievingly, and then up at the young woman and smiled. She stepped back from the car.

"Uh, thanks," Kane said. "Some place I can park?"

"By the student union," she said and pointed farther up College Avenue.

The cul-de-sac at the end of College Avenue encircled an enormous fountain that rivaled Chicago's famous waterworks. Around it, the student union, the bookshop, and a few student-run stores acted as Gradonfield's Main Street. At the far end, an administrative building tolerantly overlooked the bustling nudity of a student body gone wild. A few facilities' vehicles sat in designated spots around the cul-de-sac, others were filled by a few student-owned cars streaming with tickets, but otherwise the space was practically a park, filled with pedestrians. Kane slowly drove down the alley that led behind the student union to a tiny visitors lot.

As he and Hector walked back to the cul-de-sac, they decided to first check out the most recent student to go missing, a Terry Johansen, by questioning his roommate. Hector knew the name but not the location. After a slightly embarrassing conversation with another nudist, Hector and Kane were down the street at a Victorian revival, startling the kids playing PlayStation on the front room couch as they let themselves in and headed upstairs. At the roommate's bedroom door, Kane held up his hand.

"So, since this fellah roomed with the missing kid, he must be in the cult, right?" Kane said. Hector did not look amused. "How do you want to handle it? Shoot him first thing? Waterboard him and then shoot him? I know: I'll go siphon some gasoline out of the car and we'll burn down the house."

"I see you ain't done much work on your comedy routine," Hector said and pounded on the roommate's door.

Kane turned the handle and walked in.

On a couch so dirty its color could not be guessed, a thin, vaguely orange-skinned kid with hair like the Statue of Liberty sat naked, flipping through a book on pre-Celtic Irish art and smoking a hand-rolled cigarette of questionable contents. He looked up indignantly, at first, but seeing two grown men walking in on him, he quickly found the ash tray behind the arm of the couch.

"Can I help you, gentlemen?" he asked with the dignity of a butler receiving vagrants at the kitchen door.

"You Scott Yates?" Hector asked.

"Yeeeees," Scott Yates said without conviction.

"We've got a few questions for you, boy," Hector said and kicked the door shut.

"We'd like to talk to you about Terry Johansen," Kane said. "You roomed with him last semester, right?"

"Are you from his parents or something?" Scott Yates asked. "I thought they could give a shit about Terry."

"So you were close?" Kane said.

"No, no, like I told that other detective—and the cops—we didn't hang with the same crowd," Scott Yates said. "He was all, like, straight-edge and shit, you know? Hey, what did you say your names were?"

"I'm Kyle Broden," Kane said. "And you can call him Smithers. He hates it."

He winked at Scott Yates and Scott Yates thought it was the funniest thing he'd heard in the whole of his life. He sputtered and coughed and nearly asphyxiated trying to repeat the name Smithers. After a few abortive *The Simpsons* impressions, he settled down and re-lit his joint.

"Oh, fuck, that was funny, dude," he said. "But yeah, like I said, I didn't know the guy that well."

"We brought only the basic information on Terry," Kane said, thinking: *and how*! "We like to learn all we can first hand, for accuracy's sake. Do you know who his friends were, what classes he took, did he have a girlfriend, a boyfriend?"

"Naw man, I don't really know that stuff," Scott Yates said. "I think, like, yeah."

"Concentrate you little shit," Hector said and took a step toward him. "Or that joint is going up your boney ass."

"Easy, Smithers," Kane growled.

"Shit, man, take a hit," Scott Yates said, offering his joint.

"Did he talk about anything the last day or two you saw him?" Kane asked.

"What? Yeah, I guess," Scott Yates said. "He was, like, into some club all of a sudden, took up all his time. I don't know what it was about, but he was def off his schedule, you know? And he was a dude that never came off his schedule. You know what I'm saying?"

They knew what he was saying and didn't like it much. *A sudden interest in an unknown organization,* Kane thought, *and a few days later he goes missing.* He and Hector shared a look and then Hector demanded to see Terry's things. No dice: everything had been shipped back to his uncaring parents. Scott Yates couldn't help them on Terry's friends or schedule, either, and hit his J so hard he was losing both interest and coherence. They left and walked back to the cul-de-sac.

CHAPTER 3

INTRODUCTION
TO FINANCE

"SO NOW WE go shakedown the professor?" Hector said. "Or do you want to maybe drop by a sorority, question some coeds?"

"That Yates kid wasn't much use," Kane said, barely listening. "But he did mention another detective. I don't like it."

"Why?" Hector said. "It's a sure thing his parents would hire some private help if the local PD couldn't find their boy."

"But Yates said the parents didn't care," Kane said. "I could see them putting up a front with the police, but why throw money after it?"

"You basing this on the word of a pot head?" Hector asked. "That kid doesn't know what *he* thinks let alone what some parents he's never met are thinking."

"That's just my point," Kane said. "If that kid's level of basting is normal, it'd take a hell of a lot of complaining on Terry's part for his dislike of his parents to burn through the fog of weed and indifference. So who sent the PI?"

"Cult sending a cleanup crew?" Hector asked. He stopped Kane by the arm as they stood looking at the fountain. "I heard of that being tried by a sophisticated cult in France, once, but the Black Shroud stomped them flat. Those European Venators don't fuck around."

"I don't know," Kane said. "A weird town is usually comforting: you don't second guess yourself. This place? Something ain't right."

"Shit, it's all these fine young things walking by," Hector said. "Your monkish ass hasn't seen nineteen-year old flesh since college days, I'm guessing. No blood in your brain right now. Well, heave some up there for a second and answer me this: if we don't know anything about where and how this kid got nabbed, and know nothing about his friends and routine, how we going to track him? I say we can't and we go knock over Dr. Grendel."

"A college kid?" Kane said. "His entire life will be on Facebook. We just need to get to a computer and look."

"And we're going to do that how?" Hector said. "Go to the computer lab?"

Kane pointed to the café across the cul-de-sac. "We can borrow one," he said. "May need a bribe, though. You see what I see?"

Hector followed Kane's gaze back to the mingling nudity at the fountain's edge where, moving amongst the svelte and the curvy, the bronze and the brown and the pearly and the pink, was a decidedly overdressed young man in a hooded sweatshirt and cargo pants.

"Popular lad," Kane said.

Hector laughed with no mirth in his voice. "Yup, sure is," he said. "Shakes hands with everybody—right after they pull their wallets out of their backpacks."

Kane nodded in one direction and then made off across the cul-de-sac directly toward the hoody. Hoody caught the movement, saw the six-foot three-inch wrinkled blue suit walking toward him with that particularly authoritative stride that said, 'You owe me,' and Hoody turned the other way. He went swiftly through the crowd of sun and fountain bathers in the general direction of the café—and suddenly there was a man in front of him nearly as big as the blue suit, in a torn leather jacket thick with zippers and chains, staring bloodlust at him. Hoody recoiled back into the chest of the blue suit. He spun and found an unshaven chin an inch from his eyes.

"ID," the chin demanded.

"Wha-what?" Hoody said.

"Now, son; let's see some ID," Kane demanded. "Take your hands out of your pockets."

Hoody looked up into eyes he'd never seen on a cop before and a tremble born in his bowels shot through his liquefying guts up to his mouth. No words spilled out.

"Let's go, boy," Hector said behind him with a shove. "Show us those hands."

"And they better come out with what you've been peddling at my fountain," Kane said almost softly, "or—and this may surprise you—you'll have struck an officer of the law."

Hoody took his shaking hands out of his pockets and tried to say something about never having sold anything before, only trying to get rid of some stuff he didn't want, and on and on. Kane swiped the bag of weed out of the kid's hands and stashed it in his jacket.

He said, "I can tell this is your first time."

"It is, sir," the Hoody said. "It so is."

"Let's see your ID," Kane said and the kid handed it to him. "Ralph Blumberg. Write that down," he told Hector. Hector mouthed a certain two-word phrase over Ralph's shoulder and then pantomimed writing in a notebook. "Listen, Ralph, I don't want to see you out here again. I know we can't stop this sort of thing on campus, but we don't have to tolerate it out in the open. You make a spectacle of yourself again, I call your parents—and expel you. Capisce?"

"Totally capisce," Ralph assured him and then walked away, very tight in the seat of his trousers.

"Now why did we do that?" Hector asked quietly as they watched Ralph walk away like Charlie Chaplin, down the street and into a frat house.

"I figure a kid in the café is more likely to let us use his laptop if he doesn't think we're cops," Kane said. "You know of a surer method of explaining that than a bag of weed?"

Inside, it was enticingly cool, surprisingly quiet with a soft Latin jazz playing from nearly invisible speakers, and thinly peopled with mostly clothed patrons. Kane and Hector slid in on either side of a sparsely bearded kid typing faster than a Nigerian Prince looking for offshore financial assistance. He looked up as the two older men pressed in on either side.

"So creepy," he mumbled.

"You are one fast typing son-bitch, you know that?" Hector said.

"Computer Science major," the CS major said. "I'm coding. You guys are sitting kinda clos—"

"Let me use your laptop a second," Kane said.

"I don't lend my laptop, *sir*," CS said. Kane surreptitiously dropped the bag of weed from his jacket pocket into the minute space between them. "What? Shit, man, knock yourself out. Just let me save and log out of—"

Kane pulled the computer away and brought up the active Chrome window.

"Whoa, whoa, whoa, let me save, let me save," CS said.

"Relax," Kane said.

"No, man, not my Facebook," CS hissed.

"Relax," Kane said. "I'm just looking for someone; I won't type anything."

After a minute he'd found Terry Johansen's page but it was mostly full of well-wishes and questions about what had happened. Except for a few, the messages were all from his home town.

"You here about Terry?" CS asked.

"Yeah, you knew him?" Kane said.

"No, I mean, I just heard he was one of the students who went missing," CS said. "We've had more than our share of missing persons the last few years."

"That's true," Kane said. "We're here looking into it for a few of the families. Terry was the latest. What's your take on it?"

"Me? I don't know anything about it," CS said, holding up his hands. "It was never anyone in Computer Science who disappeared."

"Was Terry or any of the others into anything weird?" Kane asked.

"Not that I know of but look around," CS said. "Does it look like a normal campus anymore?"

"No, it don't," Hector said. "So why is it so messed up all a'sudden?"

"You mean who's behind it?" CS said. "I couldn't tell you. The nudist thing is just a fad. Some idiot figured out the laws and then had an alum with a law degree and a Maryland license hook it up: bang—studying outside became impossibly distracting."

"What about this Professor Grendel, you know him?" Hector asked. Kane clenched both fists under the table but managed to keep quiet. "He connect up anywhere?"

"What, the resident genius?" CS laughed. "I don't think so and, really, with that gut? I sure hope he doesn't join the nudists. Now, Ms. Avery, Cryptography Theory? I would cut off an arm. Or, no, I need that to code: a foot."

"So, about Terry," Kane said after mouthing 'idiot' at Hector.

"You know who he hung out with? He has the entire college friended; it doesn't help."

"Sorry dude," CS said.

"That the admin building?" Kane asked. "Student information in there?"

CS said yes and Kane stood up to leave.

"But hey," CS said as Kane and Hector stepped away. "If you're looking for weirdos, check out the Libertarians. Besides the nudist thing, they've been more and more secretive, and more and more—I don't know—pushy the past couple years. And that's saying a lot for Libertarians."

Kane thanked CS and he and Hector left.

"Time to frisk Dr. Grendel's house, right?" Hector said.

"Not just yet," Kane said. "For one, we don't know if he's home. We need his class schedule. But while we're at it, I say we get the schedules for all the missing kids. You have their names?"

Hector nodded. He said, "How are we going to get the student info? You just gave away all our weed to bribe that useless sack."

"Helen, of course," Kane said. He pulled out his smart phone and called. "Voice mail. Odd."

"So?" Hector said.

Kane shrugged and then pointed his chin at the frat house Ralph had retreated into. "Ralph's bound to have more, right? Let's collect another bribe."

They crossed the street and let themselves into Ralph's frat house. The house smelled of a cleaning crew that knew the tenants couldn't tell the difference: stale cigarettes, stale beer, and weed. Taking the stairs quietly up, they heard aggravated talking behind a far door and crept toward it. Kane pulled his Mk23 as they closed in.

"Oh, now you want to go in blazing?" Hector whispered, pulling a similarly large Auto Mag automatic. Kane smiled as he drew a silencer and screwed it into place. "Where did you get that?" Hector demanded.

"Toys R' Us," Kane whispered. He leaned close to the door and listened. A second later, he nodded to Hector and stepped to the side. Hector put his size-twelve cowboy boot into the door where the lock would engage the jamb and the door flew open. Kane sprang into the room instantly, going down the left wall, covering the center of the room and left; Hector came in and covered the center of the room and right; Kane stopped halfway down the left wall, so as to not enter Hector's field of fire, and both looked at the room's two occupants, who were nearly hysterical with fear.

Kane gave the door a nudge with his heel and it creaked closed. Ralph was in the middle of the room, tears streaking his face, as an older boy sat bolt upright on a futon, dressed in a loud Hawaiian shirt, sunglasses like Hector's, and smoking a cigarette in a long holder. He was prematurely balding and whatever he'd laced his cigarette with perfumed the air with a taint like acetone.

"Whoa, whoa, whoa," Hawaiian shirt said. "The money and the dope is right there on the table; no need to add any death-penalty crimes to the list, right boys? We're all criminals; no way we can go to the police, am I right? I know you sure as hell ain't cops—but I got no beef! No, no, take it; I'm good."

"Shut that hole in your face, boy," Hector said. He stole a look at Kane out of the corner of his eye. Kane nodded about a sixteenth of an inch. "Turn to face the far wall."

Ralph began balling in earnest as he faced the wall, thinking of a certain St. Valentine's Day he'd heard about in US History II; Hawaiian shirt turned on the futon and looked at the corner where the wall met the ceiling as if at an art gallery, his cigarette holder at full erection. Kane took a step forward and swept all the drugs and money on the table into a little insulated lunch bag with a zipper top, closed it, and then backed to the door. He and Hector were down the stairs and out on the street in seconds, walking slowly, admiring the undergraduates in the new school uniform, no sign of guns nor excitement about them. Across the cul-de-sac, they approached the Administration Building.

"I can't believe how easy that was," Hector said, thumbing through the stack of money he held concealed under his jacket. "I was running a bit low, too. Never thought to knock over drug dealers before. Should have: easy money. Easier than knocking over banks."

"You knock over banks?" Kane shouted.

"Shh, Jesus fucking Christ," Hector hissed. "Keep it down. What's wrong with you? You've never knocked over a bank? How you keep in cash?"

"Credit cards from cultists," Kane said as if to a child. "Jewelry from their houses, corpses, etc. What happens if a bank guard pulls a gun? You just shoot a working stiff, like us?"

"You don't go in during the day, jackass" Hector said, revenge condescension dripping from his mustache. "You blow the wall at night, take what you want. The rep you have and you've never done any of the fun stuff Venators are known for?"

"We're not supposed to be known at all, asshole," Kane said.

CHAPTER 4

CRIMINAL JUSTICE

THE ADMINISTRATION BUILDING had the linoleum floors and corkboards papered with photocopies common to all such buildings. The staff drinking in the break room and illicit affairs in the maintenance closet were safely tucked away; to the outsider it was the model of educational efficiency. At a reception desk near the Dean's office, a fully clothed young woman tapped on her smart phone with incredible speed, though a bored expression stilled every muscle of her face—until she saw Hector and Kane stride quickly down the hall. She finished her text, sent it, and thrust her phone to one side. After the usual polite introductions and general lying, Kane asked to see the class schedule for Terry Johansen.

"I'm sorry, I can't give out that information," the student receptionist said. "Who are you again?"

"Concerned," Kane said. "Terry wasn't the only student to go missing from Gradonfield in the last few years. Some of the parents aren't happy with the investigations conducted by the local and campus PD. We're looking into it for them."

"And they didn't give you something as basic as their kids' class schedules?" she asked, her eyes laughing at them.

Kane looked over at Hector and said, "She's smart. How'd you end up on the reception desk?"

"Money, work experience," she said. "So what's the real story? Or don't I want to know?"

Kane dropped the little padded lunch cooler on the desk and flipped back the lid. *Corrupting the youth of the city,* he thought, *isn't that why they sentenced Socrates to death?* The receptionist peeked inside. Seeing the variety of drugs available, her eyes sprang open and she came to the edge of her chair.

"Whoa, hey, I have nothing to do with, wait a sec," she said, looking at Hector's outfit. "Are you, are you bribing me or something?"

Kane perused the drug bag with walking fingers until he found a small plastic bag with a few rolled joints inside. The receptionist looked over her shoulder and then down the hall, the tip of her tongue visibly pressing her upper lip. When she reached for the weed, though, Kane snatched it away; she caught her breath and looked up at him.

"I was hoping you could help me with that class schedule for Terry Johansen," Kane said and walked around the desk. He sat on its edge, the drug bag over his far shoulder, the weed in its little plastic baggie concealed in his fist. "Maybe a few other schedules, too."

"Shit, okay," she said and grinned. She held out her hand. Kane dropped the weed into it and she stuffed it into her bag, next to her chair. She pulled her computer keyboard closer and began bringing up the info. "So, you just want his class schedule? And who else's?"

They had her call up the class schedules for all five of the missing kids. She—name of Liz—asked them what they were looking for but since they didn't really know, she suggested putting the schedules into a spreadsheet to help sort the information.

"You're trying to see where they link up, huh?" she asked. Kane nodded as he looked over her shoulder.

"Doesn't look like they do, though," he said, scanning the columns. "A few shared this or that class but otherwise, looks like no. Can you add clubs to this?"

"I can do better than that," she said. "Why don't we add the clubs they officially took part in and the class rosters for all their classes. Could be they had a few classmates in common."

"Look at you," Kane said.

"I'm a Criminal Justice major," she said. "And this is awesome, even if you are probably bounty hunters or mafia or something. Okay, here we go: for the first two and the last one—Terry—they all had at least one class with Seymour Polson; and the middle two had at least one class with Mike Barrows."

"Do they connect?" Kane asked.

"Oh yeah, I don't even have to look that up," she said, leaning back in her seat, pulling one foot onto the cushion. "They're big in the Libertarian club: Seymour, he's the one who figured out the whole town ordinance-slash-nudist-club thing."

Kane walked a few steps from the desk, trying to make the pieces fit. Hector cleared his throat and asked, "So, how come you're not a part of the fun?"

Her usual withering response to a pitiful come-on cooled her expression but she caught herself and smoothed out her features before saying, "You mean, why am I not enjoying the liberation of living as nature intended?" she said. "Believe me, if it wasn't for the job, I would be. And as soon as last period ends, I'm out of these," she added, plucking at the shoulders of her loose shirt.

"Can you call up Seymour and Mike's schedules?" Kane asked, returning to the desk and looking over her shoulder.

"Sure," she said. "They share lots of classes, naturally. Both Economics majors."

"And both have taken what looks like every class offered by Dr. Grendel," Kane said and straightened up.

"Hot damn," Hector said.

"Kind of a strange set of courses to take for an econ major, isn't it?" Kane said.

"I don't know," she said, peering at the screen and scrolling down Seymour's record. "He minors in Anthropology."

"Interesting thing to take to business school," Kane said. Pointing at the screen, he asked, "What's that code mean?"

"Senior project," Liz said. "And those are summer internships and that's a semester of field work. Hmm, all of them are with Dr. Grendel. He's been with Dr. Grendel on all of his major archeological digs, wow. He ought to swap his major and minor. That kicks the hell out of my work experience."

"What class is Seymour in now?" Kane asked.

Liz hit alt-F4, killed the spreadsheet, and then laughed behind her hand. Kane shook his head in bewilderment. "So, you don't happen to have any speed in that cooler-bag, do you?" she asked.

"What?" Kane asked.

"It's just that finals are coming up and it really helps me study," she said.

"Study for your *Criminal Justice* courses?" Kane said. "Right, gotchya."

"Hey, don't judge," she said. "I'm realistic on the subject of drug laws. Anyway, I'm just asking. If there's any little thing I can do for you, you know I'd be only too happy to oblige." The promise in her eyes was far older than her years and is not taught in any class.

"You gotta be kidding me," Hector said. "Him again? What happened to chicks diggin' bad boys?"

She had no reason to hold back the withering look this time.

"Easy, Mel," she said. Kane couldn't catch his laugh before it burst out. "Showing off your scarification and biker mustache might work down at the roadhouse, but don't think every 'chick' likes the same thing. Like being called chick, for instance. Anyway, I dig your friend. He's like a grizzled Don Draper. We should party."

Kane looked about as uncomfortable as a prostate exam conducted in the town square gazebo. "I think, I probably have, somewhere in here, I'm not sure," he said as he rifled the drug bag, beet red. "Coke?" he asked, holding up another little baggie. "Why is there a salt shaker in here?"

"Let me look," she said, pulling at the side of the bag, adding, "you are the cutest thing; a grown man blushing like that."

"On our next stal—no—uh, mission," Hector said, "we go to my kind of town. This is getting on my nerves."

"Here," Liz said, taking a prescription bottle from the bag. "See, I'm not greedy. And you're no drug dealer but I won't ask where you got the good-time bag. Let's see where Seymour is."

She called up his schedule again, found he was in a seminar, one building away, and then gave them Dr. Grendel's schedule, too.

"You sure you don't want to hang out until I'm done for the day?" she said as she handed Kane a printout of the schedules. "You could interrogate me some more. I may even know a few friends who'd like Snake Plissken over here. My roommate would eat you alive: probably bite the other arm off your jacket."

Hector threw an expression at Kane almost luminous with hope, to which Kane answered, "No, now come on. We're working, remember?" To Liz, as he backed away, "Thanks but we're on the job, right now. We'll come back if we need anything. And hey, I know our methods don't show us in the best light, but you really did help out something good here."

"I know it," she said and then pretended to ignore them as they walked out, absorbed in another tapping text.

CHAPTER 5

THE STAHL

OUTSIDE IN THE heat, Kane shook his jacket as if he'd left a sauna. Hector slapped his back.

"You're like a little girl at her first dance," he said with a snort. "You get offers like that from nineteen-year olds *so* often, do you, that you can afford to turn them down? Not a bit of consideration for your partner."

"Oh, you're my partner now, are you?" Kane said as he stepped off in the direction of the Social Science building. "Why don't you go and snap a picture of Liz with your phone and send it up to Helen, see what she thinks?"

"What's Helen got to do with anything?" Hector said, his expression of denial so comical he had to cover it with his sunglasses.

"Right," Kane said. "Did Archie get back from a stalk as you were headed out? Is that why you've been a pain in my ass the whole day?"

"There are two little words I'd like to say to you," Hector said.

"Yeah, I remember from the last time," Kane said.

"I got a whole can of them, so just let me know when you run low," Hector said. After a minute of walking, though, he slowed and said, "Shit, I wasn't thinking. Sorry. How old would she have been?"

"Who?" Kane said and took a few steps before the dime dropped. As if it didn't cost him anything, he said, "Oh. She'd have turned seventeen this past April. I wasn't thinking about her."

"Naw, not with a stalk on the hook," Hector said, nodding his approval.

They continued through the meandering crowd of the rarely clothed to another edifice of brick and wooden columns. Down carpeted hallways, past oil paintings of illustrious alumni that no one had ever heard of, the two Venators said nothing. Coming to the small suite used for senior seminars, Kane glanced inside and then leaned against the opposite wall, watching the door.

Hector whispered, "You see him in there? Recognize him?"

Kane nodded. "Just like his student ID picture in Liz's file. We can take him on his way out. And by take him, I mean maneuver him somewhere private where we can size him up. Drop a few words out of the lexicon, see if he reacts."

"Seems straight goods he's our boy," Hector said. "Been on all of Dr. Grendel's expeditions, taken all of his classes—all of his *archeology* classes, and him an econ major. Add in him sharing classes with these others that disappeared: I'm up for dropping that punk in the middle of class."

"Take it easy," Kane said. "It's provocative, I admit. And it explains this whole nudist thing. But it isn't proof."

"The nudist thing?"

"Sure," Kane said, never taking his eyes off the door. "If you can get the whole campus running around acting hedonistic and wild, any rumors of bonfires and orgies in the woods just sound like so many barbeques and biology field trips. It's like you said: hiding in plain sight."

Hector pulled his sunglasses down by the bridge so he could see over them for a second. "That hurt, didn't it?"

"I've got a couple words for you, too," Kane said. "And a whole box of them back in the glove compartment."

They snickered at each other quietly and didn't at first notice the sneaking sound of sensible flats on carpeting. A woman, too old to be a student but too young to be a full professor, came toward them leaning to one side in the attitude of someone who is either declaring that she's lost, or that you are.

"Hello?" she said quietly when she drew near. "Can I, um, help you? I'm sorry, you don't look like students."

Kane stood away from the wall, trying to block as much of Hector and his garb as he could. He bowed a little at the hips and whispered, "We're waiting for class to end; don't mean to disturb."

"Are you parents or?" she said, leaving the option open.

"We're conducting a private inquiry," Kane said.

"Into what?" she asked.

"A confidential matter," Kane said.

"A private inquiry into a confidential matter?" she said, peeking around his shoulder to look at Hector. "I think I read that in a novel once. If you're here to talk to Professor Leary, you should go through his department. If you're here to talk to one of the students, you need to go through the school. This building isn't open to the public."

"Professor, what was it?" Kane said, turning on his grin.

She crossed her arms and bounced one foot a moment before answering. "Stahl, Jane Stahl."

"Professor Stahl," Kane said. "May I call you Jane? My name is Kyle Broden and I've been asked by the parents of some of the students who've gone missing to conduct an inquiry; a *confidential* inquiry. If we went through the school, it would get out and the parents would have reporters camped out on their lawns for the next month. Mostly we want to ascertain the depth and diligence of the local investigation. We won't cause a scene, I promise," he said and upgraded the grin to a smile. "The last thing our clients want is a scene. They're looking for peace, peace of mind, closure if we can do no better."

Jane looked at her shifting feet on the carpet and then said, "Yes, of course. Those poor parents—and those kids! I had one of them in a class I taught, Sheryl Prescod. It's terrible." She took a step to her left and a quick look into the seminar suite. "You're here to talk to Seymour Polson?"

Hector stepped around Kane and said, "How'd you know that?"

"The last detective," she said and then swallowed. "I'm sorry, the last detective interviewed him, too. Apparently he knew a couple of the missing students, may have been the last person to see them. He's the big man on campus, too."

"We heard he's the one who orchestrated the, uh, shall we say *interesting* student uniform," Kane said.

Jane blushed faintly but not as if it was anything more than what was expected. "Yes," she said a little loudly, and then ducked forward before continuing in a whisper. "Yes, that was him. His older brother had a friend, an alum from here, who defended Seymour and a couple others when campus police arrested them, a few semesters ago. Turns out a town ordinance supports the club's dress code."

"We heard that part," Kane said. "He seems like a kid with some pull. We also heard he puts together certain outdoor gatherings," he lied.

"You've heard about those?" she said. "That is something I think the administration would rather keep quiet." Kane zipped his lip and threw away the key. Jane laughed lightly and said, "I'm not worried about you. But the press? Orgies in the woods? We'd have camera crews combing every inch of that little forest behind the Admin building. That's where they hold them, you know."

"Have they ever got out of hand?" Kane said.

"How do you mean, out of hand?" she said. "They're not exactly in-hand to begin with."

"I mean, people getting hurt, fights, rumors along those lines," he said.

"Oh, yes," she said. "They can get a little, um, insistent with their invitations. I've made it a habit not to stay late grading papers when I know they'll be out communing with nature."

"You know when they'll be out there?" Hector said. "Is it posted somewhere?"

"I can tell you exactly," she said. "Come with me."

She led them down the hallway and up a flight of stairs to a closet that someone insisted was an office. Unlocking the center drawer of her desk, she took out a folded and often handled slip of notebook paper. Opening it, she came around the desk and stood shoulder to shoulder with Kane.

"Apparently they think of their parties as Bacchanalias," she said.

"Take Greek culture very seriously, do they?" Kane said, examining the paper.

"As seriously as they have to, I guess," she said. "One bright lad in their group must have figured out what time of the month or year or whatever a Bacchanalia was traditionally held and then made a chart. See, it's based on the position of the stars and the moon. They have one tonight, as a matter of fact. I'm not really sure what these symbols mean, though."

Kane motioned to Hector, who closed the door, and then came over. Both of them looked a little angry, or perhaps simply intense, while they picked out certain symbols on the page.

"Where did you get this, Ms Stahl?" Hector asked.

"I, that is, I," she said and backed away from him. "I confiscated it from a student, one who'd attended a lecture drunk. It was amongst his belongings—he'd brought a bottle of vodka to class, of all things—and I just heaped everything together, and then I saw this and I knew what it was from the rumors and so I knew it was their meeting schedule and I just didn't want to be bothered by them and look over my shoulder all the time when they're out there and—"

"It's okay, Jane," Kane said, putting a hand on her shoulder. "We're not accusing you of anything. You said you took it off a student: who?"

"It was, um, no, Mike—Mike Barrows," she said.

Kane met Hector's eye and could see the Venator's malice even through the mirrored shades. The sound of Hector's muscles clenching creaked the seams of his leather jacket.

"Can I take this?" Kane said, returning to Jane. "Or borrow it?"

"Yes, go ahead," she said. "The semester is almost over and Seymour will graduate. Maybe things will calm down around here without him."

"Maybe," Kane said.

Hector opened the door as Kane thanked Jane but as he passed through, he turned and asked a last question: "Any teachers ever go out to these Bach-a-nails-and-things?"

Jane looked a little offended but composed herself and said, "I've only heard it rumored that one *professor* has ever attended. I'm not sure I believe it, or, if I do, that he was there for any other reason than to study their efforts for scholarly reasons; he is an archeologist, after all."

"Dr. Grendel," Hector said. She nodded.

CHAPTER 6

A STALK IN THE DARK

THE SYMBOLS ON Jane's paper were those found on the statuette idols used by Cthulhu Cults in their human sacrifices. When drawn properly, the symbols seem to defy the laws of geometry, causing vertigo in the sensitive and, after long exposure, madness in those of artistic temperament. The reniditions on Jane's calendar were crude enough to be viewed safely but were unmistakable. If nothing else, the paper proved that someone knowledgeable—or at least who had exposure to a Cthulhu idol—had drawn the calendar. Hector said the timing was perfect and called Helen to get a satellite photo of the woods, to see if they could pick out the spot where the so-called Bacchanalias were held; he got her voicemail again. Kane remained pensive as they made their way back to the car.

"What the hell is she so busy doing?" Hector said, sending Helen a text of their situation. "We could use some recon on this sacrificial spot. The woods aren't big, I guess; shouldn't be too hard to find once those bastards light the bonfire and start flaying poor bastards alive."

"Something isn't right," Kane said, resting a hand on the burning trunk of the Camaro.

"What are you talking about?" Hector said, snapping his fingers for the keys.

Kane handed them over unconsciously. "This whole thing," he said. "We're missing something, I just can't see it."

"You the one who put the clues together, man," Hector said, opening his duffel bag inside the trunk and withdrawing a 12-gauge Mossberg. He loaded it as he spoke. "Couldn't be better: we've got those liber'tarian shits who were involved with the missing students writing out star charts with dread symbols on them; we've got our all-too-lucky professor going out to their parties in the woods; and we've got them creating the greatest diversion since a certain wooden horse to cover it all. It's them! And tonight, they're going down." He charged the shotgun and slipped it into a gym bag padded with clothes.

"Hold on," Kane said. "We don't have enough proof to go in shooting, not yet."

"The hell we don't," Hector said.

"Listen," Kane said. "We know that Grendel brought back a large idol, right? These hedonists may just have copied some of the symbols off of it because of how weird it made them feel. These were his best students, who'd chosen him as their mentor. If Grendel is just an antiquarian with the 'Midas touch' as you put it, he may have told them stories about Cthulhu and the cults and all the rest. Venators aren't the only ones who know about the cults."

"Yeah, but we are the only one's doing something about them," Hector said. He knocked Kane's hand off his shoulder and said, "And I'm a Venator—not some half-assed private detective. What are you hesitating for?"

"You were all fired up about taking a run at Grendel since the moment we got here," Kane said. "Well, let's go take a look at him. Let's get in place now, near his house; if he's in the cult, he'll leave to go to the meeting place and we can follow him. Better yet, we can pop into his house and take a look around, first."

"Second," Hector said. "We can just as easily stakeout the woods, sneak in close, and wait for him to arrive. We see an idol, we see a ceremony that looks legit, we blast. Afterward, we can go checkout Grendel's house—and then burn it down."

Kane shook his head. "Hector, I'm not taking you to that Bacchanalia," he said. "I'm not putting you in a position to massacre a group we don't know is in the cult."

"Taking me?" Hector laughed. "Bitch, I'm going. With or without you. And if those fucks look guilty enough to me, they're going down. That's the job."

"Hector," Kane said, "listen, they could look just like a cult, dancing around out there because of Grendel's research, but not be in the cult. They may have nothing to do with Terry Johansen's disappearance or anyone else's!"

"I'm doing this," Hector said. "That paper convinced me. I'll know if it's the real thing—be real obvious if they try to kill a mo. After twenty years, I don't fool easily. You want to come with, saddle up. You want to whinge about it, fuck off."

Not waiting for a response, Hector turned on his heel and walked slowly toward the edge of the woods. Kane watched, raging internally and at himself as much as at Hector. He had worked alongside—if not actively with—Hector a half-dozen times and this moment always eventually arrived. In Odiome, Hector walked after the stalk was half finished and the final wiping out of the cult had yet to happen, forcing Kane to take them on single-handed. In Iowa, Hector had jumped the gun, gone in early, and lost an idol—which was never recovered. In Georgia, Michigan, Maine, each time Hector would reach a point where he felt he was justified to either go in early or leave. In each case, Kane had either confirmed their suspicions at the last minute or finished the mission himself. But he knew it was only a matter of time before Hector made the big mistake; before Hector took one too many things for granted and killed innocent people. Kane hadn't used the phrase "innocent people" with him because he knew how Hector would respond: he'd have said he would rather a few innocent people die than a cult slip away. And if Kane ever heard him say that, he knew he'd kill Hector Troy.

Taking four extra magazines for his Mk23 pistol, which bulged too obviously inside his jacket even with the padding he'd sown under his arm, Kane made his way cross-country toward Dr. Richard Grendel's house. As he passed through the manicured copses of trees and around perfectly constructed ponds, he thought of what Hector proposed doing. He argued both sides of the situation, that Hector did have twenty years experience—nearly twice Kane's—and hadn't, as far as Kane knew, ever made a mistake in identification (not that Helen would have told him if Hector had), that a lot of evidence pointed toward Seymour and Mike and Grendel having had something to do with the disappearances, and Grendel had been suspiciously fortunate in his research and field work. It was dark by the time Kane reached a point at the top of a low ridge that overlooked the housing development where Grendel lived. He could see the house: no lights on. *Doesn't prove a thing,* he told himself. *But proof would take time, maybe too long; maybe long enough for Hector to kill a bunch of stupid kids drinking and fucking at a theme barbeque.* Kane shouted an obscenity and ran back toward the college.

The woods were a mass of shadows, huddled on the edge of College Avenue, where live music blared at the night. The sounds of reveling youth echoed from the centuries-old buildings as if out of the ocean, out of time, a memory of human joy and pain. When they came to the woods, however, the laughter and pounding baselines and calls of friends shrank, hesitating in the face of stoic obscurity. Above, a gibbous moon grieved for what it saw below, dripping faint light upon the trees, to seep from leaf to whispering leaf and never find the earth. Kane passed between the outliers, the sentinels of darkness, weaving among them before he plunged into their realm.

For a time he walked in near total darkness, finding the space between hulking trees with each crescent step. A sound, distant yet unmistakable, furtive and not animal, slipped past him as it fled back to town: boots crunching leaves. Boots that he guessed were cowboy. Following the sound, burrowing into the sightless world, reliant on sound and feel, other noises then came to him. More quiet and no less human, they stole across the void, whispered to him, and were gone. Then, the bare field of darkness took shape as a single point of wavering orange light threw texture and shape splattering down perspective lines of trees. As they drew closer, Kane could see the form of a man, huddled low to the ground, gripping something in his hands, darting from tree to tree. The light ahead coalesced into a fire, heaped into a mound of moving color, and around it shapes capered and shouted. Some in dread, others in ecstasy so terrifying no difference between pleasure and fear existed, the voices howled at the night and the fire they made in its despite.

Kane crept closer to the huddled form, slow step by slow step, always as close to the ground as he could, always deep amongst the shadows trailing from the trees. Close enough to see but far enough not to be heard, he watched the form's movements and knew it was Hector. The shotgun slipped noiselessly from the padded bag and Kane looked desperately at the bonfire, seeking some sign that he could allow Hector to do as he wished. Then a call went up from the glad and the shouting and dancing gave way to furious movement, the purpose of which was not immediately apparent. A sound like someone jumping on a bed thumped again and again, and the fire dimmed. Too late, Kane realized what they were doing: they were throwing bags of topsoil onto the bonfire, extinguishing it.

A faint red light, the size of a quarter, suddenly jumped onto Hector's back. It made a tiny circle and settled on his spine. Kane looked to his right just as the muzzle flash of an assault rifle sent a burst of fire at the red dot—and straight into Hector. Hector jumped forward as if throwing himself against the tree, and then fell onto his back. Three other lights leaped onto his chest and a shower of bullets smacked in quick succession through the blackness left by the dead bonfire. Kane, tracing a line from the flashing muzzle up the weapon to the man who held it, watched as two tiny dull green lights rose to the surface of his sight. The green light, he knew, was the reflection of the eyepieces from a pair of nightvision goggles: one of the men who'd shot Hector was creeping forward toward the body. Kane aimed just behind the glowing green orbs and fired: with his silenced Mk23's slide locked in place, it made less noise than the distant chirping of crickits. The man's falling body and the wet sound of his lifeblood's loss drew a quick jump from Kane. Diving to the ground, he stripped the nightvision goggles from the dead man's head and pressed them to his face, surveying a world turned green by light amplification, and saw three black-clad figures stepping gingerly toward Hector—and then saw Hector raise his shotgun.

The Mossberg's roar spat sparks into the murk; a dying killer's screams filled the night with panic. Using the infrared laser sight on the side of his pistol, visible only through nightvision goggles, Kane stabbed light at the next would-be killer followed it with a .45 round. The last killer fired wildly, trying to put a tree between himself and the apparently still breathing Hector, unaware of Kane and his silenced pistol. Kane dodged around the trunk of the nearest tree, still unseen, and took the last killer through the knee. As the assassin's cries replaced his expired companion's, Kane stood and delivered the coup de grace.

The sudden noiselessness of the woods was more pregnant with fear than all the screams and bonfires and firing guns. Kane quickly panned through 360 degrees, saw no one, and then charged over bodies and brush toward Hector.

"It's me, don't shoot, Hector," Kane said as he saw the muzzle of the shotgun rise toward the sound of his steps.

"Kane," Hector barked and then coughed. "Sum-bitch."

"That's gratitude for you," Kane said. Kneeling beside Hector, he looked through the nightvision goggles at the holes in Hector's leather jacket. "Just lie still, shit. I'll see if one of these guys has a field dressing."

"Don't need it," Hector said and rolled onto all fours, coughing. "That shit's like a mule with a bad temper, man. Just need to get my breath."

"Are you crazy?" Kane said. "You've been shot a dozen times—I don't know how you're even alive."

Hector stood up, leaning on his shotgun, and took a few deep breaths. He nodded his head and tapped his chest. "I told you," he said. "This is *my* jacket."

Kane looked more closely, illuminating the infrared lamp on the side of the nightvision goggles. He could see through the holes in Hector's jacket, see the dull shine of squashed bullets.

"Is that damn thing bullet proof?" he asked.

"Ballistic nylon, boy," Hector said. "Still hurts like a mother, though."

"Grab a pair of NODS and let's go," Kane said.

CHAPTER 7

ON AN ALTAR OF SALT

THEY HUSTLED THROUGH the woods, taking a more circuitous route back to the parking lot behind the student union. Still within the woods, they stopped to conceal their two pair of NODS and Hector's shotgun in his dufflebag.

"Not that this'll do much good," Hector said, moving clothes around to make the bag shapeless. "Everyone in town will know who made those guys dead, just as soon as their bodies are found. And then the cops'll bring in some forensic genius who'll find a strand of my hair or something, get my name from that. I'm in their DNA database."

"Yup, me too," Kane said. "We gotta find that Jane woman."

"What now?" Hector said. "You think they'll know she pointed the way for us?"

"Absolutely," Kane said. "Considering she was the one who sent us there to get killed. Think about it: she just happens to walk by when we're waiting to snatch up this kid, a kid who looks so perfect for the crime it's *like he's bait*. And then she happened to have taken a star chart with dread symbols on it away from the only other suspect? And *then* she neatly implicates the most obvious person who could lure Venators to the school, Grendel, in the supposed Bacchanalia? Come on, no way. And I figured out what was bothering me: the moon. There's nothing special about the stars' configuration tonight and the moon is at least a day past even a basic observance of Cthulhu—three weeks from a sacrifice! And when have you ever seen a cult post sentries for one of their orgies? Armed with assault rifles and wearing nightvision goggles? This was an ambush."

"Son of a whore," Hector growled. "I guess you don't need anything more conclusive on this Jane-soon-to-be-dead-Stahl?"

"No way they played her," Kane said. "She was calling the shots. Now, we need to move fast. Those bodies will be found by daybreak. Cops will be all over this place. And when her assassins don't return, my guess is she'll make a break for it. We need to find her first."

"Great, now all we have to do is wish real hard until one of us thinks up her address," Hector said.

"Or we could call Helen," Kane said. "It's the middle of the night; she's got to be out of class by now."

Hector pulled out his cell phone and called. "Nothing," he said. "Voicemail. What the hell is going on up there? Is she—son of a—she must have turned off her phone and Archie—cocsukmoderuckintardsht—I'm gonna pull off his arms!"

Kane walked out into the floodlit parking lot behind the student union and toward his car, keeping ahead of Hector so Hector couldn't see his poorly concealed grin. He pulled out his smart phone as he went and said over his shoulder, "If Jane's the real cult leader down here, she's been in business since the first kid disappeared and Grendel started batting a thousand. Which means, to keep up her cover story, she probably owns a home under her alias . . . and . . . Yahtzee: she's in the white pages."

A young man in a dark, overlarge letterman's jacket and a baseball cap worn at ten o'clock came swaggering out of the alley that led to College Avenue, pulled a MAC-10 submachine gun from under his arm, and opened up with full-automatic fire at Kane and Hector.

Hector gave Kane a shove as the first rounds came chattering out of the weapon's sound suppressor. Kane tumbled to the ground, sprawling behind a low-slung Honda, tearing out his pistol as he crawled on shoulder blades and heels behind the disintegrating car. Hector, behind the car's engine block, wrestled his shotgun back out of his dufflebag. The MAC-10 spat death at a thousand rounds per minute and chewed through the Honda at horrifying speed—until it burned through its thirty-round magazine and the kid shooting it shook the dry weapon in exasperation. Kane aimed under the car and shot the kid in the ankle; as the kid screamed in rage and pain, trying to fish a fresh magazine from his huge jacket, writhing on the parking-lot asphalt, Hector slid around the Honda's bumper on one knee and shot the kid through the head.

"Who the hell was that?" Kane said, collapsing onto his back, arms spread wide. "He didn't look like the others."

"If I know anything about the seedier side of life," Hector said as he stood up, "this little punk was not connected to our other business. He's the response to our earlier financial improvement scheme. I thought it was too easy, knocking over drug dealers."

"Mental note," Kane grunted as he sat up and heaved to his feet. "Don't stay long in the city where you've robbed drug dealers. New rule. Let's get out of here. We don't have until morning now."

"We're going on foot," Hector said.

"What? Why?" Kane asked as he came around the Honda. On the other side he saw his Camaro: a dotted line of bullet holes signed the car as a witness to a shooting. Kane swore and he and Hector quickly stripped the car of ammo and ran off, away from Gradonfield College.

The State Police helicopter that had been circling the college and surrounding area since Kane and Hector crossed into the housing development, where "Jane Stahl" was listed as owning a home, began widening its search pattern, coming closer and closer to the two men responsible for all the bodies. Keeping to backyards, creeping behind sheds and around detached garages, the two fugitives wound their way to the far end of the development. Kane's silencer came in handy for shooting out streetlights when they needed to cross a road and didn't want to be seen. Late as it was, few people were awake, despite the concentrated thunder of the helicopter passing overhead. As they came to "Jane Stahl's" street, lights only burned in one house near the middle of the block. Out front, a car idled with its trunk open.

Kane and Hector, lopping along as fast as they could while crouching, stuck close to the houses they passed, using the shrubbery for concealment—until, one house away, a motion sensor above a front door flipped on flood lights, illuminating the clapboards and throwing the two Venators' shadows on them like the capture sequence in an old thirties mobster movie. A man loading something into the car's trunk sprang upright and shouted, "La! La! Mglw'nafh! Mglw'nafh! Kane! Kane!"

He flailed for his assault rifle, resting against the side of the car, but managed only to knock it over and then kick it down the driveway before a blast from Hector's shotgun threw him over the top of the car. A door inside the garage flew open and another man in a jumpsuit similar to what the assassins had worn earlier saw the two Venators as they assaulted the house. He slammed the door closed and dashed down the hallway toward the kitchen, while behind him the door splintered and snapped as shot after shot was fired through it. He reached the kitchen table, and his weapon, in time to see Hector kick in the door from the garage and rotate in on one knee, Kane leaning in above him with the other man's assault rifle. The exchange of fire was brief and to the point. But as the guard dropped riddled to the floor, a figure in black threw itself—herself—across the kitchen, somersaulting through a doorway to the basement. By the time Kane and Hector reached the door, whoever was down there was ready. Automatic fire screamed from the basement, not giving Hector even a moment's inspection of the situation below.

"Now what?" he growled to Kane as the kitchen ceiling popped with innumerable bullet holes. "You hear that, right? In the distance? Those are police cars. We don't have much time. You better have an idea or these fucks will give up to the cops and the cult will spring them from jail."

"Sure, I've got an idea," Kane shouted over the bursts of assault rifle fire. He gave the hand signal for 'pull security' and then ran back to the garage.

Hector kept out of the cultists' field of fire, listening to the helicopter overhead and the police sirens closing in. Ten seconds passed like a century before Kane came lumbering into the kitchen with a lawnmower in his arms.

"The fuck?" Hector demanded.

Kane only smiled as he set down the lawnmower at Hector's feet and then, with the deliberation and raised pinky of a fussy English butler serving tea, he unscrewed the cap on the gas tank.

"You magnificent bastard," Hector whispered.

Kane thrust the lawnmower in front of the basement doorway and turned it onto its side. Gasoline bubbled and burped from the red metal machine and met with a few unearthly curses from the cultists below. Kane and Hector backed away and then, from the door to the garage, Kane shot the puddle of gasoline. Flames swarmed up the walls and poured down the stairs; fumes in the gas tank exploded and threw the lawnmower through the kitchen table. Kane and Hector bustled through the doorway and, without consultation, split up, each taking an exterior corner of the house.

Rather than be burned to death, the cultists in the basement tried to escape through the small windows near the foundation's ceiling. Kane let the first one—an ugly scar-faced man—reach the azalea bushes before dropping him with a silent round. With Hector blasting anyone who showed at the windows on the opposite sides of the house (covering opposite corners, they could each see two sides), the three remaining cultists used what they thought was the uncovered window. Each time, Kane let them get far enough from the house so that the next escapee wouldn't see his predecessor fall. The last to scamper from the window was "Jane Stahl."

In black, head to foot, hair pulled into a tight bun, she pulled herself through the window. Before she stood, though, she noticed the three dead bodies at the far end of the backyard. She flung herself at the basement window but not before Kane squeezed off a shot. Impossible to aim accurately, the bullet took her where it took her: through the liver. She rolled onto her back and tried to shoot Kane but his next round blew her gun—and two fingers— out of her hand. He called to Hector as he dragged her away from the burning house.

"That was a nice little mousetrap you had going there, Jane," Kane said as Hector ran up. "You fed Grendel the Cthulhu artifacts and rare books to build his career, make him a target of suspicion for every Venator in the US, to draw us here and then send us out to our deaths. How many did you catch that way?"

"You think you've beaten us, Kane?" she said, ecstasy, not pain, actuating her features. "So many, so many of the faithful have fallen beneath your sword but you should never have interfered with The Followers of Dagon, for now you face us, the Legion. You believe you conquered The Followers at Odiome: you are wrong. All you have done is become known. Through your sacrilege you have earned what the faithful would give anything, do anything, kill anything to earn: Great Cthulhu's notice. Great Cthulhu as he lies dreaming in his house in mighty R'lyeh has condescended to know the name *Solomon Kane*."

Kane stumbled back a step, the sounds of helicopters above, police cars approaching, Hector swearing, and his own heart beating were swept away by a high pitched keening; a note, a cymbal's scream. Every Venator, after seeing and smashing idols of Cthulhu, eventually begins to hear the mad murmurs of the dead god in his dreams, to see the nightmare reality of R'lyeh's rise and the return of the Great Old Ones to subjugate and torture humanity for eons without rest. Instructions, though, demands, urges sent from the deeps, from the mighty city of R'lyeh beneath the waves, those are sent only to his crazed followers and the damned. To the damned.

"And he has sent to us, the Legion, the faithful beyond faith," Jane gibbered, "in dreams of anguish, your name and we will find you, we will slaughter you—as we slaughtered your family, your wife, your son, your daughter—on an altar of salt, taking your body with unspeakable agony and leaving your everlasting mind to the barest notice of Great Cthulhu, eternity of torment."

Hector ended her sentence with the last shell in his shotgun. Grabbing the nearly paralyzed Kane, he hauled him to the car in the late Jane's driveway, slamming the trunk lid as he passed, pushed Kane in through the driver's door and across to the passenger's seat, and then scrambled in after him. He rammed the car straight across the road, between two police cars screaming in from both directions, and through the yard of the neighbor across the street. Over patios, barely missing a pool, through hedges, Hector plowed on until he reached a road, leaning out the window to blow out the tires of the pursuing police cars with Kane's pistol.

Burning up the engine as they flew in an unknown direction, Hector shouted at Kane, slapped his chest, trying to bring him around. Kane could only blink, nearly comatose with fear. Hector's cell phone rang and he clawed it out of his pocket.

"Thank the fucking Venator gods," he said to himself as he saw it was Helen on the caller ID. "Helen, baby, I'm so glad it's you: we've got problem numero uno, thermo-nuclear-war problem."

"Hector, Hector, please listen," Helen whispered. "They've attacked Arkham. The University Police have been infiltrated, there are cultists everywhere, war in the streets. You've got get back here. Please, hurry."

BOOK 6

THE SIEGE OF ARKHAM

CHAPTER 1

INFILTRATION

A
N ANGRY ORANGE light darted through the trees, clawing at the trunks of the fallen. The National Guard had cut the power to Arkham but a fire had spread through the buildings across the Miskatonic River, casting flames and smoke from the farther side of the small city. Kane and Hector crept toward this beacon of Arkham's agony, running in a crouch or crawling as the forest allowed. Their prized night vision goggles aided them in passing the surrounding infantry, as did their unexpected line of march: no one expected anybody to sneak *into* Arkham.

They'd screamed north from their last stalk in Maryland, all the way to Massachusetts in a little over five hours. Along the way they had changed cars twice, bought ammunition for Hector's Mossberg, and heard the details of what the radio was calling a "terrorist attack on Arkham" in continuous news bulletins. A car bomb had been detonated outside the Arkham police station at 8:00 PM the night before, when the day shift briefed the night shift; both were lost when the explosion destroyed the building. As emergency response crews headed to the site, sniper teams positioned around Arkham made themselves known, attacking anyone in uniform or carrying a gun. Police, fire, rescue, and anyone attempting to lend a hand to the defense of Arkham, was shot from the high spots around the city. The County Sheriff's Department closed the bridges and roads into Arkham, after sniper fire had pushed them into the woods, and let neither anyone in nor out of the beleaguered city. It had taken the State Police nearly three hours to setup a hasty perimeter around Arkham and only now, two hours after that, were the National Guard mobilized enough to fill in, closing the siege lines. The Governor had released only a brief statement saying he was in consultation with the General in charge and that the situation was being handled appropriately. Kane and Hector knew what that meant. Not a damn thing.

Kane raised a fist suddenly to his shoulder, freezing both Hector and himself: through the trees ahead, not ten meters away, a small shovel had arced across the pale green mist that represented burning Arkham in Kane's nightvision goggles. Thighs burning in the strain of keeping motionless, Kane circled his head like an owl trying to judge the distance to whoever wielded the shovel; NVGs were as notorious for their diminished depth perception as for turning everything green. Behind him, Hector tightened his grip around his shotgun's slide, lest it rattle with his first step and draw fire from the surrounding National Guardsmen. *There he is*, Kane thought, *but where's his foxhole?* A few slow sidling steps over the pine-needled floor brought Kane nearly abreast of the part-time soldier, separated by four or five suddenly puny trees. Hector saw Kane jerk to one side and then crouch down, looking off toward Arkham. After a shake of his head, he waved Hector forward and they pressed on. Hector spared a glance in the soldier's direction as they moved toward Hangman's Brook: the soldier hadn't been digging a fighting position but a "cat hole" and was now squatting over it.

Hangman's Brook was only five feet wide at best and didn't show up on every map but it was the end of the world for the siege of Arkham. The National Guard had set their perimeter just back from the stream, utilizing what thin cover the woods afforded. Kane and Hector crept to the edge of the trees, a scant two feet from the muddy brook, midway between two fighting positions. Passing their monocular NVGs west and east, they saw the dim figures of sentries—only their heads showing above ground—as they watched the dark edge of Arkham. The trick would be to cross Hangman's Brook without getting shot in the back by the National Guard—or shot in the face by one of the sniper teams holding Arkham.

The slight rise from the brook to the backs of Washington Street's buildings cast a thin shadow, even in the artificial green of nightvision. Kane gave Hector a nod and then went down on his stomach; Hector paned back and forth, watching the rooftops and open windows across the way. Advancing only an inch every few seconds, Kane was a lengthening dark spot on the muddy bank as he slithered into the water. The brook, though still passing through September's summer, was icy cold. Kane's fingers didn't notice it but his chest sinking into the burbling water constricted as if he'd been tackled. Mouth wide open to keep his shuddering breath from whistling between his teeth, his pistol held flat above the water, Kane eased across Hangman's Brook fighting the urge to bolt from its frigid coils. On the other side, he stayed low and covered the bank, watching the two National Guard fighting positions in sight, as Hector followed him across. *What are you going to do if the Nasty Girls start shooting?* he asked himself. He didn't answer.

With the brook crossed, the two soaking wet and muddy Venators eased up the bank using the low shrubs for everything they were worth. Then, in a dash, they barreled down an alley in a crouch. Shots rang out all over the city, every few seconds; overhead at an indeterminate distance, helicopters flew in an endless cacophony like a stalled thunderstorm; but no shots followed Hector and Kane into Arkham. Still deep within the alley, its mouths at either end seeming hungry with expectant violence, the two stopped and sat shivering on their heels.

"Where's the safe house again?" Kane whispered through chattering teeth into Hector's ear.

"Saltonstall Street, between West and Boundary," Hector hissed. His leather jacket gleamed treacherously in the wet of the brook and the flicker of distant fire. "It's under a dry cleaner."

Kane nodded dumbly and edged toward Washington Street, his back sucking to the brick of the building behind him. At the alley's end, he went down on his side and leaned his head beyond the corner: a dozen buildings were in sight, some old row houses and some newer replacements of what had been gathered to history, all gaping with a hundred windows like dark eyes. Kane pulled back and got his feet under him. After a doubtful look at Hector, they ducked out onto the sidewalk.

A high-caliber rifle fired two blocks east, its echo as terrible as its bullet, and both men threw themselves to the ground, scrambling face down to the suspect protection of cement steps leading up to a house. Flitting their green vision across the buildings opposite them, eyes sprinting from one rooftop to the next, they found no one in sight and heard nothing but their own rattling breath and tapping pulses. Another shot punched at the night from farther into the city, closer to the University. Their street seemed dead; Kane waved them forward and they—reluctant to leave what little cover they had and more reluctant to stay on the street at all—scurried around the steps and down the sidewalk. The little voices in their heads, which had kept them alive for decades, told them to run, to break down a door and get inside, but it was just such sudden movement that would draw attention to them if one of the hundreds of windows glaring at them concealed a sniper.

Weaving around sidewalk trees and fallen garbage cans, around bodies that sprawled as if drunk or curled as if cold but were neither, the two Venators approached West Street. Kane, in front, watched the street and the buildings they moved toward; Hector, a foot behind, watched the buildings to either side—head swinging back and forth as if in adamant denial—and occasionally darted a look behind. Then something moved on a rooftop across West Street.

Kane coughed the word sniper and threw himself to the left, behind another cement staircase. Hector was practically there before Kane—and only a split second before a round pocked the sidewalk where he had crouched. Rifle blasts shouted from the rooftop again and again as the sniper began pounding the staircase. The cement was merely a veneer, plastered over a wire frame, and not nearly thick enough to hinder the high-caliber round. Huddled nearly supine, Kane and Hector couldn't bring their NVGs around far enough to see the holes knocked in the cement but they could feel the debris as it peppered their faces.

"He can't hit us this low," Kane said. "He can't get through the treads of the stairs."

"He's trying to rattle us," Hector said.

"It's working," Kane mumbled.

"Scare us into running away, down the street," Hector continued. "Hit us in the back."

"Nowhere to go, then," Kane said, rolling onto his stomach. "Can't run up the street toward him or we'll get shot in the face."

He stretched out, his head held to the side so that the steel stair tread would cover him, and tried to peek around its edge. A round skipped off the tread and shattered a cement stanchion. Hector clawed at Kane's belt, dragging him back, as Kane pushed with his arms like a man falling overboard.

"What the hell are you doing?" Hector growled. "It's a hundred yards to that building. That's a hell of a shot for a pistol, even that cannon."

"You want to try the Mossberg on him?" Kane said, wriggling around until his back was to the wall of the building.

Hector spun in a slow circle, looking at all the ways closed to them: couldn't go up the street, couldn't go down the street, the closely packed row houses might as well have been the walls of a prison, or a grave. He grabbed the window bars of a ground-floor apartment and shook them. "Maybe I can blow the brick off around these bolts," he said, "and we could yank the bars away. Move through the house and out the other side."

"It's a good idea," Kane said, sitting on his heels with his pistol pointed straight-armed out in front of him at the staircase. "Provided, of course, that you don't ricochet buckshot off the bars and kill both of us."

"What are you going to do but get shot in the head?" Hector said. "We're pinned down, man."

"I don't think that guy's a very good shot," Kane said. He rose slowly, widening his legs' angle, bringing his head closer to open space, his pistol rising between two cement stanchions. A shot and a flash winked on the corner of the rooftop and Kane could almost see the dark figures using the parapet for cover. The incoming round hit the stair's handrail in a shower of pink cement; Kane squeezed off a round, the sound of his silenced pistol undetectable underneath the trampling echoes of the sniper's shot; a puff of dust below the sniper's parapet was the only effect; the sniper's arm could be seen as he operated the bolt of his weapon and fired again; the wall to Kane's left popped as a brick seemed to implode; Kane fired again; something long and vaguely reflective dropped from the roof, smacking the sidewalk down the street with a clatter. "Go, go!" Kane shouted.

Hector was on his feet and running flat out, shotgun pointed at the rooftop hopelessly far for a shot; Kane was a second behind. A second was all it took to get closer, close enough to see two arms hanging limply over the edge of the roof. But two other arms— those of the sniper's spotter—had unslung an assault rifle. The spotter came up on a knee, out of defilade, and fired. He met a return barrage as both Venators had crossed nearly half the distance to his building. Buckshot and .45 rounds vomited up from the street as Kane and Hector wildly shot while running; the spotter fired down at them but—as he was also wearing NVGs and they are not easy to aim with—he missed. One of Hector's .33 buckshot pellets finally got lucky and threw the spotter back from the parapet.

Racing to the building—a drugstore downstairs with apartments above—Kane put two rounds into the apartment entrance lock, reloaded his pistol, and stood to one side. Hector snatched the sniper's dropped bolt-action rifle as he came up and then also stood to one side of the door. Jabbing at it with the bolt-action rifle, like a skier pushing off, Hector smashed the door open; a grenade taped to the jamb with its pin wired to the knob exploded. The thick exterior wall was just enough to take the shrapnel. Both Venators then plunged inside and up the stairs. One floor up, they slowed, dizzy with having to starve their pumping lungs of much-needed oxygen, to keep quiet, to hear. Despite a ringing in their ears so loud they would have thought it audible to passersby, every step on the old wooden stairs, every brush of fabric past fabric, roared with supernatural volume. At the top floor, they saw that the folding stairs that led to the roof were down but saw no sign of the spotter. Kane motioned for Hector to cover the stairs.

Knowing that if the spotter were still alive he'd shoot the first head to pop through the roof access, Kane had to find another way up. He used his silenced pistol again to blow the lock off an apartment door. Staying on one knee, he swiveled into the room. The eerie bleakness nightvision green lent to everything made what may have been a vibrant college kid's flat look like a squat moldering after a house fire. Kane froze in his sweep of the room when four orbs lit up like cats' eyes. There, on the far side of the room, two people huddled together under a blanket, a makeshift barricade of card table and folding chairs in front of them resembling a child's play fort, with much the same chance of stopping a bullet.

With no light in the hallway to silhouette Kane, he knew they couldn't see him just as he knew they'd heard him enter their room. He "shhh"ed to them, cooing as benignly as he could, inching closer and hoping they didn't have a gun, too.

"Easy, kids," he whispered. He could see them look toward one another, one cradling the other's head. "I'm a cop. Well, something like that. I'm here for the sniper on the roof. Just chill out and stay down. Once I get him, I'm out of here. I'll even bring you back a gun if I can. Just stay cool."

Kane could see the cradler nod almost imperceptibly. He nodded back, though the cradler couldn't see it, and then slid softly over to the window. Raising the sash inch by torturous inch, Kane stood up beside the window and slowly slid out from behind the cover of the wall, taking in the street and rooftops a sliver at a time, like slices of a pie. Once he was sure no one was waiting to shoot him from the street, Kane leaned out and looked up at the roof with its low parapet. He slipped through the window, keeping his pistol pointed up at all times, trying to find purchase with the tips of his fingers on the narrow molding over the window. It was touch and go and he nearly fell off, saved by a last minute grab at the sash, but he eventually stood on the window ledge, a couple inches below the roof. In one swift motion, he leapt up, grabbed the parapet and pulled himself up so that he hung by his armpits: there, across the tarred roof, the wounded spotter lay with a pistol in hand, pointing at the open roof hatch. He turned his NVGs toward Kane a second before Kane shot him.

After stripping the sniper and spotter of ammo and weapons, Kane dropped off the spotter's pistol to the two college kids who'd had the longest night of their lives. All they could tell Kane and Hector was what they'd heard on the radio. That and one thing more: Campus Police were in on it, had sealed off the Archeology Building and were shooting anyone who drew near. Rumor had it that they had executed the students and faculty who were caught inside, at late seminars, when the car bomb destroyed the Arkham Police Station.

Kane and Hector left and continued to the safe house on Saltonstall Street. Holstering or slinging the weapons they had brought, Kane kept point, angling the sniper's rifle to use his NVGs through the scope (which diminished their light amplification but did sort of work) when needed, while Hector, his jacket bulging with magazines, brought up the rear with his new M16A2. Up West Street, they heard much but saw little. Shots were fired continuously, sometimes close by, sometimes farther off, sometimes in volleys, sometimes singly; the single shots with nothing following rang like the tolling of a bell. Overhead, helicopters occasionally passed. One that came too close to the Miskatonic University campus earned the ire of its occupiers: a long burst of machinegun fire swept the sky with glowing red tracers, driving the National Guard helicopter away.

CHAPTER 2

THE VAULT

OWN HALF A block on Saltonstall, the dry-cleaner's windows were smashed, as were many of the windows up and down the street. Using his rifle scope, Kane looked both ways and saw dancing figures in the distance. He didn't fire, though; the figures moved with the sloppy coordination of drunkenness. They were kids, students most likely, taking advantage of the law's absence for a spree of looting. The snipers, apparently, paid them no mind. Hector tugged at Kane's sleeve and motioned down the alley. At the rear of the building, a storm cellar door was locked with a combination panel set into a steel pillar. Hector punched in the code and the door opened with a loud click. As he pulled up one side of the door, a voice hailed them from within.

"Let's hear the password, bud," the voice demanded.

"Go fry your head," Hector said and scrambled down the steep stairs.

"Close enough," the voice said.

Once inside with the doors locked, they took off their NVGs.

The small cellar was bare cinderblock with steel posts holding up the ceiling, a row of bunk beds along one wall, a tiny kitchen with a plastic work sink and microwave, and a bathroom that must have once been a closet. On one of the lower bunks, a man in a sopping flannel shirt was on his side, wheezing moistly. In the center of the room, the man with the voice, who had to duck because of the low ceiling, cradled a large magazine-fed rifle in his arms.

"Clayton!" Kane said and put out his hand. "What are you doing here? I thought some sweet Texas girl must have stolen you away from our noble bachelor ranks."

"Heh, she did," Clayton said. "Turned out her husband wasn't keen on the idea. I was healing up at a pet hospital for a spell."

Lionel Clayton could have been distantly related to either Kane or Hector, by his looks. Six-three and rangy, long hair in a tail and goatee like an upside-down red Chia Pet, Clayton looked like a right-wing survivalist except the tattoos covering his arms weren't Christian in nature but occult. Or, at least, they looked occult to the untrained eye: to other Venators, he was covered in West Indian symbols, developed to ward him from danger and proof him to the dream sendings of Cthulhu. Whether they actually worked or the placebo effect did the trick, Clayton swore by them. He'd added something small to most of the Venators he'd met, with his portable tattooing gear; often after a long bout with a glass of something strong.

"You beat us here from Texas?" Hector asked, stripping off his wet clothes after bumping fists with Clayton.

"Naw, I flew in yesterday morning," Clayton said. "Thought Helen might have a lead on something for me. Ease myself back into the business of slaughtering evil, you know. She told me to set a while. Said there was something big brewing. Didn't know she meant all this."

"No way she knew about this," Hector said as he rummaged in

a wall locker for clothes roughly his size. "She wouldn't have sent me down to help Kane, two days ago, if that were the case."

"She mentioned something big to me, too," Kane said, also stripping out of his wet clothes. "Said it was a couple months out, though. Who's that?"

Clayton turned to the man on the bunk and patted him on the shoulder. "This here's Matt Hyde," Clayton said sadly. "We had gone out when the car bomb went off last night, take a look around. We got set on by Misk-U police when we headed over there. Sons-a-bitches shot us up good—and were armed to the fucking teeth, too. Hyde took one in the right lung. I've got him setup with a flutter valve so he can breathe but he's bleeding pretty bad from it. Snuck out about two hours ago, up to St. Mary's, but someone had driven a car through the admissions door. Whole ground floor of the hospital is on fire. I tried to get in through the side but it weren't no good. A sniper took a few shots at me about then and I came back. I had a call out to Fred Hemsted, about an hour after the car bomb, and he said he and Burt Meadows were in-bound. No cell reception, now. I figure them's surrounding Arkham must've shut down the towers. It's even money Fred and Burt get here with some decent hardware before those Nasty Girls out there decide it's time to sweep the city."

Hector and Kane had finished changing by this point; Hector into fatigue trousers, boots, gray shirt, and a vest with lots of pockets; Kane into something less task-oriented.

"You've got to be kidding me," Hector said when he turned around. "Did you go to all the safe houses in Arkham and leave a suit for yourself?"

"What?" Kane said. He'd donned a black suit and a black shirt, pausing to look at himself with a tie in both hands. "We don't know where we'll be when this thing is over. We may have to blend in."

"So you're planning on blending into a damn funeral?" Hector said. "You look like a priest."

"Focus, Hector," Kane said, stuffing the tie into a pocket and kneeling down next to Hyde. "The dressing is as good as we can make it but I don't like his chances if we can't get him some blood. How's the first aid equipment here?"

"Dressings and tape, mostly," Clayton said. "Shit, I don't want to sound like a heartless son-bitch but if we try to transfuse him ourselves, without being able to stop him bleeding, he'll just bleed it out and then we have two people who can't fight. I've known Hyde for seven, eight years—and he's a good man—but I don't know what we can do for him."

"Nothing," Hector said from in front of another wall locker he'd just taken the combination lock off of. Inside there were stacks of weapons and boxes of ammunition. "We need to get to the Archeology Building. Now."

"Hell, I know that," Clayton said. "But Hyde and I already recon'd it, like I said. There must be fifty or more Campus Police there, armed fit to give the 82nd Airborne a run for its money. You figure the three of us can just shoot our way in?"

"If they could get their hands on enough explosives to destroy the police station," Hector said, jamming his pockets full of magazines, "then they could bring in enough to blow the Vault below the Arch building."

The Archeology and Ethnology Department at Miskatonic University had been the center of research into what was colloquially known as *The Great Old Ones* for over a hundred years. The flower of the Ivy League, Miskatonic University's small size had led to specialization and genius in specific areas: its dark association with The Great Old Ones, their high priest, the horrific being Cthulhu, and such evil texts as *The Necronomicon* and *Unaussprechlichen Kulten* had stemmed from the suspicious disappearances of the scholars who had studied them. The disappearances were due, no doubt, to the Cult of Cthulhu, those degenerates who hoped through human sacrifice and observance of blasphemous rituals to awaken the dead god Cthulhu, who lies dreaming in his mighty city of R'lyeh and would herald the return of the Great Old Ones, plunging mankind into eons of torment. But the cult had its enemies then, as now, and wherever they struck, the Venators followed with fire and sword. Inheritors of the ancient Praetorian Guard, in modern times they are usually the loved ones of the sacrificed, bent on revenge and protection of innocence. By their efforts, the Cult of Cthulhu never again attained the organization that it enjoyed before Rome, before the Emperors. But for their stalking of evil to remain effective, it had to remain secret. And so after each disappearance, after each extermination of a cult, no word ever spread of their deeds. Indeed, such was their secrecy that the unfinished work of the fallen scholars was soon taken up by the next great mind, and then the next, until hidden knowledge was uncovered and the Venators themselves sought the aid of the scholars they secretly defended. In 1925, the first attack was made by a cult against Miskatonic University. The Venators responded quickly but not before several irreplaceable scholars were cut down and valuable texts either stolen or burned. A Venator presence was then constant at the university. In 1978, the University was attacked with high explosives for the first time. It was covered up as a gas main leak but action had to be taken. Under the Archeology and Ethnology building, a series of caves had been discovered. The caves, in fact, had led to the first serious study of Cthulhu Cults on American soil: the caves were the ancient meeting place and sacrifice spot for the cult before the coming of Native Americans. Those wise first people of a civilized race put down the cults wherever they had found them and the cults only returned to America to search among ancient sites after European adventurers had annihilated the vast majority of Native Americans through germ warfare. With 90% of native peoples on the east coast wiped out in a single year, the cults nearly succeeded in discovering the caves then: but the Venators had followed. Rediscovered in 1902, texts found in the cave led to renewed interest of the cults. After the bombing in 1978, the rebuilding of the Arch Building included a bank vault's armored door to seal the caves. There, deep under Miskatonic University, a hundred years of research into the cults was protected by two feet of rolled armor steel. The Vault, as it was known, had independent air, food, and water to last a year, secret entrances to other caves, with other doors, and accommodations for twenty.

"Helen must have made it to The Vault," Hector said, selecting a rifle from the locker. "And since what she said looks to be true, that the Campus Police were taken over by the cult, it's only a matter of time before they blow The Vault's door and kill everyone inside. I'm not here to let that happen."

"None of us are," Kane said, standing up. "But it doesn't change the fact that fifty men guard the Arch Building. The three of us will have a hell of a time just getting there through the gauntlet of snipers, to say nothing of fighting through that many people."

"There's more than one way into the Arch Building," Hector said, slapping a magazine into an M-2 carbine.

"Take it easy, Lee Marvin," Kane said. "Where the hell did an M-2 come from, anyway?"

"You never used the safe houses before?" Clayton said. "There was a private museum outside of Smithtown, Pennsylvania, about forty years ago. Some old coot with a dealer's license had bought up all kinds of surplus Army gear and made a World War II museum. Some Venator—"

"Arnie Haskle," Hector said.

"Says his son, Benji," Clayton said, "others say it was Walter Malloy. Anyway, Arnie or Walter or someone got wind of all that gear and bet it was poorly protected. So, he up and steals a bull-dozer and knocks down one of the walls, loads up a bread truck with everything it can carry, and scoots back up here before the dust settled. There were even bazookas and flamethrowers here, up until about fifteen years ago. Most of that vintage is gone now. Safe house three, on the other side of the river, is out completely: they've got nothing but stuff like that M-16 piece of shit."

"That .45 Helen gave you," Hector said, taping a bayonet to his ankle, "the one you lost in North Cackalacky, was from this horde."

"No shit?" Kane said. "Well, if they still work, grab something and let's go. I'll stick with this bolt-action Winchester."

"Not going to do you much good once we're inside," Clayton said. "Better take a carbine for yourself. Hand me that bag, will you Hector? I've only got four-hundred rounds for the BAR but they's all in magazines."

"Yeah and weigh a ton," Hector grunted.

Armed like extras from an HBO special, the three Venators stood quietly around the unconscious but still wheezing Matt Hyde. Hector mumbled a few words in Latin, of which he only knew the rough meaning. Leaving the light on and the door locked, so if nothing else their brother would not die in the dark, even if it was his fate to die alone, the three Venators eased out of the cellar and away.

CHAPTER 3

RAIDING THE ARCH

NOT WANTING TO go north on West Street, straight to the university—because it would take them too close to Hangman's Hill and its enormous abandoned church tower full of snipers—Kane led them back down Saltonstall to Garrison Street. They moved as fast as they dared, feeling that if they assumed Kane and Hector's earlier clearing of the way had made the route safe they would pay for the assumption. Hector nevertheless pushed them to go faster now that he knew the Arch Building was invested.

Turning onto Garrison, a shot erupted immediately from three blocks away; Clayton grunted as if he'd had the wind knocked out of him, stumbled backward, and fell. Hector grabbed him by the collar with one hand and dragged him into the recessed doorway of a deli, laying down suppressive fire with his M-2, wielded with the other hand and spraying wildly. Kane dropped prone and rolled into the gutter, flipping his NVGs away from his eyes. Enough light glinted off the storefronts to cast meaningful shadows of the sniper's working arm on the wall behind him. He never finished the work. Kane put one round through the window and assailant, turned his bolt, and waited. The spotter jumped on the gun as it was slipping through the window and earned the same reward as his partner. Kane then scurried over in a crouch to see about Clayton.

"I'm good, I'm good," Clayton said, gasping. The milled steel of the BARs receiver could take being rolled over by a tank and not crack. The .308 round that had hit it had barely muffed the bluing but it had knocked the Venator sideways. He waved for them to continue on and warily they did.

Snaking from one pool of shadows to the next, taking turns covering the streets they passed as the man behind crossed it before repeating the process at the next danger area, they traversed Garrison Street as if in a giant game of armed leapfrog. Coming up to College Street, they could hear automatic weapons fire, including the steady slow whopping of a fifty-caliber machinegun like a methodical giant beating a carpet.

They took nearly two minutes—a torturous eternity for Hector who would have charged the fortifications if left to his own devices—to watch the intersection before approaching. And good thing, too: Kane spotted a sentry who had climbed down into a storm drain to use it as a makeshift fighting position. Only the sentry's head and assault rifle could be seen and even then only barely. Kane dispatched him cleanly, waiting for the next time a helicopter passed and the fifty-cal devoured all other sound.

"Why the hell do they keep flying overhead?" he whispered back at Clayton.

Clayton shrugged. "I think they haven't made up their mind whether they want to use a missile on the snipers up in Hangman Hill's church," he said. "Buzzing the Arch Building is just their way of keeping the Campus Police off guard."

"Yeah, they won't know if the helicopter is just a gag or the beginning of the assault, whenever they fly by," Hector said.

Kane shook his head, saying, "They're waiting for dawn."

Dawn was only an hour away. The one thought none of them had yet expressed was that the National Guard—and more so the State Police—wouldn't take much pains to determine who was a "terrorist" and who was a citizen fighting for his home.

Using a dull mirror taken from the safe house, Kane inched it around the corner so he could look over the Arch Building across the quad without sticking his head out into a sniper's crosshairs. The scene was grim. Many of the trees on the college green had been set aflame during the night; their burned husks looked like the fingers of a cremated body poking from a newly filled grave. A dump truck—apparently shot to pieces by a passing helicopter— had brought in a couple thousand filled sand bags and dropped them at key points around the Arch building. The Campus Police had not been idle: they had fortified the main and side entrances to the grand old brick building, wedging sandbag walls between granite columns. Ground floor windows were covered from the inside with a crazy assortment of wooden objects: some sensible tables blocked them but in other places chairs had been screwed to the window frames to bar entrance; in other windows, coat racks and display cases, their objects tumbled helter-skelter in the skewed hurry to bolt anything up as an obstacle. From many of the windows, and especially around the sandbag bunkers before each entrance, the muzzles of weapons protruded like the twitching antennae of guardian insects.

"I don't see the fifty-cal," Kane said. "Wait, there it is. They've got it in the cupola, on the roof. Stupid: the Guard won't have a qualm about putting a missile into the cupola. Otherwise, it's all bad news, fellahs. Chances are the quad is surrounded by snipers. If we so much as run across Garrison Street we're liable to catch a round. Assaulting those fortifications, against a determined defender, with the snipers shooting us in the back? I don't see how it can be done."

"Well shit, we're just going to have to try our luck," Hector said, rising to his feet.

"No the hell we don't," Kane hissed, he and Clayton pulling Hector back down into the shadow where they crouched.

"Look, I ain't waiting around anymore," Hector said, nearly a shout. "Helen called and told me to come back, she needs me—I ain't letting her down!"

"That's exactly what you'll be doing if you run out there and get yourself killed," Kane said. "This ain't—Jesus—this *isn't* a movie and you don't want to end it like Paul Newman and Robert Redford, got it? Clayton: isn't there supposed to be a couple of secret entrances to the Vault?"

"Sure but they're secret," Clayton said.

"Even from us?" Kane said.

"Only Helen and, maybe, that maintenance guy—" Hector said.

"Grady," Clayton provided.

"Yeah, Grady," Hector said, "know about them. It was a just-in-case kinda thing. Wouldn't have been safe to let us know, if the cult caught us and all that."

They looked at Kane and Kane looked at his hands, flipping the round dull mirror over his knuckles. He eyed the street ending at the college green, the buildings overlooking it, down Garrison toward Pickman and High Streets, the brook, the woods beyond; he looked ahead an hour or so to the moment when dawn—with her fingertips of rose—would touch the tops of Arkham's buildings and five-thousand National Guard Infantry would assault the tiny city, in her agony.

"Why'd they have a guy in the sewer?" Kane asked.

"Huh?" Clayton said. "He's just protecting hisself, I reckon."

"Sure, a quick and dirty foxhole," Hector said, looking at Kane, desperate to be wrong.

Kane shook his head. "Clayton, we didn't tell you but we've had a run in with these organized cultists before," he said. He started breathing more and more heavily until he had to close his eyes to get a hold of himself. Hector took and squeezed his forearm. Looking straight at the other two, monocular in their NVGs, Kane said, "They're not the usual stupidly cunning cultists. They've got their act together. They don't care about sacrificing people in the woods, hoping to earn—fuck, fuck, fuck."

Kane nearly started to hyperventilate until Hector smacked him hard across the face. "Don't think about that part, shit," Hector said. "Just solve the problem."

"What's going on, man?" Clayton asked, noticeably bringing his BAR around to point at Kane.

"Easy, Clayton," Hector said menacingly. "These bozos call themselves The Legion. Connected to The Followers of Dagon, somehow. The High Priestess we capped said that Great Fishface knows Kane's name and he's been a little shy in talking about it ever since."

"He talks to them about me in their dreams," Kane whispered.

"Shit," Clayton said, eyes wide with terror. "He, he fucking knows who you are?" He looked like he was about to make a break for it until Hector took him by the back of the neck and knocked off their NVGs.

"Listen, man," he said, staring hard into Clayton's eyes. "I don't have time for your shit. If Cthulhu wants Helen, he's going to have to drag his crabby ass out of R'lyeh and come take her from me, 'cause it ain't happenin' otherwise. Kane! Get that platinum brain of yours firing on all cylinders, boy, and find me a way into that fucking building."

"Keep your voice down," Kane gulped. He took two deep

breaths and wiped his face before continuing. "The Legion, Clayton. They're pros. They organized the bombing of the Arkham Police Station and the infiltration of the Campus Police. They have snipers on half the rooftops in town. Why put a dude in *that* storm drain? We haven't seen that anywhere else. Could be he's there because of the Arch Building, but why? With the fortifications they have? Would they need him as a listening post?"

"Sewer access," Hector said and snapped his fingers.

Kane nodded. They reattached their NVGs to their head mounts and crawled across Garrison Street to the storm drain. Going in head first, they scrambled over the dead cultist and down the strangely tall storm drain.

"They ain't getting in here, sarge," Hector mumbled, "except over my dead body."

Clayton snickered as he followed Hector over the dead cultist and down the storm drain.

Not a septic sewer filled with human waist, the storm sewer only carried rain water and refuse off the streets. It still smelled to high heaven and, though taller than usual, necessitated a crouch to traverse. The three Venators' knees burned more than their nostrils after ten minutes, which only took them down the street and across it. Kane had slung his bolt-action rifle over his back and drew his silenced .45 pistol. The others kept a distance of five meters from him and each other, Clayton bringing up the rear, pointing the BARs heavy barrel down the way they had come.

After a bend in the tunnel, and halting to listen, Kane heard a noise ahead of them. He flung up his clenched fist to bring the others to a sudden halt. Someone around the next bend was scuffing his boot against the concrete floor of the tunnel. With a deliberation of movement that made Kane's already burning muscles shake with the threat of collapse, he moved a foot forward, placed it softly, and then shifted his weight onto it. Again, as if moving in a slow-motion movie sequence, he took another painfully slow step; and then again and then again, a half-dozen times until he reached the bend in the echoing tunnel. A cautious look over his shoulder revealed that Hector and Clayton knelt where he'd left them, tense with anticipation.

Not knowing how the cultist around the corner might be equipped, Kane did not turn on the laser sight of his Mk23 pistol. Visible only through NVGs, the laser would have given him away if the cultist was wearing a pair. Leaning precariously around the corner, Kane circled with his pistol outstretched, taking an inch slice of the pie at a time, until he saw a foot. Toe, nothing, toe, nothing, toe. The scuffing foot kicked at the tunnel floor in boredom. Kane continued to take slices of the pie, edging around the bend. Up the leg, there was a hand, on an assault rifle, there was a chin, a head—bang. Or no bang. Kane's silenced pistol sighed with sudden relief as it ejected a bullet and sent the cultist into eternity. The Legion's best sentry slumped softly to the tunnel's floor and Kane was off, as quickly as relative silence allowed, to whatever the cultist was guarding: an entrance. Three concrete steps up to a metal door like a hatch on a submarine, over which read *Archeology and Ethnology Building 1979.*

Kane clicked the laser sight on his pistol so it flashed three quick dots against a wall that Hector and Clayton could see. They scrambled up to join him. There was no way to know who or what lay beyond the door so they prepared for the worst and burst in with utmost violence. The room beyond was empty. Heart rates continued to soar for a moment but they were out of the tunnel. They'd made it inside the Arch Building.

CHAPTER 4

DESCENT

THE SEWER ACCESS door connected to the century-old steamworks beneath Miskatonic University. The boilers underneath the college green fed the various university buildings via steam pipes; in the basement of each building, the pipes coupled to distributors and regulators. In the stiflingly hot maintenance corridor, pressure-release valves spewed steam; the walls ran with rivulets of rusty water. Down the cramped corridor, Kane led, ducking and weaving around the burning metal pipes.

The corridor eventually met a maintenance shop. It was about the size of a sauna and just as steamy. Three doors left the room, one going up to the Arch Building's ground floor, one to the steam tunnel and sewer access, and the last led downward. A cage filled with tools occupied the far wall. At a table smack in the middle, a guard in a Campus Police uniform sat furiously but uselessly trying to get reception on a small radio. He never heard the shot that killed him.

Slowly pushing through the doorway, Kane eased across to the door leading up to the Arch building's ground floor. The click of the lock was indecently loud. Clayton had hustled across to the stairwell leading down, as much to prevent Hector charging off on his own as to watch for people coming up. Hector was indeed impatient to go but let Kane take point, knowing he'd not relinquish his silenced pistol and it was too much of an advantage to forgo.

As they spiraled down the old cast-iron staircase, they could hear a low whine growing below. A smell like burning batteries wafted up the long shaft of the staircase. Their calves burned from taking the stairs slow enough to keep from telegraphing their approach, long before they reached halfway. Clayton put a hand out on Hector's shoulder: he needed a second to stretch. Kane leaned out over the side of the spiraling iron and looked down—and saw someone looking back. For a moment their NVGs locked; maybe the man below wasn't sure who was coming down, could have been his relief for guard duty; no one could have forced their way into the Arch Building past so many armed men, after all. Kane had led with his pistol, as always, and dropped a round from two stories up. The pistol hadn't made any more noise than the opening and closing of its slide: the man below, however, had fallen heavily when his head came apart and his assault rifle clattered loudly across the floor, echoing up and down the staircase. The three Venators crashed down the stairway like skiers trying to outrun an avalanche, desperate to get off the confined space before someone started shooting up it.

They needn't have worried. As they reached the foot of the stairs, they slowed. The low whine had grown into a grinding growl; the smell was overpowering. Far from hearing the sentry's fall, whoever was down in the caves couldn't have heard much of anything except the growl. Kane continued forward, aware of the bright light around the next corner, so intense it read as white in the NVGs perpetual green.

Slipping his dull mirror around the corner near the floor, Kane took in the sight: a dozen or so men in Campus Police uniforms stood watching two men in coveralls trying to drill into The Vault's hinged door. The armored steel was proving tougher than expected, though: two ruined drill bits the size of baseball bats lay smoking to one side. The battery power packs for the industrial drill were also smoking in the thick, hot air. From two metal stands, like IV racks, floodlights hung, illuminating the scene. Secure in the knowledge of their compatriots' fortifications on the surface, no one took any notice of anything except the struggling miners.

Kane holstered his pistol, swung his NVGs up, and took the M-2 carbine off his back. The grin that spread across Hector's face as he clicked his selector to automatic fire had no mirth in it; it was more a snarl. Kane pushed away from the wall and pointed to where he had just crouched: Clayton sprawled there, ready to throw his BAR around the edge and open up. Hector stood over him, straddling the tall rangy man, the circumstances requiring a bit of acrobatic preparation. Kane slowly slipped across the ten-foot space at the mouth of the cave, on toe tips, wanting to use the other side for cover and not make one big target of all of them firing around the same corner. Someone happened to look back when he was half-way across.

The cultist's screamed alarm was barely heard over the laboring drill and didn't sound long. Kane opened up with full automatic fire, dropping his discoverer, and then dashed to the far wall. As he slammed into the stone outcropping, Clayton let loose with his BAR and the sound of its heavy thirty-caliber rounds pounded loud enough to pierce the noise of the drill. Hector joined the firing squad as the cultists found themselves caught between a bank vault and automatic fire. They dropped to the ground and tried to bring their assault rifles to shoulder but it was no use. Scramble as they might, there simply wasn't any place to go. It was over in seconds.

As Kane and Clayton reloaded, Hector charged out into the carnage and made sure of the cultists. Never a man to stand on ceremony, or show much in the way of mercy to cultists, the thought of Helen now secured by his hand drove him wild with the need to see her. He swept over the fallen, brutally, and then hammered a fist against the door, shouting her name.

"Easy, slick," Kane shouted. "She can't hear you through that big-ass door. Clayton, cover the stairs. It's possible someone topside heard our merry-making and might come for a look."

Clayton climbed quickly, if wearily, to his feet and trotted off. Kane picked his way across the crowded floor to a spot near the door's hinge. Kneeling, he ran his hand across the stone floor.

"What are you looking for?" Hector said.

"Helen told me once that there's a connection hidden out here, in case the door is shut and you want to talk to whoever—there we are," Kane said. Opening a false stone compartment, he uncovered a USB port set into a plastic housing. He fished his phone and a USB cable out of his jacket (both having been in a plastic bag when crossing the brook earlier) and jacked into the port.

The screen of his smart phone glowed for a moment and then asked for a password.

"Son of a—"

The screen cleared a second later and a woman with thick-rimmed glasses seemed to press against the screen from the other side.

"Hello?" she asked.

"Um, yeah, this is Solomon Kane," Kane said, shrugging at Hector, who jumped to his side and leaned in to see. "Is, uh, is Helen in there with you?"

"Oh my god, Solomon Kane—and Hector!" the woman shouted. She clapped and called to the people behind her.

"Hey, it's Susan Miller," Hector said. "Susan? Susan! Is Helen in there?"

"I'm sorry, Hector, she isn't here," Susan said. "She sent the red-alert text message just after the building shook—even down here we could feel the car bomb. We closed the door immediately."

"What? With her still outside? Are you nuts?" Hector shouted.

"Please, I'm sorry, it's what she told us to do," Susan said.

"Hector, calm down," Kane said. "She probably wasn't close enough to get here quickly and didn't want to risk The Vault being left open. Do you know where she is now, Susan?"

"She should have been up on the third floor," Susan said. "She had a late seminar."

Hector stamped away, a hand on his face and slapping his carbine against his leg.

"Room 316," someone said behind Susan.

"Did you hear that?" she said. "Maybe room 316."

"She hasn't called?" Kane asked Susan.

"No," she said softly. "I'm sorry. We had internet access for only a few minutes before it was cut. The phone lines must have been disabled outside of town, to cut us off. Mr. Kane, what's going on?"

It was too much to say and there was no time to say it. Kane told her what he could in a few seconds, told her to keep the Vault closed for now and to not trust anyone in a uniform, told her to hang in there, told her goodbye. Putting away his phone, he stood and headed for the stairs.

"What now?" Hector demanded. "Where the hell is she?" He didn't look like he wanted to hear the answer he would have given anyone else in that situation.

Kane kept walking until he reached the stairs and Clayton. "We go up and have a look," he said. Hector's eyes filled with tears, his jaw set in disgust at himself and with the determination to see the thing to its end. "Look, she's tough," Kane said. "Helen's no pushover. She made the right call ordering The Vault closed: she would make the right call getting the hell away from this building, too. You'll see."

"And if she never made it that far?" Hector asked and then smacked himself across the face. "Never mind, let's roll."

CHAPTER 5

THE ASSAULT

ECTOR TOOK POINT as they trudged up the spiral staircase. At the maintenance shop, they set along the wall beside the door up to the Arch building and Kane slowly unlocked and opened it. A few seconds passed as they strained to hear over the sound of their pulses. Edging around the corner, Kane crept up the stairs, nearly prone with one hand on the steps ahead. As they ascended, the sound of sporadic gun fire trickled down to them. The heavy thud thud thud of the fifty-cal came ever-more frequently. Kane thought: *we couldn't have been down there for an hour, but it must be getting pretty damn close to dawn.*

The exit to the Arch building's ground floor was open. Laying with his NVGs just over the topmost step, Kane saw that the hall led to the front entrance and shook with each pass of the helicopter overhead, display cases rattling enough to be heard over the gun fire that swatted at the flying menace. Another sound—a strange vibration—laced through the battle as they drew near; a buzzing that swelled and receded like a tide followed by a smacking like a string of little fireworks.

"The hell is that?" Hector said.

"Minigun," Clayton said. "Them in the helicopter are shooting back. The assault must be on."

"We better get out of here soon, then," Kane said.

Sneaking out of the doorway was easy enough; the cultists in the Campus Police uniforms were far too busy with the coming assault to look behind their own lines. Down the hallway to the wide grand stairway up, the three Venators hustled without giving much time to silence. The old wood of the stairs, richly stained and with hand-lathed banisters, creaked under their running feet as they galloped up. If they couldn't come unannounced, they would at least come with utmost speed. At the third floor, they burst through the swinging double doors and a man down the hall smoking a cigarette bugged two enormous eyes at them before diving through a doorway. He screamed "Venators, Venators" as the fifty-cal machinegun in the copula above continued chattering at the strafing helicopter. Kane leapt across the hallway, taking cover behind a thick doorjamb, and bringing up his carbine; Hector dropped back into the stairwell doorway, letting off a quick burst; Clayton dropped prone and flipped down the bipod legs hanging from the BAR's muzzle.

The walls of the Arch building had originally been plaster over wooden slats, but with every passing year more renovation and repair replaced the plaster with sheet rock—and neither one stood a chance in hell of stopping a .30-06 round. Clayton shot right at the wall behind which the cultist had dived for cover. The rounds from his BAR easily passed through, pocking the hall-side of the wall and blasting off huge chunks of sheet rock inside the classroom. The cultists within (the second team for the fifty-cal, taking a break) panicked by the unexpected nakedness of their position, ran into the hallway to get away from Clayton's fire—and ran right into Kane's and Hector's. Though they fired wildly with their assault rifles and pistol, the three cultists were cut down instantly by the two spraying carbines. Clayton quickly changed magazines on the BAR and jumped to his feet to run down the hall and engage the fifty-cal up in the copula while it was busy with the helicopter, but Kane called him back.

"Leave them," he said, also reloading. "The National Guard is on their way in, and they'll be as dangerous to us as these Legion assholes. They don't know it, but as long as the Legion keeps the Nasty Girls busy, they're buying us time to find Helen and get the hell out of here. Let's go."

Down the hallway toward room 316, the three quickly plunged into every office and classroom along the way, just long enough to surprise anyone they might find, before continuing on. At 316, they stopped short. Across from the door, which hung precariously from its bottom hinge, the wall was riddled with bullet holes. In the middle of the hallway and again crumpled at the foot of the wall, a couple cultist bodies lay bloody and still. Kane—somewhat less confidently after seeing Clayton shoot through the walls—put his back to the wall next to the blasted doorway and fished out his dull mirror. Whatever he saw, he said nothing to the others. He straightened and walked slowly into the small seminar room.

Three students and two more cultists were dead on the floor. The oval table and the wooden chairs looked as if they'd gone through a wood-chipper. Kane had seen horrific carnage too many times over the years—too many times to remember, too many to allow memory to contain them all—and it wasn't the senselessness, the theft of young life, that gave him pause: slumped against the far wall under an open window, Archie's body reclined almost as if asleep.

Kane knelt beside the big Venator, touched one of the bullet holes in his neck.

"Archie, you son of a bitch," Hector whispered from the doorway. He walked around the other side of the table and knelt opposite Kane.

"Didn't know he'd recovered enough to come back from Mexico," Kane said.

"Died for her," Hector said, not hearing him. Looking away, he snatched something from the broken glass and wood and shell casings on the floor. Holding it up, it was a cell phone with a bullet hole in it. "Helen's phone."

Kane took the phone and turned it over in his hands. "We know she had it with her last night," he said, "when she called you. This must have happened shortly afterward."

"They probably tried to get out of the building," Clayton said. "Got downstairs and saw the Campus Police shooting their way in, decided to come back up."

"Maybe," Kane said. "But what happened afterwards? She's not here. Where's her body, if the bullet that passed through her phone had hit her?"

Hector's face turned red, obvious even in the bleak light of dawn. "They must have an altar somewhere," he choked out. "Took her there."

"There are no drag marks," Kane said. "And they would have taken their wounded. That guy there didn't die all at once, so why's he still here if there were any cultist survivors? I think these four cultists came up here, killed these students and Archie, but he took them with him—or Helen took them out. Her phone bought it as the firefight kicked off but she made it. Afterward, she escaped."

"Where?" Hector said.

Kane thought for a moment before saying, "Where any of us would go in Arkham, if the shit hit the fan."

"One of the safe houses," Clayton said. "The one on Saltonstall is the closest."

"Not from this room," Kane said. "These windows face north."

The sun had climbed quickly as they looked at Archie and the phone and thought. To the north, among the warehouses on River Street or across the Miskatonic River, a firefight suddenly broke out. All three turned toward it, the intensity of the new firing outstripped that of the cultists below firing at the passing helicopter.

"Either the National Guard infiltrated through North Arkham," Kane said, "or the cavalry has arrived."

"Somebody's hip deep in it, sounds like," Clayton said. "We better go get in it, too."

"If Helen made it out of here alive, we have to find her," Hector said. "There's another safe house by the river."

"It's on our way," Clayton said. "If she got out of here. Matter of fact, how we going to get out of here? Front door seems a mite crowded just now."

Kane peeked an eye through the broken window. "There's a tree practically under the window," he said. "And there's a chair missing from around this table. My guess: she threw the chair through the window and followed it out. Sounds like the way to go."

"Let's do it," Hector said and was about to pull himself up by the frame when the others yanked him back down.

"Easy, Hector," Kane said. "Let's make sure of those buildings along Church Street."

Kane backed a few steps away from the window and unslung his Winchester. Slowly circling the window, he scanned the tops of the buildings opposite. A new burst of furious gunfire broke out on the college green, along with several explosions.

"Here comes the assault, Kane," Hector said. "We've got to get a move on."

"One sec," Kane said calmly. He had tracked quickly back the other way and then knelt. Blowing all the air out of his lungs to steady his body position, he squeezed off a round, quickly cycled the bolt, and then squeezed off another. "Okay, so much for them," he said. "You want to go first?"

Hector answered by throwing himself head-first through the window. The smacking of branches and stripping of leaves was lost to the general sound of hell breaking loose around Arkham. Kane took the more leisurely feet-first approach to jumping out of a third-story window and then climbing most of the way down a tree. No sooner had he landed than Clayton broke through several branches, hung momentarily by an armpit, and then cartwheeled to a belly flop, landing beside an office chair surrounded by glass.

"Spectacular," he coughed and then heaved a few times to re-inflate his lungs.

CHAPTER 6

THE BACK DOOR

THE THREE VENATORS ran across Church Street in a mad dash, taking cover behind a parked car as a flight of Apache attack helicopters rocketed above the trees to the south west, one firing a missile into the bell tower of the abandoned church on Hangman's Hill. The rattle of chainguns engaging the fifty-cal followed the Venators down Garrison Street toward the river.

A block north, Hector cried out and crashed to the ground, clutching his side. Clayton stumbled to a halt behind him, bending over to see what was wrong when the sidewalk popped between his hand and Hector's shoulder.

"Hit, hit," Hector gulped.

Clayton, realizing what had happened, surged backward, tripped over his own exhausted feet and sat down hard on the ground. "Where is he? Where is he?" he shouted swinging his BAR from one side of the street to the other.

Another round took Hector through the chest. He choked out a cry and rolled to one side.

"Where is he, Hector?" Clayton screamed and then fired wildly at the buildings across the street.

Hector still had enough strength to raise his small carbine and add his own thirty rounds to the hopeless spray. Kane crashed into both of them a second later as another round blasted the sidewalk.

"There are still civilians trapped in those buildings," he shouted as he crawled to a parked car, dragging Hector by the arm.

Clayton threw himself forward, trying to draw his lanky form into a ball behind one wheel, replacing his empty magazine. "Where's the sniper? I can't see him."

The car door above where Kane tried to put a dressing on Hector's chest wound shook as if kicked and the metal jutted outward like a miniature volcano, as a sniper's round passed through. Another followed it, closer to Kane's head. Then another, at Clayton's elbow.

"Jesus, Kane," Clayton shouted. "That must have hit the gas tank; she's leaking. We gotta get the hell out of here."

"Stay down," Kane shouted back. "You want to get shot, too?"

Another round smashed the back window, showering them with shards of glass.

Lying across Hector's body, Kane crawled forward and a little beneath the hood of the car they used for cover. Using Hector's carbine, he shot at the car across the street. The first burst opened the gas tank; the second set it alight. A small explosion hopped the car's rear end before billowing black smoke rose into the morning sky. Crawling a little farther forward, Kane gave the same treatment to the car parked in front of the first: it exploded with the initial burst, though, shaking the street and sending a column of black smoke swirling into the air.

Under the cover of the smoke—hoping it obscured them from wherever the sniper took his shots—Kane threw Hector over his shoulders, plucked Clayton's sleeve, and ran for it. With only the few cars parked along the side of the street for cover, they had to duck down the doubtful safety of a side street before they could see to Hector's injuries. He was barely conscious and had begun to cough up blood. Clayton, for the second time in seven hours, applied a flutter valve (an improvised dressing used on a sucking chest wound, which used the plastic from the dressing's rapper to make a valve that lets blood out of the lung but seals when the patient breathes in, to avoid suffocation).

"Find her," was the only coherent thing Hector could say.

Bashing in the window of a florist, Clayton took the thick velvet covering of a tasteful table display to use as a pole-less litter. Laying Hector on the fabric, he could drag him along—like a kid on a sled—without help from Kane. Kane took point again and led the way as they tried again to make it to the safe house on River Street.

No house on River Street was safe. The searing light of burning North Arkham rippled over the street as the pale light of morning stared blindly up the river. In these competing lights, dark figures cleaved to one another in a firefight conducted from less than ten feet apart. Burning cars and fallen bodies lay everywhere. Shouts of command, of pain, of crazed fear or thoughtless rage accompanied every burst of gunfire. Not knowing immediately who was who, Kane and Clayton pulled Hector into the lee of a building. It was clear, however, that either side might overcome the other at any second, with nothing more than luck needed to decide the contest. Desperate to make sure it was not the Venators who fell —if Venators were anywhere on the street—Kane shouldered the Winchester and peered into the chaos.

"You said all the safe houses are stocked with vintage firearms?" Kane shouted.

"Except this one here, close to the river," Clayton hollered back.

"What do they have?" Kane shouted.

"Belgian—"

Kane fired, cycled the bolt, and then fired again, and then twice more. The firefight ended in a cry of "cease fire" from among the living. Out of the smoke trailing into the sky, a short, slight figure in black-and-gray camouflage and a black dew rag walked toward them, carrying a Belgian-made FN-P90, a weapon the size and shape of a closed laptop.

"Get Kim back to the safe house, Teddy," the figure said. "Marc, check them for a radio or phone but leave the rest: I think I heard the National Guard assault begin. Hey Sol, glad you made it."

"I'm glad I made it, too, Helen," Kane said, standing but keeping one shoulder pressed to the warehouse wall. "Tell me you've got a doc in the safe house nearby."

Helen teetered between footsteps for a moment before rushing around the corner and dropping to her knees next to Hector.

She was blackened in places, from smoke and grease, tired and tireless; the woman the undergraduate class believed was agoraphobic because she never left the Arch Building; the gentle voice on the phone that gave leads and led research; the closest thing the pathologically individualistic Venators ever came to an overall commander: none of it stopped her from feeling the loss of a friend—and more than a friend—when Archie had been killed the night before and none of it stopped her from seeing the same tragedy about to begin with Hector. And none of it stopped her from responding instantly.

"Clayton, get his feet," she said, coming to hers. "Sol, get his other shoulder. We've got a couple docs who managed to escape from St. Mary's during the massacre."

"They did that on purpose?" Clayton said as they carried Hector down River Street to a door beneath sidewalk level. A man in scrub trousers helped them once Helen kicked open the door.

"In case any of us were only wounded and brought in," she said.

They lifted Hector onto one of two tables. Kim—a badly scarred man in his early fifties—on the other table pounded a fist against his unwounded thigh as a haggard woman in scrubs and a burned head probed his other leg for a bullet. The first doc shooed the Venators away from Hector and began cutting away his shirt. Helen would not be shooed. She put her hand on Hectors cheek and he opened his eyes, only for a moment but his lips moved before they closed again.

"Please, I need room," the male doc said. "Catherine, just tie that off and come help me. Do you have any plasma on hand?"

"No," Helen said. After a heartbeat, she began stripping Hector's pockets of magazines, stuffing them into her LBV (load bearing vest). "We have a few blood expanders in the refrigerator. I hope they'll help. The National Guard is attacking now. If you can keep Hector alive for a few hours, they'll have an aid station set up for you. Where's Hector's weapon? I'm out of ammo for the P-90"

"Here," Clayton said, unslinging Hector's M-2 Carbine.

"Come on," she said taking the weapon as she moved toward the door. "There's another entrance to the cave they were trying to reach. It's down the street."

"Wait a sec," Kane said. "What other entrance?"

"There's a backdoor to the Vault, accessible through caves that come out on the island, in the river," she said, "and beneath a building down the street. If the forces at the Arch Building fall back after the National Guard attacks, they may try to reach the island, have another go at the back door. Clayton, do you know where the back door is, down the street?"

"Nut-uh," Clayton said.

"Okay, it's me and you then, Sol," Helen said. "Clayton, you, Marc, and Teddy keep an eye on that island; ambush anyone who makes a move toward it. Sol and I will hit the other entrance to the caves."

"Works for me," Kane said, dropping his Winchester and unslinging his M-2.

Helen went back to Hector, took his cheek in her hands as the male doc and Catherine opened the exit wound in his lung with a scalpel. She kissed Hector on the lips and his eyes opened again, merely slits. "I'm sorry," she whispered and then left.

Topside, Helen and Kane kept close to the warehouse wall, away from the river, and trotted west. Both tried not to look at burning North Arkham; even on fire, the buildings could still harbor the truly faithful among the Legion, ready to shoot.

"No where's safe," Kane mumbled as they ran.

"Not this side of the grave," she replied.

Closing in on the end of the line of warehouses, they slowed their pace—but not before a sentry in a Campus Police uniform swung his assault rifle over the trunk of a car parked at the end of a cross street and opened up on them. Kane flung himself flat at the foot of the wall, returning fire in a messy burst. Helen hit the ground rolling and with a sideways plunge got behind a truck parked on the river side of the street. She gave Kane the hand signal to lay down fire; he obliged and sprayed the car's trunk with quick bursts, pinning down the sentry. Helen ran up the far side of the parked truck until she came to the hood and then dropped prone, angling around the front tires: she killed the sentry with a single round to the head. Immediately, four more assault rifles opened fire from a stairwell going down into the sidewalk. Helen pulled further back as the truck tire blew out and the vehicle leaned precariously toward her. Crawling backwards, she reached the edge of the river and used it for cover as she circled back and joined Kane on the far side of the sentry's car.

"That's the entrance to the service tunnel that leads to the caves, the backdoor," she shouted as he tried to lay down suppressive fire on the four cultists firing from their concrete hole. "There's a pretty tough door down there; they'll have trouble unless they blow it."

A shout behind them jerked their heads around in time to see a squad of National Guard infantry spill out onto the street and take cover behind a parked car and a garbage dumpster. They opened fire a second later. But a second later, about to be caught between two fires, Kane and Helen—without a word of communication—broke around opposite sides of the sentry's car, emptying their magazines at the cultists. The cultists dropped into the concrete stairwell, ducking under the automatic fire that prevented them from returning any.

Helen continued to spray the couple inches of the stairwell's far wall that she could see from the street, every few seconds, keeping the cultists pinned. She shouted for Kane to try to dissuade the National Guard from assaulting. He didn't promise much, except to try. Now firing in both directions, a flimsy car already shot full of holes as their only cover, and running steadily out of ammo, something had to give.

"And today was going so well," Kane shouted.

"Pin them down," Helen shouted, rising up just enough to peek an eye over the trunk. "Give it everything you got."

Kane sprayed a continuous burst at the squad down the street and they pulled behind their various pieces of cover. They hesitated just long enough for him to reload and fire them up again.

"Now what?" he asked as he reloaded and continued to pin them.

"Any second now," Helen said, taking another quick peek. "When I give the word, you cover the cultists."

Kane shrugged and kept laying down fire. A moment later a shout of "frag out" came from the disheartened squad and a small, heavy object arced through the air.

"Now!" Helen shouted.

Kane spun and fired a burst at the cultists, keeping their heads down. Helen swept the dew rag off her head so she could use it to take hold of the burning barrel of her carbine. Holding the gun with her arms extended, as the grenade fell toward her and Kane, Helen stretched up to meet it like a lacrosse player receiving a pass—and knocked it right into the stairwell among the Legion cultists. A sharp cry was all that preceded the thump and fiery spurt (from an acetylene tank they'd brought to cut open the door) heralding the end of that group of cultists.

Helen flipped her carbine around to the proper position and shot the basement windows out of the building above the access tunnel. In a leap, she was on her feet, throwing her carbine in on top of the dead cultists.

"Ditch your weapons and ammo," she said, tossing her LBV in after her carbine. "Hurry, come on!"

Kane did as he was told, only a faint glimmer of what she had in mind pressing random buttons in his brain. Having disarmed themselves, Helen crawled through the broken basement window; Kane followed. Inside, she ran up the stairs, entered the ground floor, kicked in another door, crossed the front room of someone's apartment, and then kicked out a window. Kane almost went head first out it but she caught him and said, "Up stairs."

They ran up three flights of stairs and Helen stopped only long enough to remove her boots; Kane followed her example. They padded softly down the hallway until they reached a door with a corner of an envelope poking out from underneath. Helen handed Kane a lock pick. He smirked as he finally caught on and opened the lock. They said little until the door was closed and locked again. The apartment was empty.

"Now you change clothes, right?" he asked.

"While you see if there's any food," she said, walking to the bedroom. "And a drink wouldn't hurt."

Hiding her fatigues in the crawlspace, Helen donned the only dress in the apartment that fit her, one that probably belonged to a thirteen-year old girl. She looked only slightly ridiculous once she put an over-large man's sweater over it. She joined Kane at the kitchen table where he had cans of sardines, crackers, and pickles ready. And a bottle of twenty-one year old scotch.

"And now," she said as they ate, "when the National Guard sweeps the city, we'll say we were out when the bomb went off, saw people getting killed left and right, and took refuge here. I have my ID. No reason to suspect a Professor Emeritus of Miskatonic University of anything. You have some kind of cover on you?"

Kane drew out his plastic bag with his phone in it and took out a wallet. Opening it, he read, "I am apparently a Glen Tucker."

"You are the most unlikely looking Glen I've ever seen," she laughed. They touched glasses and drank to Glen.

"We found your phone," Kane said. "That looked close."

"I wear armor when I get into firefights," she said. "Unlike you cowboys. I think the shot bruised a rib, but I'll live. How much of what happened do you know?"

Kane gave her a rough outline of everything that had happened since he and Hector reached Arkham.

"But that's only what happened today," he said later. "Down in Maryland, that overly-lucky professor? It was a mousetrap. A group of cultists calling themselves The Legion had baited it to catch Venators."

"The Legion, eh?" Helen said.

"You've heard of them?" he asked. She nodded. "We wiped them out, as far as I know. That contingent, I mean. But it, well, the lieutenant or high priestess—shit."

Kane got up and walked away from the table, not facing Helen. She almost came out of her seat, too, but then held up her hands as if pressing herself back.

She took a deep silent breath and in a calm voice asked, "Sol, what happened?"

"The woman, the leader," he said, looking at the floor or his hands, shaking his head. "Before she died, she said—fuck, fuck, fuck—she said!" He couldn't make the words come out and it seemed maddening, the room was shaking under his feet, spinning, diving. He wanted to press his head against the wall but it was made of mud, of quicksand, it would draw him in. "She said, she said, she said."

Helen came out of her seat in a bound, turning him by his shoulders, and looked up steadily into his eyes. "Sol," she said, "what did she say?"

"She, she," he stuttered. With a gulp of air and a shout half swallowed, he said, "She said Cthulhu had condescended to know the name Solomon Kane."

He all but collapsed forward but she wouldn't let him fall, she caught him, kicking her feet back to take the weight, and pressed his back to the wall. "Stand," she said. "Breathe. Sol, you're afraid. You're afraid and fear is good. Don't fight it. You're afraid, say it."

"I'm afraid," he hissed into silence.

"Fear is just a sense," she said. "Like sight or smell, just a sense. It tells you what's out there, what's around you. And just as you can burn out your eyes looking into the sun or blow your hearing during a mortar barrage, you can hurt yourself with fear. Go with it, but don't let it call the shots. It's okay to fear. As long as you control it."

He was breathing deliberately now, looking over her head. "I don't want to go crazy like them," he whispered, tears spilling from both eyes. "Drop into a madness that never ends, stripped bare on an altar of salt, an eternity under the eye of Cthulhu."

"Sol, shh, it's okay, slow down," she said. "You're not going crazy. You're worried about it but crazy people don't worry about it. They don't wonder if they're crazy."

"Sure they do," he said and the last three days caught up with him at once. He was less afraid all of a sudden, and then weary, mortally weary. "I'm sorry. I haven't been able to say it without losing my mind a bit. I need a drink."

She took a trial step away and when he didn't fall, she poured him a large scotch and put it in his hand. He took only a sip before he let her lead him back to his seat.

"That'll wake you up," he said and dropped into the chair, slumping forward at the shoulders. "He does know me. Don't say otherwise, Helen, I know it. It's the only explanation why the fear hits so hard, just to say it. The idea alone isn't that frightening."

"Yes, it is," she said, taking her seat. "But you're not entirely in contact with him. Or he with you. It's not possible. We know for certain how it works now. In fact, it's connected closely with The Legion."

"Who are they?" he asked.

"You know *The Necronomicon*, of course," she said. "Well that book is merely the ramblings of the so-called 'Mad Arab' Abdul Alhazred. Ever wonder why he was mad? He had delved into arcane texts, tombs of unspeakable evil, and they changed him. That is the story but it is actually not a metaphor of how knowledge can corrupt. That's just Christian mysticism. The story is, in fact, literal. It was only one book that got him, though. I don't know its title, though I've seen the book; I don't know its contents, though I've handled the pages. Even old Abdul never saw the whole thing. As far as anyone knows, there were only four copies ever made and the original is, well," she paused and drained her glass. "The original, so they say, is down in R'lyeh."

She took a moment to fill her glass and swirl the scotch in it, watching the golden color circle in the growing light of morning. The ground was shaking with a series of explosions as Nation Guard Apache helicopters attacked the Arch Building and the church. Kane and Helen glanced toward the window in unison and then in unison tried to ignore what they could not affect.

"On Cthulhu's nightstand, no doubt," Kane joked. They both chuckled and then laughed and then cackled into a wheezing fit.

"Oh, oh that's, Jesus, that's good," she said, the strain of the last twelve hours draining out of her, despite the growing sounds of warfare. "Probably. The thing is, old Abdul saw a partial copy some cultist tried to make in Hungry. Only Cthulhu didn't take kindly to it; gave him bad dreams. The Hungarian actually, literally, chopped his own head off with a hatchet. Just kept hacking away until he decapitated himself. So, naturally, this book interested us. Well, after nearly twenty years of searching, we found one of the four."

Kane watched her from across the table. Whatever pride she took in the accomplishment was tempered with a knowledge of all that was lost, all who had been lost, to obtain it. He also wondered, not for the first time, how old she was. He was forty-two; she could have been his age; she could have been ten or maybe even twenty years older; she could have passed for thirty-five. There was nothing in her voice or movements, her mind or her spirit, that connoted age.

"We knew it was dangerous to read," she said. "And despite a couple stupidly brave volunteers, we decided not to risk it. On a hunch, we brought in the corpse of the last known person to read it and looked at his remains. Turns out, while mapping his brain structure, the computer picked up a very particular pattern in his neural pathways. We wondered. You see, every time you commit something to memory, every time you learn a new skill or hear a song, your brain creates neural pathways. This last guy to read the book-that-shall-not-be-named, his neural pathways happened to create a pattern in his brain that looks exactly like a symbol used in the lost city of Kara-Shehr. It appears carved into gemstones, engraved onto golden spheres—it's found on the Cthulhu statues you Venators are so fond of smashing. The squiggly squid head folds? It's in there. So we thought that this was odd and wondered if the book was what did it. So," she said and drained her glass again before putting the cork back in the bottle. "So—and I admit I'm a cold-hearted bitch for doing it and it's haunted me ever since—I asked Hector to kidnap a cultist for me." Kane only nodded but didn't let his face judge her. "I'm not going to excuse what we did to him, but we learned a lot. We took him, strapped him down, and did a comprehensive study of his brain. He had a few bits of the pattern here and there but it wasn't conclusive. Unsettlingly, I have more of the pattern than he did. *You* probably do to. As does every Venator who's read too much of *The Necronomicon*. Then we put him in a room and gave him the book. He devoured it, Sol. He read it in ecstasy. He raved, he wept, he gibbered. And then I shot him."

"Put him out of his misery," he said.

"Sure," she said. "Put him out of a misery I caused him."

"You know who really caused it," he said.

"Regardless," she said, dropping her hands in her lap, "regardless, we then scanned his brain again. He had the pattern complete. As the neural pathways formed, they created the pattern. In a strange way, it may be what brought on the attack. If what we surmise is true, if the pattern allows Cthulhu to *actively* dream-send into a subject's mind, then he may have learned everything our guinea pig knew; maybe homed in on his location and sent it to The Legion. The book, after all, is very valuable to them, obviously. Anyone who could survive reading it would be completely under Cthulhu's sway."

"And a few curses from it can reduce a tired old Venator to tears," Kane said. "There's one thing about all of that doesn't make sense: the cult has known about Miskatonic University's connection to the Venators for at least forty years."

"Only now, we have the book," she said.

"I guess," he said.

"But it's more than that," she said. "The big thing I told you about, on the horizon? We had the dates wrong. Two weeks ago, a comet—heretofore unknown to astronomy—appeared in the solar system, passing Neptune. It changes everything we know about the configuration of the stars necessary to attempt to open a door to R'lyeh."

"No, no, no, don't say it," Kane said.

"It isn't three months away," Helen said. "It's only a few days from now. The book may have been a big boon to The Legion but I think their real reason for attacking Arkham was to turn it into a meat grinder, to kill as many Venators as they could. They don't want us interfering. With the coming of the comet, they have their best chance in the last hundred years to open a door to R'lyeh and make the necessary sacrifices to revive Cthulhu."

BOOK 7
R'LYEH RISING

CHAPTER 1

MERRIE GLOOM

THE CARGO SHIP'S prow had begun to rise noticeably as it crested the waves of the freshening sea. Kane watched as the few Venators on deck tied down a stolen OH-58 Kiowa helicopter, bending their knees with the motion of the ship. The cargo containers *Merrie Gloom* had brought to Boston from Hong Kong via Johannesburg mostly lined the dock where the longshoremen had unloaded them; a few, though, had remained on board when Kane and the other Venators had taken the ship. Once they'd figured out how to use the crane, those few joined whatever other garbage lined the bottom of Massachusetts Bay.

The attack on *Merrie Gloom* had gone off without a hitch. By the time Kane and Helen had arrived, Oswald Greendecker, called Oz, had organized most of the southern Venators while Chico Tay and a couple charismatic west coast Venators had gotten the better of the few sailors left onboard. Chic, as the six-five and two-hundred and thirty pound Venator was affectionately known, had even recruited one of the sailors to get *Merrie Gloom* underway. Kane smiled at the ten-hour-old memory: Oz had sent the sailor swimming as they passed Martha's Vineyard.

The mad drive from Arkham didn't seem like a memory, though, more like a dream. After the Legion had attacked the quiet university town, after Kane and Hector had fought their way in to save Helen—who hadn't needed saving—and after the Massachusetts National Guard had secured the small city and finished off the cultist militia, Venators all over Arkham had had to talk their way through cordons and checkpoints, skirt outposts and lines of infantry surrounding the city, and in some rare instances—when caught—fight their way out and toward the coast. The worst of all possibilities had begun: R'Lyeh was rising.

Kane and Helen had driven out of Arkham very easily. As the head of the Archeology and Ethnology Department at Arkham University, her credentials were known and trusted. Crammed into a procured university station wagon, she drove like a banshee flies all the way to Boston, with Kane calling every Venator in the United States and Canada on both her and his cell phones as Clayton, Marc, and Teddy did likewise, hunched over in the backseat. That many Venators dropping their private stalks to gather on a dock in Boston had a look about it like the end of the world.

"Sol, wave for those guys to come up as soon as the chopper is secured," Helen said as she entered the bridge behind him.

Kane turned to see Venators filing into the cramped tower, still eyeing each other like strange dogs. He flashed the bridge lights a couple of times and then reached his arm out a window to flag those on deck. Clayton, who'd been watching beside Kane, handed Helen a cup of coffee as she put her back to the huge windows that overlooked the empty cargo ship and the darkening sky ahead.

The Venators were a cagy bunch. They came in all sizes and shapes, though rangy and tall was the most common. Unshaven but not bearded, clothes that had been washed too often but not recently, jackets that were kept like fetishes against evil long after they should have been replaced, and armed, obviously armed with everything from knives to shotguns to a few belt-fed machineguns, Venators had nothing in their lives but the stalk. A habitually solitary bunch, it was only their obvious deference to Helen that kept them together, passing sidelong looks at each other through it all.

"Gentlemen," Helen said after the door leading out was slammed against the wind, "the worst of all possible futures has come to pass: an island door to R'Lyeh is rising in the Atlantic—and The Legion is sailing toward it with all speed and a cargo hold full of victims awaiting sacrifice."

"Now hold on just a second there, Miss," a Venator with a face like a turkey said, arms akimbo. "That's the third or fourth time I've heard this word *Legion* thrown around as if it ought to mean something to me. Hell, the only Legion I know is the American Legion down by Selma, and that's mostly for drinking."

"Would you pipe down, Morton Caulfield?" an exasperated Venator next to him said. "Can't you see Helen's a-talking? She'll tell you about them Legion if you'll take the trouble to listen?"

"Shee-it, I'm so sorry I'm not as well-versed in your ancient lore," Morton shot back. "I've been stalking cultists and putting them to the torch for twenty-two years!"

"No one doubts your devotion, Morton," Helen said calmly, recalling the two Venators. "You're here, with the rest of us, sailing after The Legion even though you don't know who they are: that shows a great deal of trust, in us, in me, and I thank you. We will need every hand that can hold a gun tonight." Morton and his friend seemed placated and a general murmur of consent rippled from one side of the cramped bridge to the other. "The Legion, for those of you who've never dealt with them—which should be most of you—is in one sense like any other Cult of Cthulhu. Drawn to the worship of The Great Old Ones by dreams or lured by other cultists to gatherings around the strange statuettes by which they hope to commune with Cthulhu, The Legion's cultists differ in their organization, their lineage, and their power. Not cast-offs murdering in the swamps and deserted mountains of the world, The Legion hails from ancient times and purposes to call Cthulhu back to life through concerted action, to the world's demise.

"Like the Venators, The Legion looks back to Rome. Just as your most ancient brethren came from the Praetorian Guard and swore oaths to destroy the cults wherever they arose, to keep Cthulhu forever dead and dreaming in his sunken city of R'Lyeh, so too does The Legion hail from that time and they also have sworn oaths. The Legion, as it calls itself, first formed from the remnant of the Sixteenth Legion after the sack of Rome by the Vandals in 411 CE. Rome was gone and the Praetorian Guard had been all but annihilated defending what remained of the city. The leaders of The Legion saw their chance: many were secret worshipers of Cthulhu and hoped to open a door to R'Lyeh, devote sufficient sacrifices, and be rewarded when Cthulhu revived and took dominion over the world once more. Fools, they would have been the first devoured.

"But the Praetorian Guard had not been utterly destroyed and a section of their best fighters attacked The Legion as it attempted to seize a squadron of ships on the coast of Campania. Though defeated by the Praetorian Guard, and the chance to open a door having passed, a portion of The Legion's leadership had survived, fleeing to Sardinia and from there to Gaul. Since that time, descendants of The Legion have been trying, with military precision, to meet one of the rare risings of R'Lyeh and awaken Cthulhu with human sacrifices. And since that time, we who continue the struggle of the Praetorian Guard, in action if not in word, have always stopped them. Now we are called upon again.

"Five hours ago, The Legion took a ship—one that in all

probability they had long prepared—and with a cargo of human sacrifices cowering in the hold, has set out to these coordinates," she said, tapping a clipboard attached to the conn. "It was only the barest luck that we discovered the ship at all. It must be stopped.

"So, this is the briefing of what to expect and what we will need to do. First, the situation: The Legion ship is a similar class to ours, though from what I have been able to ascertain from a web search about each craft, we have a slight speed advantage. Gordon has also been tinkering with the engines," she said, motioning to a gray and smiling man of short stature and great girth, "so we hope to increase that advantage. The Legion has an unknown number of hostages that they intend to sacrifice. They are most likely in the hold but I suspect they will be sacrificed on deck, in view of R'Lyeh when it breaks the surface of the ocean. Be prepared, however: we may need to go below deck once we board. Their ship will probably reach the spot where R'Lyeh will rise in about three hours; we should overtake them within two but could be longer. Either way, we won't have much time so our primary goal is to stop the sacrifices by whatever means necessary."

"How certain are you, Helen?" a Venator on the far left of the gathering asked. Wearing muttonchops and sporting a leather jacket covered in zippers, he could have been Hector Troy's brother, whom they had left to an unknown fate back in Arkham. "About the sacrifices, I mean. How do we know that's the key to reviving old squid-face? I seem to remember an account of the last time The Legion got close that says otherwise."

"Yes, there is another account," Helen said. "Thank you, Kilmer. Some of you may have read the Johansen Diary, which purports to describe the last known rise of R'Lyeh: I have news for you, the diary is fake. For those of you who have not read the diary, Gustaf Johansen was second mate on the trading ship *Emma*, which left Auckland, New Zealand, on 20 February 1925. While at sea, *Emma* came across the armed yacht *Alert*. According to the Diary, *Alert* attacked *Emma* and *Emma*'s crew responded by boarding *Alert*. The battle was fierce but one-sided, with *Emma*'s crew outnumbering *Alert*'s and winning quickly. The Johansen Diary goes on to say that *Emma* had been too badly damaged and sank, so he and his crew took *Alert* and set out only to come to an island they'd never heard of before. The island held architecture of strange design and cyclopean construction. After briefly exploring the island, they came upon a door, which they examined closely, seeing horrific figures in the surrounding bas relief. Somehow they opened the door and Cthulhu came out."

A brief round of laughter battered the ceiling from one side of the bridge to the other.

"That's what it says," Kilmer shouted over the nose, though he was smiling, too.

"Then why ain't we all ate up by squid-face and all his elder gods?" Morton shouted back, slapping his knee.

"It gets better, actually," Kane said, waving for the Venators to quiet down.

"That's one way of looking at it," Helen said. "According to the Johansen Diary, he and a couple others ran for the ship, with Cthulhu apparently hot on his heels. They pushed off but Cthulhu wadded out into the ocean after them and was only defeated when Johansen bravely rammed Cthulhu with his ship. The island door to R'Lyeh then foundered again, and the diary supposes that Cthulhu—caught by the foundering island—returned to his slumber. Allow me to say, gentlemen, that the tale told in the Johansen Diary has some notes of truth but by and large it is a symphony of lies.

"After exhaustive research by both the University of Arkham and members of The Black Shroud at the Sorbonne," Helen said, crossing her arms, "the Johansen Diary was proved to be a forgery.

There *was* a Gustaf Johansen, his ship *was* attacked by *Alert,* and he and his crew no doubt came within sight of a risen door to R'Lyeh. We know that much. The door specifically. Ever since the mapping of the earth by satellite and the launch of the Hubble Space Telescope, our job of pinpointing where a door to R'Lyeh might rise and when the stars will be aligned properly for such a rising has increased by an order of magnitude. Forensic knowledge, too, has come far since 1925. The forgers of the Johansen Diary were no doubt masters in their day, but under modern examination, their art was obvious.

"We always knew that the diary had to be false, for the same reason you all laughed. If Cthulhu had truly left R'Lyeh and again strode the living world of earth, we would have all been enslaved at best, devoured or destroyed with insanity the most likely end. The point of the forgery, however, was to both throw off pursuit of the cult—particularly of The Legion, who had owned and armed *Alert*—and to reduce fear amongst the scientific community about the rising of doors to R'Lyeh. If Cthulhu seemed less dangerous, defeated by a swift yacht to the head, then why should Venators be so diligent? Why should not the scientific community welcome a chance to study the cyclopean architecture and strange pictographs of R'Lyeh?

"And that's exactly what The Legion wanted to happen, to have scientists and scholars conduct the research into when a door to R'Lyeh would rise and to have potential sacrifices bring themselves to the rising door, where The Legion could meet them and murder them to recall Cthulhu to life. There have been several attempts by The Legion over the centuries and they all have one thing in common: human sacrifice. They always bring boatloads of victims when a door to R'Lyeh rises. You know all too well—better than any other living beings—how the cults are obsessed with human sacrifice: it is an integral part of their communing with Cthulhu, with receiving his dream sendings. Make no mistake, no matter what appears in the Johansen Diary, human sacrifice is indispensable to awakening Cthulhu from his dead dreaming."

"But didn't Johansen swear before the Vice-Admiralty Court?" Kilmer asked.

"He did," Helen said. "But not in such detail as appears in his diary. Even then, though, it is possible that Johansen would have believed every word of the diary, had he seen it completed before his death. And we don't know that he did. Johansen may very well have seen the door to R'Lyeh open, and Cthulhu walk the earth—in his mind's eye.

"Which brings us to the next point," Helen said, pinching the bridge of her nose for a moment. After a sip of coffee, she continued. "Dream sendings, what are they? You've all felt them. More than simple nightmares, anyone who fights the cults in the dark and lonely places of the world, as you do, would have nightmares: dream sendings are the very whispers of Cthulhu traveling from his mighty city of R'Lyeh to plague mankind. Artists and the sensitive are particularly vulnerable to these dream sendings, but so too is anyone who has heard the name Cthulhu and all the more so anyone who knows anything of the history of the cults and the dread rituals they perform to this day. When the rising of a door to R'Lyeh is imminent, the dream sendings become prodigious—and no longer infest the sleeping minds of the sensitive but their waking hours, too. One of the signs we look for, when confirming a possible door rising, is an increase in the number of psychiatric commissions to secure facilities."

"Locking people up because they've suddenly lost their minds," Kane translated. A few heads nodded.

"Yes, people who were assumed perfectly rationally one day," Helen said, "by their friends, family, co-workers, suffering from no more than a few months of bad dreams, suddenly go mad and become a danger to themselves. Often a subject who receives these 'waking dream sendings' will rave in a language the psychiatrists do not understand, particularly if the subject was a poet or singer. But you've all heard that language before.

"It is likely that Johansen, once he and his crew landed on the risen door to R'Lyeh, in 1925, were overcome by waking dream sendings. The image of the door opening may or may not have been real but certainly Cthulhu emerging and doing battle with Johansen is preposterous. It was all in his mind. Which brings me to the last and most important point of this briefing: we shall all experience these same waking dream sendings.

"So prepare yourselves," Helen said and walked from one end of the bridge to the other, looking each Venator in the eye. "The closer we come to the door to R'Lyeh, the more perceptible the dreams will become. They will start as mere whispers in the dark, but they will grow. In intensity, in persistence, the whispers will grow. If you are unwary, unprepared, you could fall into an all encompassing delusion. Fight it! You've all experienced dream sendings in your sleep. It's an occupational hazard of the Venator. Some few Venators over the years have even had their names sent to The Legion in dreams."

A murmur shot through the gathering, of half remembered tales, of disbelief, and horror at the thought of the High Priest of The Great Old Ones knowing their mortal names. Kane scorched his tongue and throat, bolting his coffee down a suddenly dry throat and thinking of a dark night in Maryland.

"There are ways of distracting your mind from the dreams, however," Helen said. "Keep focused on the mission, for one; but focusing on anything will help. In that first attempt by The Legion to open a door to R'Lyeh, they passed very near the door in their escape. To keep his ship on track as he pursued them, Cassius Tacitus—the Venator Captain—fought the dream sendings he felt by running through his mind the teachings of Euclid. Over and over again, he ran the laws of geometry, reciting the dimensions of the Parthenon in Greece and how the length of the long side corresponded to the length of the short side, to the height of the columns, etc. In 1759, The Black Shroud stopped an attempt by The Legion near the Arctic Circle, above Norway. For some reason, their lead ship was almost entirely English and to keep their minds from being turned by the waking dream sendings of Cthulhu, they recited Shakespeare."

"Once more into the breach dear friends?" one wit asked at the back of the assembly. A few dutiful laughs followed.

"Yes, I expect so," Helen said, smiling. "I tell you this only to encourage you: use whatever works. Run math through your mind, recite your favorite movie dialogue—sing at the top of your lungs. Whatever it takes. For some of you, it won't be necessary, I expect. For others, it may be the difference between life and death. Stay focused. Focused but watchful. If you see a fellow Venator losing it badly, keep an eye on him. There are accounts of Venators so overcome by their delusions that they attack their fellows. I'm sorry, but that is the truth. Prepare yourselves for it."

"And how do The Followers of Dagon enter into all this?" someone asked from the back.

Kane shot a glance at Clayton. The large Venator hung his head.

"They don't," Kane said.

"They might," Helen said with a smile.

"I heard about you and Hector running headlong into a mousetrap," Morton said. "*The Legion*, huh? And the high holy-moly said it was on account of you two wiping out some Followers up north, back a few months."

The night in Maryland moved in Kane's mind like a stirring animal. He returned the old Venator's stare but said nothing.

"The Follower's of Dagon share certain affinities with The

Legion," Helen said. "For one, they are both considerably more organized than the—shall we say—local chapters of The Greater Cthulhu Cult. Secondly, though, they are often present together

The Legion tries to protect towns The Followers invest. Emptying such a town would have easily provided enough sacrifices for this evening."

"We don't get Followers of Dagon on the west coast," Chic said. "Not as far as we know. Don't they have some sort of jewelry fetish? And—"

"Yes," Helen said. "They use a meteoric gold-like substance in what we call Innsmouth jewelry, after its most famous appearance. Although, I suppose we could call it Odiome jewelry, now," she added with a smile at Kane. Kane wasn't smiling.

"Right, and these dudes, these Followers, think wearing the stuff will turn them into monsters?" Chic asked. A murmur shot through the bridge.

"They do," Helen said lightly. "They believe through long use of Innsmouth jewelry during ritual sacrifice that they will transform into amphibious monsters, allowing them to swim down to R'Lyeh and awaken Cthulhu without the bother of waiting for an island to rise. Do I need to tell you it's preposterous?"

"That they could revive Cthulhu when the stars aren't aligned correctly—or that they can turn into monsters?" Chic asked.

"Column A," Helen said. "I'm not going to rule out a transformation; too many of the men in this room have come across creatures that defy modern science for us to rule that out. But if The Followers are at all involved with The Legion's attempt tonight, it will be as the source of the sacrifices. And that is a far more frightening possibility."

CHAPTER 2

DEFINE CRAZY

A FEW OF THE senior Venators from the various parts of the United States, Canada, and Mexico stepped forward to say a few words of encouragement and to coordinate what they wanted from each group once the Legion ship was sighted. Though the weather beat against the angled windows of the bridge and waves shot from the prow into the lowering sky, the bridge seemed quiet as those men spoke; as if silence were a weight that they lifted with their voices and lifted with effort. Not every word seemed to reach the corners of the small room. Coordination completed, the Venators broke into shifts: surveillance, operations, and rest. Regardless of assignment, though, all eyes watched the approaching storm and sought to penetrate the depthless horizon, to see the Legion ship.

Helen motioned for Kane and Kilmer to follow her below deck. Down several flights of narrow metal stairs, grime over green paint, past the crew berths and the galley, past the store room, there was a secured berth. Not a brig, in name, but a room with a bunk and bars and a lock. It sat at the end of a short hallway, a thick door with a small circular window and then a space as narrow as a coffin, and then the cell. A guard stood outside the hall door rather than in the room, but if he thought it would give him peace from what was inside, he thought wrong. Even while on the last set of stairs, Helen and Kane and Kilmer could hear the gibbering, the pleas dissolving into sobs, the howls of mirth turning to terror that burst from the secured room.

The guard looked like he needed to be relieved and not because his patience had been tested to the limit, which it no doubt had. Kilmer clapped him on the shoulder and sent him to find a replacement. Before he left, the guard reported to Helen only that there had been no change. "Mr. Angell is as talkative as ever, Ms Helen. Not that much of it makes any sense to me. Except for a few words," he mumbled before ducking his head and slipping past. There was no need to ask which words the Venator had recognized.

Helen and Kane walked in, stood before the cage. On the floor, a young man in the remnants of a three-piece suit sprawled half rising on his hands only to throw himself toward one wall. He mumbled and spat, he screamed; eyes scanning the steel floor beneath him and then the air, he never saw his visitors, only his visions.

"He's getting worse," Kane said. "Maybe we ought to tie him down."

"He'd only pull at the restraints until his muscles tore," Helen said. "If we'd had more time to prepare, I would have brought a straightjacket. His head is bleeding but not badly. He must have hit the bars, poor man."

"How did you know he was one of the artists who would hear the dream sendings?" Kane asked. "There must be hundreds around the world right now who are in a similar state, as R'Lyeh slowly approaches the surface of the ocean."

"Oh I've known about Professor Angell for a few years now,"

she said. "He teaches Art History in Boston. Dates one of my PhD candidates. He's an artist and a good one. Over dinner in the lab one night, when he'd brought Chinese for his sweetie, I overheard him telling her this weird dream he'd had."

"When was this?" Kane asked.

Helen had to wait as Angell howled and beat the bars with his fists. After a moment he sank into a long hopeless whimper. "When you were in Louisiana," she said and winked.

"Shit," Kane said. "But that door wasn't actually rising. Those crazy shits were trying to drill through it."

"I know," Helen said. "But their intent must have been known. Known to Cthulhu."

"*Ph'nglui mglw'nafh Cthulhu R'lyeh wgah'nagl fhtagn*," Angell screamed.

Helen knelt close to the bars and tried to calm the distraught and obviously terrified young artist. If her soothing sounds and gentle touches did anything for him, though, the only sign he gave was a lapse into gibbering. She stood.

"I think that was the first time The Legion actually tangled with you," Helen said. "Then, later, they were sent a dream that the infamous Solomon Kane was responsible for Odiome," she said, lowering her voice theatrically.

"Sensational," he said.

"Which is why they came after you in Maryland," she said. "Set a trap for you, really. And I do mean, *you*. I imagine they thought that if you could wipe out The Followers in Odiome, to say nothing of that little op they had going in Louisiana, they'd better take you out of the picture before the big show."

"Yeah," Kane said quietly.

Helen turned toward him, her head on one side. "Sol?"

"I'm okay," he said. "Is that—I don't even know what to call it—the cult's language, what Angell's speaking?"

"You don't recognize it?" she said.

"The chant he just shouted, sure," he said. "I've heard that chanted in too many dark swamps and out of the way places not to recognize it. But what he's saying now? Not so much. I know I hear it in my dreams, sometimes, but it's never very clear; more of a sensation."

"Good," she said. "When it becomes clear in your dreams, you've had it: crazy time. As for poor Angell, he can't really understand what he's hearing in his head right now. He's imitating the sounds but not the words. Don't forget, human minds cannot comprehend the true thoughts of a Great Old One, or C-T-H-U-L-H-U's either. We don't possess the intellectual organs, so to speak. Once we're close enough to the island, though, when it starts to rise, the dream sendings will be going full blast and Angell will start shouting in tongues. I should be able to understand what he's saying then."

"And that's going to help us?" he said.

"Sure," she said. "Think of the dream sendings as commands sent from you-know-who to The Legion. If Angell is listening in, he'll know what those commands are and it might give us an edge."

After a last look at the muttering and agitated Angell, Helen and Kane left. Suggesting another cup of coffee, Helen led him to what had been the captain's cabin. Because of the swaying of the ship, rising up ever-higher mountains of water only to plunge down the opposite cliff, the coffee maker was a specialized pressure device. Like an espresso machine attached to a thermos, the coffee maker made a few cups of coffee at a time into a spill-proof carafe. Very good coffee in fact: the former captain must have been an enthusiast.

Kane steadied himself on the desk as the ship pitched forward down another cliff. Helen smirked over her shoulder from where she watched the coffee maker and said, "How's the stomach, Sol?"

"I wish you hadn't said that," he said, laughing with his shoulders. "I flew in a twin-prop once, through a lightning storm: it was almost as bad as this."

Helen unfastened the carafe and carefully filled a tall coffee mug about a third of the way and handed it to Kane. "This help?" she asked. He took the cup greedily. "Something about the size of the ship makes it worse. A little sail boat or Jet Ski or what-have-you wouldn't make you feel at all sick."

Kane had to hold the cup away from his nose a second after the word 'sick.' He gave Helen his evil leer and she chuckled an apology. Taking a sip of coffee, Kane said, "Hey, what's that in the corner over there? Oh look, a change of subject." Helen nodded as she sipped her coffee and sank slowly onto the couch. "I've always meant to ask, or rather I've wondered and knew there's not really an appropriate time *to* ask: how did you get into all of this? Mixed up with the Venators? It's not exactly a polite question but, shit, no sane person could expect to come back alive from this mission so this is my last and only chance. Most of us lost family to the cult," he finished softly.

"Not me," Helen said. "And I wasn't a former cultist, either. I was—and am—a scholar, an antiquarian; and when my research led to the darker parts of pre-history, I eventually came upon *The Necronomicon* and *Unaussprechlichen Kulten* and then Cthulhu. From there, meeting Venators was almost inevitable."

"That's it?" Kane said. "You actually *chose* this?"

"Can you believe that?" Helen said.

"I think that's the craziest thing I've ever heard," he said breathlessly. They laughed into their cups. He held up his thumb and forefinger and said, "Most people run for the hills if they hear *this* much."

"Well, I suppose," Helen said and then looked off to one side for a moment. "I suppose saying that family wasn't involved was true but misleading, in a sense. The first Venator I met was, shall we say, charismatic. Oh screw it: we fell in love."

"I see," Kane said. He smirked over the rim of his cup for a moment before asking: "Which one of them was it?"

"Ha, no it was neither Hector nor Archie," she said. "You know what? You were right, just now, when you said that no sane person could expect to come back from this mission alive, even if we succeed. So I want to go to my doom with my conscience clear, concealing nothing. It was Catherine Foucault."

"Oh, okay," Kane said. "Why keep it a secret, though? I know the Venators are a bit of a boy's club but I never thought of any of us as homophobic."

"You live a sheltered life, Solomon Kane," she said and chuckled.

"I do," he said. "I really do."

"But no, I don't think any of them would have really cared," she said. "At first Catherine and I kept it secret to protect ourselves; so neither of us could be used as a weapon against the other. Her being kidnapped to force me to open The Vault, for instance. Keeping my orientation a secret from the Venators was the most expedient way to rule her out in the cult's mind. People around campus knew, naturally, but not many and, of course, it was nobody's business. And these days, at least, hardly a reason to talk. After Catherine died, though," she said without completing the sentence.

Kane shook his head and held up a hand, about to speak, to tell her she didn't need to go any further. She waved him back down and took a moment while she refilled her cup.

"After she died," she said, leaning against the rolling cabin wall, "there was no one else. And then Archie and Hector started showing an interest, and I would have made it clear to them both that nothing like that was going to happen, could happen, but, well . . ."

"But intimacy is a hard thing to go without," Kane said. "Even if it's platonic."

"That's true," she said, "in this case, though, it wasn't intimacy that compelled me but ruthless self-interest. Archie and Hector were two of our best."

"Yes, they were," Kane said. "And Hector isn't a *were* just yet."

"I hope he pulls through," she said. "Someone should survive, tell the tale. But years ago, he and Archie were burning out, losing their devotion to the war, becoming reckless and not out of their usual zeal: they'd stopped caring, even about their own lives. Chasing me? I don't know. They needed it. It kept them focused, competing with each other. Stalking returned to being a job for them. Living through each mission became how they'd beat the other one: they were both waiting for the other to die on a stalk, clearing the path to me. Not that anything could have ever happened between me and either of them, though of course they didn't know that. If either of them had actually caught me, so to speak, he would have retired. As Venators, they were far too valuable for me to let that happen, to let them crash and burn or run off and find a little woman to settle down with. So I kept them interested, kept them in the war, hopelessly hoping. I've been an unimaginably manipulative asshole, Sol, and not just to Hector and Archie: to all the Venators. Part of me feels terrible about it. I've picked at other people's scabs, kept the pain fresh, reminded them of their failures in a hundred little subtle ways, promised them things they could never have, anything to keep them in the war. I'm a horror."

"You've also soothed fears and talked people off ledges," he said. "You've guided, protected, equipped, and fought beside all of us. No one has devoted as much as you, has cared for more people or lost as many friends to the cult as you have. You've done what you had to do. And it's paid off: we're going to beat these Legion bastards to the door if it's the last thing we do."

Kane put his cup in its holder on the wall and then rest a hand on Helen's shoulder. Looking into each other's eyes, they nodded their acceptance of whatever they'd done and whatever would be asked of them in the coming hours. Kane then turned and headed up to the bridge. As he left, a sly smile tugged at the corners of Helen's lips and she settled back into the couch to finish her coffee.

CHAPTER 3

SURCEASE OF SORROW

T HE VAGUE DISTANCE, opaque within the depthless night, began to glow as morning approached. The Venators would see no sun, they knew, as the marching storm-wall blotted out the east, rushing to meet them over the waves. Dark gray and rising out of sight, the boiling mass of clouds seemed to drop the ocean into a valley, cascading ever downwards. From the makeshift shack near the helicopter and from under the doubtful cover of the bridge-railing's awning and out of the countless bridge-tower windows, Venators watched the approaching storm and knew it had not been called by Nature.

As the wind increased until it played the railings and steel-corded lines like an Aeolian harp, as the waves leaped ever higher to meet *Merrie Gloom* and cast their gallons of water slithering across her deck in hissing foam, the Venators saw more than waves and heard more than wind.

"Seasons don't fear the reaper, nor do the wind, the sun, or the rain."

"What's that you're saying?"

"Oh nothing; just a song I used to listen to. One summer."

The gallows humor began, as it usually does. A whisper of doubt, a sudden image of falling into the slate gray water so cold it would shock the life out of a grown man in seconds, a cry of the wind that howled more from memory than the sky, and it began. No one's heart seemed in it, though, as it always had since they'd joined the war. There was something to Helen's warning and the first brush of madness across their consciousnesses was as ephemeral and fleeting as water tumbling down the pitching deck to shower into the ocean passing on the other side.

They huddled together in small groups. Someone would declare his lack of fear—and that his intention was only to follow Helen's advice—and then admit he'd heard something. His fellows on either side would nod or their lips would move without sound. Someone would clear his throat, an elbow would hit a rib, and someone would tell a story, usually one they'd all heard before. A bawdy tale of a wildcat in a remote roadhouse or a three-day drunk between stalks that went wrong in the funniest way possible, the stories all started with chuckles before slipping into other memories: the first sight of a cultist slitting a throat, the faint echo of mad chanting dodging through the trees of an ancient forest, the slow shaking head of a police detective on the first night of someone's war.

The Elder Gods, unknowable beyond the ken of mortal man, dead eons before the rise of civilization, called out to many and were heard by few. Under the fathomless deeps, in sunken R'Lyeh, in a temple amid that greatest of cities, greatest of horrors, dark Cthulhu stirred in his ancient sleep. Power and thought far removed from what humans could perceive, motives indescribable to man, demands that break the minds of those who resist and those who submit, a force that made night terrible, that drove man to create gentler gods in his own mind, a force that stirred beneath the waves now called and clawed at the minds of travelers who drew near.

"Out of the night that covers me, black as the pit from pole to pole, I thank whatever gods may be for my unconquerable soul."

"You hear them? You hear them, too, Jack, they keep shouting at me!"

"It's normal, it's what Helen told us about. Look at me! Keep your mind focused, okay? Talk to me."

On the bridge, every set of eyes gazed through binoculars or night vision scopes to search the ocean ahead, sparing only seconds to check compass heading or radar. The dark gray of the clouds allowed no appreciation of distance; night was removed without the coming of day. Somewhere ahead, though, somewhere a similar ship drove into the clouds meeting the sea.

"There, eleven-thirty!" Kilmer shouted. "We're almost directly behind them."

"Where?" several voices asked as half a dozen people swarmed to Kilmer's side, trying to orient their binoculars to his.

He leaned to one side to see the surface search radar screen. "That's them, alright," he said. "It's hard to tell with the storm kicking up so much interference but that's them. The white of their bridge tower shows up better against the clouds than against black night, if you can believe it."

"I can," Helen said, standing next to him and adjusting her night vision scope. "We're gaining, too."

"I told you we would," Gordon, in his auto mechanic's coveralls, said triumphantly from behind everyone. "Those bastards won't escape me."

Helen smiled over her shoulder at the mechanic and slipped her arm through the press to bump fists with him. "Oz, have your men get the helicopter ready," she said. "The wind is bad but it'll get worse the closer we come to that storm. We only have this small window; let's not waste it."

"You got it, Helen," Oz said, motioning for another man to follow him out the door and down to the wind-swept deck below.

"Marc, get Siegfried and the guys for the chopper," she said before returning to watch the Legion ship, several miles ahead.

The men huddling in the shack pulled up their hoods and pulled on their gloves as Oz ran toward them. The helicopter would need to remain tied to the deck until its rotor was spinning but the blades would need to be unsecured and the tarp taken off. They swarmed over the helicopter, one man working numb and soaked fingers to untie a line while the man behind him held him in place with one hand and tried to keep them both from sliding off the deck and into the drink with his other. Orders were nearly impossible to give outside of hand signals, the wind was so bad, and those unhitching the aircraft wondered if the pilot would even be able to get it into the blowing sky.

One of Oz's southern Venators working on the helicopter suddenly fell to his knees and covered his ears.

"You okay?" Morton Caulfield shouted at him from six inches away.

Morton shook the man but he only kept pressing his ears and mumbling. Morton looked over to Oz; Oz motioned to drag him into the shack. As soon as Morton took hold of the man's jacket, the man broke free and ran toward the edge of the ship. Morton and a couple others tackled him before he could go over. All they could hear him saying, as they pried his fingers from the steel railing, was, "Dreams that you dare to dream really do come true."

"It's started," Helen said quietly from the bridge, no longer following The Legion ship with her eyes, turning them instead to the men she'd brought into the storm.

"I got news for you," Clayton said from the rear of the bridge:

"it started long before that feller lost it." She looked back to see Clayton white from hairline to collar. "I've been seeing my sister dragged out of our basement window and shouting for me to save her for about an hour now. No, no! Don't come over here. I'm good. I'm doing what you said, I'm thinking. I'm thinking real good, Helen. 1, 2, 4, 8, 16, 32, 64, 128, 256, 512 . . ."

Kane slid slowly into Helen's field of vision, a question on his face. She met his eyes for a moment before saying to Clayton, "You're doing beautifully, Clay."

"Hey, uh, everyone," Marc said as he wrestled open the heavy steel door from the companionway. "Siegfried is all ready to go, aren't you pal?"

A tall, mustachioed man in a flight suit with a network news insignia on the pocket came in stumbling with the motion of the ship. He had a flight bag in his hands, hands that shook. He was covered in sweat.

"Siegfried," she said. "We've got some lovely flying weather for you. Up for it?"

"Eagerly I wished the morrow;—vainly I had sought to borrow," he said, "from my books surcease of sorrow—sorrow for the lost Laura." He nodded as if that was all that needed to be said.

"Anybody else know how to fly?" Kane asked.

"He's fine," Helen said. "He's dealing with it—aren't you, Siegfried? Just nod."

Siegfried opened his mouth and then nodded. Helen took him by the arm and guided him to the front windows, holding up the night vision scope for him to see The Legion ship.

"There's the target," she said. "The rest of the chopper crew is at the bottom of the stairs, on deck."

He handed her back the scope, said, "Nameless here for evermore," and then hurried to the door out. Pausing there, he nodded in the direction of The Legion ship and said, "Darkness there and nothing more." The wind blowing in the door as he left scattered any reply those left on the bridge might have made.

Along with three other men—one carrying a machinegun and the other two carrying what looked like a fifty-five gallon drum—Siegfried hurried with drunken grace across the pitching ship. They then wrestled the drum into the rear of the helicopter, one of the two carriers sitting beside it, while the one with the machinegun sat in the front seat to the Siegfried's right. The remaining carrier began to return to the bridge when he seemed to become distracted by something in the distance. Slowly, he shuffled toward the edge of the ship.

"Shit," Kane swore under his breath and dashed out into the wind. The air pressure was like a body check, plowing Kane into the superstructure of the bridge as he pulled himself hand over hand down the stairs' railing, watching the unknown Venator's halting steps draw closer to the now plunging side of the ship. A sudden plateau leveled the deck for an instant and Kane threw himself toward the man, reaching him just as *Merrie Gloom* dropped over the side of a wave. They both careened into the railing, the jar seeming to awaken the sleepwalking man. He looked around wildly, as if surprised to find himself on a ship at sea, but with Kane hauling him inside, shouting for him to focus, some echo of reality returned to him and he followed. Inside the bridge door, though, he collapsed.

"Is he alright?" Helen asked from the windows.

"No," Kane said between gasps.

"I'll be okay," the man said. "Just need a second to clear my head. I haven't been hearing voices at all and then bang. I usually don't have those crazy dreams, you know?"

"It's okay," Helen said. "Go get some dry clothes on, if you can find any."

The man stumbled off. Kane shed his dripping parka and hung

it by the door, wiping his hair back and coming away with a handful of water.

"You never did say why you dressed up like Johnny Cash for this stalk, Kane," Kilmer said. He chuckled and spit into a Styrofoam cup; he chewed tobacco.

"They were the only clothes that fit me in the safe house in Arkham," Kane said for the fiftieth time. He joined Helen, looking down at the helicopter with its now turning rotor. "How is this supposed to go again? That machinegun Freddy Tuller brought isn't going to do much against a ship."

"That's for the bridge crew," Helen said. "There she goes. Siegfried may be losing his shit but he can still fly."

The helicopter strained against the cords lashing her to the ship until Siegfried motioned to Oz. The cords were loosed from the deck and the OH-58 lurched into the sky, dodging quickly to one side to avoid collision with *Merrie Gloom's* bridge. Once she'd gained a little altitude, Siegfried ran her straight for the Legion ship.

"Nguyen—in back with the drum—" Helen said, "he's got something for their ship. The drum is a sort of makeshift depth charge. They rigged a detonator that should go off when the drum is only a couple of feet below water. Hopefully it'll take out the Legion ship's screw and leave her adrift. Even if it just disables her rudder, we'd have an advantage: no one is steering a straight line in a sea this rough. Once they drop the charge, Siegfried will circle their bridge and Freddy will let them have it with the M240. Even if he can't kill everyone onboard, if he can just keep them from steering, we'll catch up that much sooner and launch the assault craft."

"Freddy said he only had a thousand rounds for the two-forty," Kilmer said and spat. "He didn't seem to think it was enough."

"If he doesn't play Rambo it'll be fine," Helen said. "We only need *this* much advantage." She picked up the handset for the overhead radio and keyed the mic. "Sig this is Helen, how we doing, over?"

"Deep into that darkness peering," came the chanted response, "long I stood there wondering, fearing, doubting, dreaming dreams no mortal ever dared to dream before."

"Stay focused, Sig," Helen said. "Concentrate on your flying. You're almost there."

"Is that hoo-ha he's ranting from *The Raven*?" Kilmer asked.

"Yeah," Kane said and looked at Clayton monitoring the surface search radar.

"2097152," Clayton mumbled, "4194304, 8388608, 16777216 . . ."

The helicopter rose and fell over invisible cliffs of air, spun on jabs from the rising storm, but still her mad pilot and desperate crew sped their way to the Legion ship. *Merrie Gloom's* bridge grew crowded as Venators pushed in to see, hoping their first strike would be the only one needed. Some muttered to themselves, some grinded their teeth so viciously that it could be heard over other sounds of the bridge, some wept, with shame or unconcern or no awareness that what ran from their cheeks came not from the storm.

"We're coming up on her now, Helen, over," Freddy said through the radio. His sudden voice barking in the speechless silence of the bridge was like a brick through a window; a couple Venators ducked; someone cursed.

"What's it look like, Freddy, over?" Helen asked through the handset.

"Kinda like our *Merrie Gloom*," Freddy replied, "only not so big. The deck is clear of people and cargo containers but there's something else I can't quite make out. Hold this ping-pong ball steady, will you, Sig?"

A few seconds passed as the OH-58 drew nearer to the Legion

ship and Freddy peered through a night vision scope at its murk-shrouded deck.

"Oh Jesus," Freddy said quietly, the crackle of static nearly drowning his voice.

"Freddy?" Helen said. "Freddy, what do you see, over?"

"Altars," Freddy said and gulped. "Jesus, Helen, the deck, the deck is covered with altars."

"Altars of salt," Kane said. All eyes turned toward him as they listened to Freddy's open mic pouring static and rotor noise into the bridge.

"There must be a hundred or more," Freddy said.

"Graven with images both foul and ancient," Kane said.

"They all have what look like long thick candles attached to them," Freddy said. "And are carved with something on their sides; I can't make it out this far away."

"Sol?" Helen asked.

Kane took a long shuddering breath, continued to gaze across the leagues of the sea toward The Legion ship. "Cthulhu has been showing me those altars," he said. "Since Maryland."

"Holy shit," Kilmer shouted into the stillness, twisting his night vision scope for better magnification.

"Helen, Helen," Freddy screamed through the radio. "They've got an anti-aircraft gun."

Flashes could be seen in the distance, angry and orange against the dirty gray of the storm.

"On this home by Horror haunted—tell me truly, I implore," Siegfried cried through the radio, the pop of rounds striking his little helicopter drumming time to his chant. "Is there—is there balm in Gilead?—tell me—tell me, I implore!"

"We're hit," Freddy shouted.

Even at that distance, the flash of the OH-58's engine flaming out could be seen from *Merrie Gloom*. Still the orange and red stars burst into being and died atop the bridge of The Legion ship, shooting stars of white fire arcing through the sky, following the helicopter as it fell.

"Siegfried!" Helen shouted through the radio. "Siegfried, auto-rotate. Do you hear me? Auto-rotate the helicopter. Siegfried!"

"And his eyes have all the seeming of a demon's that is dreaming," Siegfried wept in the final seconds. "And my soul from out that shadow that lies floating on the floor shall be lifted—Laura, Laura I'm coming!"

The waves took the helicopter without a sound, without a splash; the moment of three men's deaths not precisely known to those who watched. Seconds afterward—seconds past without words, without breath—the depth charge detonated and a column of water reached like an outthrust arm toward the stooping sky and then fell back, formless into the churning oblivion of the ocean.

Only the adagio drumming of spray against the windows and the empty static of dead air over the radio ignored the silence observed on *Merrie Gloom*'s bridge. Even Clayton and the others who talked themselves away from waking dreams stilled their mumbling lips for a moment. Helen then shut off the radio and dragged them back to the mission.

"Kilmer?" she asked quietly.

"Yeah?" he said.

"Can you guess anything about that antiaircraft gun?" she asked.

"33554432, 67108864, 134217728 . . ."

Kilmer steadied himself as the ship dropped down the face of another steep wave. He shrugged, almost an apology, and said, "From this distance? The only place I've ever heard that sound, though, was in the movies. That pom, pom, pom noise, like a kid beating an oil drum. I heard it in old documentaries about World War II and Korea. It's from a 40mm Bofors AA gun. Used on ships at first, during Korea they mounted them in place of the turret on light tanks. They must have taken it from a museum or something. I doubt anyone would have bothered busting the firing mechanism. Where the hell they got the ammo for it, I couldn't guess."

"Explosive?" she asked.

"Maybe back in World War II," Kilmer said. "Those rounds we heard through the radio sure weren't. Maybe they manufactured them? Ordered them from one of those machine shop-turned-illicit-weapons-maker you sometimes read about in third-world countries. Or the warheads are just too old and didn't blow, when they attacked Siegfried and all."

"Just running scared," someone sang quietly in one corner. Kilmer looked over his shoulder briefly and saw it was Chic Tay, fighting tooth and nail to keep his mind on what was being said. "Each place we go. Running scared, do you love him so."

"Roy Orbison?" Kilmer said.

"Kilmer," Helen said.

"Yeah, that's about all I can think of, Helen," he said. "That and it's a crew-served gun: one guy aims and fires the thing while two or more other guys slip these huge four-round ammo clips into two hoppers on the top of the gun. You aim the thing by turning a couple of wheels." He pantomimed rotating a pair of small wheels turned by perpendicular handles as he looked upward through an invisible sight.

"It's going to make boarding that ship a whole lot more exciting," Kane said. He'd wiped his hand across his face and again came away with a fist-full of moisture. "It won't take a big honking AA gun to sink either of the two rubber assault craft we brought."

"That's true," Helen conceded, turning back to watch as they closed on the still distant Legion ship. "We'll need to get as close as we can and then launch one boat to either side of their ship. It'll take time to wheel the AA gun from one target to the other. Hopefully that'll be enough time for at least one of the assault craft to draw alongside and use the bulk of their ship to block the AA gun's line of fire."

With that slim hope, most of the Venators left the bridge to descend mumbling to the berths below or to the galley for much-needed coffee. The few who stayed watched as the towering storm wall finally enveloped their enemy. Soon after, *Merrie Gloom* plunged into its churning netherworld.

CHAPTER 4

A HOLE IN THE OCEAN

WHILE APPROACHING THE storm, the crashing waves had been steep and vigorous—but nothing compared to the rancor of Plutonic power that awaited the two ships within. *Merrie Gloom* reeled so far back on her haunches as she rode up cliffs of water that those at her helm were brought to the deck, leaning against it as if against a wall. And then down the following side, into a deep cleft of ocean like a wound cleaved by the moon, invisible in the darkness of the storm, and *Merrie Gloom*'s deck was so awash with water that it appeared she would go under, submerge and join the centuries upon centuries of ships devoured by the menace of the sea.

As the madness of the storm howled around the ship, within *Merrie Gloom* madness began to scream down her corridors. At first, the shrill cries merely whitened the faces of those who heard them, reminding them of what they thrust so violently from their own thoughts. Into those screams, however, crept also words of torment. Not the agonizing memories of loved ones lost or tortures and sacrifices witness in the long-dead innocence of the past, no: into their screams came the chanted words of horror, the prologue of madness.

Ph'nglui mglw'nafh Cthulhu R'lyeh wgah'nagl fhtagn.

For some, the images welling from beneath the ocean, from the dreaming mind of dead Cthulhu, could no longer be proscribed. Into their minds' eyes came eons of torment, came the unimaginable will of The Great Old Ones as they once stood, without challenge, beyond mastery of little earth. The great city of R'Lyeh as it had been, both a part of earth and yet something beyond, streets running from what now is Bangkok to what once was Carthage made traversable by bridges whose geometry broke the minds of its travelers. Blood-soaked temples gleaming moistly in a sun whose very color bent to the will of the High Priest Cthulhu now wavered in the minds of the approaching Venators, sinking beneath a green sea, nestling soundlessly into the ocean floor to wait, eons if necessary, for all to come to pass as it had been foretold. The slime of innumerable ages clung to the great cyclopean edifices of R'Lyeh; down avenues of stone that once saw enslaved multitudes driven to sacrifice by unheard commands now swam monstrosities that the surface world has forgotten; in the great temple, whose size cannot be guessed because its very shape is unknowable to man, on a bed of meteoric gold, mighty Cthulhu lies dead and dreaming.

Madness began to take the Venators. Some huddled in corners, frantic in their mantras of reality and the past, helpless to unseat from their minds the whispered calling of Cthulhu. Others no longer existed within *Merrie Gloom* except in body, their minds fleeing down passages of horror, wound with spells of inescapable cruelty. In their madness, they acted. Some charged out onto the deck and, with clenched fists, screamed words of rebuke at the drenching sky, words of malice, of indecipherable acceptance, until the waves took them overboard and under. Others tried to restrain them, to drag them to the infirmary or lock them in rooms: the mere touch of their skin seemed to infect their saviors with madness and together they joined the storm-rocked sea. Whether locked away by door and bolt or chained to some portion of the ship by muddled visions of what had been and what was said to be, others surrendered to the maddening calls of Cthulhu through imitation. Impossible to hide from visions of past miseries or horrors to come—to all mankind for all eternity—those who could not close their eyes to the madness sheared off their own eyelids and stood under the pouring sky to wash the blood from their sockets. Others cut the bones from their feet or hands, or searched their self-inflicted vivisections for some lost thing they could not describe, while still others carved into their flesh hieroglyphics of an unknown language. The ship became a nightmare of gibbering and blood.

Not all the Venators submitted to the calls of anguish and coming destruction. Those few, through power of will or irrational incredulity or absence of fate, contained their cursed fellows as best they could, guided *Merrie Gloom* through the battering ocean, and watched as they drew ever closer, league upon league, to The Legion's ship of sacrifice.

Helen was bent double and puffing hard after wrestling another fallen brother to the ground. Kane had secured the raving man with zip-ties and stuffed him into a closet. Only Clayton and Kilmer remained with them on the bridge. Kilmer had begun mumbling, clenching his teeth and avoiding eye contact if anyone came near him; he still watched The Legion ship, though, and guided *Merrie Gloom* toward it. Clayton had had to start over many times during the past hour, and had occasionally sank to the floor and pounded his palms against his temples, but he had arisen again each time and, with tears in his eyes, had not given up.

"I don't know how many of us are left," Kane said from where he stood panting, back to the door leading down into the tower, "but it isn't much. How's the idea of ramming their ship sound to you now, Helen?"

She straightened and flexed her back, forcibly calming her breathing. "I'd say it sounded pretty good, Sol," she said, "except for that AA gun. We'd have to get in front of them, or at least along side, in order to get enough speed where a collision would breach their hull. Otherwise, tapping the back of their ship isn't likely to do much except push them to R'Lyeh all the faster. With that AA gun firing at us the whole time? I'm guessing eventually, if they have enough rounds for it, they could chew through our hull and sink us. This isn't a warship, after all."

"One of us in each assault craft then, huh?" Kane said and smiled. "I'm excited to be a part of this plan."

She rolled her eyes and turned to look out the front windows, but she smiled all the same.

"Look!" Kilmer shouted.

Ahead, the billowing clouds and mists broke and *Merrie Gloom* shot out into suddenly calmed waters. Around them in an enormous arc, the storm still rolled but all within was calm.

"The eye of the storm," Helen whispered.

Overhead, the clouds enclosed the wide spot in the ocean like the vaulted roof of the Pantheon, though mobile and somehow giving the impression of greater weight. Glowing like an ember, the overarching clouds parted for a moment in spots and rays of sunlight stabbed to the ocean beneath like searchlights or the gaze of something that scoured the sea with malevolent intent. At an unknown distance, in the center of the storm's swirling calm, a vortex slowly churned the ocean's surface.

"And there're our Legion friends now," Kane said, pointing.

Having weathered the storm better than *Merrie Gloom*, it seemed, the Legion ship had nevertheless lost ground and was closer than ever.

"Helen," Clayton said quietly. She looked, fearfully expecting that madness had overcome the gentle man at last, but following the line of his arm out to their right, she saw another ship in the distance.

"Who the hell are they?" Kane said as he stepped to the other side of Clayton and raised a pair of binoculars.

"I don't know but they're on course to come between us and The Legion ship," Helen said. "Okay, Sol: go below and see how many people are still fit to fight. Whoever you can find, bring out to the assault boats and get them prepped. We may not get more than one shot at this. Kilmer, push *Merrie* as hard as she can go; if we can beat that other ship to her, all the better."

"They might not even be involved in this," Kilmer said through clenched teeth. "Could have just got caught in the storm; thinking they'd ride it out in here."

"Let's cling to that hope," she said, raising a pair of binoculars as Kane rushed out. "And that their radio is damaged and that's why they aren't hailing us."

Kane went down the corridors, checking berths and the galley, the day room and the engine room, and every nook and cranny he could think of. While there was no shortage of cowering or gibbering Venators, huddled and rocking in corners and under tables, Kane was still able to pull together nearly a dozen men, all more or less cogent. Whether trying to distract themselves with some private mantra or trying to expel the insanity with which the dream sendings of Cthulhu infected them, the file of frantic resolve that followed Kane murmured as it wound its way up to the deck.

Helen, after watching the new and strange ship pass between *Merrie Gloom* and the Legion ship, in sudden remembrance, ran down to the makeshift brig. The posted guard was nowhere to be found; taken by Kane or madness, it was impossible for her to guess. Inside, Angell writhed face down on the floor, still caged, still weeping. His voice had subtly changed, however, and he spoke never again in English or any other language of man. What he spoke, though, Helen could piece together from her store of knowledge of Cthulhu.

"Where's Kane?" Helen shouted as she burst onto the bridge. Both Clayton and Kilmer jumped and swore; Kilmer pointed to the deck. "Shit."

Helen rushed to the door leading to the outside railing and shouted, "Kane! Kane, leave the boats inside. Shut the doors and get everyone up here, now—now!"

She waved emphatically and called again and again. The confused Venators, opening two small cargo containers in which the two assault craft waited to be joined to their outboard engines, passed glances back and forth, questioning whether Helen had finally cracked, too. Kane could hear the alarm in her voice but no note of insanity; no more than was in all their voices since entering the storm. He motioned for the others to secure the cargo containers and follow him back to the bridge.

Once the dozen men were crowded inside, the inevitable question was posed.

"I just remembered Angell," Helen said. "Downstairs. He's begun to talk in tongues and I think I can guess what that ship is about."

"It's out of the way, now," Kilmer said. "Look. It passed between us but then kept on going. Maybe their crew has gone nuts."

"No, I think it's more likely—" Helen began to say.

Two gouts of fire spilled from the fore and aft of the strange ship and an instant later flames raced over the water away from it. In a wide circle the flames ran, into the distance; smoke rose in a black curtain, blocking all sight of the Legion ship. When the flames grew to a roar so loud it could be heard even half a mile away, their heat—or poor handling of what had started them—found the hold of the strange ship and it exploded in a plume of fire and debris.

"Whoa, what in the hell is going on?" Kane said, slipping past Helen and all but pressing his face to the window.

"It's what Angell said," Helen told him. "Something about bandits at the crossroads of the seas—which I think means Somali pirates—and a fire ship to cloak the bearer of sacrifices. Something like that; it doesn't translate exactly. The African Venators have been saying for the past couple of years that Cthulhu cults have been trying to infiltrate the Somali pirates. Looks like they succeeded. They must have stolen an oil tanker."

"That's fucking great, man," Chic said. "What's going to happen to old *Merrie* when she tries to sail through a flaming oil slick?"

Every eye not consumed by a dream sending turned to Helen. Her eyes scanned the ocean ahead—writhing in orange and coughing black—and tried to speak, to start the sentence that would solve the problem, that would see them through, but nothing came. The fire had destroyed the Somali ship, why not them? The fire swept an impenetrable arc across the ocean; how could they go around? Was there time? Her mind held the pieces before her face as she tried to fit them together but nothing came; nothing except a mumbled voice, as if from far away or deep under the ocean, filled with a slow patient mirth, which now began to rise with wakefulness.

"We go right the hell through it," Kane said and then slapped Chic hard enough for the others to look at him instead of Helen. He grinned at their surprise.

"You know Solomon Kane isn't hearing voices," Chic said, rubbing his cheek: "he was crazy before we even started."

"Like a fox, my friend, like a fox," Kane said. "Now run down to the engine room—I think Gordon is still more or less with us—tell him to shut off the air. I don't want *Merrie* drawing anything from outside of the ship. Everyone else, get as deep below deck as you can and wait for my call. It might get a little hot but it's the smoke that's our biggest problem."

"Is that all?" Clayton said, shuffling toward the stairwell down with the others.

"I rarely ask anything of you, Clay," Kane said. "All you have to do is not breathe."

"Sol, the fire," Helen said, holding him back. "It will detonate our fuel."

"Yeah, it might," he said. "If we're cruising fast enough, though, I don't think it'll get hot enough. I figure that other ship blew because the fire crept up the stream of fuel they were pouring over the side. If you can come up with a better plan in the next thirty seconds, I'd be eager to hear it."

"We don't really have a choice, do we?" she said, looking over her shoulder.

"We never do," he said.

As the black mass of the oil slick's smoke drew closer, Kane pushed the throttles as far forward as they would go and locked the helm in position before rushing after Helen, down the stairs and deep into *Merrie Gloom*.

In the corridor leading to the engine room, the last of the functioning Venators sat huddled on the floor. The drone of the engines beyond was a welcome oblivion from the omnipresent whispers, the incessant memories, and the mumbled attempts by their fellows to stave off madness with compulsion. Then the engines strained and raced and then howled and died in a hissing seizure. The Venators half rose to their feet or slumped further to the ground, casting around for what next they could do. Kane watched the engine room door until it opened. Gordon shuffled through, tossing up his hands.

"It's the smoke," he said. "I'm really sorry, Miss Helen. The engine's got to breathe, too, you know."

"Are we still inside the fire ring?" she asked, stepping gingerly between outstretched legs.

"Can't say," Gordon admitted. "Could be. But we're still moving. The ocean was calm enough and a ship the size of *Merrie Gloom* is like to hold onto her momentum for a spell."

Helen looked back and Kane ran for the stairs up.

The slowing of the ship was perceptible but so was its forward movement. As Kane took the stairs two at a time, he saw in shadowed corners or rooms off to either side a floating darkness and beneath it, the mad Venators who had breathed their last. The smoke was noxious; every cough was a plume of acid in Kane's lungs until he reached the bridge. There, looking out the windows, he saw that *Merrie Gloom* had pressed through the ring of fire and now slid, a little to one side, into the narrowed arena surrounding the vortex in the sea. The Legion ship had slowed, seeming to orient itself at some special angle to the vortex. Kane punched the intercom button and called everyone who could still fight up to the deck.

CHAPTER 5

R'LYEH RISING

LAMES STILL CLUNG to the side of *Merrie Gloom* and the air still stung with burning fumes, when the Venators ran across her deck to the storage containers. The steel deck beneath their feet was warm, even through their shoes, and so they had to be careful not to let the rubber assault craft touch the ground. Carrying each to opposite sides of the ship, they dropped the small boats overboard, holding them close with ropes, and then descended the steel ladders attached to the sides of *Merrie Gloom*, to board. Kane took half the men with him in one boat; Helen, the other half. They also took two hand-held radios from the ship. In minutes, both assault craft were racing across the mirror-still waters surrounding the vortex.

"Clara?" Kane said, wondering why the house was so quiet. "Clara are you home?"

Clayton shook him by the shoulder and said, "32768, 65536."

"Kane, push out a little further from my boat," Helen said over the radio. "They'll see us soon enough and when that AA gun opens up on us, I don't want to make it easy to shoot at both of us."

"Roger that," Kane said quietly. He shook his head, saw the ocean around him again, smelled the salt air, felt the spray, and then repeated his confirmation more loudly and told Gordon to put another couple boat-lengths between them and Helen's assault craft. Kane tried to think of something, to focus on The Legion ship, anything to keep the flashbacks at bay. He wondered for a moment if it was sent deliberately and a sound not unlike laughter and not at all similar to human speech or thought displaced all sound for a throbbing few seconds.

The two assault craft skimmed the ocean at full speed. In their bows, Venators lay stretched out as far forward as they could with binoculars scouring The Legion ship's deck. And then they saw them. Legionnaires dragged dozens upon dozens of frightened, hysterical, or dazed captives across the deck, soon to be sacrificed. But it was not the horror they were prepared for that made the Venators scream.

"Kane, Kane!" Clayton shouted from their assault craft's bow. "There's something, there's something walking around with the captives—I ain't seeing things, neither!"

Kane lifted his binoculars and focused on The Legion ship's deck. There, walking between the graven altars of salt, stooped in posture yet hulking in size, bereft of the humanity to which they had been born, Followers of Dagon.

"Shit, Helen," he shouted into his radio. "Followers, Followers of Dagon on The Legion ship. And they're not human, not anymore."

"What? Say again," she said.

"The rumors," Kane said, half standing to keep his binos steady in the speed of his craft. "The crazy beliefs of The Followers, that they can transform if they sacrifice enough people while wearing the Innsmouth Jewelry: it's true. There are a dozen or more. They're huge. Their heads—their mouths!"

"Steady," she said. "I should have guessed. It doesn't change the mission."

"No," Kane said. "Okay, out." To the Venators in his boat, he shouted: "Morphed Followers of Dagon. What old-school Venators used to call frogboys. I don't think anybody's seen one in a hundred years. Doesn't change what we've come to do. We shoot those amphibious sons of bitches just like everybody else."

"They've seen us!" Chic shouted.

A second later, Helen came across the radio shouting the same thing. The Legion ship had spotted the assault craft or finally decided they'd come too close. A crew of two Legionnaires and four frogboys ran up to the AA gun, atop their bridge tower, and traversed it around toward the Venator assault craft.

"Okay, Gordon," Kane shouted. "Time to dance this little boat. Don't make it easy on them."

The 40mm Bofors anti-aircraft gun depressed its twin barrels and in an instant dirty orange bursts popped from each. There was no noise, at first, no indication of firing except for the muzzle flashes. Then the first rounds landed close to the two assault craft, boring into the water between them as they zigged and zagged across the ocean; little plops like jumping fish. But as they drew ever closer to The Legion ship, the concentrated fire from the AA gun came closer. Rippling over the water like the steps of some invisible entity, Kane's boat was only missed by a few feet as Gordon threw the little craft from side to side; every Venator held on with both hands. Though they all wanted to raise their weapons, to return fire, it was impossible. More than the evasive maneuvers of the assault craft, the vortex had increased now to a tremendous churning and its waves throttled the ocean around it. The two assault craft leapt and swerved and were battered from side to side as they tried to avoid the AA gun and reach The Legion ship. And then a line of fire from the gun ran across Helen's boat.

The sound was impossibly loud. The sudden escape of air from the inflatable boat was as loud as an explosion; the explosion of the engine, a dirty cough. Some of the Venators had been hit as well but all were dead, in time. The boat sank beneath them, disintegrating to a black floating mass like the long locks of a woman's hair.

"Helen!" Kane shouted into the radio. He could still see her, treading water, keeping the radio above the waves.

"Kane, get out of here," she said. "Don't come back for us; remember the mission. We all knew we weren't coming back alive. Make an end. Don't fail me." And then the waves took her.

Venators near the sunken assault craft swam toward the Legion ship, those who still could, but the water was too cold. Long before they would reach the ship, their muscles would seize, they would sink beneath the rising ocean. Every Venator in Kane's boat looked between their fellows and Kane, waiting for the order to rescue them, knowing it would not come.

"Blood," Kane said. "There's blood all over the kitchen floor: what the hell happened?"

The assault craft raced on, bounding over the waves and drawing so close to The Legion ship that the AA gun could not depress its barrels enough to fire at them. As it came alongside The Legion ship, Legionnaires on deck leaned over the gunwale and opened fire. Slower now, trying to tie off, the Venators could risk firing back and fire they did. Hours of bombardment by dream sending, hours of horror and watching their fellows fall, hours of nothing to do but take it and try to hold on until this moment arrived, the Venators forgot their madness as a new madness took them: the madness for vengeance.

Lashing their boat to the side of the Legion ship, a few Venators crouched in the front and returned fire with an M60 machine gun and a couple assault rifles as Kane led the charge up a steel ladder to the Legion ship's deck. With his heavy .45 automatic in one hand,

Kane scrambled as fast as he could, never looking down, taking shots at anyone who appeared at the ladder's head or at the guns they held over the side in a desperate attempt to repel the boarders. Some of their shots found targets, though, and a couple Venators fell back into the assault craft or, worse, into the ocean. But as the M60 ran out of ammo, Kane reached the top of the ladder, threw himself over the gunwale, and found himself face to face with six armed Legionnaires.

A heartbeat passed as Legionnaire and Venator crouched inches apart, staring into each others eyes, before Kane stabbed his pistol into the foremost Legionnaire's face and squeezed off his last round. The others raised their weapons or dived for cover but Kane was amongst them, his pistol now a club, swinging wildly, trying to smack their weapons aside and cover their arms with his body. They beat on him with their fists, kicked, shot passed his face, but the scrum lasted the three precious seconds Kane needed: in the next instant, Chic was over the gunwale and carefully pressed the muzzle of his shotgun to the head of each of Kane's wrestlers before blasting them into eternity.

The roar of Chic's shotgun nearly deafened Kane but from farther down the deck, and from the bridge tower, more Legionnaires still fought, firing from behind the numerous altars of salt or over the railings above. There were dozens of Legionnaires; some fought, some still manned the AA gun, others herded their captives out of the crossfire or threw them over altars to quickly sacrifice them with a bellowed prayer and a slash of the throat. There were less than five Venators left.

Pressed to the side of the bridge tower, the Venators fired in all directions. Clayton, having run dry with the M60, clung to the side of the ship, using the gunwale for cover, and fired an M-2 carbine one-handed at the attackers above. Chic dropped to his stomach and began worming his way around the altars of salt, blasting as he

went. Kane pulled an AKM assault rifle from the tangle of Legionnaire bodies and tried to climb the stairs into the bridge tower.
Again and again he was forced to leap back, as rounds drummed
on the risers, fired from beneath or above. Again and again he shot
Legionnaires who leaned too far over the railings overhead, their
bodies falling like heaps of snow off a heavily laden roof. Then the
ship heaved to one side and for a moment, all gunfire stopped.
R'Lyeh had risen.

Stabbing through the churning vortex, the tallest tower of
R'Lyeh—draped in the fetid slime of the ocean floor—soared into
the air once again. Less than a hundred meters away, the city's glory
was beheld in the mind's eye as well as the body's by all aboard The
Legion ship. The cyclopean stonework of the buildings was laid
with skill beyond the ability of mankind. The streets ran in arcs and
slashes, following some design whose geometry would drive mad
any who attempted to compass it. Some streets appeared to descend
and rise in more than one direction simultaneously; some seemed
to lead back in time; some led to arches wherethrough gleamed
galaxies unseen, pits of fire, or places without description, too weird
in their amorphousness for man to comprehend. And in its midst,
the tallest tower, the Temple of Cthulhu stood looming over all as
a god before supplicants. In that city slithering with the filth of the
ocean bottom, only the door to the Temple of Cthulhu glowed.
And upon it, amid the angles that defied geometry, graven into a
metal unknown on earth, hieroglyphics of blasphemy, of horror,
blazed in their terrifying familiarity. Those symbols every Venator
had seen during a lifetime of stalking the cult; they appeared on
every figurine that the cult prayed to as it sacrificed the innocent
to bring about this day.

The Legion, seeing its hour had come, gave a shout of lust, or
madness, or hopelessness, and dragged its victims to the altars of
salt. The morphed Followers of Dagon then showed themselves.

Crouching where they had been at the bow of the ship, they launched themselves with their frog-like legs back to the huddled mass of screaming victims, there to use their hatred-enhanced strength to position the victims on the altars. What remained of the Venators saw that time itself was on the verge of death: they left what cover they had and charged.

Kane fired wildly overhead at the Legionnaires still holding the bridge tower and could cut down his Venators from above, until his weapon ran dry. He leaped to the railing then and pulled himself up, using a body hanging over the side to cover his ascent. Pulling from it another weapon, he fought his way onto the railing and then circled it to the front of the bridge tower. Below, he saw the battle fought at point-blank range. The madness of Cthulhu's proximity seemed to have taken its toll most heavily upon his own followers, though. The Legion, enraptured by the madness of their dread lord's coming, threw themselves with splayed jaws at the last few Venators, and were cut down like stalks of wheat before the farmer's scythe. The fury of the Venator charge was such that they overwhelmed the first few ranks of The Legion and even the frogboys had to pause in their sacrifices to throw themselves at these most persistent intruders. Their amazing strength and terrible arms were hurtled at the Venators as they fought. From where he stood on the tower railing, Kane had the advantage of height and fired down with precision upon the monsters changed by their devotion to hate.

The sacrificial victims also felt the insanity that stirred in its long sleep, a hundred meters away, deep within R'Lyeh's great temple. Some cowered in heaps, others ran about the deck either heedless of the combat or desperate to catch a bullet and thus end their torment. From above the bridge tower, though, the crew of the AA gun would not surrender an inch and depressed their cannons as far as they would go and opened up on both Venators and Legionnaires alike.

Kane snatched a fresh weapon from amongst the dead and charged into the bridge, snaking around equipment until he came to the ladder up to the roof. There was no time to think of whether a guard or a booby trap awaited him at the top of the ladder; he flung open the hatch to the roof. With only his right arm above the level of the floor, wielding the heavy assault rifle one-handed, he let off a burst of fire into the nearest frogboy loading ammo into the antiquated AA gun. The crew stopped firing immediately and dived for their discarded weapons or threw themselves at Kane. His weapon's magazine held out long enough to kill the two humans and one of the frogboys before it gave out. The terrible prospect of failing after having come so close seemed to grip the frogboys as badly as it did the remnant of the Venators. Two powerful hands then wrapped themselves around Kane's throat and lifted him from the ladder.

His legs kicked free above the bridge roof, the sound of gunfire lost to the pounding of his oxygen-starved heart, Kane looked unblinking as the other remaining frogboy drew near. Its head had increased in size, its mouth now a wide maw dripping with the froth of a fanatic. Its bulging eyes could no longer close and had pushed out to either side of its misshapen head; hatred burned from each. It watched, fascinated by the death of Solomon Kane—and did not notice Kane sweep a dagger out of his boot.

Slashing first the blubberous throat of the gloating frogboy before him, Kane then stabbed over his shoulder and into one hideous eye of the creature that strangled him. It reeled back, swatting at its ruined head, as Kane sprawled amongst the dead. As it ripped the thin razor-edged weapon from its face, with its remaining eye it saw Kane snatch a weapon from the heap of bodies. Swinging a hasty burst around, Kane ended the creature and then turned the last five rounds in the gun on the gurgling frogboy he'd slashed.

Gasping for breath, Kane scrambled to the edge of the roof and looked down in time to see that what remained of the other frog-boys were leaping into the ocean. Only Clayton was still standing, from among the Venators who'd attacked the Legion ship. Kane could see Chic sprawled on the deck, surrounded by a circle of dead or dying Legionnaires; Chic's one arm still beat the deck but whether he was in the last throes of his death or overcome by the dream sendings of awakening Cthulhu, it could not be guessed. The captives too had lost many of their number, but those that remained still huddled on one side of the deck.

Clayton was out of ammo and was grappling with the last of the Legionnaires, both wielding knives. Kane dropped to the floor and untangled another weapon from the fallen gun crew and returned to the tower's edge in time to see Clayton reeling back with a wound to his face. Kane took careful aim as the last of the Legionnaires lunged forward for the kill. Kane dropped him with a single shot, despite the shifting deck. Clayton looked up and grinned his thanks before collapsing on his back. He held up one thumb and then covered his face with both hands.

"I'm coming, Clayton," Kane shouted. "Hold on."

"You've come to me at last, my love, my husband," a voice said behind Kane and he froze.

It was then that what The Followers were doing became apparent. They had not been jumping to their deaths in the frigid ocean but playing their part in the orchestrated blasphemy of resurrecting Cthulhu: they had swam to R'Lyeh and were now swarming to the temple in its midst. Some were already there, touching the bas relief, chanting and capering, and the doors began to shake with impeding movement.

"Even if they wrench open that door," he said quietly, unable to turn, "you won't get the human sacrifices you need. We've killed off your little army."

"And I killed our little children, Sol," she said. "I know you think the cult had come and kidnapped us from our home; just random bad luck that those silly insane cultists should choose our home. It was otherwise, Sol, my love. I was one of them. I danced in that far glade where you found us, many times before that night. I felt the warm blood of a sacrificed child cascading over my flesh and knew that as it pleased my lord so too did it give me the ultimate pain, the inescapable pleasure of wrongness. And I knew the only way to enhance it further was to sacrifice our babies, Sol. It was so naughty of you to interrupt."

Kane broke from the grip of those words and dashed to the AA gun. Dropping into the seat, he used the hand wheels to bring the gun to bear on the frogboys slithering over the door to the Temple of Cthulhu. Squeezing the trigger, two rounds fired and then the gun went silent. Spinning in his seat, he did not see the specter of his wife; he saw the huge crates of ammunition behind the AA gun. Remembering what Kilmer said of the weapon's operation, Kane hefted two of the enormous four-round clips and fed them into the two hoppers atop the gun. He then yanked back on the charging handles and leaned forward to fire the gun again. Again the huge gun fired from both barrels but for eight rounds only. Through luck or fate, some of those rounds found targets amongst the myriad frogboys in R'Lyeh but to no avail. The door to Cthulhu's temple swung open at last.

"You still don't have your sacrifices," he shouted, pulling off one shoe. He took the lace from it and tied the trigger of the AA gun in the fire position. He then raced around to the ammo crates and picked up two more clips.

"Now is the time: come to me, Solomon, my love," she said behind him. "Come to me and we shall be together for all eternity. I want you to know the pain that I have known. I want to strip the skin from your body and bathe in your heart's blood. I want us to lie together forever in a bliss of agony, listening to your screams and the last begging moments of our children's torment. Wouldn't that be the best of all possible worlds, my love, my husband."

"Never going to happen, you sick fuck," Kane said, gritting his teeth. He ripped back the charging handles and instantly the gun leapt to life. He kept feeding the guns as they fired, the shaky mounting and swaying ship sending the rounds flying in a wide beaten zone, which found mark after mark at the now open Temple of Cthulhu. The frogboys were nearly eradicated. "They won't be coming back to finish the job."

"They don't need to, silly," she said.

Kane stopped feeding the AA gun and hobbled to the edge of the roof. Looking down he saw the final madness that awaited mankind. The would-be sacrificial victims, from where they huddled on one side of the deck, now rose—weeping or screaming or chanting in a tongue they could not possibly understand—and walked haltingly to the altars of salt. There they lay themselves across the obscenely prepared monoliths and took up the sacrificial blades that hung in intricate scabbards, ready for the moment. And then the victims sacrificed themselves. Tearing at their own bellies, they disemboweled themselves, screaming the chanted words of madness until their life's blood drained and what was left of their minds went wherever eternity took them. Again and again a victim would rise and stumble slowly forward to lay across an altar and finish by his own hand what his murderers were now prevented from doing.

"They will me to return," she said. "And verily, my love, my husband, I come."

Kane, his mind now ringing with the shattering of all hope, screamed until his lungs bled but then threw himself back at the gun. Wheeling madly, he brought the barrels to bear on the deck below; he loaded the hoppers again and wrenched back on the charging handles; instantly the gun coughed to life as rounds blasted at the steel deck. Kane was a machine, weeping and sputtering words he could not consciously form, he fed the AA gun from the crates of ammo, and the gun, safe from all madness in its murderous perfection, continued to fire into the deck of The Legion ship. Clip after clip went into the weapon; round after round fired into the deck; and then through the deck; and then through the structure beneath and before even half of the insane victims could drag themselves to the altars of salt, The Legion ship began to sink.

Heaving to one side as the hold filed with water, some of the altars of salt broke from their fixtures and tumbled down the slanting deck and into the ocean. Of the now insane victims, some still huddled and shielded their heads as if to drive away with flailing hands the impossible echoes from time and space that demanded their ritual deaths. Others sought a release from madness in the frigid embrace of oblivion, diving over the side. For some, the reeling ship hurled them into the same embrace.

Kane spun round from where he stood panting, seeing that less than half of the ritual murders had taken place and now, no matter the metamorphosized Followers of Dagon, those sacrifices would never take place. He searched the bridge roof, looking for the blasphemous image of what could not be his wife, despite her voice, to laugh in his last moments at having denied the ancient evil its rebirth. But there was no image. The voice, however, the voice remained behind him, whispering over his shoulder.

"You have gained nothing with your insolence," she said calmly. "You are the truly mad, the insane beyond reason. Extending my rest is futile, doomed to final defeat. For your kind must succeed every time, prevent every attempt to recall me to life, must attain that most inhuman quality: perfection. My followers need only succeed once and I return. What is a thousand years to one who has dreamt eons, to the deathless who may return? If not this day, Solomon Kane, another. In time; inevitable. One day."

Made in the USA
Middletown, DE
05 March 2023

26243481R00255